AF098967

CROOKED

Copyright © 2025 by Vi Keeland and Penelope Ward

All rights reserved. No part of this publication may be reproduced, distributed, or transmitted in any form or by any means, including photocopying, recording, or other electronic or mechanical methods, without the prior written permission of the publisher, except in the case of brief quotations embodied in critical reviews and certain other noncommercial uses permitted by copyright law. No part of this book may be reproduced, stored, or transmitted in any form or by any means, including for the purpose of training artificial intelligence technologies, without the prior written permission of the author.

This book is a work of fiction. All names, characters, locations, and incidents are products of the authors' imaginations. Any resemblance to actual persons, things, living or dead, locales, or events is entirely coincidental.

CROOKED
Cover Designer: Sommer Stein, Perfect Pear Creative
Editing: Jessica Royer Ocken
Formatting and Proofreading: Elaine York, Allusion Publishing
Proofreading: Julia Griffis
Cover Photographer: Michelle Lancaster, @lanefotograf
Cover Model: Andrew Murray

CROOKED

VI KEELAND
PENELOPE WARD

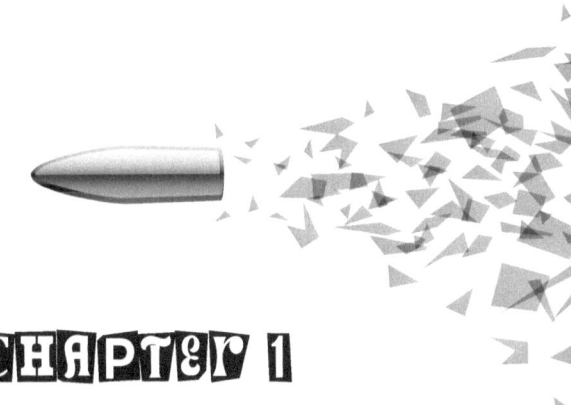

CHAPTER 1

Juliette

Ugh. What the heck time is it?

I pushed my sleep mask up onto my forehead and reached over to the nightstand to unplug my ringing cell from the charger. *Arlo Quinn* flashed on the screen, and unless I'd slept eighteen hours, he was calling me at five fifteen AM.

"Hello?" My voice cracked with morning grog.

"Hey, Jules. It's Arlo. I'm sorry to wake you this early."

"If you aren't calling to tell me there's a wildfire heading straight for my house, I'm hanging up."

He sighed. "Bradley doesn't like the rewrites you did."

I sprang upright. "What? How is that possible? It's the fourth set of rewrites I've done for those scenes, and I barely even wrote any of the words. Bradley dictated how he wanted the entire thing to go."

"I know. I'm sorry. He can be...difficult sometimes."

"Parallel parking in front of The Ivy while being watched by a table of movie stars is difficult. Figuring out what to wear when someone tells you dinner is *smart casual* is difficult. Bradley Wilson? That man is a giant *asshole*."

Arlo chuckled. "He wants to meet with you at six in his trailer at the studio."

"That's in forty-five minutes."

"I know. He just woke me up to have me call you."

I shook my head and ripped the covers from my body, dragging myself out of bed. "Does Sam know he asked for rewrites again?"

"I'm not sure."

Translation—the director has no freaking clue. These constant rewrites had become a control game for Bradley, a power trip of sorts. The director's team spends hours planning the next day's shoot, only to have the star show up ten minutes before call time and drop twenty pages of rewrites in their laps. After, he struts back to his trailer to sip his stupid grande, iced, half-caff, ristretto, sugar-free vanilla, oat milk macchiato with no foam and enjoy a one-hour massage. I had no clue why the director put up with it. Actually, that wasn't true. He probably did it for the same reason I did. Because Bradley Wilson was—*Lord knows why*—one of Hollywood's biggest A-list actors at the moment, and the jerk had a lot of industry pull.

Annoyed, I padded into the kitchen to the coffeemaker. "I'll be there, Arlo. But you have to invite Sam, too, or at least one of the assistant directors. They need to be in the loop from now on."

"Okay. I'll make some calls."

I breathed out on a huff. "Thank you."

"There's one more thing..."

"I'm afraid to ask. What?"

"Bradley requested you stop at Robeks and pick up his morning energy drink."

My eyes bulged. "Are you freaking kidding me?"

The poor assistant sighed. "I'm afraid not."

"No." I shook my head vigorously. "I'm not doing it. I'm a screenplay writer, not his damn gopher."

"I would do it myself, but my girlfriend and I share a car, and she works the night shift. She doesn't get home until seven."

"Why can't he have his drink delivered from Uber Eats?"

"He doesn't trust the drivers."

"What does he think is going to happen? They're going to poison him? Wait, on second thought, maybe I will pick up his energy drink, with a side of cyanide."

"I'll take an Uber and get it for him. I really am sorry to keep calling you with all his requests, Jules."

I took a deep breath in and let it out. It wasn't Arlo's fault. And the poor guy probably made minimum wage for dealing with his asshole boss all day long. "I'll pick up his drink. There's a Robeks on my way to the studio."

"Are you sure?"

"I can't guarantee I won't add some laxatives so he's stuck in the bathroom half the day, but yeah. I'm sure."

"Thanks, Jules. I'll text you his order. It's sort of long."

Of course it is... After I hung up, I brewed a cup of coffee and took a three-minute shower. I did not wash my hair. Looking in the half-fogged mirror, I gave myself a quick internal pep talk. *Think on the bright side. Your day can't get much worse than being woken up at five AM and having a spoiled actor's breakfast order to fetch.*

Unfortunately, the universe must've taken my attempt at *manifesting* a better day as more of a *challenge*. Because when I climbed into my car at twenty minutes to six, my cell phone rang a second time. And the name on the screen this time was probably the only person I wanted to speak to *less* at this hour than Bradley Wilson—my father.

I debated not picking it up, but the last time I'd avoided Dad for a half day, he'd sent one of his goons to my house to knock on my door. So I took yet another deep breath and told myself dealing with my father would be good practice for my meeting with Bradley—a primer in staying calm.

"Hi, Dad."

"Glad I'm not having a heart attack, or I'd be dead waiting for you to answer the damn phone."

I steadied myself. "I'm glad you're not having a heart attack, too. What can I do for you?"

"For starters, you could move back to New York where you belong."

I was *not* about to have this conversation again. So I closed my eyes, counted to three, then opened them and shifted the car into drive. Pulling away from the curb, I attempted to redirect the bad start to our conversation. "How's your sciatica? Feeling any better than last week?"

But Dad ignored my question. "I'm having some trouble at the pizzeria."

Oh Jesus. This was going to be one of *those* calls, the kind where I had to decipher what the heck we were talking about. My father really did own a pizzeria back in Mill Basin, but when he talked about trouble at the *pizzeria*, it was never really about a broken oven or a bad batch of dough. Gino's Pizza was a front for the crooked Ginocassi family, one of the infamous *five families*.

"The oven is running really *hot*," he said. "So hot that I'm going to need to keep an eye on it. You know how it goes—too much heat and *boom!* The place can explode."

I shook my head. Even the feds could figure out my father was telling me a war was heating up between him and his rivals. I was never sure how to respond to his cryptic messages, so I stuck with the oven storyline. "I'm sorry to hear that. You know me... I like my pizza better the second day, when it's cold."

"There's also a sauce problem."

I had absolutely no clue what that meant. "Oh?"

"Yeah. The competition really wants to get our *sauce recipe*. But you know my sauce means everything to me. I don't even want anyone looking at my recipe, much less touching my sauce."

Still clueless, I kept up the charade. "Umm... Yeah. You make good sauce, Dad."

"I'm glad you agree. One of my men will be there today."

"Your men? Where?"

"In LA, to protect the sauce."

Oh no! I'm the sauce! "No, Dad. The sauce is good. No one knows the..." I was about to say no one knows the sauce's last name—I'd stopped using Ginocassi and started using Grecco, my mother's maiden name, when I'd moved out to California—but that sentence made no sense if someone was actually listening in on our call. "Dad, you don't need to worry about the sauce. It's very secure where it is. No one even knows where you keep the sauce recipe."

"*Juliette!*" my father barked, and I instantly felt like I was seven years old instead of twenty-seven. He'd always had a way of silencing a room with a single stern word, and growing up, that word had often been my name. "You will not give me a hard time about this. I have enough going on to worry about."

"But, Dad—"

"It's not up for discussion." He stopped with the cryptic talk. "You might call yourself by another name, but you will always be Juliette Ginocassi. And it's my job to make sure you're always safe."

"But—"

"Enough!" I heard a loud bang and knew he'd just pounded his fist on the table. "It's done."

Before I could say another word, the line went dead. I pulled my cell from my ear and stared at the screen. *Call Ended.*

No, we were *not* done. I didn't want one of his goons hanging around. I'd worked too hard to make a new life out here in California—one where no one knew who my father was. My heart pounded in my chest as I hit the button to call him back. But the call went straight to voicemail. When it happened a second time, I waited until I got to a red light and thumbed off a text. I stared down at my phone, waiting as the message went from *Delivered* to *Read*. Eventually the car behind me honked because I hadn't noticed the light change, so I drove the rest of the way to Robeks. Just as I was getting out of the car, my cell buzzed with an incoming message.

> Arlo: Triple shot matcha mega-charged power surge smoothie. Sub coconut for water and oat milk for half and half. Add a scoop of bee pollen, a half scoop of probiotic

> blend, and one pump of agave, and blend it with half a banana and only two ice cubes.

Fury surged through my veins; I felt like a pot ready to blow its lid. I didn't even get a chance to calm myself before a second text came in.

> Arlo: Don't ask me how, but if they blend it with more than two cubes, he'll know.

My fingers clenched around my iPhone. With each second that ticked by, a slow burn of heat spread across my cheeks and behind my eyes. Bradley Wilson was annoying, but my father was impossible. *Totally impossible* to deal with. Yet I made one more attempt to call him. Of course, I went right to voicemail.

"Unbelievable," I muttered.

Yanking the keys from the ignition, I flung open the door to my Prius and stomped each foot out of the car. The moment I stood—*crack*! My ankle twisted. I began to stumble, yet somehow, I managed to catch myself on the frame of the car door. I looked down at my foot. My heel had broken off, snapped straight from the bottom of my pump.

"Are you freaking serious right now?"

I kicked the shoe from my foot, bent, and without thinking, hurled it toward Robeks. *Stupid freaking Robeks.* It landed on the sidewalk with a satisfying clank, but that wasn't enough to calm me down. My cell phone was still in my hand, so I wound up and threw that too. It landed with more of a thud than a clank, which was likely because my phone didn't hit the ground...

It hit a person.

A man walking from the car parked behind mine rubbed his jaw as he turned to look at me. I hadn't noticed him or his vehicle until that moment. Once I did, it was hard to notice anything else. He was tall and broad-shouldered, with the kind of rugged good looks that made you do a double take. I covered my heart with my hand for more reasons than one. "Oh my God! I hit you in the face?"

"Why the hell did you throw your phone at me?"

"It was an accident. I was angry, and I didn't see you there." I limped toward him wearing one heel. "Are you okay? Should I call 9-1-1?"

He bent and scooped my cell from the ground. "I think maybe you should call a therapist, sweetheart."

My eyes narrowed. "You don't need to be a jerk about it. I'm already having a bad day."

"That makes two of us." He shook his head. "You need to learn to control your anger."

He was right, of course, but in the moment, I didn't need a lecture. "I was frustrated. Someone hung up on me."

He smirked. "Not surprised, with your attitude."

I froze. "What did you just say?"

"If this is how you act when someone pisses you off, I get why they'd hang up on you."

"You don't even *know* me."

"I've seen enough to know your type."

"Wow. And I guess you're better than *my type*?"

"Haven't hit any strangers today, so..."

I limped the two steps separating us and grabbed my phone from his hand. "Thanks for the free behavior analysis."

He shrugged. "No charge."

I briefly considered taking off my other shoe and hitting him on purpose this time. But instead, I showed him my pearly whites. "You have a wonderful rest of your day."

"I'd say the chances of that are pretty damn slim. Not when I'll be spending it with you."

"With *me*? I think maybe my phone did more damage to your head than it appears."

He gave me a look. "Name's Wes Callahan, Juliette. Your dad sent me. I'm your new bodyguard."

CHAPTER 2

Juliette

What a day.

I walked out of Bradley Wilson's trailer at five o'clock after a long, shitty day. Arlo had not, in fact, called the director this morning to inform him that his lead actor was demanding another set of rewrites. So when he showed up at nine to start shooting, all hell broke loose.

I wound up working ten hours on rewrites in Bradley's trailer, while he did stupid shit like gargle with rose petals and get a lymphatic neck massage from a massage therapist who cracked his knuckles every five minutes and told his patient that his "*lymph nodes hold rage.*" Not to mention, I had to play charades to guess the changes Bradley mimed because his throat was a little *scratchy*, and he worried he'd lose his voice during filming.

So, the very last thing I needed at the end of this day was to find Wes Callahan, the guy from this morning, parked next to me in the studio parking lot.

He watched me as I walked to my car, but didn't roll down his window until I knocked on it.

"How did you even get past the guards at the gate?" I asked. "You can't get onto the property unless you're on the pre-approved list."

"Don't worry about it."

I rolled my eyes. He might be better looking than the others, with his chiseled jaw and enviably full lips, but this guy was one of my father's goons all right. That was exactly the type of response Vince Ginocassi, or any of his men, gave whenever I asked a question.

"You're fired."

The jackass smirked. And I hated that my eyes lingered on his mouth for a beat too long.

"You can't fire someone you didn't hire, sweetheart."

"Well, you can't just follow me around. That's harassment. I'll go to the police."

"We don't know each other yet, but trust me when I say that won't stop me."

Ugh. The jerk might have a jawline that rivaled Henry Cavill's, but he was no different than my father's regular crew. I knew there was no point in arguing with him, so I didn't waste my breath. I got into my car and pulled out. As I waited at the guard's station for the parking gate to go up, I called my father. Not surprisingly, he still didn't answer.

That did not change the fact that the last thing I wanted was one of my dad's people following me around, so when I got out to the main road, I made a sharp U-turn and hit the gas instead of taking my usual left. I weaved in and out of side streets with my heart racing until Wes's car was no longer behind me.

I felt a little high at having lost him, at least until I pulled up in front of my house and found the jerk blocking my driveway with his car. He leaned against the driver's side door, tossing his keys into the air and catching them. He smirked again when he saw me, and I decided I officially hated him—especially because he looked annoyingly hot, and my body reacted.

I rolled down my window and growled at him, *not* noticing his broad shoulders. "Move!"

"Say please."

"I am *not* saying please."

He tossed the keys into the air and caught them again. "Then looks like you're going to have to park somewhere else."

I slammed the car into reverse and nailed the gas, causing the tires to chirp. Steam practically billowed from my nose as I parked in front of the house and got out. Wes had his truck open now and was unloading a suitcase.

"Uh... What do you think you're doing?" I asked.

"Moving in with you."

"Like hell you are!"

Maybe I shouldn't have made him sleep in the car. It was a little bit chilly last night—for me at least. But even if he wasn't cold out there, he had to have been uncomfortable.

My father had some nerve sending this guy here, but I knew it wasn't Wes's fault. He'd just been doing his job. I realized how demanding Dad was, and this guy likely had no choice but to go along with all of this. His life could literally depend on it.

I should go outside and tell him to come in.

But first, coffee. I couldn't deal with him—or anything else, for that matter—until I was properly caffeinated.

I was just about to pour myself a cup when there was a knock at the door. Assuming it was Wes, I cinched my silk robe tighter. When I opened, Wes was indeed standing there, but next to a cop.

My heart dropped. "What's going on here?" This had to have something to do with my father.

"Your neighbor called to report a suspicious car parked in front of your place, ma'am," the officer said. He pointed to Wes. "I just spoke to the occupant. This gentleman here says he's your boyfriend, and the two of you got into an argument last night, so you made him sleep in the car..."

Oh my goodness. But relief washed over me that this had nothing to do with my father causing trouble.

Having no good options, I cleared my throat. "Yes, that's right. We got into a bit of a tiff, so I kicked him out for the night so I could have some space."

The cop arched a brow. "Just to confirm, no one laid a hand on the other person, correct?"

I shook my head. "No, no. He would never."

I glanced over at Wes, who grinned at me smugly. "Just a little lover's spat," he said.

"Been there," the officer said, patting Wes on the shoulder. "Okay, as long as everything is copacetic now. I'm gonna head out and let you two sort out your issues."

I nodded. "Thank you, Officer. I appreciate you checking in."

"Well, thank your neighbor. She was looking out for you. Rare to find people who care these days."

I managed a smile. Actually, I wished Pam and the other neighbors would mind their own damn business, considering the circumstances of my life. Pam was my book club buddy and friend, but she was damn nosy—always after more details than I wanted to give her. All I needed was for someone to find out what was really going on. Why didn't my father realize that assigning a bodyguard would only draw more attention to me?

After the police officer left, Wes stood before me in all of his fuck-hot glory, with his hands in his pockets and his tight white T-shirt practically painted onto his muscular chest. His hair was a little messed up and flattened from what I was sure hadn't been a pleasant night's sleep.

"Sorry for making up that story," he said. "But I didn't know what else to tell him. Wasn't like I could admit the real reason I'm here looking out for you."

I crossed my arms. "Maybe you should've, and he could've carted you away, so I don't have to deal with any of this."

"Now, now. Is that how you talk to your loving boyfriend?" He winked.

"Please don't repeat that." *Especially in that annoyingly seductive voice.*

"Well, you don't think at some point we're gonna have to pretend to be something to each other? People are going to wonder who the hell I am. How else are you going to explain me, if I'm not your boyfriend?"

"I'm hoping not to have to explain you at all because I'm counting on this arrangement ending soon."

"Well, if you'd let me sleep inside like you should've, I wouldn't have attracted the neighbor's attention."

"I will admit that making you sleep outside was a mistake, in hindsight." I rubbed my pounding temples. "Do you want some coffee? I need to get a cup before my head explodes."

He smiled wide. "I would love some."

God, those dimples.

Had they been there yesterday?

Of course they had.

Again, I needed coffee.

After I filled two mugs, I handed him one. "As you just saw, my neighbor is very nosy. You need to keep a low profile. That means no hanging around outside my house unless absolutely necessary. She'll try to talk to you."

"I'll be fine if she does. I'm a pretty good liar."

"How commendable."

He shrugged. "I don't make a habit of it. But in this business, you have to be able to stretch the truth with a straight face."

Putting my coffee down, I crossed my arms. "We have to set some ground rules."

Wes grinned from behind his mug. "Okay…"

He'd better be taking this seriously. I took another long sip of coffee. "One, you have to sleep on the couch. I only have one bedroom. So…"

"All right. I was expecting that. No big deal. I've slept on worse things."

"Not even gonna ask." I sighed. "Also, no walking around without your clothes on."

Wes raised a brow and laughed. "Why would I do that?"

"I don't know. You seem like the type who might be comfortable enough in your skin to want to flaunt it or something. Just letting you know I won't appreciate that."

"No naked ass. Got it." He nodded. "What else?"

"No eating anything in my refrigerator that belongs to me. I just went to Erewhon to stock up. Practically spent a week's salary." I opened the fridge and began moving my items to the right, leaving spots on the left of the top two shelves empty. "You can keep your stuff on this side."

"How generous of you..." He grinned.

I tilted my head. "Are you mocking me?"

"No." He pursed his lips, probably to keep from laughing.

I sighed. Maybe I did need to calm down. This situation was making me more high-strung than usual.

After a moment, he asked, "Are you done?"

"I'll let you know if I think of anything else."

"Look..." he said. "I don't wanna be here any more than you want me here. So let's just try to make the best of it."

"We don't need to *make the best* of it. We need to stay out of each other's way and not make each other insane." I downed the last of my cup of joe.

Wes's expression dampened. Had I hurt his feelings? This situation stressed me out and made me less than pleasant. My father's antics brought out the worst in me. I felt like I needed a time out.

On that note, I took my own advice and ventured back to my room to have my second cup of coffee in peace.

When I walked back out into the living room about fifteen minutes later, my jaw dropped. It was like I'd walked onto the set of *Love Island*. Wes was sitting on the couch with his feet up on the ottoman—shirtless, with every beautiful contour of his bronzed chest on full display.

What. The. Heck. I gulped. "What are you doing?"

He stood, looking confused. "What do you mean? I'm just sitting here."

"You've only been here a matter of minutes, and you've already broken a rule." I scoffed. "The most important one, I might add."

He drew in his brows. "What rule?"

I glared. "Naked?"

He looked down at his chest. "I'm not naked."

"You took your shirt off."

"That's shirtless. Not naked. You say *naked*, and I think…junk hanging out. This is *not* naked."

I shook my head. "You need to wear a shirt in this house."

He stalked toward me. "It's hot as Hades in here. Does your air conditioner even work?"

"I don't like it too cold. I freeze easily."

"I guess that's what happens to people who are already cold enough."

As he stood there with his hands on his hips, I did feel oddly warm, actually. And it had nothing to do with the air-conditioner setting.

He smirked. A chill ran down my spine.

Fuck. Those dimples.

I'm going to kill my father for hiring this guy.

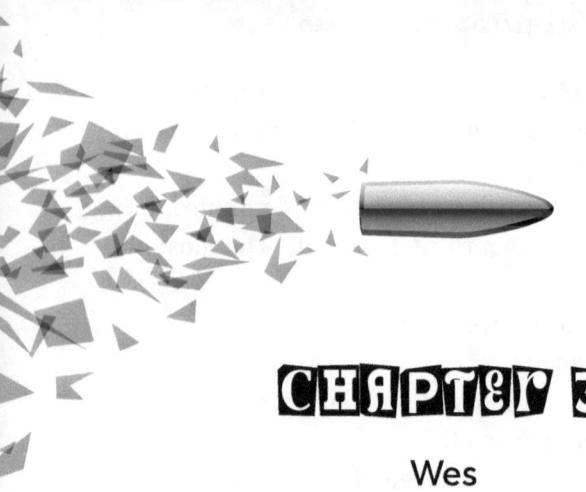

CHAPTER 3

Wes

That afternoon, the business phone rang while I was parked across the street from the building where Juliette had gone to work, waiting for her to get out of a meeting.

I had two phones, and whenever the first one rang, I knew I had to brace myself. Because it could only be one person.

I picked up. "Hey, Vince."

"How's it going over there?"

"Do we need to talk about pizza or…?"

"No," he said. "We're good."

"Okay." I ran my hand through my hair. "Everything is going well, actually. But your daughter runs a tight ship."

"What's that supposed to mean?"

"Just that she's very regimented. Everything has to be a certain way."

"Well, good. She probably gets that from me." He paused. "Anyway, you're not there to make friends."

"I wasn't planning on it."

"No funny business. You get what I'm saying? I'm not stupid. I know my daughter is a very attractive woman."

I had to laugh at that. Not because Juliette wasn't attractive, because she sure as hell was. But Juliette wouldn't let me near her with a ten-foot pole. I chuckled under my breath. "She doesn't seem to like me very much."

"Good. Keep it that way. Your job is not to make her like you. It's to protect her."

"Understood." I tugged at my hair. "I take my job very seriously, sir."

"Juliette and I got off to a rough start in our relationship," he said. "But she's the most precious thing to me. I've done a lot of things wrong, but Juliette is something good that's come from my life."

I had to smile at the rare moment of softness coming from a man who was normally tough as nails. It didn't last long, of course.

"So, if anything happens to her, you won't see the light of day," he added.

"Nothing's going to happen to her," I assured him. *And if it does, it will be because her stubborn ass can't get out of her own way.*

"Well, glad to hear you're confident in your abilities. Don't let your guard down. And keep me apprised of anything suspicious."

"Yes, sir."

"I'll be checking in again soon."

"Looking forward to it," I lied as he hung up.

I let out a long breath and rested my head against the back of the seat. The call with Vince had left me feeling a little rattled. Not sure why. Maybe I was still getting used to the fact that my life wasn't really my own anymore. Anytime I had to talk to him, it was a stark reminder of my new reality.

The passenger-side door suddenly opened, and Juliette slid into the car. I'd been so preoccupied, I hadn't noticed her walking toward me, which wasn't good. My eyes should've been on her from the moment she left the building until she was safely in the car.

"What's gotten into you?" she asked, likely noticing that I was on edge.

"Nothing." I started the engine and glanced over at her. "Put your seatbelt on."

She reluctantly followed my order. "I was going to..."

It surprised me that she didn't give me shit for telling her what to do. Still tense, I chewed on my bottom lip as I drove.

"Did something happen today?" she asked.

"No." My tone was curt.

"Wes..."

"What?" I snapped.

"If we're gonna do this, you need to be honest with me. Am I in danger?"

Shit. I didn't want her to think that. I also didn't want to admit that her father made me nervous, but I didn't want to freak her out for no reason, either.

"Nothing's wrong, Juliette. Truly. Your dad called to check in. That's all. I told him everything was fine."

"If everything is fine, then why are you in a mood?"

"Because I'm not a machine," I answered. "When someone reminds me what's at stake, I can't help but react. But there's nothing new. Nothing to worry about. The call was just a kick in the ass for me to remember why I'm here, even if you make it easy to forget sometimes."

She blushed. "Was that a compliment?"

"I guess you could say that. There are worse places I could be than hanging out with you, even if you're cranky. You're a good distraction. And this still beats a lot of other gigs."

"So I'm one step up from guarding a laundromat that's a front for money laundering?"

I chuckled. "Many steps up from that."

"Oh good." She winked.

She seemed to be getting more comfortable with me, and that was a win that might just cancel out the call from Vince. I calmed down for the ride back to her place. But the calm was short-lived.

When we returned to the house, Juliette noticed that I'd turned down the temperature—quite a bit—before we left this morning.

"What the hell? It feels like Antarctica in here, Wes."

"It was hotter than hell earlier. You said you didn't want me to take off my shirt. I turned down the temperature so that wouldn't be an issue when we got back."

She placed her hands on her hips. "You don't have the right to do that."

"Well, if the thermostat is off-limits, then I do have a right to take off my damn shirt when it's hot in here."

Juliette proceeded to adjust the temperature back and storm off to her bedroom. She only came out once to grab something from the fridge and take it to her room.

I'd picked up some food while Juliette was at work earlier, so I made myself dinner and took advantage of the space she'd allotted me.

After my meal, the temperature became too much to bear again. So, I slipped my tee over my head.

When Juliette finally emerged around eight PM, her eyes went wide. She didn't even have to speak before I defended myself.

"Look, like I told you, as long as it's hot as balls in here, I'm gonna be shirtless. You need to get used to it."

She mumbled something under her breath as she headed for the fridge.

And I waited.

Here it comes.

"What the?"

I flashed a mischievous grin. "I did a little rearranging."

I'd put all of Juliette's stuff on the left side to mess with her, moving mine to the right. But all of her precious Erewhon food was still intact. I just wanted to shake things up a little. As she stood there with her mouth agape, I asked, "What exactly happens if your stuff is on the left, Juliette? Does the world end? Don't worry. I didn't touch any of your food except to move it."

"What the hell is that smell?"

Crap. I knew she'd call that out. "It's smoked Portuguese sausage. There's this guy in West Hollywood who has a smoker in his yard. I found him on Reddit. He smokes the meat all day and sells it."

"When did you have time to get smoked meat?"

"I swung over there really quick after I dropped you at your meeting. It was in the trunk, which is probably why you didn't smell it when you got in the car."

She shook her head and took out a few berries. She washed them before popping one into her mouth. She winced and nearly spit it out. "These taste like smoke! Berries are porous, you know."

"Well, your rules said nothing about freshly smoked meats, so I thought it was okay."

"You need to keep that crap out of the fridge. I feel like I'm eating a blueberry-flavored chimney." This time she spit a berry into the trash.

I stifled laughter as she once again stormed away to her room. I hadn't realized how pungent the smoked chorizo would be. She was right—you couldn't smell much else in the fridge. That was my bad and an unintended consequence.

I vowed to make up for it tomorrow by cleaning out the fridge and restocking it with her frou-frou berries and anything else that might've been impacted by the unfortunate smoked-sausage takeover.

Once nine PM rolled around and she hadn't re-emerged, I figured it was safe to get comfortable in my sleeping spot for the night. I took off my pants and lay down in my boxer briefs.

I was halfway into a movie on Netflix when the doorbell rang.

Shit. Who the fuck is here at this hour?

I peeked through the peephole and found an innocent-looking woman standing there. Redhead, mid-thirties, and a penchant for wearing green apparently. I recognized her as Juliette's neighbor. I bet she was the one who'd called the cops. Without thinking it through too much, I opened the door and said, "Can I help you?"

She looked me up and down, and her eyes slowly widened. I'd sort of forgotten I wasn't wearing pants. *Whoops.*

She cleared her throat. "I'm Pam from next door. Officer Horton explained to me what happened last night. I wanted to apologize for causing a scene. I didn't realize Juliette had a boyfriend staying here. We don't have too many unfamiliar cars in this neighborhood, and we try to look out for each other." She looked me up and down again. "Please accept my sincerest apologies for intruding."

I nodded. "No problem at all."

A second later, I heard Juliette's voice behind me. "What the hell is going on?"

I turned to find her eyes scrolling my body before they landed on my crotch.

I guess my *smoked* sausage wasn't the one she was most concerned about anymore.

CHAPTER 4

Juliette

I yanked the belt of my robe tighter as I got to the door and forced a smile. "I got this. Thanks, Wes."

He grinned. "No problem, babe."

He was barely out of earshot when Pam leaned in. "I want all the dirt on the new hottie right now."

I shook my head. "There isn't anything to tell. He's... a family friend."

"I saw the police officer coming out of your house this morning. He said you'd had an argument with your *boyfriend*."

Shit. This was why I didn't lie. One led to two, and before long you were caught in a web of them. But I really didn't want Pam to think Wes was my boyfriend. I considered her a friend, but she was a pretty big gossip, and we both worked in the entertainment industry. "That was just Wes and his odd sense of humor. He got in late and didn't want to wake me, so he crashed in his car."

Pam's mouth curved to a grin. "So that sizzle stick is single?"

Her comment irked me. "I think he might have a girlfriend back home."

She shrugged. "No ring means I'm still in the running."

I had to work to hide my frown. "I should get back to sleep. I have an early day tomorrow. Were you just coming to check on me, or..."

"Oh! I almost forgot. I stopped over to ask you for a favor. My brain got a little frazzled by that six-pack."

It's more of an eight-pack. Trust me, I've counted. "What's up?"

"Would you mind swinging by Brewer's tomorrow night? I ordered finger sandwiches for book club, but I'm going to be cutting it close on time because I have a late-day meeting. I don't want people showing up before I get home."

Shoot. I forgot all about book club. "Umm... Yeah, sure. I can pick up the food from Brewer's for you."

Pam dug into her purse and pulled out a receipt. "Great. It's all paid for."

"Okay."

"One more thing. Do you think you could go over to the house and set up, too? Put out the food and paper goods? Maybe set up the circle and stuff?"

"Sure."

Pam hugged me. "You're a lifesaver. The spare key is still under the flowerpot."

I nodded. "Have a good night."

"You too, honey. And good luck with that author tomorrow. I still think you should go for it and ask the man out." She winked. "Lord knows I would." Pam cupped her hands around her mouth and yelled over my shoulder. "You're invited to book club, too, hot stuff!

You don't have to read the book. Just come for the cocktails—and the cock!"

I practically shoved her back and shut the door, praying Wes had gone to the bathroom and hadn't heard any of that. But of course, I found him standing in the living room—*still* with his shirt off and now with his hands on his hips.

"What the hell was that last comment about? Does your book club have strippers or something?"

"No. The book they picked to read this month is a romance novel."

He flashed a dirty grin. "Oh yeah? Is it steamy?"

"I wouldn't know. I didn't read it. To be honest, I don't read half the books they pick. My job is reading and writing all day long, so I need to be in the right mood to read for pleasure these days. I pretty much go to the meetings for the cocktails and food."

He shrugged. "I guess we'll both be taking a back seat and sipping a cocktail during the discussion then."

"Ummm... No. You will *not* be going."

"Why not? I was invited."

"Because I don't want to have to answer a million questions about you, that's why."

"Probably be less questions if I'm sitting with you than there would be with me outside in the car watching the house."

"You can just stay here. It's right next door."

He shook his head. "It's not a secure location."

"You left and ran errands while I was at my meeting this afternoon."

"Because that building has tight security, and anyone who walks in has to go through metal detectors.

And I also spoke to the guards before I left—both are ex-cops."

"You *went into* the building where I was for my meeting?"

"I needed to determine how secure it was. Speaking of which, it would make my job a lot easier if you could give me the addresses of the places you're going a day ahead of time so I can look into the security beforehand."

I felt heat crawling up my neck. "I've worked very hard to create a new identity out here—one not associated with my father and his business. People are going to talk if you're following me around, asking questions every place I go."

"I'm discreet."

I flailed my arms in the air. "Discreet? There is *nothing* discreet about you!"

Wes folded his arms across his chest, and my stupid eyes followed. *Damn*, his forearms were veiny and sexy, too. Pissed off for even thinking that, I shook my head and marched back to my room. "You know what? I'm going back to bed. Don't answer the door anymore. And for God's sake, *put a damn shirt on*!"

Slam!

A half hour later, I was lying in bed in the dark, feeling too riled up to sleep. I decided to download the audiobook my book club would be discussing tomorrow night and listen. At least I'd know what the story was about, even if I didn't make it through the entire thing. I popped in my AirPods and settled back, hoping the narrators were good and the story would help me relax enough to drift off.

But it only took a few chapters to realize what I was listening to was *not* going to help me relax. It was going to do the exact opposite because the damn book was about a celebrity who had an affair with her bodyguard. *Great. Just freaking great.*

The following morning, I woke up thinking about a steamy scene between the heroine and her bodyguard, so I hoped to avoid Wes. But of course, he was already up and making himself breakfast in the kitchen. I guess I should've counted myself lucky—he at least had a shirt on. The smell of bacon wafted through the air as I went to the coffeemaker.

"Morning, sunshine." He smiled.

I rolled my eyes. "Morning." Noticing the Erewhon label on the half-empty package of bacon on the counter, I tried to remember if I'd bought any. I didn't think I had. "Is that mine?"

"Nope. Did a little food shopping earlier this morning."

"You can't leave me next door for my book club, but you can go downtown to food shop and leave me alone in the house?"

He lowered the flame on the two burners he had going and turned to face me. "I had the house covered for an hour by an associate of mine. I wanted to go get you new berries before you woke up. I also tossed my smelly chorizo and cleaned out the refrigerator to get rid of the smell."

"Oh."

He smirked. "It pisses you off when you don't have anything to complain to me about, doesn't it?"

I narrowed my eyes. "You enjoy pushing my buttons, don't you?"

Wes chuckled and went back to cooking. "You want some breakfast, sunshine?"

I looked over at the sizzling bacon and scrambled eggs. "It's okay. You made it for yourself."

"There's enough for two. Sit."

My initial impulse was to argue, but then he lifted the bacon pan, and I got another delicious whiff, so I took a seat. I'd never admit it, but it was kind of nice to have someone make me breakfast in the morning. Lord knows it had been a while since any other man had stayed over.

Wes plated bacon and eggs for both of us and took the seat across from me. "So, what's on the agenda for today?" he asked.

My mouth was already watering, so I picked up a slice of bacon and bit off a piece. "I have a meeting with an author whose book I'm turning into a script for a movie."

"The author you're supposed to ask out?"

I stopped chewing. "How did you know?"

"Your neighbor mentioned it yesterday." Wes shrugged. "I overheard."

Damn. I had completely forgotten about that, since Pam's *cock* comment had taken center stage after she left. I wasn't about to girl-talk with Wes about the crush I'd had for way too long. Instead, I changed the subject. "How did you get into bodyguarding?"

"I used to work for the NYPD."

"Wow. Really?" My father normally wanted *nothing* to do with the police. "You were a cop?"

Wes nodded.

"Did you not like it?"

"I loved it."

"So...why are you not working there anymore?"

Wes sighed. "Long story."

I waited to see if he was going to share that *long story*, but he didn't say anything more. And the way he was now avoiding eye contact told me it was a subject he didn't want to discuss. Yet I sniffed around a bit more. "How long have you been working for my dad?"

"Two years."

"Who are you related to?"

Wes looked up from his plate. "What do you mean?"

"Everyone in my father's organization is either family, or the family of someone in his crooked inner circle. There aren't any outsiders."

Wes shrugged. "I'm not related to anyone."

"Really?"

"Really." He finished his food and leaned back in his chair. "How did you get into screenwriting?"

"Well, I was a movie junkie growing up. We had a small theater in the basement of our house, and I used to go there to escape the chaos upstairs. Whenever my dad was home, he was either barking at someone on a burner phone, or his buddies were over and he'd play super-loud music so they could talk in private, in case the feds were listening in."

Wes frowned. "That must've been hard."

"It wasn't your normal childhood, let's just say that. But at least it pushed me toward a field I love working in. Anyway, I went to NYU and got a BFA and an MFA in dramatic writing. While I was in school, I interned for one of the bigger production companies that has a bunch of in-house writers. The internship turned into a full-time job, and I worked there for three years before I went out on my own."

"Do you write a specific genre of screenplays, or just whatever comes up? I'm not sure how it works."

"I write in my two favorite genres: thriller and horror."

Wes's brows jumped. "No shit. Horror?"

"Why do you look so surprised?"

"I don't know. I guess I expected you to say romance or women's fiction, like Nicholas Sparks type shit."

"Nope. I like to write the kind of stuff that makes me nervous to be in my own house alone at night." I smiled. "I'm sure Dr. Freud would have a lot to say about that with my family."

Wes chuckled. "What's the name of the guy you're too chicken to ask out?"

"I am *not* too chicken." *Here I thought our conversation was finally going well...* "And his name is none of your business."

"Actually, it is my business. It's my *only* business these days. I wasn't digging into your personal life. I'm asking because it's my job to know who you're with and where you are at all times, until the boss tells me otherwise."

"Oh."

He pushed his chair back and stood, taking his plate with him. "Yeah, oh."

"Do you see someone you know?" Jett asked. He turned and looked over his shoulder toward the bar, where Wes was now sitting.

Great. Now I was lying *and* being rude because of that man. Why the hell did Wes need to come inside the restaurant? He'd been in the car out front when I'd walked in.

"Sorry. No. I must've gotten lost in thought, picturing what the movie might look like. Your ideas gave me such a good visual." *Great. More lies...* Weren't bodyguards supposed to watch but not be seen?

At least Jett seemed happy with my response. He smiled and nodded. "Yeah, *The Hunted* begs for a cinematic adaptation, especially with it being set in Charleston."

We spent another hour talking about his ideas for the book-to-film screenplay I'd be writing. This would be the second project Jett Bradbury and I had worked on together. The first had been eighteen months ago, which was when I'd developed my secret crush on him. But he'd been dating someone—a pretty big Hollywood actress—until very recently. This was actually the first time I'd seen him since his breakup.

Jett was in the middle of describing how he visualized the ending of the movie when I noticed a tall blonde sidle up to Wes at the bar. I tried my best to keep my eyes on Jett, but the task wasn't easy. Through my peripheral vision, I watched as Wes and the woman spoke for a few minutes, and then the woman handed him her phone. He typed something into it and gave it back with a smile before she disappeared. That annoyed me, though I obviously had no reason to feel annoyed, and I couldn't shake my bristly mood through the rest of my lunch meeting and the entire drive home.

"Who was the woman you were speaking to at the bar?" I finally asked Wes once we were back in my kitchen.

"Her name was Clover," he said. "I think."

"*Clover*? What kind of a name is Clover?"

He shrugged.

"You met her for the first time today? It looked like you gave her your phone number."

He shrugged. "She asked for it."

"*Clover* just walked up to you—a complete stranger—and asked for your phone number?"

"Yep."

Jesus, and I don't even have the balls to ask Jett out for a drink—a man I've known for a year and a half.

"How was your lunch meeting?" Wes asked.

"Good. Jett likes to be involved in the adaptation of his books. Sometimes that makes the process more difficult, but he has really good ideas."

"What's his deal? Is he married or something?"

"No, why?"

"Then why hasn't he asked you out?"

"I don't think I'm his type."

Wes looked me up and down, and his brows dipped. "Why not?"

"Because he likes statuesque blondes with big boobs who wear dresses with glitter."

Wes opened his mouth to say something, then shut it. When it became apparent he was done with the conversation, I decided to go get some work done. "You're in for a boring afternoon," I told him. "I'm going to be writing at my desk for most of it."

"I'll be out here if you need me."

Hours later, I emerged from my bedroom. Wes was sitting on the couch looking down at his phone. I glanced over his shoulder as I passed and noticed he was texting. I immediately wondered if he was texting the woman he'd met earlier—not that it should've mattered to me.

Wes tossed his phone on the couch. "I was beginning to wonder if you fell asleep. I didn't hear a peep, and you were in there for a long time."

"When I get on a roll, I don't take breaks."

"I take it that means your writing went well?"

"It did, actually. I really like how the first few scenes came out. I'm excited to show them to Jett."

Wes made a face. "*Jett*. What kind of dumb name is that?"

"I kinda like it. Beats *Clover*." I grabbed a water bottle out of the fridge and chugged half of it. "I have to run out to Brewer's to pick up the food Pam ordered for book club tonight."

"All right." He stood. "Where is that?"

"It's at The Grove." I grabbed my keys from the hook near the door and slipped on my shoes. "The parking there is horrible, so I might have to circle the block for a while."

"Why don't I just drive, and you can run in while I wait? I'll double park and move if I'm in anyone's way."

"Oh. That would be great, if you don't mind."

The drive to Brewer's was only about fifteen minutes, and surprisingly, there was a spot right in front.

"It must be our lucky day," I told Wes. "I usually have to circle the shopping center for ten minutes, and then I wind up walking three blocks after I finally accept that I'm never going to find a close place to park."

Wes winked. "They probably knew I was coming."

He parallel parked like a pro, and I was surprised when he got out of the car and jogged around to open my door.

"Thank you. Is this part of your bodyguard duties?"

"Doesn't need to be in the job description for a man to treat a lady like she should be treated."

His answer made me smile. "I'll be right back."

When I returned, Wes was leaning against the passenger door. He pushed off and took the sandwich platter from my hands, settling it in the backseat before opening the passenger door for me. I'd started to fold into the car when a man's voice stopped me.

"Jules?"

None other than Jett was standing on the sidewalk. He walked over to kiss my cheek. "I thought that was you."

Wes folded his arms across his chest and stood taller. I'd never thought Jett was short or thin, but standing next to Wes, he looked a little of both. Wes's shoulders were almost twice the size of his. Jett looked at Wes, and I had no choice but to introduce them. "Jett, this is Wes...a family friend."

Jett held out his hand, and for a second, Wes just stared at it. I thought he was going to embarrass me, but eventually he shook. "How ya doing?"

Jett nodded.

"I spent all day working on *The Hunted*," I told him. "I can't wait to share it with you."

"Awesome. I can't wait to read it." Jett pointed to the restaurant next door to Brewer's. "I'm meeting Arnie Edmunds for drinks. Are you guys going to Mesita?"

"No, I just picked up some food for my book club tonight."

"Nice." He looked at his watch. "I'm already late, so I have to run. It's never good to keep actors waiting. You know how they are."

I smiled. "I do."

Jett kissed my cheek again and waved to Wes, who gave him a curt nod.

The drive home was quiet, until Wes's phone rang. He picked it up and held it to his ear. "Hey. What's up?"

I heard someone talking on the other end but couldn't make out most of what they said. Though I thought I heard, "*Landed at LAX.*" We pulled up to my house just as Wes hung up, and his jaw seemed pretty tense.

"Is everything all right?" I asked.

"Yep." He jumped out of the car and looked around the street before opening my door. Then he took the sandwich tray out of the backseat. I held out my hands to take it, but he shook his head. "I got it."

"We discussed this already. You're not coming to my book club meeting."

"I'm at least going to check out the house. Your friend's not home yet anyway. Her car isn't in the driveway."

"Do you really think someone broke into Pam's house and is hiding there to get me when I go to my *book club*?"

"Just let me do my damn job, and both our lives will be easier."

I huffed. "Fine. But you only have two minutes."

Inside Pam's house, Wes did a full sweep—going from room to room while I stood in the kitchen.

"Was the boogeyman waiting for me?" I asked when he returned.

Wes shook his head. "I'll be outside in the car."

I rolled my eyes. "Whatever..."

After I was alone, I went about setting everything up. People started to arrive just as I set the last chair into place. And at seven, our official start time, Pam walked in. Unfortunately, she wasn't alone. Her arm was linked with Wes's.

"I saw this handsome man sitting outside in his car," she said. "And I insisted he come in."

I walked over and took Wes's other arm. "I must've forgotten to give him my key again. Excuse us for a moment." I practically shoved him back out the front door.

"You're *not* coming to book club," I hissed, attempting to keep my voice down.

"Fine with me. I only came in because your friend practically dragged me out of the car. She's a pushy one."

I shook my head. "Just go next door. You already checked out the house, and you know I'm not in any danger. You'll be thirty feet away."

"I'll stay outside, but I'll be in my car or sitting on the porch."

"Why are you being such an ass about this?"

"You want to know why? I'll tell you why. Because that call I got in the car a little while ago was someone letting me know that your father's enemies have landed in LA, specifically two guys who have been arrested for murder more than once but always seem to get off, even though they shouldn't. So you're lucky I'm even saying I'll sit out here because I shouldn't let you out of my damn sight."

Shit. "People are going to be coming and going all night. I don't want them feeling uncomfortable with some guy watching their every move."

The front door swung open. Pam smiled and held out two glasses of wine. "Hey, you two. Allison has to leave by eight to relieve her sitter, so we're going to get started."

"I'll be right in."

"Wes, honey, you should come too. Lord knows we could use some testosterone at our book club full of ladies." Her eyes sparkled. "Maybe we can even get you to read a little of the male part from the book we're discussing. I bet you'd play a great bodyguard."

Wes's eyes narrowed. "Excuse me?"

"The book we read this month," Pam said. "The heroine has a steamy affair with her burly bodyguard."

Wes looked at me. "Is she serious?"

I grabbed his arm and tried to turn him to leave, but the big oaf didn't budge. "Wes has somewhere to be. I don't want to make him late."

"Actually..." He grinned from ear to ear. "I don't mind being late. I think I'll come in for a while."

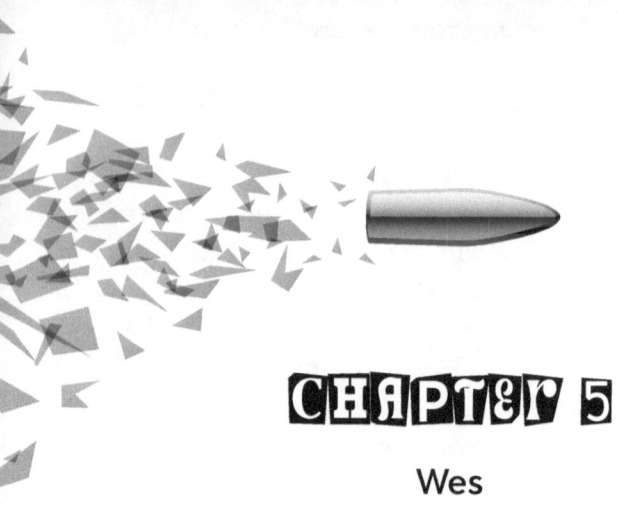

CHAPTER 5

Wes

This was too freaking good to be true. I loved messing with Juliette, but usually I had to be creative. *This* situation? It had been handed to me on a silver platter. This job was tough, so if I could have a little fun with it, that made it somewhat tolerable. And tonight? I planned to have some fun, despite remaining on high alert.

I made my way into the living room, where Juliette had set up the food. I could get used to this. Not only was it going to be awesome making Juliette blush, but the snacks here? Top notch. I'd been missing out on the book club game all these years. Cheese and crackers. Shrimp cocktail. Cured meats—my favorite. The last time I'd seen a spread this good was the buffet on the Carnival cruise I took with my family when I was fourteen. While I wouldn't be taking advantage of the alcohol tonight, since I had to be at the top of my game, I would most definitely be stuffing my face full of prosciutto.

The seats were arranged in a circle. Seemed so...formal.

Taking my full plate over to the chair next to Juliette, I bumped her arm with mine. "You should eat."

She crossed her arms. "I'm not hungry in the least."

I narrowed my eyes. "Why not?"

"I lost my appetite the moment you decided to stay."

I looked around, then leaned in to whisper in her ear, "Ready for the circle jerk?"

She rolled her eyes.

I chuckled. "I mean, what the fuck is this? Who sits in a circle like this?" When her serious expression wouldn't budge, I popped an olive into my mouth. "Oh, come on. Lighten up. You're apparently the only one who doesn't want me here."

She spoke under her breath. "They're a bunch of horned-up women. They only want you here because you're cute. You should have more self-respect than to allow them to objectify you."

I licked some salt off my finger. "Being objectified is better than somebody who acts like my shirtless chest is the anti-Christ. We're going from one extreme to the other."

While Juliette remained stoic, I did my best to enjoy myself, continuing to devour my food while everyone gathered around. It *was* a little strange being the only dude here. But hey, I'd take one for the team anyway. I supposed I was here…repping bodyguards.

Just as I shoved a piece of spanakopita into my mouth, I heard someone say, "Mine was the part where he pretended to be an intruder, tied her up, and blindfolded her. Then she realized it was him. And they ended up having butt sex. They roleplayed the very thing he was supposed to be protecting her from. Ohhh, that was so hot."

Say what?

Roleplay?

Butt sex?

This was a bit different than the book I'd imagined.

I whispered to Juliette again. "Can you imagine if *I* pretended to be an intruder? Pretty sure I'd be in for a swift kick in the balls, or worse, instead of what the guy in the book got for pulling the same shit."

Juliette laughed a little that time, which pleased me. *Figures she'd laugh at a visual of me getting kicked in the balls, though.*

"Juliette?" Pam said. "It's your turn."

Juliette straightened in her seat. "What's that?"

"It's your turn to tell us your favorite scene. You told me earlier you'd highlighted one. Might you want to read it for us?"

"I listened to the audiobook mostly," she said. "But I highlighted a particular scene I liked on my Kindle." She swallowed.

Juliette hadn't planned for me to be here and didn't look enthused in the least about having to participate in this part of the evening. She opened her Kindle and pulled something up but stared down at it for several seconds without saying anything. Finally, she looked up. "I think I'm gonna pass, though, on sharing it."

"Oh, come on," I said with my mouth full. "That's no fun."

She gritted her teeth. "Neither is you being here, Wes."

"You seriously want me to leave?" I put my plate on the floor. "I will, if that'll make you happy."

"Please don't leave," some random woman begged.

"Jesus Christ." I snatched the Kindle from Juliette. "*I'll* read the scene, if you want."

Juliette's mouth dropped open, her face turning crimson. She held her hand out. "Give that back to me."

I kept it firmly in my hands. A quick glance down at the highlighted scene told me *exactly* why she was blushing. *Holy fuck.*

My eyes widened as I looked over at her. She gulped.

My mom read romance novels, too. I cringed at the thought that she might be reading something like this.

"*You* should read the scene for us, Wes," someone said.

Now *I* was the one feeling embarrassed—and I was normally a pretty bold motherfucker. It was hard to make me blush. But this? Reading it aloud in front of these thirsty women? *I don't know.*

Ultimately, I decided it would be worth it just to get a rise out of Juliette. Although, she might not forgive me for this one. I wiped my mouth with a napkin and cleared my throat. "Okay then." I flashed Juliette a wicked grin.

She turned her gaze away, while every other set of eyes in the room remained firmly on me as I began to read aloud.

"*Jonah wrapped his hands around Brooke's arms, both of them clearly spooked by the crashing sound, which turned out to be a false alarm. But there was nothing false about the need erupting between them as they held each other. Brooke could feel Jonah's heart beating against her chest. That wasn't all she could feel.*" I paused, trying to keep a straight face. "*He was throbbing against her, causing her panties to slowly melt with each second that passed. Once they realized they were safe, a desperate need for each other took over...*"

For the next several minutes, I recited what could only be described as straight-up porn, which included (among other things) three C-words I never imagined uttering aloud among a group of mostly older women: *cock, cum,* and *cunt.* Excuse me: *beautiful* cunt.

When I finished and looked up at my audience, I was a little freaked out. Every woman in the room remained entirely focused on me. One was licking something and sort of looked like she was imagining it could be me. Some of them seemed to be drooling or foaming at the mouth. Everyone stared—except Juliette. She still looked away, sinking into her chair as if she were trying to disappear into the cushion.

Pam fanned herself with a napkin. "That was...wow. That was something, Wes."

"You have an open invitation to be our official live reader," someone else said.

Another woman chimed in. "You should consider audio narration. You have the perfect deep voice for it."

I laughed awkwardly. "Not sure Juliette agrees."

But whether she agreed or not was irrelevant because she wasn't saying a damn word. She'd gone mute since my live reading.

And the walk home later was no different. Juliette remained quiet.

The silent treatment continued until the moment the door to her house closed behind us. Then she turned to me. Finally, she'd come alive, but not in a good way. She looked ready to spew venom.

"Did you *really* have to insert yourself into my book club like that?"

"You need to lighten up. It was all in good fun. And I mean, come on...the subject matter of that book? I was meant to be at this one. It was written in the stars. What were the chances?"

"The chances were very good, actually. Bodyguard and client is a popular romance trope."

My eyes went wide. "It is? I thought we just got lucky."

"It's a stupid trope, if you ask me. But yeah."

I squinted. "Stupid? Why?"

I found that a little insulting. Like, she thought it was so far-fetched that someone could find their bodyguard attractive? *Pfft*.

"You wanna know why it's stupid?" She arched a brow. "Because that doesn't happen in real life. A client falling for her bodyguard is a contrived situation—convenient. In reality, the situation would be inappropriate, messy at best, and unlikely to happen."

"But couldn't you argue that's *why* it's a fantasy? That could be why it's so fucking hot to them because it *is* inappropriate and not something you see every day in real life." I'd raised my voice a little louder than intended. Damn, was I butthurt over this or something? I needed to get a grip.

She shook her head. "Yeah, well, it's not my thing."

"You seemed to like that scene you highlighted, though," I cracked.

"There were probably a ton of other scenes that were better, more emotional. But these ladies always eat up the dirty parts. It was a lazy choice, though I knew they'd like it. I had to pick something, so I didn't show up empty-handed."

"Actually, that was more of a *one-handed* scene, if you know what I mean." I wriggled my brows. "You sure you didn't practice with it before you picked?"

Her cheeks turned pinker. "Yes, I'm sure."

I smirked. "You're turning red, so I have my doubts." When she didn't respond, I tried another question. "Okay...if bodyguard romance isn't your thing, what *is* your thing? What gets you off?"

"I like dark romance."

Hmm... "Like, horror shit? The kind of stuff you write screenplays for?"

She bit her bottom lip. "Not quite."

I plopped down on the couch and kicked my feet up. "Is it kinkier than what I read tonight?"

She went silent for a few moments. "Yes, it can be kinkier and also just..." She hesitated. "Never mind."

I pulled out my phone and started googling *dark romance*. Some of the things I found included morally gray hero, serial killers, kink, and BDSM.

"Damn." I looked up from my phone. "Little does Vince know what his daughter likes."

"Vince will *never* know what I read."

"It's nothing to be ashamed of. We all have fantasies."

"I didn't say I was ashamed." She turned away suddenly. "Goodnight, Wes."

Damn. That's it? I wasn't ready for the night to be over.

Juliette retreated to her room, leaving me alone. I wasn't tired at all yet—wired was more like it. So I flipped through the channels. I missed arguing with Juliette, though. Or maybe I enjoyed her company. All I knew was that it felt pretty damn lonely out here without her, though she was only in the next room.

Later that evening, she finally emerged. Juliette went to brush her teeth in the bathroom, leaving the door open. I decided to brush mine right alongside her.

For a while we stared at each other in the mirror. I smiled while she just looked…pissed.

Juliette spit out some toothpaste. "What are you doing?"

She had white, foamy liquid dribbling down her chin. And my mind? Straight into the gutter. My dick twitched, a little too excited for its own good by the toothpaste facial she'd given herself. I didn't mean for my head to venture to a dirty place—it just did. This was a clear indication that I needed to get laid, and certainly not with the current subject of my arousal.

"I'm just brushing my teeth, like you are," I said.

"Can you please wait your turn?"

"You had the door open. Unless the door is closed, the bathroom is fair game. That's my new rule. So close the door next time if you don't want company. Otherwise, I'll assume you're okay with it."

She rolled her eyes at me, and I smirked at her through the mirror.

After another minute of silence, I stopped brushing for a moment and asked, "Do women actually like it when a man refers to her pussy as a cunt?"

Juliette spit again, but refused to answer my question.

"I'm being serious. I want to know. For my own purposes…" Laughing, I added, "Call it research."

She rinsed, shut off the water, and said, "Go put a shirt on."

"Why does me being shirtless bother you so much?" I tilted my head. "Are you a bit flustered after all that sex talk tonight?"

"Go to hell."

"Hell is the temperature you keep this damn house at!" I glared. "Thus, the reason I continue to wear no shirt."

For the first time, I looked down and noticed Juliette wasn't wearing a bra. She didn't usually walk around without one, but the cami she had on tonight was thinner than usual, and I could see she didn't have anything on underneath. I looked up again. God, she was pretty. Actually, *pretty* wasn't a strong-enough word. Juliette Ginocassi was absolutely fucking stunning. Once again, my eyes traveled to her chest. I couldn't help it. Either her nipples were naturally prominent, or they were hard. And unfortunately, that made *me* hard.

Time to leave the bathroom *now*. I exited before she could notice my pants tightening.

One thing was for certain: I didn't need a damn book to get me off. All I'd had to do lately was think about Juliette, which was pretty messed up, all things considered. *Shit*. I'd been teasing her about the book turning her on, but it seemed *I* was actually the one riled up tonight.

Back on the couch, I kept thinking about how gorgeous she'd looked in that bathroom, her dark hair all wild from the humidity. And those damn nipples. They were like steel. The fucking toothpaste on her chin. And now that I knew she had a kinky side? Hard to forget. Very damn hard. It'd been a challenge not to see her in a sexual way before, but tonight had made it even worse. Tonight had been...*enlightening*, to say the least. And I'd also be lying if I said I hadn't briefly imagined her and me when reading that excerpt earlier. I'm sure she would've *loved* to know that tidbit. I'd have to keep it to myself.

I laughed. There's a story idea: a bodyguard romance where the bodyguard gets his balls shot off for crossing the line with the daughter of a mob boss. And not by the mobster, but by said daughter.

The next morning, I awoke to a loud bang. And not the kind of bang I'd had in my dreams—a loud and jarring one that sounded like it had come from somewhere in the house.

Fuck! What was that?

Adrenaline pumping, I jumped off the couch and reached over for my gun.

My heart pounded as I burst through Juliette's bedroom to check on her.

"What the fuck are you doing?" she screamed.

Panting, I held the gun up. "You didn't hear that?"

"Hear what?" she asked groggily, placing her hand on her chest. "And get that gun away from me."

"There was a loud bang. I thought someone had burst through your bedroom window or something."

She rubbed her eyes. "I didn't hear anything."

Was I hallucinating? "Stay put. Do *not* leave this room," I ordered.

Holding my gun close, I tiptoed around the house, sweeping the place. Finding nothing, I cautiously headed out the door to survey the front. Then I walked around the side of the house, which happened to be closest to where I'd been sitting in the living room. There I found a garbage can tipped over. Two raccoons were ransacking the garbage, though they fled the scene when I appeared. *Well, fuck.*

Laughter rang out behind me. Juliette looked all too amused by my discovery.

"What are you laughing at?" I grimaced.

"Thanks for rescuing me from those...evil perpetrators." She burst out laughing again.

"I'm glad you think it's so funny."

Her joking annoyed me. But that feeling was quickly replaced when I looked down and saw she'd never put a damn bra on. Just like that, I was feeling something *else* again.

"How about I treat you to breakfast for saving me, big guy?" She winked.

God, I wished she wouldn't wink at me like that. I was still too damn sensitized after last night. I cleared my throat. "I accept."

While we were out for coffee that morning, I noticed Juliette was in a *much* better mood. "You seem happier today," I told her. "Perhaps you let some of that tension go? Maybe your wrist is a little tired from thinking about the last book you read?"

She scowled. "I did no such thing."

That makes one of us. I sure as hell had used my hand. "Well, even if you did, it's natural." I shrugged. "I do it all the time."

"You'd *better* not be doing it on my couch."

Time to change the subject. "What's on tap for today?" I asked as I sipped my coffee.

She wiped her mouth with a napkin. "I have a yoga class."

"Oh, sounds like fun." I beamed.

Juliette looked a little scared. "You're *not* coming inside with me."

That's what you think.

CHAPTER 6

Wes

This is the day from hell.
It was barely noon, and I was already being subjected to my third round of torture. The first had been another braless morning at home. This time, the camisole was white, and I could clearly make out Juliette's areolas as she pranced around making a damn smoothie. Thankfully, she'd changed before going to yoga, and the new outfit wasn't see-through. But watching her stick her ass in the air during an hour-long class was definitely torture round two—and the gift that kept on giving. Because now that I knew how limber her body was, I couldn't stop imagining all the positions I could bend her into. Still, this third round of punishment was the worst of them all—watching her eat lunch with *Jett*.

I'd known the guy would take a renewed interest in Juliette the moment he saw me with her. The way he'd sized me up the other day told me he was one of those guys who liked to keep his options open and only paid attention when he felt threatened. So I wasn't surprised when Juliette's phone rang as we were walking into the house after yoga.

What pissed me off was that she immediately rearranged her whole day to accommodate him. Still, even that irritation didn't compare to what I was feeling now as I sat in my car, watching the jerk check out another woman's ass while Juliette was busy looking at the menu.

I sat, stewing and watching Juliette toss her hair around and laugh for almost an hour. Then, because apparently my shitty day could only get worse, my phone buzzed. *Vince. Great. Just fucking great.*

I took a deep breath and answered. "Hello?"

"I hear it's going to be *hot* out there today."

Vince Ginocassi did not call anyone to shoot the shit about the weather, so he had to be referring to something else—something I didn't like the sound of. I sat up straighter and kept my eyes on Juliette as we spoke. "Oh yeah. How hot?"

"*Blistering.* You should stay indoors."

"How long is this heat wave supposed to last?"

"*How the hell would I know? I'm not a fucking weatherman.* Just stay inside until the UV rays come down. Until then, I'm gonna ship you another gallon or two of sunscreen."

"I got it covered. I don't need more sunscreen."

He raised his voice. "*You need what I tell you that you fucking need.*"

Blood pumped through my veins. It was insulting he thought I couldn't handle protecting his daughter, especially if we were on freaking lockdown. Yet I swallowed the urge to argue. "Have you told our mutual friend?"

"That's *your* job."

Great. I had to give the news to Juliette.

"The line sounds staticky," Vince said. "Maybe you should get a new phone. When you do, text Frankie Knuckles the number. Make it soon."

"Got it."

"Good."

The line went dead without so much as a goodbye. I glanced around the street. Juliette wasn't exactly safe sitting at an outside table on Hollywood Boulevard, but with people and cars everywhere, they'd have to be idiots to take a shot at her here. Then again, these guys weren't the brightest. As I watched, the waiter walked over to their table and handed her lunch date what I assumed was the check. I figured I'd let her finish up and then break the good news about lockdown at home.

Ten minutes later, Juliette walked down the block to where I was parked behind her. That asshole Jett didn't even walk her to her car.

I turned on the ignition and rolled down my window. "I need to make a quick stop before we head home."

She smiled. "Okay."

Great, she's in a good mood for a change, and I get to ruin it. "Follow me."

I made a pit stop at a 7-Eleven, keeping a hawk's eye on Juliette's car in the parking lot while I paid for a burner phone.

When I walked out and she saw what I'd purchased, she rolled down her window. "What's wrong?"

"Let's talk when we get home."

She frowned, and I climbed into my car and fired off a text to Frankie with my new number before following her home. When we walked in, I asked her to wait just inside the door.

"Why?"

"Just give me a minute, please." I did a quick sweep, then nodded. "We're good."

She huffed. "Can you tell me what's going on now?"

I opened my mouth to speak, but the burner rang in my pocket. I held up a finger. "Give me another minute."

Juliette rolled her eyes. "Like I have a choice..."

I brought the phone into the bathroom for privacy. "What's up?"

"Blue Ford Mustang GT. Consider it the only car that's safe until you hear otherwise," Frankie said. "Eddie G and Tommy just picked it up as a rental. They'll park on the block and be your extra set of eyes. I'll text you their numbers after we hang up so you can reach them, if you need to."

"What's going on?"

"Direct threat to the boss's family. Juliette was specifically mentioned. We got intel that Sonny Altieri is on the move, searching for her. Look him up so you know his face. His mug shots shouldn't be hard to find."

I raked a hand through my hair. "All right."

"I'll call this phone when I have an update."

"Okay."

"Oh, and Wes, the boss asked me to pass along one more message."

"What's that?"

"Lockdown is not an opportunity to become *friendly* with his daughter."

I clenched my teeth. "Anything else?"

"Nope. Just do your job." *Click.*

Was there anyone in that organization who knew how to end a conversation like a human? I shook my head and walked out of the bathroom.

Juliette was waiting with her arms crossed in the kitchen. "What's going on?"

"We're on lockdown."

Her eyes flared. "*What?* For how long?"

I shrugged. "I don't know."

"This is ridiculous!" She flailed her arms, then smacked them down at her sides. "I have a date with Jett tomorrow night!"

At least there's one good thing about this situation... I shrugged. "Looks like you're going to have to cancel."

"I am *not* canceling." She dug into her purse and pulled out her cell phone. "I'm calling my father."

"Go right ahead. This wasn't my decision. I'm just doing what I was told."

Juliette tapped a few buttons on her phone, then held it to her ear, glaring at me the whole time. When I heard a voice start talking, I figured she'd been sent to voicemail. She growled and tried again—same result. On her third attempt, her face turned bright red with frustration. Without a word, she marched into her bedroom and slammed the door.

I didn't hear from her for hours after that—not until she walked out to the living room with her hair blown out, a full face of makeup, and a little black one-shoulder dress that stirred something in me instantly.

"Where do you think you're going?"

She lifted her chin into the air, marched to the table, and swiped up her purse. "Karaoke with Pam and a few friends. We go every other week."

I shook my head. "Well, you're not going this week."

Ignoring me, Juliette strutted to the front door and grabbed her keys from the hook. I stepped in front of her, planting myself between her and the door. "I'm sorry you can't go. But the only way you're going out without me is by walking over my dead body."

Juliette's eyes narrowed, and she took a step forward. "If you insist..."

Her chest heaved up, and she looked about as pissed as a person could get—but damn, she smelled good. And that spark in her eye? It only made her sexier. Being this close was messing with my head. My body reacted and clouded every rational thought.

I had to take a step back, put some room between us before I did something stupid—like grab a fistful of her hair and kiss the living shit out of her. *Oh boy*. Make that two steps. I definitely needed two.

"You're not leaving this house, Juliette. If I have to tie you up to keep you inside, that's what I'm going to do." *Crap*. Now I was picturing her with her arms spread wide, wrists tied to her headboard—so yeah, I needed a better strategy than restraining her. That might be even more dangerous than letting her walk out the door.

"Fine..." She huffed. "I'm going to call all of my *uncles*, until someone puts me on the phone with my father, and he puts an end to this ridiculousness." Turning around, she marched toward the back of the house, where her bedroom and bathroom were. "But first I need to pee."

I waited a few minutes, expecting to hear her yell or maybe throw her phone, but it stayed quiet—*too quiet*. So I walked to the back and knocked on the closed bathroom door.

"Juliette?"

No answer.

"*Juliette?*"

Still no answer. I reached for the door handle, expecting it to be locked, but it turned. And Juliette wasn't inside.

Fuck.

I ran to her room, but that was empty too. *Goddammit!*

She must've climbed out the bathroom window or slipped out the back door. Either way, I needed to find her. *Now.* I bolted out the front door in a panic and spotted her standing at the neighbor's front door. I reached her just as it swung open.

Pam glanced between us and grinned. "Ooh. Hot stuff is coming too?"

Juliette opened her mouth to respond, but her words fell by the wayside as I wrapped a hand around her waist and pulled her close.

"I'm sorry, Pam," I said softly. "I came to apologize for making your friend stay in with me. I just got her to agree a few minutes ago. I really want a night alone with her."

Pam's eyes widened. "A night alone?"

"She's been so busy since I got here. You understand, right?"

A grin spread across Pam's face. "Of course."

"Thanks, Pam."

"You two have a great time." She winked at Juliette. "Don't do anything I wouldn't do."

We walked back to the house with my arm still tightly around Juliette. She hadn't said a word, but I suspected I was in for an earful once we were alone.

Boy, was I right. The minute I shut the door behind us, she threw her purse at me. I caught it, which only pissed her off more.

"How dare you do that in front of my friend?" she hissed.

"You didn't leave me any choice, sneaking out like that. What are you, twelve?"

The vein in her neck bulged. "Maybe I act like that because I'm *treated* that way."

I was pissed that she'd ditched me, yet I could understand why she was so upset. The woman had done everything she could to break free of her father, and somehow his shit still blew back on her. I spoke with a calm voice. "I get it. I really do. But my priority is keeping you safe, even if doing so also happens to make you miserable."

"Tell me what's going on. Why are we on lockdown?"

Vince had never instructed me to keep her in the dark, and I sort of thought she had a right to know anyway. "I don't know that many details. Just that we have some extra eyes watching the house, and a guy named Sonny is a threat."

Juliette's face fell. "Sonny Altieri?"

I nodded. "You know him?"

All the anger was suddenly gone, and it seemed like she was on the verge of tears. She looked away. "I'm going to my room."

I waited a few hours before knocking on her bedroom door. "Juliette? You okay?"

Her voice was small. "I'm fine."

I pressed my ear to her door. "Can I come in?"

A few beats passed. "Yeah."

She was lying in bed, curled in the fetal position, and didn't sit up when I entered. "What happened earlier? I said a name, and you lost all your fight."

"There's nothing left to fight for."

I pointed to the foot of the bed. "Can I sit down?"

She shrugged. "Whatever."

When I did, Juliette sat up a little, leaning her back against the headboard and wrapping her arms around her knees.

"Are you scared?" I asked.

She shook her head. "I'm used to lockdowns and threats."

"Then what is it?"

"The name you mentioned. I haven't heard it in a long time."

I hadn't needed Frankie to tell me to look up Sonny Altieri. I already knew he was a soldier for a rival family, one who seemed to be coated with Teflon. He'd been indicted for murder three times in the last fifteen years—and got off on every charge. Though I wasn't sure why the mention of his name would upset Juliette, unless she was scared.

"Did he do something to you?"

She nodded. "Not directly, but to someone I loved."

I waited for her to say more, but she just kept staring at her knees.

"One of the men he was indicted for killing?"

She shook her head. "He was never charged for killing Nick. I'm sure there's a laundry list of other horrible things he's gotten away with."

"Was Nick a relative of yours?"

"He was my boyfriend. My high school sweetheart. He was shot in front of my father's pizzeria."

Oh shit. I remembered the story now. God knows I'd read everything I could get my hands on when I'd started working for Vince Ginocassi. Nick Spagnoli, the eighteen-year-old son of Big Nicky, one of her father's underbosses, was killed in broad daylight walking out of Gino's Pizza with his dad. It was assumed he'd been caught in mob-related crossfire, and as far as I knew, no one had ever been arrested for the murder.

"I'm sorry, Juliette."

She sniffled back tears. "I haven't thought about Nick in a long time, and hearing you say Sonny's name made me feel guilty for that."

I wasn't sure what to say, but I wanted to make her feel better. "Did Nick love you?"

Juliette nodded.

"Then he wouldn't want you to carry grief with you every day. He'd want you to find peace and move on."

"Thanks." She wiped a tear and tried to force a smile, but it looked more like a wilted flower. "Would you mind giving me a few minutes alone?"

"Of course."

After I closed her door, I stood there a moment, listening. It sounded like the floodgates had opened. Part of me wanted to go back in and hold her, but I decided to respect her privacy.

Out in the living room, I sat for a while. Juliette hadn't eaten any dinner yet, so I thought about making something in case she got hungry. Then a better idea hit me. Frankie had texted me the numbers of the two guys watching the house. I'd seen their car outside earlier, so I went to the front door to check that it was still there before calling.

"Hey. It's Wes."

"Everything good?"

"Yeah, everything's fine. But I need a few things from the store, and I have to stay here. Can you make a run for me?"

"I don't know. We're supposed to be watching the house."

"Vince knows I'm sending you," I lied.

"All right then. What do you need?"

"I'll text you a list."

Forty-five minutes later, there was a light knock on the door. I'd watched the Mustang come back down the block, but I checked the peephole before answering anyway.

A guy I recognized as Eddie Guiliano shook his head. "What the hell do you need all this shit for?"

I took the bags. "Don't worry about it."

The guy shrugged. "Whatever. You know where to find me."

Juliette still hadn't come out of her room, so I had time to set up alone. When I was done, I knocked on her door again. "Juliette?"

"Yeah?"

"Can you come out for a minute?"

"Do I have to?"

I paused. "No. But I'd appreciate it if you did."

She padded from her room wearing ratty sweatpants, her eyes pink and puffy from crying. When she saw the living room, her little nose scrunched up. "What's all this?"

"You couldn't go out to karaoke and cocktails tonight, so I brought karaoke and cocktails to you."

I'd hung two strings of white lights in the living room, set up a margarita maker and glasses, and connected the new karaoke machine to the TV, which now read *Juliette's Karaoke Party*.

"Where did all this stuff come from? I don't have a karaoke machine or a margarita maker."

I winked. "I have my ways."

"You did all this for me?" Her face softened. "That is so sweet."

There should have been warning bells going off in my head for making nice with this woman, considering who her father was. But instead, her smile soothed me.

"Take a seat and scroll through the playlist. I'll make you a drink."

One drink led to two, and two led to three, and before long Juliette was hiccupping between giggles. I'd just finished singing "Friends in Low Places" by Garth Brooks.

"You are soooo bad." *Hiccup.*

I chuckled. "Thanks a lot."

"Anytime."

"Even if I could carry a tune, I'd still sound like shit compared to you. You sing like that *American Idol* woman—Kelly something. Where'd you learn to belt like that?"

"My mom." *Hiccup.* She giggled again and covered her mouth. "She was a lounge singer. That's how she met my dad."

"A *sling*er, huh?" I smiled. "Not a singer?"

My comment sent her into another fit of giggles. The sound made my chest feel warm. "How are you not slurring your words?" she asked. "You drank as many margs as I did."

"Mine were virgin. I can't drink and do my job."

"Oh. Virgin." She picked up her glass and held it out with a goofy smile. "That means more tequila for me!"

"I don't know about that. I think you might've reached your limit."

She pouted. "Pleeaassssse."

I shook my head, unable to contain my own smile. "One more, lightweight."

Juliette flopped back on the couch. "I'll just wait right here."

"You do that..."

In the kitchen, I dumped the old mix into the sink and added fresh ice for a new batch. This time, I only added enough tequila to make it *smell* like alcohol before blending.

When I came back with a practically virgin margarita, I found Juliette fast asleep.

I grabbed the blanket draped over the back of the couch and covered her up. For a moment, I stood watching her. A tiny smile threatened at the corner of her lips, making me smile too.

I thought I'd understood the dangers of this job. But standing here, looking down at Juliette Ginocassi's beautiful face, I realized *she* was the real threat.

And God help me, I wanted her anyway.

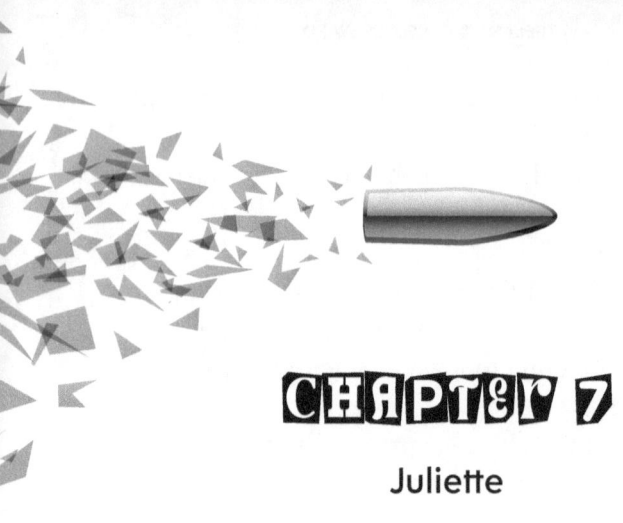

CHAPTER 7

Juliette

I rubbed my tired head the next morning. "Who called?"

"It was your father." Wes sighed. "He said the threat is over. I guess Altieri and his people were in town for a wedding. It's been confirmed that they've left LA."

I yawned. "Good riddance."

Although, there were certainly worse things than being holed up with Wes. Despite having too much to drink last night, I'd actually had fun. Wes had *made it* fun.

In fact, the more time I spent with the guy, the more I saw good in him. What he'd done for me last night had taken not only creativity, but heart. And it wasn't anything I'd soon forget.

But alas, I really should try to forget the feelings that seemed to be brewing for Wes. The last thing I needed was to let my little crush on him grow any bigger.

After I had my coffee, I decided to text Jett to confirm our date tonight.

Juliette: Hey! Still on for tonight?

The little dots moved around as he typed.

Jett: Absolutely. Looking forward to it.

Juliette: Where should we meet?

Jett: How about Rosa's on Sunset at 7?

Juliette: Sounds perfect. Love that place.

Jett: See you then.

Juliette: Looking forward to it.

Jett: See you soon. xo

I exhaled. Well, that was that.

Wes startled me as he came up from behind. "What's the plan for later today?"

I hated having to admit where I was going. But I couldn't lie. "I have a date tonight, remember? With Jett."

His expression fell a bit. Or was that my imagination? He definitely didn't look happy.

"I guess that's happening, huh?" Wes cocked his head. "Where are you headed?"

"Rosa's on Sunset."

He nodded. "Okay. I'll go in with you and sit at the opposite end of the restaurant."

"You can't go in with me." I frowned. "He'll recognize you."

"Not if I wear my shades and sit far enough away. I'll stay out of your way."

I placed my hands on my hips. "No, Wes. I'm putting my foot down. You can't come in."

He gritted his teeth and fell silent.

"You wait outside when I'm at work," I pointed out. "How is this different?"

After a long hesitation, he finally conceded. "I'll wait outside, but if I can't find parking right across the street, I'm coming in. So you'd better hope I find a spot."

From there, Wes gave me the silent treatment for most of the day—a stark contrast to last night's jovial mood. I guess I'd pissed him off by asking for space.

That evening, after I got all dolled up in a sexy yellow sundress and matching shoes, I announced to Wes that I was ready to leave. He grabbed his keys but said nothing as he followed me out the door.

The tension lingered the entire ride over to the restaurant as Wes said nothing.

Leaving him waiting in the car, I headed inside Rosa's. There was no sign of Jett. That surprised me, since I was a couple of minutes late and assumed he'd be waiting. I was pretty sure Wes had taken his sweet time getting here on purpose in order to make me late. Hopefully, Jett wouldn't be too much longer. I hated when dates were late. It showed apathy, although I couldn't be sure he hadn't hit LA traffic. That would be the only acceptable excuse.

More than ten minutes passed before I spotted Jett walking in the door. He ran a hand through his hair, looking flustered, but his mouth curved into a smile once he noticed me.

Grinning, I waved him over to the table.

"Sorry I'm late." He sat down across from me. "Traffic."

At least he had a good excuse. "I figured."

He placed his napkin in his lap, leaned back in the chair, and grinned. "You look absolutely stunning, Juliette," he said, seeming a little out of breath. "Yellow is most definitely your color. It accentuates your dark hair beautifully."

"Thank you." I felt my cheeks heat.

Jett and I ordered drinks, and it seemed like things were going well, the conversation flowing easily. But then the tide shifted as I looked over at the entrance and found Wes stalking toward our table. My pulse raced. *What the hell is he doing?* Anger raced through me, leaving a trail of heat. I couldn't believe he'd gone against his word.

"Hey, friend!" He flashed a fake smile as he approached the table. "Didn't expect to run into you tonight!"

"What are you doing here?" I gritted my teeth.

"Well, I was in the area and decided to come in for a bite." He pulled out a chair and made himself comfortable. "You don't mind if I join, do you?"

I opened my mouth, and then closed it. What could I possibly say? The nerve of him after he'd specifically promised he'd wait in the car. I wanted to tell him to beat it, but Jett thought Wes was a family friend, so my reaction needed to be in accordance with that story. I had to suck it up, as it would've seemed rude to kick him to the curb.

Wes leaned back in his chair and scratched his chin as he perused the menu. Jett stared at him incredulously.

After Wes ordered a drink, I did my best to turn my attention back to Jett. We talked shop for a while, basically ignoring Wes, until my trusty bodyguard finally spoke.

"Do you mind if I interrupt?" Wes cleared his throat.

My stomach sank. *I'm seriously going to kill him.* It was bad enough that I had to deal with having a bodyguard, but had I given Wes the impression that my life was a toy he could play with? Had I been too nice to him, and he thought he could do whatever he wanted now? He would be getting the biggest piece of my mind later.

Jett narrowed his eyes. "Something tells me you're going to interrupt regardless of my answer, so go right ahead."

Wes leveled him with an incendiary stare. "I have a question for you, Jett..."

Jett took a sip of his drink and crossed his arms. "Okay..."

"Do you always suck face with one woman right before going out on a date with another?"

I immediately looked up.

Jett's face went white. His mouth opened and closed a few times.

Wes continued, "Like, literally a minute before your date with someone else?"

Jett remained silent as Wes took out his phone. He slammed it down on the table so that both Jett and I could see. It was, indeed, an image of Jett kissing a woman. He was wearing the same shirt he had on now, and the photo had been taken just outside on Sunset Boulevard.

Holy crap. Wes wasn't joking.

"Juliette," Jett finally said. "I'm not sure what to say. I'm certainly not going to deny what's obvious. I was with a date before I came here." He shook his head. "But it's not serious. So technically, I don't owe her, or anyone else, an explanation for meeting you after. But I can understand why this would be upsetting."

I just sat there, my mouth agape.

No, Jett wasn't my boyfriend. We weren't exclusive. We were just on a casual date. But kissing someone a literal minute before coming in to meet me? I was certain he'd probably told that woman he had a business meeting or something. He'd likely be going back to her or someone else later. This was a giant red flag. Jett was now someone I didn't feel deserved my time.

"You know what?" I stood. "I've had a rough week. Rather than sit here and try to figure out whether this is right or wrong or how to respond to you, I'm gonna protect my peace." I nodded once. "So, if you'll excuse me, I'm leaving. Have a good rest of your evening. Hope it's as exciting as your afternoon seemed to be."

I lifted my chin high and walked straight toward the entrance without looking back.

I headed over to where Wes had left the car across the street. The car door was unlocked. *Hmm...* That was unlike Wes. I did a quick sweep of the vehicle to make sure no one was hiding in it. Then I got in and leaned my head against the backrest, taking a moment to sit in quiet and recover from whatever the hell that had been.

When I heard the driver's side door open a few minutes later, I opened my eyes to find a somber-looking Wes.

"Juliette, I'm really sorr—"

"No. No. Don't you dare apologize. You did me a favor. I should thank you for intervening. I don't want anything to do with someone who operates like that. You saved me hours of my life, maybe more—time that would've been totally wasted."

"Well, I'm glad you're not mad. I sat here and debated it for a while before I went in. But I couldn't let you sit across from that guy without giving you the opportunity to make an informed decision about it."

I had to laugh. "I was ready to kill you when you walked in."

He nodded. "I knew you would be. I hated those minutes where you thought I was just being an insensitive jerk who didn't care about boundaries." He chuckled. "I mean, I know I *can* come across that way sometimes, but I wouldn't have stooped to that level for no good reason."

"What took you so long to come back out?" I asked.

He shrugged. "I gave him a little piece of my mind before I left."

Nice. I turned toward him. "You left the car unlocked. That's not like you."

His face turned red. "My head wasn't on straight. I wanted to fucking kill that guy for disrespecting you."

Something like a jolt of electricity shot through me. It was one thing for a man to protect me because he'd been hired to do so. But Wes looking out for me today now seemed totally different. And I wasn't used to that.

Wes started the car, and as he pulled into traffic, I remained quiet, looking out the window. "Please just take me home," I said after a moment.

"Are you sure? It's a nice night and still pretty early."

I shook my head. "I'm not in the mood to do anything."

When he passed the exit for my house, I turned to him. "Where are you going? I said I wanted to go home…"

"Will you trust me?" he asked, glancing over. "I promise you'll like it."

When I noticed the signs for Venice Beach, I couldn't help but smile. I hadn't been there in a long time, and maybe it was just the thing to take my mind off this. *Screw it.* I was wearing my pretty yellow dress, and the weather was gorgeous.

After we parked, Wes came around to the passenger side before I had the chance to exit the car. He smiled as I stood. "They have the best churros here." His eyes sparkled, almost like a child's.

"I'm just glad you didn't take me to West Hollywood for smoked Portuguese sausage."

"The night is young." He winked.

I smiled, grateful that he hadn't let me go home and mope. Lord knows my father wasn't one to care whether his workers were kind. But it seemed I'd gotten a good one.

Wes and I scored his beloved churros and walked around for a bit. We then stopped at a cute shop that sold blown-glass trinkets, among other things.

After a few minutes, Wes ventured to the counter to purchase something. I tried to see what he was up to, but he kept his back to me.

He held up a small gift bag as we walked out of the place. "I bought you a present."

"Oh! I assumed you were buying something for yourself."

He handed me the bag, with a snicker. The small box inside held a tiny pendant made of glass on a silver rope chain. My eyes widened. "You bought me a penis pendant?"

"Ah." He laughed. "That's what it looks like, doesn't it?"

"It's *not* a penis?"

"No, dirty girl. It's not. It's supposed to be a cactus."

"A cactus does not have two balls at the base."

"Those are not balls. Those are two other tiny cactuses growing next to the big one."

"You expect me to believe that?" I laughed.

"I asked the owner! Because I wasn't sure myself."

I rubbed my thumb over the shiny glass. "Well, thank you...I think?"

"It has a deeper meaning," he said.

"Oh? And what exactly is the deep meaning of this cactus cock here?"

"When you think back to this day when that jerkoff double-timed you, instead of focusing on that, you'll remember it as the day I gave you this ridiculous necklace. The cactus cock will forever serve as a reminder that you deserve better, Juliette."

My cheeks hurt from smiling. "Will you put it on me?"

"Of course." He took it from me and opened the clasp. "Just don't tell Vince it was from me," he said as he wrapped it around my neck. "He'd never believe it's a cactus."

The warmth of Wes's hands on my body sent a moment of heat through me. "Thanks again. That was sweet," I said, looking down at it.

Next, we walked along the shore. I took my shoes off and held them in my hand, digging my bare toes into the sand as we went.

"Do you ever miss being a cop?" I asked him.

Wes looked up at the sky. "All the time."

"Do you want to talk about what led you to working for my father?"

He slipped his hands in his pockets. "Not right now, no."

"Okay," I murmured.

I knew it had to be pretty damn bad for Wes to have ended up working for Dad. I didn't envy anyone who had to deal with his wrath—myself included.

"But I will say this," Wes suddenly added. "You don't get too many moments like this one being a cop.

So I have to take the good with the bad when it comes to this gig, you know?"

"I hear you." I shielded my eyes from the sun as I looked up at him. "You're good at what you do, Wes. I know I haven't made it easy on you. I was very resistant to the idea of you in the beginning. But I've had more pleasant moments than bad ones with you."

"I'll take that as a compliment." He smiled.

"You should."

"And if I may compliment *you* for a moment, Juliette..."

"Please do..."

"You're handling this whole thing as well as can be expected. I know it can't be easy having a guard twenty-four-seven."

"Well...it's not easy. But...I'm glad it's you," I told him.

After a moment, he said quietly, "I'm glad it's me, too."

Why am I getting butterflies right now? Foolish.

We sat down on the sand and almost immediately, seagulls swarmed us. The next thing I knew, one of the birds had snatched my shoe and flown off with it.

"Oh my God! My shoe!"

Wes cackled. "Here I was thinking I could protect you from anything. But that right there was as covert an operation as I've ever seen."

I cracked up, too. It sucked to lose a shoe, but it would always make for a good story. And it felt really good to laugh.

When it was time to walk back to the car, Wes carried me across the lot, since it skeeved me out to walk on the pavement with my bare foot. I felt light as a feather in his arms and wouldn't have minded if the walk had lasted a bit longer.

I was so relaxed on the ride home that I nearly fell asleep. It had turned out to be a wonderful evening, thanks to Wes.

When he came around to let me out of the car, I hopped on one foot to the door. We cracked up all over again at the ridiculousness of it.

But our laughter came to an abrupt end as the lights of an approaching car registered.

Wes placed his arm around me protectively before shielding me. A window rolled down, and Wes reached for his gun.

Then we realized who it was.

"Where have you two been, and where the hell is your shoe?" my father bellowed.

CHAPTER 8

Wes

What the fuck?

The pulse in my neck throbbed as I sat in the car, listening to Vince and Juliette scream at each other inside the house. I'd never been a fan of Vince Ginocassi, but hearing that asshole bark at his daughter like she worked for him sent fire coursing through my veins. Who talks to their kid like that? It took every ounce of my self-control not to storm in there and break up their argument. But a glance in my rearview at the two goons sitting in the car behind me reminded me why I wasn't making a move. Across the street was a second SUV parked with two more men—four guys in total. Vince usually traveled with just one bodyguard, so something must've happened if he needed this much security.

After another tense ten minutes, Juliette's front door finally whipped open. Vince stomped down the porch steps and headed straight to my car, sliding into the passenger seat without asking.

"Are you even capable of not thinking with your dick around my daughter?" he roared.

Heat rushed to my face as I fought to maintain my composure. "I've been nothing but professional around Juliette."

"Didn't look very professional from where I was sitting when you two pulled up," he scoffed. "Looked like you were having a good ol' time."

My jaw flexed. "What's going on? I know you didn't come all the way out to California to make sure I wasn't smiling around Juliette. If you didn't trust me, I wouldn't be sitting here."

Vince stared at me before he spoke again. He was trying to intimidate me, but I wasn't going to kiss his feet, no matter who the hell he was. "Things have gotten hot," he said. "Boiling."

"You told me this morning that Altieri and his men had left town, and I didn't need to keep Juliette locked up in the house anymore."

"*That was fucking this morning!*" he bellowed. "Tonight, things are different."

"What happened?"

His eyes narrowed. "What are you, writing a fucking book?"

I clenched my teeth, rather than my fists, but I was about two seconds away from punching this asshole in the face. "I can't do my job unless I know what I'm looking out for."

He heaved a sigh. "Everything. Anything. One of my men's kids got popped. Thirteen fucking years old. And he wasn't collateral damage. It was a direct hit, aimed right at the boy. The old rules are gone—families aren't off-limits anymore. The next generation coming up are a bunch of damn animals." He looked over at Juliette's house. "I got word that Juliette's a target, and they know where she lives."

Shit. "What's the plan?"

"I want her off the grid for a while, at least until things cool down. So pack your shit. You're flying private. I'm not taking any chances that someone follows her out of town. The plane leaves Van Nuys Airport in two hours."

"Where are we going?"

He held out an envelope. "Ortigia."

Vince opened the car door and started to get out, then turned back with a raised finger. "If you so much as touch my daughter, I'll have your dick cut off and stuffed for my mantel. Do you understand me?"

This time, my fists actually balled at my sides, but I managed to grind out a single word. "Yes."

"Good." He leaned down before shutting the door. "Get her on that plane. No matter what it takes."

The door slammed shut before I could ask where the fuck Ortigia even was. I sat in the car and googled it as I watched Vince and his army drive off. *Ortigia is a small island off the coast of southeastern Sicily. It is part of the city of Syracuse and is connected to the mainland by two bridges.*

Great. I don't speak Italian. I'd have to worry about that later, considering I only had two hours to get to the damn airport. I shoved the envelope Vince had given me in my back pocket, checked my surroundings, and headed into the house.

Juliette was sitting at the kitchen table, eating what looked like a bowl of ice cream. My brows drew together. "Why aren't you packing?"

"Because I'm not going."

Great. Just fucking great.

I heard crunching, so I leaned in for a closer look at what she was chomping on. "What's in there?"

"Cinnamon Toast Crunch, vanilla ice cream, and caramel syrup."

I made a face that told her what I thought of the combination, and Juliette went off.

"Mind your own business about my ice cream! And while you're at it, keep your nose out of anything to do with the men I date, too!"

An hour ago, she'd been thanking me for showing her what an asshole her date was. But clearly now was *not* the time to point that out.

She pushed back from the table, chair scraping against the tile, and marched over to the garbage, dumping her ice cream—bowl, spoon, and all.

"*And I'm not going to Ortigia!* So just leave me alone!"

I counted to ten, but it wasn't enough. I still needed to cool down before I tried to talk some sense into her. So instead, I went to the garbage and fished out the ceramic bowl she'd tossed. The day must've gotten to me, because before I could think better of it, I'd scooped some of the crap she was eating into my mouth.

I shrugged. *Not bad.* I rinsed the dish before knocking lightly at Juliette's bedroom door.

"Go away!"

"I hope you're decent because I'm coming in."

She didn't answer, so I creaked open the door and found her sitting on the bed.

I spoke calmly. "We have to go. You're in danger."

"I don't want to go anywhere!"

a bunch of damn animals." He looked over at Juliette's house. "I got word that Juliette's a target, and they know where she lives."

Shit. "What's the plan?"

"I want her off the grid for a while, at least until things cool down. So pack your shit. You're flying private. I'm not taking any chances that someone follows her out of town. The plane leaves Van Nuys Airport in two hours."

"Where are we going?"

He held out an envelope. "Ortigia."

Vince opened the car door and started to get out, then turned back with a raised finger. "If you so much as touch my daughter, I'll have your dick cut off and stuffed for my mantel. Do you understand me?"

This time, my fists actually balled at my sides, but I managed to grind out a single word. "Yes."

"Good." He leaned down before shutting the door. "Get her on that plane. No matter what it takes."

The door slammed shut before I could ask where the fuck Ortigia even was. I sat in the car and googled it as I watched Vince and his army drive off. *Ortigia is a small island off the coast of southeastern Sicily. It is part of the city of Syracuse and is connected to the mainland by two bridges.*

Great. I don't speak Italian. I'd have to worry about that later, considering I only had two hours to get to the damn airport. I shoved the envelope Vince had given me in my back pocket, checked my surroundings, and headed into the house.

Juliette was sitting at the kitchen table, eating what looked like a bowl of ice cream. My brows drew together. "Why aren't you packing?"

"Because I'm not going."

Great. Just fucking great.

I heard crunching, so I leaned in for a closer look at what she was chomping on. "What's in there?"

"Cinnamon Toast Crunch, vanilla ice cream, and caramel syrup."

I made a face that told her what I thought of the combination, and Juliette went off.

"Mind your own business about my ice cream! And while you're at it, keep your nose out of anything to do with the men I date, too!"

An hour ago, she'd been thanking me for showing her what an asshole her date was. But clearly now was *not* the time to point that out.

She pushed back from the table, chair scraping against the tile, and marched over to the garbage, dumping her ice cream—bowl, spoon, and all.

"*And I'm not going to Ortigia!* So just leave me alone!"

I counted to ten, but it wasn't enough. I still needed to cool down before I tried to talk some sense into her. So instead, I went to the garbage and fished out the ceramic bowl she'd tossed. The day must've gotten to me, because before I could think better of it, I'd scooped some of the crap she was eating into my mouth.

I shrugged. *Not bad.* I rinsed the dish before knocking lightly at Juliette's bedroom door.

"Go away!"

"I hope you're decent because I'm coming in."

She didn't answer, so I creaked open the door and found her sitting on the bed.

I spoke calmly. "We have to go. You're in danger."

"I don't want to go anywhere!"

"I know you don't, and I don't blame you. It sucks that you constantly have to deal with the fallout from something you've worked hard to keep your distance from."

When she looked up, tears welled in her eyes. "I have a life here. A job, friends...commitments. What would I even tell people?"

"Maybe you can say someone in your family is ill, and you have to take an unplanned trip."

She seemed to consider it for a moment, but she shook her head. "No, I'm not going."

I could try to reason with her some more or toss her over my shoulder and carry her ass to the plane. The latter would probably be easier, but I suspected it would raise more than a few eyebrows. So I took a deep breath before walking to the bed and sitting down. Telling her she wasn't safe hadn't worked, so I switched tactics.

"What's it going to take to get you on that plane, Juliette? Because if I don't get you to Ortigia safely, it's gonna be my ass."

She met my eyes and held my gaze for a few beats. "Tell me what my father has over you to get you to work for him."

Fuck. Vince would not be happy if he found out I'd told his daughter the story of how we'd connected, but I looked at my watch—an hour and fifty minutes to go, and it would probably take an hour to get to the airport with LA traffic. "You'll pack and get on the plane if I tell you?"

She nodded.

"Fine." I centered myself for a moment. "When I was a cop, I responded to a domestic violence report of a man abusing his wife. I busted through the door and found a three-hundred-pound asshole beating a five-foot-nothing woman. He had one hand around her neck, holding her against the wall, and the other was pummeling her face. The guy was so out of his mind, he didn't even hear me come in. He punched her again before I could get to him, and I heard the crack of her nose." I paused, seeing the woman's bloody face again like she was right in front of me. "My father used to beat my mother when I was a kid, so I guess it brought back a lot of bad memories, and I lost it on the guy. I took him down to the floor and beat the crap out of him. When backup arrived, they had to pull me off of him, and he was a bloodier mess than his wife was. Long story short, I got fired from the force, and the district attorney charged me criminally for using excessive force. Turned out, the woman being beaten was Vince's cousin."

Juliette gasped. "Oh my God. Antoinette?"

I nodded.

"I remember that. It was in the news. I'd called my dad to see if she was okay."

"A few days later, Vince showed up at my door and told me he respected what I'd done for his cousin. Then he laid out a deal. Antoinette would change her story— say she'd smashed her husband in the face with a frying pan after he started beating her, and that her husband had pulled a gun on me. That version would clear me. In exchange, I'd owe Vince. He wanted me working security for him. Said he liked the idea of a trained cop on his payroll." I shrugged. "Prison isn't easy for regular people. It's a different kind of hell for cops. So I took the deal."

Juliette reached over and squeezed my hand. Then she got up and took out a suitcase. "I'll be ready in fifteen minutes."

"Have you ever been to Ortigia?" Juliette asked once our plane had leveled out at flying altitude.

I'd been too busy strangling the armrests to talk until now. I wasn't a fan of planes, especially not little ones like this, even if the inside was fancy. I shook my head. "Never been to Italy."

"You're going to love it. It's beautiful."

"What's in Ortigia? The little bit I read about it said it was a pretty small island."

She nodded. "It is. My grandmother lived there. When I was growing up, we went once a year, and I loved it. It was the only time I felt like I had a normal family. My dad wasn't the boss yet, so things were calmer. Though he always had a posse of men around. His..." She made air quotes. "...*associates* didn't come with us to Ortigia, so it was just my mom and dad and me. We'd do simple things like go to the beach and take bike rides, and my dad wasn't busy looking over his shoulder all the time."

I smiled. "That sounds nice. When did you stop going?"

"When I was sixteen. The last time I was there was for my grandmother's funeral. But my dad still goes back from time to time. Do you know where we're staying?"

I reached into my back pocket and took out the envelope Vince had given me. Inside was a thick stack of hundreds and a paper with an address on it. I handed the paper to Juliette.

She nodded. "This is my grandmother's house. I'm excited to see it."

"Yeah? Then maybe you shouldn't have given me such a hard time about going."

She stuck her tongue out.

I chuckled. "Mature."

Juliette sighed and looked out the window. "I didn't even know what my father really did for a living until I was twelve. Can you believe that?"

"How'd you find out?"

"Career day. We had to write a paper about someone we admired and tell about their job. My mom didn't work, so I wrote it about my dad."

My brows drew down. "What did you think he did?"

She rolled her eyes. "Garbage man. What else? I stood in front of the whole freaking class and told them how my father wore a suit to work every day, then changed into his uniform once he got there so he wouldn't come home smelling bad. That's what he'd told me when I asked why he didn't wear a uniform like the guys who picked up the garbage at our house. At the end, we had to take questions from the class, and Danny Donnolly raised his hand and asked if I really didn't know my father was in the mob."

"Shit."

"I marched straight to the pizzeria after school that afternoon. That's where my father went every day after he supposedly went to work. My uncle Pietro owned it back then, and I had no idea Gino's was a front either. Apparently, when they kill your uncle and you become the head of a crime family, the job comes with a free pizza place." Juliette shook her head. "Anyway, I confronted my dad and told him what Danny Donnolly had said."

"How'd that go?"

"He ruffled my hair and laughed. Then he said, '*Little Danny got half the story right. I do take out trash. Just not the kind that goes in the can.*' All his cronies started laughing like it was the funniest thing in the world. Meanwhile, everything I thought I knew about my family had just blown up in my face."

I shook my head. "I'm sorry. That must've been tough."

"Anything to do with my father is tough." She caught my eye. "But I guess you know that by now."

Family was complicated—you could bitch about them, curse their name, and drone on to anyone who would listen about how horrible they were. But the moment someone from the outside did it, you bared your teeth. So rather than share how I really felt about Vince Ginocassi, I nodded and kept my mouth shut.

Eventually Juliette went back to staring out the window. "Can I ask you something about the story you told me earlier?" she asked a little while later.

I shrugged. "You can ask."

"How long do you have to work for my dad to pay him back?"

I was quiet for a long time before meeting Juliette's eyes. "Forever."

She frowned. "That's what I was afraid of. Once you're in, he swallows you whole. That's why I had to move three-thousand miles away. Is there anything else he required of you, aside from working as a bodyguard?"

I met her eyes again. "Yeah. Not to lay a finger on you."

The drive from Catania-Fontanarossa Airport to the Ortigia causeway was about an hour. A few fishing boats bobbed close to the bridge, and up ahead the village looked different than the ones we'd passed on the way. Terracotta roofs and pale stone buildings were stacked together tightly, and domed churches caught the end of the daylight.

When we reached the other side, I pressed the button on the rental car's GPS, which hadn't moved since we left the mainland. "I think this thing is frozen. It's not giving me directions anymore. I'm going to pull over and see if I can get them on my phone."

"It's okay. I can get us there."

"You sure?"

"Positive. My dad and I used to ride bikes down to this bridge all the time to fish."

"I can't picture your dad on a bike."

Juliette smiled. "I can't anymore either. A lot has changed since those days."

Some of the streets in the village were so narrow, it was hard to believe they weren't one way. Juliette's grandmother's house was tucked at the end of a tiny lane, hidden behind a set of heavy wooden doors that opened to a stone courtyard with a fountain running in the middle. I figured someone must maintain the place since everything was so neat and tidy. We parked and got out, and the smell of the sea carried through the air.

I looked around. "It's quiet."

"That it definitely is."

I unloaded our suitcases from the trunk, and it dawned on me that Vince hadn't given me a key. "Do you have the keys?"

She shook her head and pointed to a flowerpot next to the door with a lemon tree in it. "It's in there. You might have to dig around."

I raised a brow. "Seriously?"

Juliette laughed. "That's where my grandmother always kept it. But my father also texted me before we took off. He said the caretaker was coming today to air the house out, and she'd leave the key in the usual spot. He also said she'd pick up some groceries for us, at least to carry us through the first day or two."

"Oh. All right, good."

After digging in the dirt for a few minutes, I found the key and opened the door. Inside, the ceilings arched high with dark wooden beams that were probably a hundred years older than I was. All the windows were open, the breeze blowing around sheer curtains. A long, heavy table sat in the center of the kitchen with mismatched chairs tucked in around it. One wall held an oversized cabinet filled with dishes and glasses, and copper pans hung from hooks above the stove. I walked around, making sure things were secure, then told Juliette to wait while I checked upstairs.

She laughed at me. "The tooth fairy can't even find this place. Trust me, I lost a molar when I was ten and got stiffed."

I was pretty sure she was right, but I'd much rather err on the side of caution. After I finished sweeping the three bedrooms upstairs, I came back down. Double doors leading to the backyard were open, and Juliette was looking out at a small in-ground pool.

"This is one of only a handful of pools on the island," she said. "I'm not sure why more people don't have them. Maybe because the properties are so small, and it's unnecessary since the sea is within walking distance from wherever you are. But my father had it put in when I was little. I remember it was the talk of the town. Did you bring a bathing suit?"

I shook my head.

Juliette shrugged. "We can pick one up in the village tomorrow."

While the gesture was nice, the last thing I needed to do was frolic in a pool with Juliette in a bathing suit. My eyes dropped to her T-shirt, and I immediately noticed that her nipples had come out to enjoy the breeze. *Yeah, definitely not having pool parties with this woman.*

In fact, I needed a little distance right now. "I'm going to go unpack. Which room should I take?"

"Any of them."

"All right. I'll bring your suitcase up and leave it in the hall."

"Thank you."

There were two rooms on the second floor that overlooked the yard. Both had French doors with balconies. I chose the smaller of the two and unpacked my stuff. After, I lay down on the bed and attempted to unwind from the stress of the day—Vince showing up, traveling for fifteen hours...being alone with Juliette in a place that looked like it was the setting of a romance movie.

But I couldn't seem to relax. I'd noticed a few bottles of wine in the kitchen, so eventually I went back downstairs. The back doors were still open, and now Juliette was swimming in the pool. I scrubbed my hands over my face and grumbled to myself, "Why? Why does it have to have a fucking pool?"

Grabbing one of the bottles of wine, I went to the door. I was relieved that the only thing I could see was Juliette's head. "Is it all right if I open this?"

"Sure." She treaded water. "I'll have some when I'm done swimming, too."

Back inside, I swallowed the first glass like it was a shot. The second, I decided to take back to my room, just to avoid being around when Juliette came out with a wet bathing suit clinging to her body. But after only a few minutes upstairs, I wandered over to the French doors and glanced out at her in the pool. Like a good little pervert, I stayed back far enough so she couldn't see me. Ten minutes went by. My second glass of wine was gone, but my eyes remained glued to the woman in the pool. Juliette swam to the ladder and climbed out, water streaming down her gorgeous body. Her red bikini was smoking hot, and her body was even better than I'd pictured at night when I went to bed. Maybe it was my imagination, but she seemed to move in slow motion, every shift of her body exaggerated and deliberate. She leaned her head back, shook water from her hair, and slowly strolled to the edge of the pool before turning her back to me.

Great. A thong, too.

I knew I should move, get the hell away from the door before I got caught. But I just couldn't. My gaze stayed solely on the curve of her ass. I was too fixated to notice what her hands were doing until she'd tugged the tie at her neck loose and tossed her top on the ground. Then her bottoms slid down, pooling at her feet. For a moment, I thought I had to be hallucinating, that this couldn't really be happening—until Juliette's voice cut through the haze and snapped me out of it.

"If you're going to stare," she yelled without turning around. "You might as well have something worth staring at."

Then she dove back into the pool naked.

Jesus freaking Christ. I was screwed. Doing the twenty years in prison might've been easier than keeping my promise to Vince.

CHAPTER 9

Juliette

"There are worse things than being stuck here, that's for sure." I sipped my cappuccino.

Wes stretched his legs out. "I'd have to agree with you on that."

We'd just parked ourselves at a table in front of a café in Fanusa, a neighboring village, after picking up a bathing suit for Wes. He'd been oddly resistant, but we got the task done.

We'd spent the morning on a bike ride exploring the area and were on our way back to Ortigia. The bikes had been in storage at my grandmother's property, and it seemed a shame not to put them to use. I'd nearly forgotten how beautiful it was here: the sun-bleached limestone streets, turquoise water, and open-air markets.

I turned to him. "I don't think I realized how damn stressful it's been living in the States lately until I got here. It's exhausting feeling like I have to watch my back every second."

He nodded. "I do understand what it's like to watch your back every second. That's my job."

"My literal backside you mean?" I winked. "I don't think *that* was part of the job."

It was bad enough that I'd given Wes that poolside burlesque show yesterday after we arrived. Did I need to pour salt in the wound by bringing it up? It was just too much fun to mess with him.

"Keep your literal backside and your literal front side to yourself from now on, please. Maybe get a swimsuit that actually covers your ass, while you're at it. For someone who was hung up on my shirtless chest for so long, you sure as hell changed your tune."

"It's Italy." I shrugged. "I feel like a new woman here."

"Yeah, well, tell her to cover up, whoever she is." He scoffed.

I chuckled and looked around. "Have you ever seen such beautiful architecture in your life?"

Wes licked foam from the corner of his mouth. "An earthquake decimated this place back in the late 1600s. Everything had to be rebuilt. All of the intricate ironwork and beautiful designs you see today come from that."

I raised my brow. "Someone's been studying the history of Ortigia?"

"I was up for a bit last night reading about it online. Had trouble sleeping."

"Any particular reason you had trouble sleeping last night?"

"Not one you'd be interested in." He crushed his empty cup.

I sighed as I sipped the last of my coffee. "Any guesses on how long we'll be here?"

"No clue. Vince hasn't given me any guidance on that."

"Well, just for the record..." I held up my empty cup in a salute. "I'm in no rush to head back."

"This from someone who didn't even want to get on the plane." Wes laughed.

I waved that away. "That was mostly defiance over my father controlling my life. But I'd also forgotten how peaceful it is here. Seriously, why would anyone choose to live where we do when you can live like *this* every day?"

"Money?" He chuckled. "It's a little expensive for most people to just take off and live someplace like this. Unless you can find work here, I suppose."

"I guess you're right."

"Or in my case..." he continued. "I can't live where I want because I'm indebted to a mobster for life. I just happened to get lucky when he sent us here."

"Well, I'm also bound to him for life. So we have that in common." I sighed. "I don't know if I'll have a job to go back to in California. I'm missing so much work being here."

"Can't you do some of it remotely? I mean, I would think you can write screenplays from anywhere."

"I can, but I'm constantly getting called into meetings, and in Hollywood, they like to do everything in person over expensive coffee, so I can only get by for so long being MIA."

"I hear you..."

We eventually got back on our bikes and returned to the house. I was ready for an afternoon nap when there was a knock at the door.

Wes's body immediately went rigid. We should've been safe here, but it was a bit jarring since we weren't expecting anyone; we knew no one here.

Wes headed to the door and cautiously opened it. "Can I help you?" he asked.

A woman with dark hair pulled back into a bun stood at the threshold. She held a plate of something. "Ah, you are American. I suspected that," she said in an Italian accent.

"And you are?" he asked.

"I'm your neighbor, Natalia Romano."

She seemed safe enough, so I stepped forward and introduced myself.

"I'm Juliette." I turned to him. "And this is Wes."

"Are you visiting, or have you moved here?"

"Visiting." I smiled. "Well, it's a bit longer than a quick visit, but not permanent, either."

"An extended stay," Wes chimed in.

"Well, I wanted to welcome you." She set the plate on the entry table. "I brought you some bread I baked. Our houses are so close together, it felt wrong not to stop by. There's rarely anyone here. I know the woman who takes care of the property for the owners, and she mostly just keeps the place clean."

"Thank you so much for the bread. That's very kind," I said. "How long have you lived in the house next door?"

"Only a year. The house belonged to my grandmother. My mother inherited it after Nonna died, and I bought it from Mama. My husband, Mario, owns one of the shops here in the town."

"Oh, we'd love to visit his store." I beamed, deciding to keep my own grandmother story private. "What does your husband sell?"

"What *doesn't* he sell is more like it—ceramics, jewelry, perfumes..."

"Does he sell one-piece bathing suits?" Wes asked her. I rolled my eyes.

"Never mind him." I shook my head. "We'll definitely check the store out. What's the name of it?"

"La Conchiglia. It means the seashell in English."

Wes turned to me. "Maybe we can get you an early anniversary present there."

I narrowed my eyes. He was pretending to be my partner. We hadn't discussed how to explain ourselves to people here. And now he'd made the decision for us.

"How long have you two been married?" she asked.

I began to explain, "Oh, we're not married—"

"We've been dating for five years," Wes interrupted.

"How nice..." She grinned.

"Yeah..." I muttered.

"Do you have plans for dinner tonight? I'd love to have you over."

"We don't, actually," I answered. What the hell? She seemed nice.

"I'm making fried eggplant, pasta, and ricotta salad."

"That sounds absolutely delicious." My stomach growled just thinking about it. "What can we bring?"

"Please. Just yourselves."

"Nonsense," Wes said. "We'll pick up dessert at that bakery down the road."

"If you must..." She shrugged.

"What time should we be there?" I asked.

"Nine thirty? Does that sound good?"

"Sounds wonderful." I grinned.

"See you then!" Natalia waved before heading back toward her house.

After the door shut, Wes chuckled. "Nine thirty for dinner? That's a little late, isn't it?"

"Not in Italy. Dinner is later here than in the US."

"Ah, yeah. I should've known."

I crossed my arms. "Why did you tell her we were a couple?"

"Are you forgetting that people aren't supposed to know what we're doing here together? There's no other explanation that would make sense."

"You could've said you were my brother or something..."

"That would be weird. I'm not *that good* of an actor."

"If we have to pretend anyway, what's the difference?" I tilted my head.

"Because I probably don't look at you like you're my sister. And it would be creepy if they caught me checking out my sibling."

"Ah, so now you admit to checking me out."

"And you now like testing me." He glared. "I'm only human."

"You weren't testing *me* every time you walked around the house without a shirt on?"

"No, I truly wasn't, Juliette," he said, not a hint of sarcasm on his face.

Actually, I believed that, and I needed to stop while I was ahead.

I changed the subject. "Well, now that we're going to dinner at the neighbor's house, we have to come up with a story and make sure we're both on the same page. Who should we be tonight?"

"You already gave her our real names, which was dumb. But as far as who we should be... Let's be who we *wish* we could be..."

"Who's that for you?"

He paused for a moment. "I'm a cop. Let's say in LA—since we have to be in the same city in order for this to work out. We probably don't live together yet because you keep the damn house too hot." He winked. "I own a modest, ranch-style home in a quiet neighborhood right down the road from you. I have a big German shepherd named Knight. You and I will probably move in together eventually, once we're engaged, but that hasn't happened yet. Life is good, honestly." He raised his chin. "What about you?"

I closed my eyes and allowed myself to fantasize for a moment. "I just sold my first screenplay for a major motion picture. My parents are so proud of me—they're together back in New York. My father is a used-car salesman with no rap sheet. My mother is a teacher. I had a pretty uneventful childhood in a loving, happy home. I met you when you stopped me for speeding, but we didn't start dating until you recognized me at a bar a month later."

"Nice." He laughed. "I think that's a good start on the basic fundamentals. We can wing the rest."

That sounded dangerous.

"How long will you stay?" Natalia asked us from across the table.

"We're not sure yet." I turned to Wes and smiled. "We're sort of seeing where the wind takes us with this trip."

Their house was gorgeous, featuring high ceilings with dark wooden beams and ceramic-tile floors. Vibrant artwork covered the walls, which were painted in bright colors like terracotta and aqua. While they had two children—a twelve-year-old girl and ten-year-old boy—the kids hadn't wanted to join us for dinner, each retreating to their room to do homework after briefly coming out to meet us.

Mario turned to Wes. "How were you able to get time off from your work as a cop?"

That was a damn good question.

Wes cleared his throat. "Some...stuff happened on the job that I don't really want to get into. I asked for a leave of absence for my mental health, and they were nice enough to grant my request. I think everyone should take a break once in a while, if they need it." Wes turned to me and smiled. "And thankfully, she can work remotely."

I smiled. It all sounded so logical.

Natalia asked how we met, and Wes proceeded to tell the story of how he'd pulled me over for speeding.

"When I saw her in a bar about a month later, I couldn't believe it. She caught me staring, and I knew *I* was the one busted this time."

Nice one, liar.

"She smirked at me, and then I swallowed my pride and went over to speak with her. Honestly, the rest is history." Wes shook his head. "For some reason, that night I knew she was the one."

I blushed. He looked dead serious. Wes was definitely the better actor in our pairing. I mostly just sat back and nodded while he lied. *Some team.*

"Five years is no small feat," Mario said as he poured us more wine. "Any plans for marriage?"

I gulped and looked over at Wes. *Why am I nervous about his answer? This whole thing is fake. Delulu.*

"We have our differences," he said, placing his arm around me. "She likes to keep the temperature super hot at her house. But when you care about someone... you live with these little things. And I definitely think we've been wise to take our time, to get to know each other's quirks. That way, we're all the more ready for marriage when it happens. And it *will* happen, yes. I just have to think of the right time and place to pop the question. Pretty sure she knows it's coming."

"Well, I think Ortigia is the perfect place for an engagement." Natalia winked over at me as if she were doing me a favor by putting ideas in my "boyfriend's" head.

Don't waste your time, Natalia. You're being punked.

As they continued to chat, I found myself falling into a daydream, wishing this story were somehow true, that our lives really were that simple.

Natalia served dessert as Mario poured more wine. Wes was definitely partaking tonight, which was not like him at all. He'd always insisted he couldn't drink on the job. It was the first time I'd ever seen him this buzzed, and I was happy he'd let loose for one night.

After we thanked Natalia and Mario for dinner, we bid the sweet couple goodbye and walked back over to the house next door. Wes had his arm around me as we strolled the short distance. My body felt warm from the contact, despite the light chill in the air outside. I knew sober Wes might have thought twice about this physical contact, so I was grateful for his loss of inhibitions.

"That was fun." He smiled as he entered the house, his eyes hazy.

"I have to say, it was. You did a great job with your performance. You nearly had me convinced you were boyfriend of the year."

Wes plopped down on the couch and bent his head back. "I can't do this again."

"Do what?"

He turned to me. "Drink like that..."

"It's not a big deal. It's not like we were even out in public. We were in the safety of their home."

"I can't be sure no one will find out where we are, Juliette. We're never totally safe."

"You can't expect to be in Italy for God knows how long and not drink wine, Wes. I get that you're technically on the job, but you have to live a little."

He jumped to his feet. "Actually, that's not true. I have to be a hundred percent all the time. If I let my guard down even once and something happens, I'll never be able to live with myself. There's no true relaxing on this job. I'm happy you're comfortable enough here not to have to think about the situation we're in. And I'm happy if I've helped you forget." He shook his head. "But I can't slip like that again."

That felt like a slap in the face. I'd been so happy to see Wes let loose. I'd hoped we might have more nights like this one.

As tension lingered between us, depression seeped in. For a moment this had felt like a vacation, but it wasn't. This was a hideout. That was the harsh truth. It was only a matter of time before reality would come back to bite us in the ass.

I started to cry.

"Whoa. What's going on?" He stepped toward me.

Wiping my eyes, I sniffled. "Nothing. I think I had too much to drink."

"Too much wine doesn't make someone cry, Juliette." He frowned. "Did I say something to upset you?"

"You just woke me from whatever delusion I'd been allowing myself since we arrived." I shook my head. "As you lied to their faces tonight, I really tried to imagine it was true. It felt good to just be a normal damn person for one night, Wes."

His expression softened. "I'm sorry for getting snippy with you. And I'm sorry for everything you have to go through because of your father's fucking poor decisions." He hung his head. "I wish I could somehow...get you out of this. You don't deserve it."

"Neither do you," I whispered.

Silence lingered between us, and I felt the floodgates open within me. "I used to think I'd have at least one child someday, give them the kind of upbringing I couldn't have. But the more time passes, I don't think that's possible. I don't think I could bring a child into this world in good conscience if it means they'll also have to deal with this. The same goes for a partner. I think I'm going to have to end up alone, Wes. How could I inflict this life upon someone I love, have them live in constant fear?"

He didn't say anything for the longest time.

"You'd be worth it, Juliette," he finally murmured. "Any real man would take the chance."

My heart fluttered. Why did this guy have to be so damn level-headed *and* off-limits? Why did he also have to be so smoking hot, especially tonight? His eyes were drunk with something that looked an awful lot like desire, his hair tousled from running his hand through it as he lied through his teeth. Fuck, it felt like the wine had just gone straight from my head to my vagina.

"I'm sorry I made you cry," he said.

"You didn't. It was the wine. And the reality check."

To my utter shock, Wes moved toward me, wrapping his muscular arms around my body. The very arms hired to protect me were doing just that—protecting me, but this time not in a physical sense. Now he protected me from my own pain, self-doubt, and anger. Wes's touch comforted me, even as my hungry body starved for him. But the logical side of my brain knew he'd never cross the line. That made the torturous need inside me even worse.

His heart beat against mine, showing me I wasn't the only one with complicated feelings here. Or maybe it was the alcohol. Either way, I didn't know what to make of it. I just knew I had to cherish his touch before the buzz wore off and he came to his full senses again.

Then, just like that, he pulled back and the moment was over. Cold filled the space between us.

"I'm heading to bed," he said before disappearing up the stairs to his room.

My heart was still going a mile a minute.

If Wes had been up all night with insomnia yesterday, tonight was going to be my turn.

CHAPTER 10

Juliette

The next morning, I sat in the kitchen drinking coffee while Wes swam laps in the pool. The double doors were wide open, giving me a clear view, and I enjoyed the sight of his muscular arms slicing through the water. After about ten minutes, he swam to the ladder and climbed out. It all happened in slow motion. Water streamed down his chiseled pecs, tracing every line of muscle across his torso. His hair was slicked back, darker from the water, which made his jaw look even more sculpted than usual. His shoulders were broad, waist narrow, and his skin glistened in the early-morning sunlight. I licked my lips as I imagined catching the droplets with my tongue.

Eyes still glued to the man outside, I'd lifted my mug for another gulp of coffee when the phone rang, jolting me so hard the liquid nearly sloshed over the rim. *Jeez, I really need to get a hold of myself.* I swiped the cell from the table and answered.

"Hello?"

"I really hope I dialed the wrong number," a woman's snarky voice said.

I didn't recognize it. "Umm... I think you might have. Who are you looking for?"

"Wes."

Wes? Who the heck would call my phone looking for... Oh wait. I pulled the cell away from my ear and flipped it over. We both had iPhones with black cases—mine glossy, his matte, and this one had no shine to it.

I lifted the cell back to my ear. "Hang on a second. I'll get him for you." I stood to take the phone outside, but curiosity got the best of me. "Umm... Can I tell him who this is, please?"

She huffed. "Amber."

I rolled my eyes. *Of course, it's Amber.*

Out in the yard, I held out the phone while covering the mouthpiece. "Sorry. I answered your phone thinking it was mine. It's someone named Amber."

Wes frowned, and I wasn't sure if it was because of the person calling or because I'd answered. Either way, it wasn't my problem. I went back inside to give him some privacy. A few minutes later, he came into the kitchen and went to the cappuccino maker.

"Sorry about that," I said. "Hope I didn't get you in any trouble."

He glanced at me, then went back to making his espresso. "It's fine."

I waited through the gurgle of the water being pulled through, the hiss of the espresso pour, and the sharp spit of the steamed frothing milk. By the time he was done, my cheeks were probably as hot as his stupid coffee. "So...who's Amber?"

Wes turned and narrowed his eyes. "Did she give you a hard time or something?"

"No, but she wasn't exactly Miss Sunshine."

He nodded. "Sorry about that."

"It's fine. Is she...a girlfriend?"

He leaned a hip against the kitchen counter, sipping his cappuccino and watching me over the brim. "Just someone I used to see from time to time."

"What does that mean? A booty call?"

"Just a casual relationship I had back in New York."

I scoffed. "Booty call."

He narrowed his eyes again. "You make it sound like something bad. It wasn't a one-sided thing, if that's what you're thinking. She's older and just got out of a divorce, and she didn't want more than a physical relationship either."

"She knows you're not in New York anymore?"

"She does. I told her before I left."

"Well, if she's calling you when she thinks you're three-thousand miles away, it doesn't sound like she's *only* interested in something physical."

"Actually..." He sipped his cappuccino. "I'd told her I was going to be out in California for a while. She works in sales and was calling to let me know she's going to be in the LA area next week for a business trip. She was seeing if I'd be interested in meeting up. So, I believe her call *was* for something physical, not to shoot the shit. Though it's a moot point since I'm here."

My stomach twisted. "Would you have met her if we were still in California?"

"That's irrelevant because we aren't."

"But if we were there..."

"Even if we were, I'm responsible for your safety twenty-four-seven on this job."

The word *job* felt like a smack in the face, and I felt my skin heat. I stood. "I'm sorry if your *job* gets in the way of your sex life." I turned and went straight to my room.

An hour later, I was still lying on my bed feeling prickly when Wes knocked on my door. "What?"

He opened the door. "Put a bathing suit on and pack a bag. I made plans for us."

I frowned. "I'm not in the mood."

"How the hell do you know if you're in the mood when I haven't even told you what the plans are?"

"Because I'm not in the mood to do anything."

"Welp. Too bad, because I already made the plans, and I had to pay for things upfront. So, find a way to get in the mood."

I gave him my best pissed-off look.

Wes chuckled. "Is that the best you can do? Sweetheart, I work for some scary-ass men. Now lose the mood and get a bathing suit on."

"Do whatever you made plans to do by yourself."

He sighed. "Don't make me carry your ass down to the car. It might give poor Natalia and Mario next door a heart attack."

"Fine. Get out so I can change."

He smirked. "Since you asked so nicely..."

Half an hour later, we pulled up at a small marina. "What are we doing here?"

"I rented us a boat," Wes said. "I read about these caves we can snorkel in that are only a ten-minute boat ride."

"Do you know how to drive a boat?"

He nodded. "My uncle had one out on Long Island. He taught me. We used to go clamming all the time. I'm pretty sure he only taught me because then he could drink beer all day while I drove the boat, but we always had a good time anyway."

"I've never snorkeled."

"It's easy. I'll teach you. I rented equipment from the guy who rents the boats."

I hesitated, but eventually I got out of the car. "If I have a panic attack in the water, don't say I didn't warn you."

We stopped at the rental shack, and Wes signed a bunch of paperwork before paying and collecting keys and the snorkeling gear. The boat was navy and white, probably about twenty-five-feet long, and had a small canopy over the driver's console for a bit of shade. But otherwise, it was open to the sun. Its deck was clean and uncluttered, with cushioned bench seats along the sides and a cooler tucked under the captain's chair. Wes held out a hand to help me on, then lifted a compartment door in the bow and stowed the snorkel gear.

"You good to go?" he asked as he took off his shirt.

Miraculously, my mood started to improve. "Yep."

He put the key in and turned it, and the engine hummed to life. "I'm just going to punch the coordinates of the cave into the GPS before we go."

It was a gorgeous day, with the sun shining in a perfect blue sky. As we started to drive, the smell of the saltwater made me forget whatever I'd been annoyed about earlier. We went slow until we got out of the marina area, past the docked boats, and then Wes yelled, "You ready to hit the gas?"

I smiled. "Yes!"

He pushed the throttle, and we shot forward, the boat slicing through the water. I hadn't thought to bring a hair tie since I didn't know where we were going, so the wind whipped my hair all around. But it felt exhilarating—so freeing. Saltwater sprayed as we crossed over the back of another boat's wake, making me squeal.

After a while, we slowed as we approached a hidden cove. The water inside it glowed bright turquoise. Wes killed the engine, and we drifted for a moment, listening to the gentle lap of water against the hull before he got the anchor out of another compartment in the back.

Once he was done setting it, he turned to me with a big smile. "Beautiful, right?"

I looked over the side and saw sand at the bottom. "How deep is it?"

He checked the electronic depth finder on the dash. "Twenty feet."

"Wow. It looks like I can stand."

"It will probably get shallower as we get closer to the cave entrance. But there's a lot of coral, so don't try to reach for the bottom or touch the reef. It can be razor sharp."

"Oh. Okay." I glanced over the side of the boat again, feeling wary.

"You ready?"

I took a deep breath and nodded, even though my heart pounded. When I stood, I could see fish swimming around the boat. I liked marine life, but generally on my plate or in an aquarium. Though, at least part of me was excited to try something new with Wes. We put on our fins and snorkels and then stood on the ledge at the side of the boat together.

"On three?" he asked.

I bit my bottom lip but nodded.

"One. Two. Three!"

We jumped in at the same time. The cool water was a shock, and I squealed as I surfaced. Wes popped up beside me, grinning. "You good?"

"I'm sort of terrified." I laughed.

"I won't let anything hurt you, in or out of the water." He held out his hand. "Come on. We'll swim into the cave together."

Goggles and snorkel ready, I took a deep breath and stuck my face into the ocean, kicking my legs behind me. The water was so crystal clear, I could see all the way to the rocks of the cave up ahead. Tiny yellow and black fish swam around us as we moved toward it. Wes squeezed my hand and pointed to a bright blue fish with yellow and black fins that looked exactly like Dory from *Finding Nemo*, and soon I forgot to be nervous anymore. Together, we snorkeled for more than two hours before climbing back onto the boat.

"That was incredible!" I tugged off my mask. "It felt like we were on our own little planet, just us and schools of fish."

Wes rubbed a towel over his wet hair and smiled. "You were a natural out there."

He handed me a towel, and while I dried off, he stowed the snorkel gear back in a cabinet. When he bent forward, I noticed how red his back was.

I pointed. "I think you're getting burned."

He twisted and looked over his shoulder. "Shit. Yeah."

"I have sunscreen. Want me to put it on you so it doesn't get any worse?"

"If you don't mind."

I definitely didn't mind putting my hands on his muscular back. And I was glad I'd brought the type of lotion you had to rub in, rather than the spray kind. I dug into my bag for the bottle. "Turn around."

My palms glided over his smooth, sun-heated skin, and I felt ripples of muscles tighten beneath my fingers. I told myself to focus on what I was doing, but it was impossible to rub his broad shoulders and not imagine the way they might look hovering over me. The quiet moment grew intimate and stretched into something that felt charged.

When I finished, Wes cleared his throat. "Thanks. I'll pull the anchor so we can head back."

Neither of us said much on the ride to the marina, and I started to wonder if maybe it was just me who had felt the spark. Once we were docked, Wes looked at his watch. "We have the boat for another two hours. I noticed a liquor store a couple of blocks back when we drove in. How about I run over and grab us a bottle of wine, and we can watch the sunset from here?"

"That sounds great. I thought you said you weren't going to drink anymore, though?"

"I'll stop at one this time." He winked.

While Wes was gone, I fussed with my hair, using the faint reflection off the silver trim of the electronics console as a mirror. He came back a few minutes later, holding a bottle of wine and two plastic glasses.

"They even uncorked it for me."

"I probably wouldn't have thought of that until I was back on the boat."

Wes poured us each a glass and held his up for a toast. "To surviving your first snorkel."

I smiled as we clinked plastic. "I had a great time."

He sipped. "I'm surprised you've never snorkeled before."

"I only started going in the pool again a few years ago."

"Why is that? Did you have a scare of some sort?"

I looked away before answering. "Yes, but probably not the kind you're thinking of. I didn't nearly drown or anything."

"What happened then?"

I sighed. "Growing up, we had an in-ground pool at our house. I used to spend the entire summer swimming in it when I was little. The day after my tenth birthday, I got up early and let the dog out in the yard. Buddy started barking the way he always did when he saw squirrels or geese, only he wouldn't stop. I went outside to see what was riling him up so much, and I found a dead body floating in the pool."

"Jesus."

"I didn't go in it for the rest of the summer. Even the next year, I couldn't bring myself to go near the water, so my mother finally had the entire pool drained and refilled. But it wasn't really about the water. Every time I looked at that pool, all I saw was that man's gray, bloated face."

"Did you know him?"

I shook my head. "Years later, I was watching *Law & Order*, and a character drowned in a pool. The police and the medical examiner came, and it hit me for the first time that no one had come to our house except for my dad's friends. It was never on the news, and no one ever spoke about what had happened again."

"That must've been hard to understand as a kid."

I smiled sadly. "I still don't understand most things that have to do with my father. Namely, why he chooses to lead the life he does."

"I'm not making excuses for him, but I'm guessing it's what he knew. His father and uncles were in that life, and sometimes when you grow up around crazy shit, it starts to seem normal."

"I think that was true for me when I was little. I didn't realize other dads didn't hold business meetings at home while blasting music, just in case the house was bugged. But the older I got, the more I understood, and the more distance I wanted from my dad."

Wes smiled. "Can't get much farther apart than New York to California and still be in the US."

"I probably should've moved to Hawaii."

The sun started to sink, casting a golden hue over the marina. Wes and I sat in comfortable silence, watching a sailboat pull in and dock.

"What about you?" I asked. "Did you go into the family business? Was your dad a cop? Is that why he got away with abusing your mom?"

He shook his head. "My dad's an electrician. At least that's what he was before he took off when I was ten."

"That must've been difficult."

"Not really. I was relieved he couldn't touch my mother anymore." He shrugged. "And my mom gave us a damn good life."

"What made you want to become a policeman?"

Wes finished the rest of the wine in his cup. "When I was fourteen, my older brother didn't come home one night. Luke was seventeen, and unlike most brothers who are close in age, we were tight. I wanted to be just like him. That night, he was walking home after a party and passed a gas station where a guy was yelling at his wife and getting in her face. Luke stepped in, and a fight broke out. The guy wound up stabbing my brother eight times."

My hand covered my heart. "Oh my God. I'm so sorry."

Wes nodded. "It took the police twenty minutes to show up after it happened, and my brother bled out—he couldn't be saved. All I remember from that night is sitting in the hospital with my mom, and she kept asking over and over why no one came sooner. Nobody had an answer. I decided right then that I wanted to be the reason someone's brother made it home."

"You're pretty amazing, Wes. You know that?"

He caught my gaze. "So are you."

We watched the beautiful sunset until the sky's show was over.

"It's really nice to be able to talk to someone and be so open and honest," I said. "My entire life, I've had to pretend my father is an upstanding businessman. It's such a relief to just be myself."

Wes's eyes dropped to my lips. They lingered for a long time before he abruptly stood. "We should get going."

"Oh. Okay."

He unloaded the snorkel equipment we had to return and held a hand out to help me off the boat. The wine and sun must've hit me harder than I thought, because when I stepped off, I lost my balance and tripped. Wes caught me in his arms. Our faces were close, and I debated leaning in and pressing a kiss to his lips. But before I could find the courage to do it, Wes was already pulling back.

The ride home was quiet, which seemed to have become a pattern with us. We'd grow close, and then Wes would put distance between us, sometimes while we were still physically next to each other. The silence continued in the house as we walked up the stairs to our respective rooms.

"Thanks again for today," I said.

Wes nodded. "You're welcome."

I opened the door to my bedroom, but Wes stopped me from going in.

"Juliette?"

I turned.

"I wouldn't have met up with her."

I felt my forehead wrinkle. "Who?"

"My booty call from earlier. Even if I'd been in California, I wouldn't have gone."

CHAPTER 11

Juliette

The following morning, I walked out of my bedroom to find Wes on the phone with someone. My first inclination was to admire his shirtless physique, and the way his hair was beautifully messy in the morning. But immediately I could see that something was off.

He paced repeatedly, seeming nervous, running his hand through his hair.

Oh no. What's happening?

Wes was muttering, so I couldn't hear anything clearly, and he was mostly listening to what the other person had to say.

My stomach sank. *Are we in danger?* All the worst-case scenarios ran through my mind.

Someone found us here.

Something happened to my father.

The moment he hung up, I charged toward him. "What's wrong, Wes? Tell me what's going on."

"It's not about us," he said, letting out a long breath. "It's my grandmother." His voice shook. "She's not doing well. They don't think she's going to be alive much longer." His eyes glistened.

"Oh no." I covered my mouth. "I'm so sorry. Has she been ill for a while?"

Wes nodded. "Lung cancer. She's lived a decade longer than the doctors predicted. But it's finally gotten to be too much for her. They think she only has days to live."

I placed my hand on my chest. "How old is she?"

"Seventy-nine."

"You should go see her..."

He shook his head. "Juliette... I don't need to tell you that's not possible right now. I can't just leave you here." He exhaled, looking tormented.

"Where does she live?"

"Same place as my mom. Down the shore."

I rushed back to my room to grab my phone.

"What are you doing?"

"Calling my father."

Wes hung his head, but he didn't try to stop me. He might have been hesitant to piss my father off, but I had *no* problem doing that.

"Juliette," my father said as he picked up. "Is everything okay?"

"Wes and I need to leave Ortigia as soon as possible," I stated matter-of-factly. "His grandmother is dying, and he needs to be able to say goodbye. I won't take no for an answer. You need to let him go see her without penalty."

My father let out a long sigh. "And what about your safety?"

"I'll be with him. No one's gonna find us there. His family lives down the Jersey Shore, far away from the city. We can come right back here after."

"I'm worried about this, Juliette." He paused. "But I can't let a guy not see his nonna before she dies."

"Exactly." I expelled a relieved breath. "Thank you for understanding."

"Listen to me," he ordered, his tone growing stern. "You need to make sure you stick with him. And you'll fly back private again. We don't need you wandering around airports right now. You'll check in with me before you leave Jersey. Most likely you'll head back to Italy, unless I tell you otherwise. But don't book any flights without consulting me first. You hear me?"

"Okay." I exhaled. "Thanks, Dad."

"Wait. Don't hang up. Put Wes on."

I handed Wes my phone.

He took it. "Yes, sir."

Wes just kept nodding and yessing my father. "Thank you again," he finally said.

After he hung up, he exhaled and smiled softly at me. "Thank *you*."

"Of course." I headed toward my room. "Now let's get the hell out of here. We don't have time to waste."

"I'll arrange for a car to come get us," he called.

As I threw my clothes into a suitcase, sadness washed over me.

Leaving Italy would be a harsh return to reality, like being forced to wake up from a dream you wished would never end.

I'd miss our little Ortigia bubble.

The drive to the airport in Catania had taken a little over an hour. Luckily, my father was able to get us a flight that departed not too long after we arrived.

My nerves calmed considerably once we were safely in the air headed for Newark. About halfway through our flight, Wes bounced his legs as he looked out the window. I placed my hand on his knee, prompting him to look at me.

"Hey," he said softly.

"It's gonna be okay, Wes. Think positive. We're gonna make it in time."

He blew out a breath and forced a smile, but there was sadness in his eyes.

"So..." I said. "We should probably use this time to talk about what our story is going to be when we get to your mom's. Things will be emotional for you, and you shouldn't have to worry about it then. We have the time now, so let's talk about it."

"Yeah." He nodded. "Of course."

The fact that he hadn't brought up a game plan yet showed me just how distraught he was. Who could blame him?

"What exactly does your mom think you're doing for a living right now?" I asked.

"All she knows is that I'm working privately as a bodyguard after leaving the force. She doesn't have a clue how dangerous my job really is or the shit I've gotten into with your father, and I want to keep it that way." He shrugged. "Not that being a cop wasn't dangerous, but you know..."

I sighed. "Unfortunately, I *do* know."

He scratched his chin. "But yeah, we should get our stories straight—yet again."

"Not to pat ourselves on the back, but I think we did a great job with Natalia and Mario in Ortigia."

"Oscar worthy." He laughed.

"So, should we tell your mom I'm some damsel in distress with a lot of money, hiring you to look after me?"

He shook his head. "Actually, I don't think we should say you're a client at all. It's best if we just pretend we're dating. I don't want to bring the job home at a time like this. Even saying you're a client is a little too close to the situation, if you know what I mean. It's better to keep everyone in the dark, since knowing anything at all can potentially put people in danger."

"You have a point there. The less people who know anything, the better." I nodded. "Okay, so we pretend to be a couple again... That's old hat for us at this point."

"My mother might interrogate you a little. She's not used to me bringing anyone home. I've always kept my personal life pretty private, with the exception of one girlfriend. We should probably just say we met on a dating app and that it's fairly new, but you wanted to come to support me."

"Okay..." I nodded. "It doesn't have to be more complicated than that. I'll be honest about what I do for a living, so no need to pull stuff out of my ass about some pretend career. I'll just be Juliette. We shouldn't have to fake too much, aside from the actual nature of our relationship."

I'd been curious about Wes's family but never thought I'd have the opportunity to see where he came from. He'd given me bits and pieces of his past, like the tragedy of losing his brother. I knew his dad was MIA and had been abusive to his mother. But it would be interesting to see firsthand what she was like.

"Anything I need to know about your mom or anything else?" I asked.

"Not really. She lives in a modest house, the same one I grew up in. I don't come from money or anything."

I drew in my brows. "Why do you feel the need to clarify that?"

"Just making sure you know what to expect."

"I'd give every red cent my father ever made for a modest house with a normal mom and no crazy-ass father who ruined my life."

"I get it." He offered a sympathetic smile.

After a few minutes, he started bouncing his legs again.

"Are you still anxious that we won't get there in time?"

"Yeah. It's pretty much all I can think about."

"Have faith, Wes. It'll work out. Every second that passes, we're one step closer to being with your grandma." I held out my hand, and he took it.

The feel of his fingers intertwining with mine sent a burst of awareness through me. He squeezed my hand. Touching him felt so natural now. After about a minute, I reluctantly let go. Though I'd felt like I needed that contact, too. *Why am I so damn anxious to meet Wes's mother if our relationship is a sham?*

It still felt meaningful somehow. Wes meant a lot to me, even if I couldn't express to him how much.

After we landed in Newark, we picked up our rental car and headed to the Jersey Shore as fast as we could. The drive to the shore from the city was about an hour. Thankfully, we didn't run into too much traffic.

I'd never been down to the Jersey Shore, which was pretty crazy considering I'd grown up in nearby

New York and had been to Jersey many times. When I was younger, we'd always gone out to Montauk or East Hampton during the summers. Like many, I supposed, my ideas about the Jersey Shore came from that old MTV show I used to watch when I was a preteen.

It was around seven thirty PM when we finally got to Wes's grandmother's house.

The moment the hospice nurse let us in, Wes raced to his grandmother's room where a hospital bed had been set up. Religious statues surrounded it, and some rosary beads lay on the table next to her.

"Hi, Grandma." He ran to her and broke into tears as he laid his head on the edge of her bed.

The relief I knew he felt in that moment was tangible.

We made it.

She reached her hand out and placed it on his head.

And he wasn't the only one relieved. I finally felt my pulse calm a bit. I'd assured him that everything would turn out okay, but the truth was, there were no guarantees. It was only by the grace of God that my promise to him had come true, and I couldn't imagine what it would've been like if she had died before we got here.

His grandma could barely open her eyes, but at one point, she did. "Wes," she whispered.

"I came all the way from Italy when I found out you weren't doing well," he told her. "I love you so much. And I'm not going anywhere."

"My Wes," she murmured.

I stayed in a corner of the room and watched as Wes held her hand and whispered to her. Understandably, she wasn't saying much, since it was a struggle for her to breathe, but she managed a few words here and there.

At one point, she opened her eyes and turned toward where I was standing. "Who's this?" she said in a raspy voice, barely audible.

Wes turned to me and smiled before returning his gaze to her. "That's Juliette."

Her mouth curved into a smile as she looked at me for several seconds. "Let me guess. You're Romeo?"

Wes and I smiled at each other and laughed.

"You're beautiful," she added, looking over at me.

"Thank you, Rose," I said, grateful that I'd asked Wes for her name, since I couldn't exactly call her Grandma.

She didn't say much else after that.

I stayed standing in the same corner of the room, not wanting to interrupt Wes's time with her. I was happy that she knew he was here and that he was able to tell her over and over how much he loved her.

My heart clenched. If only everyone got that privilege before a loved one passed.

Wes's mother greeted us at the door when we arrived at her house a little after nine PM that night.

He let out a nervous breath. "Mom, this is Juliette."

She looked me up and down and smiled. "Juliette, very nice to meet you. I'm Joanna." After she reached out to hug me, her eyes lingered on me for a bit.

"Stop staring, Ma." Wes laughed. "That's creepy."

Joanna shook her head. "I'm sorry. I just never thought I'd see the day you brought someone home, let alone someone as absolutely gorgeous as this raven-haired beauty."

Wes's face turned red. "Ma…"

"Thank you so much. You're very kind," I said. "It's so wonderful to meet Wes's family."

The house was cozy and warm. She had jarred candles lit on the mantel and the coffee table. It smelled like something made with cinnamon was baking.

Family photos covered the walls. There was one of Wes that must've been taken when he was about thirteen. His cheeks were a bit chubby, and he hadn't developed the beautiful angles of his manly face yet. I smiled as I took it all in. I also noticed photos of another boy, who must have been his brother. He looked a lot like Wes. That made me so very sad.

There was a tan sectional with colorful pillows and a big ceiling fan in the center of the living room, which opened to the small kitchen. A hallway led to what looked like a couple of bedrooms.

"I made your favorite cinnamon rolls, Wes," she said. "You guys must be hungry. But it's also late, so I wasn't sure if you'd already eaten. I can also heat up the lasagna I made earlier..."

Wes looked over at me. "You hungry?"

"Not too much."

He rubbed his stomach. "Maybe I'll just have a cinnamon roll before bed." He smiled at me. "You need to try one, Juliette."

I nodded in agreement. "They smell delicious."

As we sat in the kitchen, Joanna served us cinnamon rolls. She placed a tall glass of milk in front of Wes without even asking what he wanted, which I thought was adorable. I opted for water, since it was too late for anything else.

Joanna leaned her elbows against the table. "What do you eat for breakfast, Juliette? I want to be prepared in the morning."

"Oh, I'm pretty easy. Anything is fine."

She crossed her arms. "I know California girls like fruity-nutty stuff."

Wes's eyes widened as he chuckled. "You're fruity-nutty, Ma."

Joanna laughed. "You know what I mean. People from California tend to be health conscious." She snapped her fingers. "What do they drink over there? Wheatgrass shots? Tried that once and almost heaved. Burped up grass for three days." She yawned. "I don't have much in the house because I was planning on shopping tomorrow. But I do have eggs and bacon. And coffee, of course. We drink lots of coffee around here."

"My kind of place." I grinned. "And all of that sounds perfect."

I hadn't had a chance yet to explain that I was a New York girl and not a "fruity-nutty" chick from California. I did like clean eating, but I could enjoy greasy food with the best of them.

Joanna grinned. "I know it's late, so feel free to ditch me and head to bed. We can get to know each other more over breakfast and coffee in the morning." She turned to Wes. "How was Grandma tonight?"

His smile faded. "As sick as I imagined, but she said a few words and knew I was there. That was probably the best I could hope for."

"It's been hard." She shook her head slowly. "Your grandmother loves you so much. I'm so happy you made it back."

Wes reached for my hand in a way that seemed genuine. "Well, you can thank Juliette. She was the one who encouraged me to hop on the plane as fast as we did."

"Really?" Joanna turned to me. "Well, you're a sweetheart for that. Wes is lucky to have you."

A warm feeling came over me. "I'm the lucky one. Your son is the most protective and kind man I've ever met. I know the circumstances aren't ideal, but it's truly an honor to get to see where he came from."

Our relationship may have been a lie, but there was nothing disingenuous about that statement. Both his mom and grandmother had made me feel special in the brief time I'd known them. It was hard not to wish this experience was genuine. I felt safe here. And I felt the love his family had for each other. It created a deep longing inside of me for the same.

"Anyway, I got the spare bedroom ready for you," she said. "I know you must be tired, so I'll get out of your hair. We can catch up more tomorrow."

Oh.

Why was this the first time it had occurred to me?

Wes and I would be sharing a bedroom.

CHAPTER 12

Juliette

I wasn't sure what to do.

Wes and I stared at each other a moment before he stood and walked over behind me. "Why don't you go up, babe?" he said, rubbing my shoulders. "I'm going to go out front and shoot hoops for a while. I'll probably be done before you finish your half-hour-long skincare routine."

My night routine did take forever, but I couldn't figure out if he actually knew that or had just made it up for his mom's sake.

Joanna smiled and patted her son's arm. "If you two ever live together, you're going to need a basketball hoop out front. Since he was a little boy, Wes has been going outside to shoot hoops whenever he has a problem. Sometimes he would spend hours out there." She gave his forearm a squeeze and her voice softened. "Sadly, I don't think Grandma's problem is solvable, Wes. Don't stay out there too long."

He nodded, but I knew Wes had more than one problem to work on tonight. We'd been next to each other the entire long day, though, and I figured he could use some time alone. So I said goodnight and followed Joanna up to the spare bedroom.

The rhythmic thump of a basketball bouncing out front sounded faintly in the background as I got ready for bed. I washed my face, applied my serums and creams, and brushed my teeth. But instead of finishing barefaced the way I usually did at night, I leaned close to the mirror and swiped on a fresh coat of mascara, then fixed my hair a bit. Ridiculous, I know. I never wore makeup to bed. Still, I told myself it was because I was going to have to see Wes's mother again in the morning—not because I wanted to look nice for her son. Though of course, I knew better.

Wes came in fifteen minutes later, just as I finished making up a bed on the floor. His shirt was tucked in his back pocket, and his chest glistened with sweat. He lifted his chin, gesturing to the makeshift bed. "I don't need two pillows."

I glanced over at the setup. "Oh. The floor is for me, not for you."

He frowned and shook his head. "No, it's not."

"I'm fine on the floor," I assured him. "Once I even fell asleep during shavasana at yoga because I'm so comfortable there. The instructor had to wake me."

"You're not sleeping on the floor, Juliette."

"But—"

He cut me off with a look. "There's no point in arguing, because it's not happening. I'm going to take a quick shower. When I come out, your ass better be in that bed."

I must have been losing it because the way he said *"your ass better be in that bed"* sent tingles running through me. I slid under the covers as he disappeared into the bathroom.

A few minutes later, the sound of running water filled the silence. I told myself not to picture him behind the frosted glass, his broad shoulders slick and head tipped back beneath the spray. I failed miserably. To make matters worse, he walked back into the room smelling clean, with a towel wrapped low on his hips. I'd never found the scent of soap particularly sexy before, but on him it was intoxicating.

Wes grabbed his bag and returned to the bathroom to get dressed, emerging wearing no shirt and a pair of sweatpants. I really wanted to know if he had underwear on under there. But sadly, he flicked off the light before climbing into his bed on the floor.

"Goodnight," Wes said.

"Goodnight."

I rolled to my side and pulled the blanket up to my shoulders. Fifteen minutes went by, and I was still wide awake. Sleep wasn't going to come easily with Wes so near. Every time I closed my eyes, I heard him shifting. He was definitely not comfortable on the floor. I tried to ignore it by rolling to my other side, but after what felt like an hour of torture, I whispered into the dark. "Wes? Are you awake?"

"Yeah."

"This is silly. I hear you tossing and turning, and I'm staring at the ceiling feeling guilty about you down there on the floor. We're both adults. There's plenty of room in this bed. Why don't we share it?"

"That's not a good idea."

"Why not?"

Long seconds of silence ticked by. "It's just not."

"I also noticed that there's no lock on our door. Your mom is very nice, but she sort of seems like the type who might pop her head in to say breakfast is ready in the morning. We're supposed to be a couple."

Wes stayed quiet for so long I thought he might've fallen asleep. Eventually, I whispered again. "Wes? Are you still awake?"

"Yeah, I'm awake. I'm just sitting here thinking of the time she walked in at an inappropriate moment when I was a teenager and had Missy Callaway over. You would've thought she'd learned her lesson then, but a few months later she walked in on me while I was getting dressed."

I kind of hated Missy Callaway at the moment. Nevertheless, I sat up and started moving pillows around. "Come on. I'm making a wall between us."

It surprised me when Wes got up and walked around to the other side of the bed. He sat down and started to swing his feet up, but his body jerked, and he cursed under his breath. "Fuck."

"What's the matter? Are you okay?"

He winced, lowering himself slowly. "I threw out my back shooting hoops. I have a disc that pops in and out ever since I took a hit playing football in my senior year of high school."

"Then why the heck did you try to sleep on the floor?"

He made pained sounds as he eased down into the mattress. "Because I didn't want you to."

He was in pain, yet he'd still insisted on being a gentleman. Stupid, yet it warmed me. "How do you get the disc to go back into place? Do you go to a chiropractor or something?"

"No, I tried that a few times, but it didn't help. I usually go to this medical massage therapist. She's able to relax all the muscles around it, and within a day or two, things go back into place."

"I'm pretty good at giving massages..."

"That is *definitely* not a good idea."

I got defensive. "Why not?"

"Because there's a line I can't cross with you."

"You're being ridiculous. Do you worry about crossing a line with your massage therapist?"

"No, but..."

"But what?"

"She's a professional."

"I might not have a license, but what do you think I'm going to do? Try to give you a happy ending?"

After a moment, Wes blew out a deep breath. "Fine."

The way he said it, you'd think I'd asked him to walk before a firing squad, not enjoy a back rub. I rolled my eyes and sat up. "Roll over."

The groans he made as he flipped onto his stomach had me second-guessing my assurance that I wouldn't try to give him a happy ending. They were low, guttural, and so damn sexy that I had to imagine they were a lot like the sounds he made during sex.

Fuck my life. What had I gotten myself into? I needed a minute to regroup. "I'm going to wash my hands and get some lotion out of my bag."

When I came back, Wes's face was buried in the pillow, arms loose at his sides. I pumped some cream into my palms and rubbed them together before setting my hands on his shoulders. His muscles tightened instantly.

"Relax," I whispered.

"Trying."

I kneaded slowly down his back, fingers pressing into the ridges of tense muscles. When I hit a spot close to his kidneys, his breath hitched.

"Here?"

"Yeah."

I took my time in that area, slowly pressing harder and harder. "Good?"

"Mmm..." Every response was a single word.

After the area felt looser, I moved to the spine, circling over the knots at the base. Wes let out a half-groan, half-growl that shot straight between my legs.

I cleared my throat. "Should I go deeper here?"

It took a moment for him to answer. "Yeah."

I bent to his ear, smiling. "Are you always this talkative?"

"Depends."

"On what?"

"On who's touching me."

Lord, *I* was going to need a massage to relax after we finished this little session. My body felt like it had been plugged into a socket. But I tried to ignore that and focus on alleviating his pain.

I spent a good half hour releasing the tension from Wes's muscles. Toward the end, I eased the pressure and glided my hands over his back, rubbing in the last of the lotion. "There, how was that?"

"Great."

I smiled at yet another one-word answer and capped the lotion. Sliding back under the covers, I pulled the blanket up to my chin. After a few minutes of silence, Wes still hadn't moved.

"Are you sleeping?" I whispered quietly.

"No."

He turned his head to face me, but kept his eyes shut.

"Aren't you going to roll over?" I asked. "When my back hurts, I find it helps to sleep on my back, let the spine straighten itself out."

Wes cracked one eye open. "Can't."

"Can't? Do you need help?"

"Nope."

He looked over at my face and must've read the confusion because he sighed. "My body hasn't gotten over how much it liked the massage, Juliette."

"Oh," I answered before the meaning sank in. "*Oh!*"

Wes gave a tiny shake of his head, almost amused, before his eyes closed again. I lay with my eyes open, staring at his face in the dim light. He looked so handsome, even half asleep. My pulse quickened with thoughts I probably shouldn't have indulged. What would he do if I leaned in right now and kissed him? Would he kiss me back? Would he flip me onto my back and pin my wrists over my head? I knew he would be the kind of lover who didn't ask, but *took*. Rough, commanding. Addictive. And God help me, I'd love every second of it.

My dirty thoughts kept me wired long after Wes turned over and drifted off, his breaths evening out into a steady rhythm of sleep. Desperate for something to quiet my own mind, I inched closer and gently rested my head on his chest.

The next morning, Wes slept in. I went downstairs in search of some coffee and wound up sitting at the kitchen table with his mom for more than an hour. She told me half a dozen stories from Wes's teen and tween years, each one funnier than the last. Apparently, he'd started noticing girls at a young age.

"Then when he was eleven, he got this crush on one of his brother's friends," Joanna continued, smiling. "She was three years older, like Luke, and Wes decided that if he grew some muscles, maybe she wouldn't notice that he hadn't even started puberty yet. He asked me to buy him some weights, but I wasn't sure if boys that young should be pumping iron, so I told him to wait a year or two." She shook her head. "But Wes was determined. He usually walked home after school with some friends because I worked until five o'clock, but one day I came home early and saw that the boy next door had come home, but Wes hadn't. I asked Billy where my son was, and he said Wes had started going to Costco every day after school. I thought that was strange, so I took a ride over—and found Wes lifting the display weights."

We both laughed, and Wes walked in mid-cackle, frowning as his head ping-ponged between us. "Oh, this can't be good..."

I grinned. "I'm glad you're up. I was thinking about going to the gym. Maybe we can go together."

He cocked his head, like he was waiting for the other shoe to drop. "Okay..."

"Or maybe you'd like to go to Costco instead?"

Wes shut his eyes. "I'm going to kill you, Ma. How many stories have you told her?"

"Oh, just one or two."

I chuckled. "Or six."

"Great." He crossed over to open a cabinet, pulling out a mug and filling it with coffee from the pot. "Just what I needed."

He carried the mug to the table and sat down opposite his mother, who looked between us and smiled. "How did you two meet?"

I opened my mouth to tell the story we'd told Mario and Natalia—how Wes had pulled me over for a traffic stop, and we later met at the bar. But I didn't think that timeline would make sense, as his mother probably knew he'd been off the force for a while. So I extended a hand to Wes. "I'll let Wes do the honors. It's so much funnier when he tells it."

Without missing a beat, Wes spoke with a straight face. "I saved her ass."

His mom chuckled. "What does that mean?"

"I was in Dunkin Donuts getting my morning coffee, when the woman ahead of me in line darted to the ladies' room. I figured she really had to go." He shrugged and sipped his coffee. "A few minutes later she came back, and there were like six more customers in line, so I told her she could cut in front of me since she'd been there before I was. When she did, I noticed her entire ass was hanging out. She'd accidentally tucked the back of her skirt into her underwear."

My eyes widened, mortified.

The corner of Wes's lip twitched. "She also had some toilet paper in there."

I blinked at him, unsure if I should be impressed that he'd made up that story so quickly, or a little scared.

Joanna patted my arm. "It happens." She looked over at her son. "Did you not sleep well, Wes? You look tired, and it's not like you to sleep so late."

"I had a little trouble falling asleep."

"You did?" I asked. "I thought you fell asleep pretty quick."

Wes shook his head slowly. "Nope, but you did. You were out cold. I think I had a pile of drool on my chest when I finally fell asleep about four o'clock."

Oh shit. I thought he'd been asleep when I snuggled up to him. Wes had a sparkle in his eyes as he looked at me across the table, and I was grateful when Joanna changed the subject.

"What are your plans for today, honey?" she asked.

Wes shrugged. "Not much, other than going over to visit Grandma."

"Did you have a certain time in mind?"

"I figured I'd give Juliette some time to shower and get ready, then head over. Maybe an hour or two. Is that all right?"

"That's perfect. I'll go over and see her now and then stop back later tonight. That way she has visitors throughout the day."

"Sounds good." Wes nodded.

Joanna finished her coffee and stood. "All right, you two. I'll see you later on."

After Wes's mom left, he rinsed our empty mugs in the sink and leaned a hip against the kitchen counter. "Why don't you go shower first, since you take longer to get ready?"

"Okay. How's your back feeling today?"

"Great. Thank you for last night."

I smiled. "And thank you for letting me use you as a pillow."

Upstairs, the shower felt incredible. One thing I missed about living on the East Coast was the water pressure. My rental didn't compare to this or what I'd had at home in New York. I lingered longer than usual and let the pounding water unwind the tension in my shoulders. When I finally stepped out, I realized I'd done the same thing as Wes had last night: left my bag in the other room. So I walked out in my towel.

Wes was making the bed. When he turned, he froze, and his eyes raked up and down my body. After a long, heated stare, he looked away. "You should get dressed. You already broke my no-touching rule by sleeping on top of me."

My eyes narrowed. "I didn't sleep on top of you. I rested my head gently."

He met my gaze. "And that turned into wrapping your arms and legs around me about ten seconds after you fell asleep."

"Oh."

"Yeah—*oh*." He shook his head. "I'm trying to be good, Juliette. And you're not making it easy. I can't be on my game to protect you if I'm distracted."

"Maybe...we would be less distracted if we took care of our pent-up frustrations."

"Absolutely not."

I sighed, and in a moment of utter insanity, I untied the knot of my towel. It fell to the floor, pooling around my feet. "I'll be here if you change your mind."

The car was quiet on the drive over to Wes's grandmother's house. In fact, he'd barely said two words to me since storming out of the bedroom. I thought about apologizing, but really, why should I? I wasn't sorry. I liked Wes, maybe too much. My physical attraction to him was off the charts. And I knew in my bones that he felt the same way.

But yet again, my father was in the way of my life.

We pulled up to his grandmother's house, and, as always, Wes told me to stay in the car until he determined it was safe. I watched as he scoped out the block before opening my door. As I climbed out, our arms brushed, and a bolt of electricity shot through me. Wes's eyes jumped to meet mine, and I had no doubt he'd felt it, too. He looked away quickly, but I decided right then and there that he and I were going to have a talk later.

Inside, the house was quiet. His grandmother's hospice nurse was just coming out of the bedroom. Her face fell when she saw us, and I knew what was coming before she even spoke.

"I'm so sorry," she said softly. "Your grandmother just passed."

CHAPTER 13

Wes

Engulfed in sadness, I lay on my bed, staring into space. I'd told Juliette I wanted to be alone after we got back from my grandmother's.

I found myself more grateful than ever that we'd gotten to New Jersey when we had. Just one more day, and I wouldn't have had the chance to say goodbye. I could thank Juliette for that opportunity. I also wondered if Grandma had waited to see me before letting go.

Despite finding some comfort in the fact that I'd gotten to see her before she died, I was in shock. I'd been thinking I'd talk to her again today, yet instead of spending time with her, I'd sat with her lifeless body as we waited for the medical examiner to arrive. Still, it was an honor to be by her side.

Mom had met us there as soon as I called to tell her about Grandma's passing. My mother seemed to be handling that better than I was, maybe because she'd been here day in and day out and had seen how my grandmother had declined, how little she could enjoy her life. At least Grandma wasn't suffering anymore.

The strange thing was, despite feeling distraught, I hadn't cried yet. I felt like I *should've* been crying. I was in immense pain, after losing one of the most important people in my life, but for some reason, the tears wouldn't fall.

After about ninety minutes in my room alone, I heard a knock at the door.

"Wes, can I come in?" Juliette asked.

"Yes," I answered, straightening against the headboard.

She smiled sadly as she entered the room.

"What have you been doing all this time?" I asked.

"Well, your mom just got home from meeting with the funeral director. But I thought I'd make sure she returned to a clean and tidy house. So, before she got here, I put all the dishes away, scrubbed the sink and countertop, and neatened up the living room."

I forced a smile. "That was really nice of you. Thank you for doing that."

Juliette lay next to me on the bed. "I waited as long as I could before coming to bug you."

"You never bug me." I briefly placed my hand on her leg. "But thank you for giving me a little space. I thought I was going to break down, and didn't want you to see that, but strangely, I haven't been able to cry."

"We can't control how we react to these kinds of situations. I find that the tears tend to creep up on you at random times, not when you necessarily expect them."

I nodded.

I'd been so sad earlier that I didn't really appreciate how beautiful Juliette looked today. She'd curled her hair a little differently, and her lips were a deeper shade of pink than usual, even without lipstick. While I'd only now taken notice of that, something else *had* been playing on repeat in my head: the memory of her naked body after she'd unknotted that towel this morning. That image had permeated even my deepest grief.

As if she'd read my mind, she said, "I feel like I need to apologize for being so brazen earlier…" She shook her head. "I don't know what came over me. I think I'm just angry at the situation my father put us in, and I'm taking it out on you, in a way."

While I'd have loved nothing more than for Juliette to take out *all* of her anger on me in ways she probably couldn't imagine, I had to resist.

Before I could respond, she spoke again.

"Anyway, I don't want to talk about it because it's not the appropriate time. I just wanted to clear the air a little because things were awkward between us in the car this morning—and rightfully so. I want you to feel like you can lean on me right now."

"You want me to feel like it's safe to lean on you without you randomly disrobing." I smiled. "Got it."

"Basically, yes." She laughed.

Things went quiet for a bit, and Juliette leaned her head on my shoulder. "I'm so sorry about Grandma Rose, Wes."

I closed my eyes for a moment. "I think what bothers me the most is that…" I paused. "She was so damn proud of me when I was working as a cop. A lot of her family had been cops. In Grandma's eyes, there wasn't a more honorable job." I sighed. "If she knew the truth about who I was working for now…" I shook my head.

"Well, she might've passed a lot sooner. Let's just put it that way."

"She knew as much as your mother does?"

I nodded. "Pretty much. She didn't know the whole story of why I left the force, either."

"I think if she truly understood, she'd still be proud of you. Just for different reasons."

"I don't know." I looked away. "Her greatest wish was that I settle into a stable job, get married, and have a family someday. I don't think any of that is in the cards for me now."

"You don't see yourself ever settling down?"

"As long as I'm in this job?" I shook my head. "No. How would that even be possible?"

Juliette turned her whole body toward me. "Listen, Wes..." Her eyes glistened. "Wherever your grandmother is now, I believe she does know the truth. I believe she fully understands that everything you've ever done, you did with good intentions, with the goal of protecting people. I have the honor of getting to experience that firsthand." Her eyes filled with emotion. "You put your life on the line for me every day. How many people willingly do that for someone else? I know you feel obligated to my father. But that doesn't change the fact that you're a hero. And your grandma *is* proud of you, in this very moment, wherever she is."

And *that* caused me to get choked up.

Fuck.

It's happening.

A tear fell. It figured I'd cry around Juliette. She always made me feel things.

"Well, here are the damn tears that wouldn't fall earlier." I sniffled and wiped my eyes. "So much for the manly man who's supposed to protect you."

"I think it's a beautiful thing when a man allows himself to cry," she whispered.

We sat quietly for a long moment.

"Listen, now that my grandmother has passed, we can leave Jersey, if you want."

Her eyes widened. "You can't leave before the wake and funeral..."

I shrugged. "Those events are for other people, not the person who died. Wakes make me angry, in fact. Sometimes it's a bunch of jerks talking and laughing while the dead body is right there in the room. Half the time I want to punch people for being so damn disrespectful." I groaned.

"Well, that's true..." she agreed.

"The only thing that matters to me was getting to see her before she died and to make sure she knew I loved her," I said. "I'm at peace with that."

"Okay, but I still don't think we should up and leave," she added. "It would be important to your mom to have you by her side, don't you think?"

I exhaled. She was right. "Yeah. We'll stay." I wiped my eyes one last time. "Listen, you need to somehow erase my crying episode from your memory, okay?"

"Deal, if you erase my towel drop from yours."

I flashed a mischievous grin. "No chance in hell..."

Grandma's wake a couple of days later was just as uncomfortable as I'd imagined, with lines of people, some of whom I recognized and others who were complete strangers. I couldn't tell you how many hands I'd shaken in that receiving line, and it looked like flowers had exploded everywhere. My grandmother knew a lot of people and had always been a social butterfly, so the amount of locals coming to pay their respects wasn't surprising. It was overwhelming, though, to see so many faces I hadn't come across in years.

Even a few of my exes from high school and beyond had showed up. Awkward but touching. While I'd only had one serious relationship, I'd dated a lot. I kept noticing Juliette looking over at me whenever I talked to one of them. Not sure why some sick part of me liked the idea that she might have been jealous. If I knew nothing was going to happen between us, why did that matter?

At one point, when the line finally died down, my mother placed her hand on my shoulder. "How are you holding up?"

"I'm okay." I shrugged. "I'm looking forward to this being over, though. It just feels like something I wish you and I could've done in private."

She nodded. "I know. But your grandmother knew a lot of people, and I didn't want them to feel slighted. You don't get a do-over with these things."

I turned around toward the open casket and knelt there. Even though Grandma was pretty frail in her final days, the funeral home had done a good job with her makeup and hair. Her hands were crossed one over the other, looking a bit orangey and hardened, and she held a set of rosary beads. I had to keep reminding myself that the body was no longer my grandmother. She was an angel now, and hopefully fully able-bodied, healthy, and playing bingo in the sky.

Eventually several people lined up again to greet us, so it was back to business. A little while later I realized I'd gotten distracted and hadn't noticed that Juliette had disappeared from her seat. She and I hadn't really discussed safety tonight, but I'd assumed it went without saying that she shouldn't leave my sight. She'd probably just had to go to the bathroom and would be right back. I tried not to panic—yet.

Twenty minutes later, though, the wake was winding down and there was still no sign of Juliette. *Now* I could panic. My mother knew nothing about the real nature of my relationship to Juliette, yet she seemed concerned, too, when I pointed out that it was odd Juliette hadn't returned from the bathroom. I excused myself and left the viewing room.

Sweat beaded on my forehead as I searched the funeral parlor in a frenzy. I'd never forgive myself if something happened to her, even if I had good reason to be distracted tonight.

I entered every bathroom on the premises, but there was no sign of her. Next, I ran out toward the front and around back to the parking lot. No Juliette.

When I reached for my phone, I remembered I'd stupidly given it to her to hold in her purse during the wake since it barely fit in the small pockets of my dress pants.

Fuck!

How could I have been so irresponsible?

I went down to the funeral home basement again, where the bathrooms were. The sound of knocking coming from the back corner caught my attention. Actually, it was more like banging.

"Help!" I heard someone say.

Juliette?

Oh my God.

What the fuck?

I ran over to the door and frantically tried to open it. "Are you okay?" I yelled.

"Yes. But I'm stuck in here because the door won't budge!" she said. "It locked behind me, and I can't get out."

I pushed and pulled on the door again with no luck.

"Hang on. The door is fucking jammed. I'm getting help."

I went in search of someone who worked for the funeral home. When I finally found a guy, I explained that my friend was locked inside one of the rooms.

"There is a door that gets stuck from time to time," he said. "We've been trying to get someone to fix it."

The man brought out some tools and finally got the door open.

Juliette's face was red as she stepped out, and what I saw inside shocked the shit out of me, although it probably shouldn't have: a body covered with a sheet atop what looked like an operating table. *For fuck's sake. She locked herself in the damn embalming room?*

"I'm very sorry," Juliette told the man. "I was curious about what was in here, and well, you know the rest."

"No worries." He chuckled as he locked the door. "I'm sure you learned your lesson with that one. I don't expect you'll do that again."

"What the hell were you thinking?" I asked as we walked away.

Her voice shook. "I've always been kind of fascinated by funeral homes. That sort of ties into my interest in horror. I only meant to use the bathroom when I came down here, but then I saw this door and decided to peek inside. I quickly realized what it was and tried to leave. Though for some reason, the door locked behind me, and I couldn't get out."

"You had me scared shitless."

"*You* were scared?" She laughed angrily. "I'm not sure I'll ever get over that trauma."

I rubbed her back. "Damn, I'm sorry."

She blew a breath into her hair. "It's my own damn fault."

We went back upstairs to let my mother know what happened. She managed a laugh, despite the somber mood of the evening.

Juliette and I left soon thereafter, stopping to pick up a couple of pizzas on the way home.

I turned to her in the passenger seat while we waited. "So, did that guy under the sheet have anything interesting to say while you were locked in there with him?"

"I flashed him, and he had more of a reaction than you," Juliette cracked.

I chuckled. "Good one."

She winked. "At least someone wants me."

Tense silence settled between us.

"You think I don't want you?" I asked after a moment, gritting my teeth. "*Far* from it, Juliette."

She leaned her head against the seat and looked out the window. The ride remained quiet the rest of the way home.

After we returned to Mom's, Juliette and I demolished most of a large pizza.

When my mother came home, she joined us at the table and ate a couple of slices from the second box.

It had been a long night, so Mom retreated to her room early.

Back in our shared bedroom, Juliette brought up the subject of my ex-girlfriends. I was surprised it had taken her this long.

"So, there were parts of tonight that reminded me of *The Bachelor*," she said. "Women were lining up to kiss you on the cheek. I'm assuming you dated some of them?"

I raised a brow. "Why would you assume that?"

She glared at me. "They were attractive and clearly still into you."

"A few of them were people I dated years back, yeah," I confessed. "I hadn't seen any of them in forever."

"None were significant relationships?"

I shook my head. "Nope."

"Well, it's a testament to the way you treat women that they would want to come and pay their respects to your grandmother all these years later." After a moment, she added, "I can't help being a little jealous of them."

"Why?"

"Because they got to experience a side of you that I never will." She sat at the edge of the bed. "I guess I just don't know how to separate my feelings from reality. On a rational level, I know nothing can happen between us. But too often you make me forget that, Wes. And being here with you during this emotional time in your life, seeing how you comfort your mom..." She shook her head. "I don't know. I don't know what I'm saying."

I knew what she was saying. Wanting someone you couldn't have was torture. I couldn't really fathom how the future with Juliette would play out. Eventually she'd find someone, and I'd have to sit back and watch. Or maybe I could somehow get out of this particular gig and ask to be reassigned. Although, I couldn't imagine leaving her, either. I wasn't sure I trusted anyone else to protect her. And that was telling.

As she sat there rubbing her temples, I felt what could only be described as a magnetic pull that urged me to go to her, to hold her. Still, I tightened every muscle in my body and resisted. "I'm sorry things aren't different," I finally said.

Juliette looked up at me and murmured, "Me, too."

Then my phone rang. "It's your father," I said before picking up. "Vince. How's it going?"

"How are things down the shore?"

I hesitated. "My grandmother passed away. But I had the chance to see her before she died. So thank you again for clearing us to come."

"I'm sorry for your loss."

"Thank you."

I noticed Juliette turn around and begin changing into her sleep clothes. I moved to the farthest corner of the room to give her some privacy.

"I wanted to let you know that things have calmed down," Vince said. "You and Juliette are free to return to California. But you should still be on high alert—just no need to go back to Italy."

I ran my hand through my hair. "Okay. I'll let her know."

"Very good, then. Take care of my baby girl."

"Of course. Thanks, Vince."

I was still looking down at the phone when Juliette asked, "What's going on?"

After I filled her in, Juliette looked like someone had pissed in her Cheerios. "I was actually hoping to go back to Italy, believe it or not," she said. "Although this is probably best for me workwise."

"I hear you. A part of me was kind of hoping for that, too."

My feelings on the matter were starting to mess with my head. So were Juliette's nipples, which I could see clear as day through the thin shirt I was pretty sure she'd put on to torture me tonight.

CHAPTER 14

Juliette

I couldn't sleep.

It had been close to an hour since Wes had turned off the light, and I was still staring up at the ceiling, feeling wide awake despite the long day. I'd assumed Wes would conk out pretty quickly, considering the day's emotional toll, but I hadn't heard his breathing smooth out yet.

"Wes?" I whispered. "Are you still awake?"

"Yeah."

I turned to face him and tucked my hands under my cheek. "Where would you see yourself in five years, if you didn't work for my father?"

He was quiet a moment. "If we're playing in the land of make believe, then I'm back on the force. Maybe in a different unit and with a higher rank that comes with more pay."

I smiled. "What unit would you want to be in?"

Wes had been lying on his back, but he now turned to face me. It was dark, but not so much that I wasn't reminded how handsome he was.

"I always thought I might want to go into the Special Victims Unit—work with women and children who were abused."

I didn't have to ask why that would interest him, not after finding out how his father had treated his mother.

"Do you think you'd be married with children?"

"Maybe. I'd like to have a couple of kids someday." He lifted his chin. "What about you? Where would you like to be?"

"Well, I'll be thirty-two in five years, so I'd love to be married and have a child. Possibly even pregnant with a second." I smiled, imagining it. "I'd love to continue working, too. Maybe part time. To me, that would be the best of both worlds. My mom never worked, and I feel like her identity was her family, and she could've used something of her own to be passionate about."

"That sounds nice."

I sighed. "Too bad it will likely never happen."

"Why not?"

"Well, for starters, since I moved out to California, I haven't even told a man my real last name. Imagine dating me for a while and then one day I drop a bomb that my last name isn't what I go by and oh, by the way, my dad is Vince Ginocassi, head of one of the five families." I scoffed. "I'm pretty sure Jett would've run the other way if I'd told him."

Wes scoffed. "Jett's a weasel. I told you, any real man won't care about who your family is. He'll take you for who you are, no matter what obstacles come with it."

"I guess I haven't met any real men then yet." I placed a palm on Wes's chest. "Present company excluded."

He didn't respond, but I heard his breathing grow labored. My heart pumped faster.

"As long as we're living in the land of make believe," I said. "Could you…see yourself coming home to me?"

"I thought I was a cop."

I smiled. "You are. I didn't mean come home to me because you work for my dad. I meant because you want to."

"Juliette…"

"What? You said in the car that wanting me wasn't a problem. Are you attracted to me?"

"I think you know the answer to that."

"Maybe. But I'd really like to hear you say it."

Wes was quiet for a long time again. When he spoke, his voice was gritty. "You're unbearably beautiful. When I look at you, it's impossible to think of anything else. A lack of attraction is probably the one issue we don't have."

My heart thumped. "I'm very attracted to you, too."

Maybe I was a glutton for rejection, but I couldn't help myself lately. "We could…spend one night in the land of make believe and go back to reality tomorrow." I gnawed on my bottom lip and lowered my voice. "I really want to touch you right now, Wes."

He let out a loud, painstaking groan. "Fuck."

"What? Don't you want to touch me?"

"It doesn't matter what I want, Juliette."

"Because of my dad?"

"Because I can't get involved with someone I'm protecting. That's dangerous for more than one reason. I need to keep my mind and emotions sharp, not clouded with things that distract me from doing my job."

Because of the way I grew up, I could understand that, at least in theory. Though in reality, I wasn't able to let go of my idea. "What about when you're done protecting me? When I'm no longer your job. Would you let me touch you then?"

Wes abruptly shot upright. "I'm sorry. I need to go sleep on the couch. I can't stay in the room with you tonight."

"What? No. What about your mom? What will she think?"

He stood from the bed and grabbed a pillow. "I'll tell her I didn't want to wake you with my snoring."

I rose to my knees on the bed. "No, don't go. I'll back off, I promise."

Wes shifted the pillow to under one arm and grabbed his cell phone from the nightstand. When he pulled it from the charger it illuminated, allowing me to see him more clearly. And what I saw made my eyes grow wide. Wes was wearing sweats, but he very obviously had an erection. A long, thick one. I licked my lips.

Wes groaned. "Fuck. Don't look at me like that, Juliette. I have to go. *Now*."

The following day felt endless. We attended Wes's grandmother's funeral, then flew back to California. By the time we made it to my place, it was almost ten at night, even with the three-hour time change. Things between Wes and I had been strained ever since he'd gone to sleep on the couch last night. He'd pretty much kept three feet of distance between us at all times. Before we boarded the plane, we'd had two aisle seats across from one another. But when we'd checked in, Wes had moved to a window seat so there was a man separating us for the entire six-hour flight.

It was finally just the two of us in my house now, yet it still felt like we were a mile apart.

I fixed myself a bowl of Cinnamon Toast Crunch, vanilla ice cream, and caramel syrup, and offered to make one for Wes. Instead of his usual sarcasm about what I was eating, he politely declined. I'd turned the air conditioning off before we left, so it was a zillion degrees in the house, yet Wes didn't take off his shirt, even though sweat beaded on his forehead.

I couldn't take the awkwardness anymore and was trying to figure out how to fix what I'd done to us when my phone rang. It was my mom. Ten here meant one AM at home, so I quickly swiped to answer. "Hi, Mom. Is everything okay?"

"Other than having one week left in my fifties, it's fine."

"You don't look like you're even fifty yet, so no one has to know."

She sighed. "I feel old."

"Are you sure everything is okay? You don't usually call so late."

"Everything's fine, sweetie. Your dad asked me today what I wanted for my birthday next week, and I told him I wanted to be off lockdown and see my baby. I miss you."

I'd been so wrapped up in myself, I hadn't given any thought to the idea that my mom was likely on lockdown, too. My heart squeezed. "I miss you, too, Mom."

"Good. Because I booked us a spa day at some fancy place in Beverly Hills."

"Oh. Okay. That sounds great. You're coming to LA then?"

"I am."

"When?"

"Tomorrow. Or rather today, since it's past midnight here."

"You're coming…tomorrow?"

"I take off at seven AM New York time. Dad booked me a private flight. I'm packing as we speak. It'll be a quick trip, but I want to see you."

"Wow. Okay." I had a million things to do now that I was finally back home, but I guess it would all still be there after she left. I tried to sound enthusiastic, though I had mixed feelings about my mom coming for a visit. Our relationship had been strained the last few years. Unfortunately, my disconnecting from my father's life had spilled over to my mom's life as well. "That's great, Mom. I can't wait to see you."

"I should be to you about noon, your time."

"Perfect."

"Gotta pack. See you soon, baby."

"Goodnight, Mom. Safe travels."

Wes came into the kitchen just as I hung up the phone. I sighed. "You might want to prepare for a storm that's rolling in tomorrow."

Wes lifted his phone and pressed a few buttons, then turned it to show me the screen. "Says it's going to be eighty and beautiful tomorrow. Just like every other day out here."

I shook my head. "The storm isn't the weather. It's Frannie Ginocassi. My mother is coming tomorrow."

Francesca Concetta Grecco Ginocassi didn't do things halfway.

My mother arrived at my house at two in the afternoon, two hours later than she'd told me on the phone last night, wearing a leopard-print wrap dress, four-inch heels, and big gold hoop earrings. Her dark hair was teased high—frozen in place with Aqua Net, no doubt—and her long nails were painted fire-engine red. She looked like she'd just stepped off an old episode of *The Real Housewives of New Jersey*. She held four big shopping bags in one hand, a pink pastry box from her favorite bakery in Brooklyn in the other— surely filled with cannolis—and tucked under the same arm like an accessory was none other than Chester, her Siamese cat.

"Hi, Mom." I kissed her cheek, and Chester gave me the side-eye. He was extremely territorial. "Are you moving in? I didn't realize you were bringing your cat."

She set down the shopping bags and stroked the top of her feline best friend's head. "Sorry I'm late. I passed this strip of amazing boutiques, and I couldn't help myself. I did a little shopping for you."

"Shopping for *me*?" Oh no. My mom meant well, but that meant rhinestone belts and animal prints. My taste was simpler and understated.

Wes came out of the kitchen. "Mom, this is Wes Callahan."

"Hi, Mrs. Ginocassi." He extended a hand. "It's nice to—" His words were cut short by a sneeze. Then another. And still a third. He pulled his hand back. "Sorry. I'm a little allergic to..." He sneezed once more. "Cats."

I raised a brow. "A little? Your eyes are already red and watering."

Mom put her hand over her heart. "I'm sorry. Everyone usually loves my Chester."

"It's fine," Wes said. "I'll just go in the other room. It was nice to meet you."

But Wes lived on my couch, so it wasn't like he had anywhere to hide. "Why don't you go into my room?"

"Thanks. Good idea."

Ten minutes later, I could still hear him sneezing through the door. "We need to leave, Mom. Let's go to your hotel to hang out."

"All right."

I went to my room to let Wes know we'd be relocating. His eyes were now puffy, and he held a ball of wadded-up tissues. "I'm so sorry about this. I had no idea she was bringing her cat."

He shrugged. "No big deal."

Even his voice had a wheeze. "Boy, you're really allergic."

"The beginning is always the worst part."

"Well, regardless, we're going to go to my mom's hotel. Mom's bodyguard is out in the car. He can keep an eye on both of us so you can rest."

Wes shook his head. "You go, I go."

I sighed. "If you must."

Outside, Mom's driver was leaning against their rental car. I'd met Paulie before. He was a mountain of a man, and today was clad in a black leather jacket and mirrored shades. If Mom looked like she belonged on the *Housewives*, Paulie Distefano looked like he'd walked straight out of *Goodfellas*.

Great. The neighbors will all be talking. As I approached, he opened the front and rear car doors and nodded. "Ms. Ginocassi."

"Hi, Paulie. Would you please not refer to me as that here? I go by Grecco now. Even better, call me Juliette."

He shrugged. "Whatever you want." Paulie looked to the man standing next to me. "How you doing, Wes?"

"Hanging in there."

I gestured to the open car door. "I'm going to ride with Wes."

Wes and I followed behind Mom and Paulie. "I guess you've met Paulie before?"

Wes nodded. "A few times. He's with your father a lot." He glanced over at me before turning right at my corner. "I'm surprised I've never met your mom before. I've been to the house a bunch of times."

"That's probably because my mother doesn't live with my father, not in the main house anyway."

Wes's brows furrowed. "Where does she live?"

"In the pool house in the yard. My parents have a bizarre relationship."

"They don't get along?"

"No, they actually get along really well. But my dad has at least two girlfriends at a time, sometimes more. And my mom is in love with her best friend, who is gay."

Wes blinked. "Come again?"

I chuckled. "It's funny, when I'm home it all seems almost normal. But when I say it out loud, I realize it's not."

"So your parents have what...an open relationship?"

"I'm not sure what you'd call it. Basically, my mom knows my dad has girlfriends, and she's okay with it as long as she doesn't have to see it. But my mom would never cheat on my dad because that's a sin."

"She's just in love with a gay man?"

I smiled. "That's right."

"And she lives in the pool house by herself or with the gay guy?"

"Alone. Timothy is married."

"To...a man?"

"Who else would he be married to if he's gay?"

"I don't know. It seems like nothing we're talking about makes too much sense."

I laughed. "I guess you have a point."

Ten minutes later, we pulled up at the Ritz-Carlton. One good thing about my mom's visit was that it seemed to have gotten my relationship with Wes back on track. Who knew my parents' nutty situation could be the ice-breaker we needed?

Wes stayed downstairs in the lobby, and Paulie went upstairs with us. He had the room next to Mom's, so the two of us were alone in her suite. Chester took his spot in the middle of the bed, and Mom and I stayed out in the living area.

"How are you, Mom?"

"Old. Tired. Hungry." She smiled. "Let's order room service. Hot wings?"

I smiled back. "With bleu cheese."

"You got it." She picked up the phone and placed the order. Then she covered the receiver. "Anything else? A drink or something?"

"I'll have whatever you're having."

Mom grinned and returned to the phone. "Two bottles of merlot, please. And two straws."

I chuckled. "Actually, Mom, do you think you can get some wings delivered to Wes in the lobby, too?"

"It's the Ritz-Carlton." She shrugged. "We can get anything we want."

After she finished ordering, Mom slipped off her shoes.

"How are things at home?" I asked. "How's Timothy?"

My mom's face lit up. "He just got a big promotion at work. He's the vice president of the bank now."

"Oh, that's great. What about Ken?"

I regretted asking when my mom's face faltered. Ken was Timothy's husband. "He's fine. Redecorating again and wasting more of Timothy's hard-earned money."

I wasn't about to point out that my mom's full-time job was redecorating our family home—the one she didn't even sleep in anymore. "What about Dad?"

"He's very stressed. He would love it if you would move back home. So would I."

"Mom…let's not go there. I'm happy out here in LA."

"Are you seeing anyone?"

"I don't need a man to make me happy."

"So that's a no."

I rolled my eyes. But then I realized my mother was probably the only person on the planet who understood my situation, and I could talk freely with her. It might be good to discuss how to handle things with Wes. So I took a deep breath. "There actually is someone I'm interested in."

Mom's eyes sparkled. She tucked her feet under her butt and leaned in. "Tell me all about him."

"Well, he's handsome and smart, has a good sense of humor."

"Sounds amazing so far. What does he do for work?"

I chewed on my bottom lip before answering. "He's a bodyguard."

"Ooh, interesting. For someone famous out here in Hollywood?"

"Not really."

"Someone with a lot of money then?"

"Definitely not."

"Why does the person need a bodyguard if they're not rich or famous?"

I met my mother's eyes. "Because her father is a kingpin."

My mother's brows dipped, and then her eyes grew wide. "You and Wes?"

"Well, there isn't really a *me and Wes*." I sighed. "But yeah. I've grown feelings for him."

"He's a real looker."

"And he wants nothing to do with me—at least not in a romantic way."

My mother looked offended. "Why not?"

"You know why…"

Mom frowned. "Oh. Of course. I wasn't thinking. Your father must've given him the *touch my daughter and die* speech. I bet it was the same one he gave poor Evan Roberts."

"Evan Roberts? My prom date?"

Mom nodded. "I was so mad at him for pulling a gun on an eighteen-year-old."

My eyes flared. "Are you kidding me? Mom, I had no idea Dad threatened Evan. You know he wouldn't even dance with me at the prom, and he ditched me the minute it was over. All these years, I thought he didn't like me."

"How could anyone not like you?"

I shook my head and blew out a big breath. "Whatever. But yeah…Dad told Wes I was off-limits."

Mom patted my hand. "I'm sorry, honey. But it's probably for the best."

"It's best that I wind up an old maid because everyone in the world is afraid of Dad?"

"No, best because Wes works for your father. Even if Wes had Dad's blessing, you know what would happen. You'd get sucked back into that life because your man's life would be tied to your father. You moved three-thousand miles away to escape that world."

My shoulders slumped. Mom was probably right. The men in my father's world didn't go to work at nine and come home at five, leaving their job behind. They were in deep. And half the guys who lived that life wound up in jail or...worse. Right now it was easy to pretend Wes was just a guy who did private security. But what would his next job be? I wasn't sure I wanted to know what my father had him doing before this either.

"Maybe Dad could release him from the job, and Wes could do private security out here in LA. I'm sure there are tons of celebrities who hire security."

"There is no release from that world, honey. Look at me."

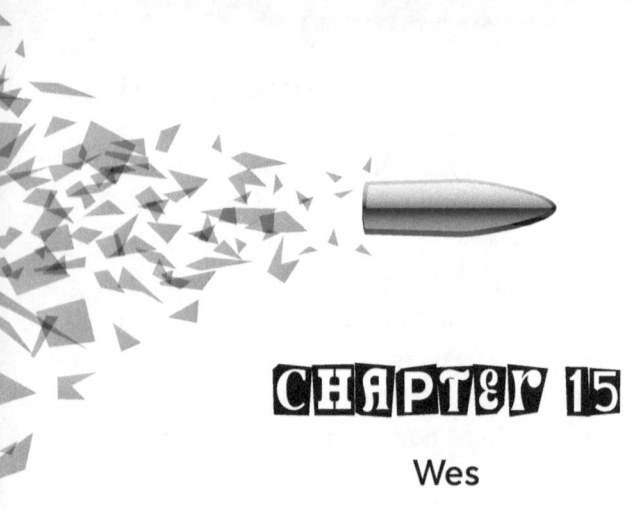

CHAPTER 15

Wes

The next morning, Juliette was still sleeping when there was a knock at the door. My body went rigid, and I went over to the peephole to check it.

Frannie Ginocassi and her bodyguard. What the hell are they doing here so early?

I took a deep breath to gear myself up for this. Opening the door, I feigned a smile. "Good morning."

Frannie gave me a once-over and brushed past my shirtless body into the house. "We left the cat at the hotel to spare you. I wanted to be here when my daughter woke up."

Paulie followed her inside.

I closed the door. "Well, you know she likes to sleep in."

Paulie smacked me on the back. "Frannie, I'll wait for you out in the car. I have some phone calls to make."

"Take your time, Paulie." She turned to me after he left. "I sort of figured Juliette might be sleeping." She lowered her voice. "Actually, I was hoping you and I could talk before she woke up."

I stiffened. "All right." Running a hand through my hair, I said, "I haven't had my coffee yet. Can I make you one?"

"Please." She followed me into the kitchen. "Heavy on the cream. No sugar."

"You got it."

As I reached for two mugs and got the coffee going, I considered what she could possibly want to talk to me about. Couldn't be good, whatever it was.

While the coffee was brewing, I took a seat across from her.

Frannie cocked her head. "Do you have feelings for my daughter?"

Well, all right then. Maybe I should've seen that coming. My eyes widened. "You couldn't have waited until I'd had my coffee to hit me with that?"

"It's a yes or no response."

"No."

"Considering you're turning various shades of red right now, I think I have my answer." She smirked. "How long have you had feelings for her?" When I remained silent, she added, "You can trust that anything you tell me will not get back to Vince. I know my daughter is fond of you. And she's my number-one priority. I wouldn't abuse her trust or put you in danger."

The gurgling sound of the coffee finishing prompted me to stand. I was thankful for the brief reprieve. I nervously prepared her coffee, clanking the spoon against the ceramic a little too loudly while I stirred in her cream.

As I set the cup of joe in front of her, she stared at me like she'd been waiting for my answer to her question the entire time. Rather than give her what she wanted,

I returned to the coffee station and took my sweet time preparing my own mug.

Sitting back down, I took a long sip, which didn't go to my head fast enough. I sighed. "My feelings for Juliette aren't relevant to the current situation."

She blew on her coffee and took a sip. "Take the situation out of the equation. I understand your predicament. Anyone working for Vince is under the gun—literally. But try to put that aside. I'll ask again... Do you have feelings for my daughter?"

"What good is putting the facts aside? That's not realistic." I shook my head. "Admitting to you that I have feelings for Juliette isn't going to change how I have to proceed."

She leaned in. "But you do, right?"

"Mrs. Ginocassi—"

"Call me Frannie...please."

I lowered my voice. "Frannie." Looking down into my mug, I said, "Your daughter is obviously gorgeous. Of course I find her incredibly attractive. But she's also..." I paused, trying to find the right words. "She's real, vulnerable, funny, honest...caring." I closed my eyes for a moment. "She makes me laugh." I chuckled. "Every day." I sighed. "I could go on. But yes, I have found myself wishing things were different, because any guy would be lucky to have Juliette."

"Wow, it's even worse than I thought." She smiled in satisfaction, as if she'd already known everything I just told her. "I commend you for holding your ground. And you're right on the money. Nothing good could come from her getting involved with one of Vince's guys."

"Was that the point of this conversation, to reiterate the obvious?" I scoffed.

She shook her head. "Well, my attitude is a little different than Vince's. My husband doesn't give a shit how people feel. But *I* recognize that the people who work for him are still human. I was just curious whether this situation is a struggle for you, like it is for Juliette."

Pretty sure she shouldn't have admitted that to me. Clearly, she and Juliette had been talking.

"Still, despite your feelings, you're doing what you know is best for my daughter," Frannie continued. "And I greatly appreciate that."

My hand tightened around the mug. "It's not just what's best for her. It's my damn job. Your husband has made it clear numerous times that he'll kill me if I ever lay a hand on her. So there's not exactly room for error. I just…" I looked away, hesitant to continue.

She tilted her head. "What?"

Letting out a long exhale, I said, "I just wish Juliette could somehow escape her ties to him. She doesn't deserve to live her life in the shadow of evil. She deserves so much more than that. And yeah, maybe as a bodyguard I'm not supposed to care so damn much about my client. But I can't help it." I ran my thumb along the mug. "Juliette makes it easy. I'd give anything for her to be able to live in peace."

"Well, you risk your life for her every day. And I'm indebted to you for that." She frowned. "And I'm sorry that you and Juliette have to deny your obvious feelings for each other. Even if you're not admitting it in so many words, it's clear to me that you're smitten with my daughter. There's no greater torture than wanting someone you can't have."

I couldn't help myself as I arched a brow. "Like you and Timothy?" *I'm going to hell.*

Her jaw dropped open. "Who told you about that?"

"Who do you think?" I chuckled. "It's okay. I won't tell anyone."

Frannie rolled her eyes. "There's about as much hope for Timothy and me as my husband being sainted."

I laughed. "Ain't that the damn truth."

Juliette entered the kitchen and rubbed her eyes. "Oh boy. The two of you talking behind my back..." Her hair was knotted and wild. She was so damn beautiful.

Frannie beamed. "Good morning, darling. I couldn't wait to see you. So I decided to stop by." She narrowed her eyes. "Do you always walk around here with no bra on?"

Shush, Frannie. It's all I have.

"Where's Paulie?" Juliette rubbed her eyes again, her voice groggy.

"He's in the car. He likes his privacy whenever he can get it."

Juliette yawned and walked over to the coffee machine to pour herself a mug.

Thankfully, as she prepared her coffee, she didn't ask what her mother and I had been talking about. I couldn't be sure Frannie wouldn't bring up my feelings for Juliette again. And that would be so fucking awkward.

"You're full of crap, Mom," she finally said as she joined us at the table.

Frannie's face turned red. "What do you mean?"

"I don't believe you came by this early just to see me. I think you were torturing Wes." Juliette turned to me. "Am I right?"

Maybe I'm not getting out of this conversation after all.

I tried to keep a poker face, and thankfully this time Juliette dropped the subject for good.

After a bit, Frannie suggested that we all go out to breakfast. Juliette agreed, so Paulie and I sat at a corner table at the restaurant to give her and her mother some privacy while still keeping close tabs on them. Together they were a double target, and we had to be especially vigilant.

Paulie was an interesting guy—a bit of an oddball. He was pretty quiet and only spoke when spoken to, even with me. I couldn't quite figure out his deal, except that he seemed ambivalent overall. Still, I was kind of hoping to talk to him. It would be nice to chat with someone else in the same predicament as me. It wasn't every day you got to sit down with other bodyguards working for the mob, let alone for the same guy.

After we ordered, I leaned back in my chair. "How are you holding up?"

"What do you mean?" he asked, seeming genuinely confused.

"Working for Vince."

He shrugged. "It's all right."

I raised a brow. "Just all right?"

"It's a job."

I squinted, finding his attitude hard to believe. "It's not just a job, and you know it."

Paulie shrugged again. "I don't sweat it too much."

I continued my inquisition. "How did you end up working for him?"

"My father owed him a favor."

Ah. Should've known.

I nodded. "Well, I wish I could be like you...looking at this as just a job." I shook my head. "I feel like I'm on edge every second of the day."

As I took a sip of coffee, it hit me. Paulie's ability to view this gig as just a job was directly related to the fact that he didn't have personal feelings for Frannie. If something happened to her, it would be a failure from a business perspective, but it likely wouldn't shatter him. If something happened to Juliette, I knew it would wreck me. Juliette had never felt like just a client, even in the beginning, but especially not now as we'd gotten closer. Her life felt like my life. And that was pretty damn eye opening.

A waiter brought our food, and Paulie happily escaped into his eggs rather than encouraging deeper conversation with me about the plight of the mob bodyguard.

After they finished their breakfast, Juliette and her mother came walking toward our table.

"We should go pick up the cat and get to the airport, Paulie."

"Yes, ma'am." Paulie stood from the table.

"I already paid for all of us," Frannie announced.

I nodded. "That was very nice of you. Thank you."

Frannie placed her hand on my arm. "It's the least I can do with how well you take care of my baby."

I watched as Juliette and her mother embraced. After, I gave Frannie a hug and clasped hands with Paulie.

"Call me when you get home, Mom."

"I will, my darling."

After they left, Juliette and I walked to the car together.

"What were you and my mother talking about this morning before I woke up?"

Damn. I hoped we'd gotten past that. "Nothing. Just shooting the shit."

She gave me a look. She knew I was lying. Of course, Frannie told her how she'd confronted me. There weren't many secrets between those two.

"Your mother's advice to me this morning only solidified the fact that I need to keep things purely business with you."

Juliette sniffed. "Well, she had no right to interfere."

We got in the car, but I didn't start the engine. Instead, I turned to Juliette. "What made her ask me if I had feelings for you? Did you tell her we've crossed the line?"

She blushed. "I might've mentioned that things are a little complicated."

"The feelings might be complicated, but the course of action isn't. There's not a choice," I said, maybe a little too gruffly. But I started the engine and took off.

Juliette crossed her arms and looked out her window for the rest of the ride. Once again, you could cut the tension between us with a knife.

Maybe it was good that she was mad. We were getting too close—especially after Jersey. Frannie's warning was the reality check I needed. She wasn't telling me anything I didn't already know, but hearing it from someone else was a reminder to stay on course.

When we got back to the house, Juliette went straight to her room while I lay on the couch watching TV. As I flipped through the channels, though, I remained preoccupied with the fact that I'd upset her. I knew my harsh stance on the matter was just as much for my own benefit, to remind myself of the boundaries I'd been so bad at respecting lately. I talked a good talk, but ultimately, I never *felt* in control around her.

Juliette didn't come out of her room for most of the day. I ended up nodding off, and by the time I woke up, it was dark out.

I walked back to check on her. Running a hand through my hair, I knocked on her bedroom door—but there was no answer.

"Juliette?" I called. *Is she asleep?*

While I tried not to enter her room without permission, the fact that she didn't answer was troubling. I finally opened the door, only to find that her room was empty.

"Juliette!" I yelled as I stormed around the house.

I called her, but there was no answer.

What the fuck?

Pacing, I pondered whether I should go in search of her or stay put in case she came back. But I truly had no clue where she could've gone. Wherever it was, though, there was no doubt in my mind that Juliette had left because she was mad at me. This was my fault—because I'd turned so damn cold on the way home earlier—and I wouldn't forgive myself if something happened to her.

Ready to pull my hair out, I decided I couldn't take it anymore. I rushed out to my car and drove off in search of her, roaming the streets of LA. In the midst of my panic, I realized I wasn't thinking about the job or whether Vince might kill me for losing track of his daughter. The only important thing was Juliette and her safety.

No matter how much I tried to tell myself our relationship needed to be purely business, it wasn't. Juliette mattered to me more than anything. Before meeting her, this whole thing had been, in the words of Paulie, "just a job." But it was so much more to me now.

With no luck finding Juliette, I finally returned to the house. As I entered, my stomach dropped when I realized she still wasn't home. I'd tried her phone three times while I was on the road, but I tried calling her again.

No answer.

Several minutes later, the door opened, and Juliette strolled in.

"Where the hell have you been?" Springing to my feet from the couch, I stalked toward her.

"I was next door at Pam's," she said casually, as if she hadn't almost given me a heart attack.

"Why the fuck didn't you answer your phone?" I started to pace.

"I left my phone here to charge."

"I called you multiple times." I placed my hands on my hips. "Why didn't I hear it ring?"

"I had it on vibrate while I was napping earlier. I guess I forgot to turn the ringer back on."

"You should always take your phone with you," I scolded. "And you should never have it on vibrate."

"Well, it wasn't intentional. I was just thinking—"

"You *weren't* thinking. That's the fucking problem!"

Her face reddened. "Calm your fucking balls, Wes. I didn't mean to scare you. You were sleeping, and I didn't want to wake you. I'd told Pam she could borrow my book. So I took it over to her, and then she asked me to stay for a glass of wine. That was it. Relax!"

As adrenaline coursed through me, I stormed toward her again. "I *won't* fucking relax. You had me worried sick, thinking something had happened to you." I inched closer. "Do you have any idea how scared I was that you could've been hurt—or worse?"

Her face softened as she looked into my eyes.

And somehow, I was certain she saw it.

The truth.

That this wasn't *just* about my duty as her protector.

I couldn't let my guard down like this. I forced myself to harden as I spewed words at her that I didn't really mean. I just had to overshadow my own vulnerability.

"You are the most selfish person I know," I lied.

"Selfish? What the fuck are you talking about, Wes? I can't even do what I please in life because of this mess. How is that selfish?"

It isn't. I'm just being a dick, so you can't tell how damn crazy I am about you.

Her nostrils flared. "If you think I'm selfish, why don't you tell my father you want a reassignment? I'm sure there are other things he could use your help with. Maybe he'll assign a real man who won't be so scared of me." She pointed at my chest. "How can I be selfish when I can't even live my life without you stuck to my ass all the time?"

I moved in, backing her up against the wall. "You *wish* I was stuck to your ass. That's the problem, isn't it, Juliette? You wish I was *in* your ass right now."

Her mouth slowly widened. "Fuck you."

"I know you want to..." I murmured.

That's when I felt a firm slap across my face. I placed my hand on my cheek, realizing I'd taken it too far. But apparently there was still room to take it further.

Because the next thing I did was lean in and take her mouth with mine.

CHAPTER 16

Juliette

Wes abruptly pulled away, the sudden loss knocking the breath from my lungs, as if someone had yanked the rug out from under me. I touched my lips, the taste of him still lingering. "Wh...why did you stop?"

He shook his head. "Because that was a mistake and shouldn't have happened."

The words landed like a slap. "A mistake? Are you kidding me? *You* kiss *me* like that and have the nerve to stand there and tell me it was a *mistake*?"

"You know it was, Juliette."

"A mistake is sending a text to the person you're talking about instead of the one you were talking about them with." I'd spent weeks listening to this man say one thing while his actions told me another, and I was done letting him hide behind excuses. "No, I don't know that it was a mistake. What I know is that *nothing* has ever felt as good as that kiss. Nothing."

He shook his head again. "It doesn't matter how it felt."

"Of course it does!" I yelled. "All that matters in life is how much you *felt*! When you're lying on your deathbed, do you really want to think back to all the times you followed the rules? Or do you want to remember the moments that set your blood on fire, the ones that made your heart race and reminded you that you were alive?" My chest heaved, and unshed tears stung the corners of my eyes. "In the end, feelings are all we get to take with us."

Wes pulled his hair at the root and paced. "I can't protect you if I'm emotionally involved."

"I didn't think you were a coward."

He stopped in his tracks. "What did you just call me?"

I walked straight up to him, pushed to my tippy toes, and spoke in his face. "*A coward.*"

"How am I a damn coward?"

"You're using not wanting to get emotionally involved as an excuse. You're *already* emotionally involved. Can you honestly look me in the eyes and tell me you don't have feelings for me, that emotions aren't involved just because we haven't had sex?"

Wes's chest rose and fell, his breaths uneven. Turmoil flickered in his eyes, and I saw it all—anger, denial, *longing*. "I'm not—" he started, then looked away. "I don't have feelings for you like that."

My heart twisted, even knowing that was a damn lie. I grabbed his chin and held it so he was forced to meet my gaze. "That's bullshit, and you know it. Stop being a damn *coward*."

His nostrils flared, the muscle in his cheek ticcing. "Stop."

"No. *You* stop. Stop fighting what you feel."

We stared at each other for a long moment, the only sound between us our ragged breathing. I shook my head. "Coward."

Wes's eyes darkened. But he still didn't budge.

So I leaned closer and whispered in his face. "Coward!"

I saw the exact moment he broke. If I hadn't already been out of my mind, I might've been a little nervous at the determination on his face. Wes stepped forward, forcing me to take a step back, then another and another—until my back hit the kitchen wall. "Is this really what you want? Me to fuck you while I'm pissed off?"

"No." I moved in so close our noses were touching. "I want you to fuck me like you hate me."

His eyes flared, but before I could say another word, his hands were on my face and his mouth crushed against mine. I'd never felt such passion, such raw need. The kiss was fierce, borderline punishing, yet underneath I caught what he was trying to hide: Relief. Surrender. The weight of all the things I already knew were true, but he couldn't yet allow himself to accept. I fisted his shirt, dragging him closer, and kissed him back with everything I had.

Wes reached down, gripped beneath my thigh, and suddenly my feet left the ground. My legs wrapped around his waist, holding on as his body pinned mine against the wall. He wound his hand into my hair and yanked my head back, making me gasp. Sucking his way down my neck, his teeth grazed along sensitive skin. He moved lower and nipped at my collarbone.

I let out a sound that was somewhere between a cry and a moan, and Wes responded by growling and sinking his teeth into the flesh of my shoulder. It was sharp enough to sting, yet I loved it. *Loved, loved, loved it.* Clawing at his back, I understood exactly how he felt—desperate to leave marks.

Wes's breaths were ragged bursts as he continued lower, working his mouth along the top of my exposed cleavage. My nipples hardened, straining against the fabric of my shirt, desperate for attention. One hand stayed locked under me, keeping me supported, while the other slipped between us. I heard the scrape of the metal as he unbuckled his belt, followed by the rasp of his zipper lowering. The sound left me trembling with need, a hungry pulse throbbing between my legs.

He shoved his jeans down just enough, and then his fingers hooked into my panties and yanked them aside. He groaned. "Christ, you're soaked, and I haven't even touched you yet."

"That means you don't need to waste time," I breathed. "I need you inside me now, Wes."

"You trust me to always protect you?"

"Yes."

"Then you're getting me raw. Need to feel every bit of you when you come around my cock."

My body hummed like a live wire, electric currents racing through me. He wasn't even inside yet, and I was already barreling toward orgasm. "I'm on the pill."

He fisted his cock and guided it to my opening. Surging forward, he slid into me in one deep, claiming thrust. The picture on the wall next to us rattled and nearly fell off the hook, but even the house falling down wouldn't have stopped us. With a string of curses, Wes pulled almost all the way out, then slammed back in. He did it again and again, over and over. It was hard, fast, and unrelenting, but exactly the way we both needed it.

Every thrust slammed me against the wall, every grind sent fire racing through me.

Wes took my mouth again, kissing me with the same desperation that had him driving into me. My nails dug into his shoulders, and I rocked with him.

"Fuck. Need my cum deep inside you." He gripped one thigh and lifted it higher, pushing in at a slight angle that rubbed against the perfect spot inside me.

My body began pulsing on its own. "Yes...yes...just like that." I arched into him, moaning, letting my orgasm swallow my words.

"I feel you," he growled. "Feel you gripping me like a fist."

Wes kept going, fucking me until my body shattered and I had nothing left. With a roar, he pumped once, twice, then sank deep and stilled, jerking inside of me as he unloaded. I could feel the heat seeping through my body.

After, we collapsed onto the kitchen floor together. I offered a spent, goofy smile. "It's about damn time."

Wes's laugh was a deep rumble. "You're going to be the death of me. If not one way, then the other."

I poked my finger to his chest. "That's not even funny."

He slipped his hands under my ass and lifted, taking me with him as he climbed to his feet. "That shouldn't have happened like that."

I stiffened. "What are you talking about?"

He smirked and kissed my nose, walking toward the bedroom, still cradling me. "Relax, woman. I mean it shouldn't have happened against the wall and full of anger. You deserve better than that."

"I didn't mind."

He kicked the bedroom door open with his foot and set me down gently in the middle of the bed. "I want to see every part of you, taste every inch."

My body had just quaked through a near-violent orgasm, yet a couple of words from this man had me riled up all over again. Both our clothes were still on, so Wes took his time undressing me before starting to strip himself. I'd seen him shirtless plenty of times, but getting a close-up view of the full package was something else entirely. His shoulders were broad, his arms thick with muscle and corded veins, and his chest was sculpted to damn near perfection. I'd never had a lover with such an incredible physique.

I licked my lips. "God, your body is amazing. I've been drooling over it for so long. I can't believe I finally get to touch it."

Wes smiled. He'd pulled his jeans up enough to walk, but the button and zipper were still undone. Hooking his fingers into the waistband, he yanked them down in one swift motion, pulling his underwear off at the same time.

I swallowed. "Jesus, even that thing looks like it lifts weights. How is it still hard?"

Wes chuckled and lifted a knee onto the mattress, draping himself over me. When he pressed his lips to mine, a sigh of relief rolled through my body. This kiss was filled with so much more than desire; it was filled with emotion and unspoken words. I hadn't realized I'd needed anything more than what we'd already done, but my heart suddenly ached for it.

I spread my legs wide, inviting him in, and Wes took his time. All the muscles in his face strained as he dipped his cock inside of me and slowly rocked in and out. It didn't take long for things to build to a frenzy again, but now Wes looked into my eyes with every stroke.

We moved in unison, rocking back and forth together, while we kissed like we were starving. I'd never experienced something so beautifully intense. We felt like one—mind, body, and soul.

"Fuck," Wes gritted. "I want to stay inside you forever, but I can't hold back much longer."

The sound of his voice straining and the way he looked me in the eyes while he spoke had a second orgasm brewing inside me like a hurricane. I was right there on the edge. My breathing picked up, and my eyes shut as it took hold.

"Open, sweetheart. I want to watch you come undone."

That did the trick. My body exploded—legs throbbing, toes curling, nails digging into his back. "Wes…"

"Beautiful," he groaned. "Fucking beautiful, baby."

His jaw flexed as he picked up the pace while my body pulsed all around him. Once I went slack, he thrust deep and came inside me again.

After, I expected him to collapse. What man can have two orgasms so close together and still be semi hard? Apparently, the answer is *Wes*. He glided in and out, moving at a leisurely pace as he smiled down at me.

"You're screwed, woman."

I offered a goofy smile. "Yes, deliciously so."

Wes brushed hair from my face. "I meant you're going to be stuck in the house with me an awful lot. Now that I know how good it feels to be inside you, you might be walking funny."

"It's okay. It'll be worth it."

"Yeah, babe." He kissed my lips. "I'll make sure it is."

The next morning, I woke to find Wes sitting in the chair next to my bed, watching me.

"Creepy..." I grinned and pulled the blanket up. "What time is it?"

He shrugged and looked out the window. "Sun just came up a little while ago, so I'd guess about seven."

I turned onto my side and tucked my hands under my cheek. "How long have you been awake?"

"An hour or two."

"And you were sitting there like that the whole time?"

He shrugged again. "I was thinking."

The look in his eyes made my chest tighten. "Do you regret last night?"

"No."

"What's bothering you then? I can see the turmoil in your eyes."

He sighed. "I don't want to hurt you, Juliette. But I'm not sure how this could ever work."

"What if I talk to my father? He's always wanted me to be daddy's little girl, so he could give me anything I wanted—a pony, a car, whatever to spoil me. Except, of course, he couldn't give me what I wanted most: a normal father and a normal life. I'll tell him I want *you*, and he needs to set you free."

"A pony, a car—those are things he wanted you to have. He doesn't want you with me, Juliette."

"How do you know that?"

"Well, for starters, he told me if I laid a finger on you, he'd chop off my dick and stuff it for his mantel."

I cringed. "I'm sorry."

"Don't apologize for him. Ever."

"What if I told my dad we'd never touched? That I've fallen for you, and he has to set you free because you won't even give me a chance while you work for him."

Wes rubbed the back of his neck. "No."

"Why not?"

"It's not a good idea. Your father is in the middle of a war, and the last thing he wants to deal with is one of his people falling for his only daughter."

"But…"

"It's just not the right time."

I didn't like it, but maybe Wes was right. Maybe after whatever was going on was over, my dad would be in a better place—more reasonable. He tended to be more difficult than usual when he was under stress. Which I suppose is why he'd been difficult the last decade because being the head of a crime family was the definition of tension.

"Okay…but when the time is right?"

Wes frowned. "I don't know when that'll be, Juliette. I don't want to promise you something I don't have control over."

"But I want more than to be your secret fling."

Wes seemed to contemplate what I'd said for a minute. "Like what? What is more?"

"I don't know. Simple things. I want to go out on dates, go to the movies, hold your hand in public. Be a couple, so we can see if this could really work."

Before he could respond, my cell phone buzzed on the nightstand. Wes and I looked over at the same time.

He frowned. "Why is that putz calling you so early?"

"We've discussed that we both like to write first thing in the morning, so he probably assumed I was up."

It buzzed again, and Wes held my eyes. "I'll go get coffee and give you a minute."

When he walked out of the room, I figured I might as well get the call over with.

"Hello?"

"Hey, Jules. I didn't wake you, did I?"

I sat up, back against the headboard. "No, I was up. What's going on?"

"I woke up at five feeling like I'd been shot out of a cannon. I must've written a dozen pages of notes for the screenplay."

"Oh. That's great."

"Could we get together today? I want to talk about it while it's all fresh in my head."

"Ummm..." I looked over at the bedroom door before responding. "Yeah, I guess so."

"You don't sound so happy about it. Are you still upset with me for what went down a few weeks ago?"

Wes came back into the room carrying two mugs and sat on the chair next to the bed again. I looked at him while I spoke to Jett. "No, I'm okay."

"Great. How about twelve at Lazaro's?"

"Okay. I'll see you then."

Swiping the phone off, I tossed it on the bed next to me, and Wes held out my coffee. "Thank you."

He sipped his and watched me over the brim. "Hot date?"

"Funny. But Jett does want to get together today, to discuss the book I'm turning into a screenplay."

"Right."

My eyes narrowed. "What does that mean?"

"It means that guy's a douche, and I don't trust anything he says."

I sighed. "I could see why you would think that after what he did. But I don't believe he's a bad guy. He just let his last movie's success go to his head, and he thinks he's all..." I made air quotes. "Hollywood."

Wes was quiet for a beat. "What if having lunch to discuss his book is a ruse, and he wants more from you than just to talk business?"

I climbed from the bed, taking the sheet with me, and sat on Wes's lap. "See? There's another benefit of getting my dad to let you out of your deal. Then I can tell Jett I'm seeing someone."

Later in the afternoon, I was listening to Jett drone on about the hundredth thing he wanted me to incorporate into the screenplay, but I was only half listening because I was distracted by the man sitting fifteen feet away at the bar. Wes didn't even try to hide how intently he was watching me, and I couldn't stop wondering if the jealousy I saw on his face might turn into something explosive when I got home. That thought had my thighs squeezing together. We'd had sex three times since last night, and it hadn't even begun to quench the thirst I had for the man.

At one point, Jett's phone rang. It was his agent, so he said he needed to take it.

"I have to go to the bathroom anyway. I'll give you some privacy."

The ladies' room was at the back of the restaurant, down a long hall. Inside, there were two stalls, but the one next to me was empty. Which turned out to be a damn good thing, because when I stepped out, a man was standing there.

"Wes? Is everything okay?"

He turned the lock on the outer door. The loud clank echoed, causing all the little hairs on my body to stand at attention. "Hands on the sink."

My heart started to race. "Really? What if someone needs to use the bathroom?"

"Then they can wait. If I have to sit there and watch that asshole gawk at your cleavage every time you look down to write notes, you're going to do it with my cum leaking out of you."

My jaw dropped open. Yet... *God, that's hot.*

"Hands on the sink, sweetheart."

I loved it so much when he used terms of endearment like that, and even more so when he was telling me to hold on so he could fuck me hard and fast. I planted my hands on the sink basin.

Five minutes later, I went back to my meeting flush-faced and freshly fucked. Thankfully, I'd worn a long skirt, because Wes hadn't let me wipe off, and I could feel him dripping down my leg.

Jett smiled, none the wiser. "Sorry about that. I had some quick business to take care of."

I smiled back with two wet thighs. "Yup. Me too."

CHAPTER 17

Wes

What the hell have I done?

Two days after I'd lost control with Juliette, the guilt had really started to set in. In these quiet moments alone in the morning while she was still sleeping, I found myself ruminating the most. When Juliette was right in front of me, on the other hand, it was much easier to forget our dilemma and focus on her. I couldn't wait for her to wake up today, so I could escape into her beautiful face and forget everything else again.

My phone rang—my mother. I moved outside to the front of the house to avoid waking Juliette. "Hey, Ma."

"Hi, honey. I wanted to check on you. We haven't spoken much since Grandma's funeral."

I waved to a neighbor rolling his garbage cans out. "I know. I'm sorry. I've been busy with work." I sighed. "How are you holding up?"

"It's been quite the job cleaning out her house. So much stuff to go through, deciding what to keep, what to donate..."

"I bet. I'm sorry I can't be there to help you."

"You can't imagine how many old photos I've come across of you and your brother. She loved you both so much."

That made me smile and feel a little sad at the same time. "She kept everything, so that doesn't surprise me."

"So..." She paused. "How are things with Juliette?"

While I'd lied to my mother about the nature of my relationship with Juliette, ironically, after recent events, the lie didn't seem like all that much of a stretch anymore.

"Things are still going well," I finally said. *Better than ever.* But also, so very bad.

I wished I could tell my mother everything. I'd always valued her advice. Would she tell me to run from this situation before I got myself killed? Or would she believe that my feelings for Juliette superseded everything? One thing I knew: even if it didn't work out between Juliette and me, I couldn't leave her behind. I couldn't trust anyone else to protect her.

I shook my head, unable to contain the truth. "Actually, things *aren't* perfect, Ma."

"What's wrong?"

I hesitated. "I can't tell you everything. But...I wasn't completely honest about how Juliette and I met." I paused. "She's related to a client of mine, and we've been hiding our relationship. That's the most I'm able to say due to..." I paused again. "A non-disclosure agreement I signed."

That was the most honest I'd been with my mother in a long while.

"Okay..." she said. "So you're torn between doing the right thing for your career or following your heart?"

Much more complicated than that, but she got the gist. "Basically, yes." I scratched my chin.

"There are always jobs, Wes. But there's only one Juliette. And if you care about her, then fuck the job. That's my opinion. Nothing else should matter."

If only it were that simple. *Fuck the job*. I chuckled, though, since my mother rarely cussed. Hearing her say that gave me renewed hope that somehow, some way, I could figure this out. I wished I could *fuck this job* straight to hell.

"She seemed really great," my mother added. "She makes you smile, which was nice to see."

"She *is* great," I agreed.

After we hung up, I went back inside and continued to ruminate about whether I'd made a colossal mistake with Juliette. I had a bad feeling I couldn't shake about how this was going to play out. That's why every single day we had together mattered. I couldn't control the future, but I could control her memories of me. I could control today. Today felt safe, and I would cherish every second.

Juliette interrupted my thoughts as she emerged from her room, rubbing her eyes. She stretched her arms and yawned. "I overslept."

"I sure as hell wasn't going to wake you." I winked. "Anyway, it's my fault. I kept you up late last night."

She smiled. "What's the plan for today?"

"We're going on a trip." I decided this in that very moment, my mouth slowly curving into a smile. "Just for the night."

Her eyes went wide. "Where?"

"It's a...surprise." *A surprise even for me. I need to figure this out.* Needing to buy myself some time to make plans, I decided to make this fun for her. "Give me a few, all right?"

She narrowed her eyes suspiciously and went to make her coffee.

A little while later, I met Juliette in the kitchen as she finished her cereal.

"I'm sending you around the house on a little scavenger hunt," I announced. "When you get to the last step, you'll find out where we're going."

"Really?" Her face lit up. "Where's my first clue?"

"I'll *give* you the first one." I handed her a piece of paper.

Grinning from ear to ear, she read the message aloud. "I won't tell you everything, just a smidge. You'll find out more when you head to the fridge."

Juliette got up from her seat and went over to the refrigerator. Earlier, I'd come in here and pretended I wanted orange juice, but really just stuck one of the notes to a carton of almond milk.

She peeled off the note and read it aloud. "There shall be mountains galore. Head to the toilet for more." Juliette giggled as she left the kitchen.

I followed her to the bathroom.

She found the note lying next to the sink and read it. "It's only a hundred miles from here. Next clue is on the chandelier." She scratched her chin. "Hmm... A hundred miles. I'm trying to think..."

Juliette made her way to the chandelier that hung in the entryway. She picked the sticky note off one of the bulbs and read, "The location is east. Now go to the room you like least."

She looked up at me. "The laundry room?"

Crossing my arms, I shrugged and played dumb. "You tell me..."

She raced to the small laundry area and found the note I'd left on top of the dryer.

Juliette covered her mouth in laughter. "By now, you know it's not France. Final answer is in Wes's pants."

She turned to me and glanced down at my package. "You didn't..."

I smirked. "I did."

Juliette inched toward me and undid my belt. She slowly unzipped my jeans to peek inside. Right on my boxer briefs was a sticky note that read: **We're going to Palm Springs!**

"Clever, Wes." She shook her head. "All that just to get me to stick my hands in your pants? You didn't need to send me on a wild goose chase." She wrapped her arms around my neck. "Palm Springs sounds amazing!" She kissed my lips.

Our tongues collided for several seconds, and I immediately grew hard. It didn't take much.

She spoke over my mouth. "When do we have to leave?"

"Any time now, but no rush," I said.

"So we have a little time?"

I arched a brow. "Time for what?"

She flashed a mischievous grin as she ran her finger seductively over my lips.

Already horned up, I flipped her around, pressing my cock against her ass.

Juliette braced her hands against the washing machine as I kissed down the back of her neck.

My cock went rigid. "I can't get enough of you."

She pushed her ass back against my throbbing dick.

"You really want to get fucked right now, don't you?" I groaned.

"I do." She let out a long breath, reaching back to rub her hand along my erection. "But I'm also in the mood for something else..."

My curiosity was officially piqued.

Juliette turned and dropped to her knees, sliding my belt out of the loops and throwing it aside with a loud clank. She pulled my pants down to my knees.

"What are you doing?" I murmured, even if I knew damn well what was happening. And *fuck yes*.

She looked up at me. "I want you to fuck my mouth."

Shit. Hearing her say it that way nearly made me come on the spot.

Juliette lowered my boxer briefs, and my cock bobbed out to greet her. She wrapped her hands around my swollen shaft and took me straight into her hot, wet mouth.

For so long, this very thing had been one of my biggest fantasies. The past couple of days had felt like a dream. I never wanted this to end.

I bent my head back, and my eyes followed. No dream could do justice to the reality of what it felt like to move in and out of her beautiful mouth, to slide down her throat. Pure ecstasy.

Fisting her thick hair, I looked down and kept my eyes on her, relishing every second. "You're so fucking good at this..." I had to tighten my abs to keep from exploding down her throat.

She moaned, and it vibrated down my shaft, causing me to lose control and come faster than I'd wanted. I watched in awe as Juliette swallowed every last drop. My chest rose and fell as I recovered from that mind-blowing orgasm.

She licked her lips and stood. I wanted to burn that sight into my memory.

Juliette kissed me, and I could taste myself on her tongue. "Let's get out of here…" she whispered.

I couldn't wait to get to Palm Springs so I could bury myself inside of her again.

As we exited the laundry room, she said, "I've never been to Palm Springs, you know."

"Me neither." I kissed her forehead. "Pack your bag."

After Juliette and I threw our stuff together, we headed to the rental car place where I'd reserved a convertible. The weather was supposed to be perfect, so I figured, why not?

We drove with the top down for the nearly two-hour journey to Palm Springs, blasting the music. Juliette lifted her arms into the air numerous times, her hair blowing in the wind. This was what freedom felt like, even if it was only for a couple of days. *True* freedom with Juliette was likely a pipe dream. But I needed to put the negativity aside for a little while.

Once we got to Palm Springs, we dropped our stuff at the Airbnb before taking a tram ride from the desert to the mountains. Juliette was a bit scared of heights, so I held her hand the entire time. We had dinner at a mountaintop restaurant as we watched the sun set overlooking the Coachella Valley below. Our escape so far had been everything I'd hoped it would be.

After we returned to our Airbnb for the night, Juliette and I sat outside for a bit to gaze at the stars. I'd lit the firepit, which counteracted the chill in the air. We sat together in the same lounge chair, Juliette resting her back against my chest.

"This is the most peaceful I've felt since Ortigia," she said.

"That's sort of what I was going for." I kissed the back of her head. "I wanted to give you a little bit of that peace back, since our Italy trip was cut short."

She sighed. "Maybe we just need to keep running from reality." She turned around to face me. "I can't imagine going through this without you, Wes." She chuckled. "And I don't know what my father was thinking, sending *you* and expecting me not to fall..." She hesitated.

Even though Juliette stopped short of actually saying the word *love*, her admission shocked me, although it probably shouldn't have; I was falling, too. Before I could conjure a response, Juliette shook her head. "I didn't mean to, um..." She exhaled.

Even in the darkness, I could see her face turn red as she waited for my reaction. And yet, I couldn't find the words. More than that, I wasn't sure if it was wise to unleash them, afraid to give her false hope in what seemed like a hopeless predicament.

I'd let the silence go on too long before I stammered, "Juliette, I—"

"I'm gonna go shower," she said, getting up before I could respond.

Shit. My heart ached as I continued to sit outside by the fire. I couldn't let her go to sleep tonight thinking I didn't feel the same way about her. If anything, my feelings for Juliette might've even been stronger than hers were for me. I just hadn't categorized it as love because I couldn't dare go there. But that was a protective mechanism and had no bearing on how I *actually* felt about her.

She was already in bed when I went into the house. I took a quick shower and gathered my thoughts as the warm water rained down on me. But I knew there was no way to rehearse this. I needed to speak from the heart and hope I didn't sound like a blubbering idiot.

After, I slipped into bed and wrapped my arms around her from behind. Juliette's body went rigid at my touch. She was so damn tense, and I didn't have to wonder why.

"You're not the only one, Juliette," I whispered. "I've never felt this way about anyone."

She turned to face me and placed a gentle kiss on my lips. But when she pulled back, I noticed a look of worry in her eyes, as if somehow in the time she'd spent lying in bed alone, she'd realized a little of what I was already concerned about.

The following morning, the tension from the night before had thankfully dissipated.

After mind-blowing morning sex, Juliette and I had coffee together out on the patio, flanked by palm trees and a cool morning breeze.

We decided to try a breakfast place that had great reviews online.

The outdoor seating area was crowded by the time we got there. Once we found a table, Juliette ordered the chocolate chip pancakes while I opted for eggs, bacon, and toast.

We were in the middle of our meal when I spotted what looked like a man holding a camera in the nearby bushes. The lens seemed to be aimed straight at us.

Adrenaline raced through me. "Stay right here," I told Juliette as I got up. My eardrums throbbed as I stalked toward the bushes. "What the fuck are you doing?" I yelled as I jumped him, ripping the camera out of his hands and placing him in a chokehold.

"Get off me!" He coughed.

He couldn't have been more than twenty-two and looked like he was about to shit his pants.

"Not until you tell me what you were doing taking photos of us," I seethed. "Did Vince hire you?" I let him go long enough to speak.

"Who the fuck is Vince?" He panted. "And I wasn't taking photos of you! See for yourself."

I scrolled through his camera, and sure enough, all the photos were of the couple seated behind us. My breathing calmed, and I felt a bit stupid, to be honest.

"I was hired to take photos of Lindsay Appleton," he said. "You know...the actress."

I vaguely recalled her as an up-and-coming star.

My shoulders slumped. "Man, I'm sorry."

"Who the hell are you? And why should I be taking photos of you anyway?"

I shook my head. "You don't want to know." I handed him back the camera, then reached into my wallet and took out a hundred-dollar bill. I offered it to him. "We good?"

He took it and ran a hand through his hair. "Yeah, man."

Hanging my head in shame, I returned to the table where Juliette waited with fear in her eyes.

"What the hell just happened, Wes?"

"It's all good. It was a false alarm," I muttered, shoveling some eggs into my mouth.

"Explain," she demanded.

I put my fork down and sighed. "I thought someone was taking photos of you and me. I assumed your father had hired someone." I lowered my voice. "But Lindsay Appleton is at the table behind us. That's who the guy was snapping."

Juliette turned around. "Oh my God. I had no idea." She chuckled. "I guess we're not that important."

I shook my head. "I was sure Vince had us followed."

"Well, better a camera than a gun?" She arched her brow.

I glared at her.

"Too soon?" She reached out her hand. "I'm sorry that happened. We'd been having such a peaceful morning."

As long as Juliette's life was in my hands, I could never let my guard down. I needed to remember that. One slip, and we could both end up dead.

CHAPTER 18

Wes

"I really like when you cook at the stove wearing a robe with nothing underneath." I came up behind Juliette, tugged the tie on her robe so it came loose, and cupped both her breasts.

She laughed and pushed her ass out to force me to take a few steps back, but that only turned me on more.

"This is even better." I groaned and slid my hands around to her ass. "Bend a little more. Grab on to the stove."

"You're a fiend." She giggled and turned around, holding the spatula up. "I'm frying bacon, so my robe needs to be closed and my face far away from the sizzle. Now go sit. We're going to eat in a few minutes."

I pouted but sat my ass in a chair at the table. My spot had the newspaper folded and a vitamin waiting for me on the napkin. Juliette had teased me last week when I'd mentioned that I missed reading a physical newspaper, yet a few days later, when I sat down to breakfast, there was a copy of the *New York Post* waiting for me. Apparently, you can get it delivered out here in California. I opened the paper from the back, last page forward, to get to the sports section and started reading. But not even halfway through an article about the Mets' rookie pitcher, my eyes found their way back to the lady standing at the stove. Juliette and I had settled into what felt a hell of a lot like domestic bliss lately. She made me breakfast and did my laundry. I fixed the dishwasher and took out the garbage, and we went food shopping together. We were practically an old married couple, and I hated to admit it, but I loved every mundane task when I was with her.

But for every minute I let myself enjoy playing house, there were twice as many sleepless ones spent staring at the ceiling, trying to figure out how the hell to get out of the mess I was in. Leave the country with her and never come back? That idea was starting to seem less ridiculous by the day. Though I had no doubt that Vince Ginocassi would scour the Earth to find his only daughter.

Even in moments like this—when I felt content and my heart was full, I couldn't shake the shadow of a bad feeling, like something was bound to go wrong. Some days, it took everything I had just to let myself live in the moment here and there.

Juliette set pancakes and bacon on the table, then took the seat across from me.

I folded the newspaper and set it aside. "What's on the agenda for today?"

"I have to go meet Bradley Wilson."

"The asshole actor you were doing rewrites for when we first met?"

She nodded. "I thought I was finally done with them. They're almost to the end of filming, but he's decided to change the ending now. I'm sure the author of the book is going to love that."

"What time do you need to be there?"

"Ten." She looked at the time on her phone. "Which is in an hour, and I didn't even shower yet."

"Me neither." I grinned. "Sounds like we should save time and do that together."

"That will *not* save time. It will make me late," she replied. "Besides, we had sex an hour ago."

"I know, but I'm still turned on from watching you at the stove."

"You're insatiable." Juliette chuckled. "We're meeting at the studio offices instead of on set. So at least you won't be bothered about being on the lot today."

An hour later, after a quickie in the shower, we were on the road, and I caught myself whistling. *Whistling*. I wasn't a damn whistler. But I guess two rounds of morning sex before ten AM will do that to a man. Though my whistle was cut short when I glanced in the rearview mirror and noticed that a black sedan three car-lengths back changed lanes right after I did. Tinted windows. Same car I'd clocked when we first hit the highway. I didn't want to alarm Juliette, since it was probably nothing, but I sat up straighter, my hands tightening on the wheel as I sharpened my focus.

When I got off at the next exit, the sedan did, too, though it was now back five lengths. At the first light, I turned left, and the car kept going straight, so I breathed a little easier. Five minutes later, we pulled up to the studio office. I parked in the loading zone in front of the building, hoping no one would hassle me since I was staying in the car. If they did, I'd have to pull the ex-cop card and hope I got a courtesy.

While Juliette unbuckled and gathered her things, I jogged around the car to open her door.

"I'm probably going to be here most of the day," she said, stepping out. "Nothing to do with Bradley Wilson is quick."

I shrugged. "It's fine. I'll be here waiting."

"Thanks. I'll see you later." She leaned in and kissed me.

At first, it didn't even register. Kissing her goodbye felt natural at this point. But then a heavy feeling washed over me. What if one of Vince's guys had eyes on us? What if that simple gesture got me killed and ruined her life because she'd have to carry the burden forever?

We needed to be smarter. I'd have to remind Juliette about that when she got back.

I returned to the driver's seat and scanned the street. Everything ahead looked clear. But when I checked the rearview mirror, I froze. The black sedan with tinted windows was now parked four cars back. Had it been there when we pulled up and I'd missed it? Or had it crept to the curb while I was busy kissing Juliette goodbye?

Suddenly on high alert, I adjusted the mirror, my eyes darting all over the cars behind me. Which was probably why I didn't notice the figure closing in on the passenger side.

The door yanked open, and before I could react, someone slipped into the seat beside me.

I didn't even get a chance to breathe a sigh of relief once I saw it wasn't Vince or any of his men. Because it was someone worse.

My boss.

Captain Dana Rourke.

"What the *fuck* do you think you're doing?" she yelled.

Fuck! Fuck! Fuuuck! I played dumb. Stupid move, considering I knew her well enough to know it'd only piss her off more. "What are you talking about? I'm parked here because Juliette's inside."

"I'm talking about *kissing the suspect's daughter*! What the fuck's going on, Callahan? You trying to blow our entire sting operation because you need to get your dick wet?"

The shock of having my NYPD captain slide into the car started to fade, just enough for me to realize something else. A cop being here in my car was more dangerous than kissing Vince's daughter. I glanced toward the building Juliette had gone into, then scanned the street and sidewalks all around me. "*Me* blow it? Juliette could see you. Or worse, Vince's guys could be lurking around."

"It's not my first day on the job, Callahan," she snapped. "I know what I'm doing. I have four of LA's finest in cars keeping an eye on the area to make sure it's secure."

I raked a hand through my hair. "What are you doing here?"

"First, you answer *my* questions. Are you fucking that mob princess?"

My teeth clenched, and I lied right through them. Who wasn't I lying to at this point? My mother, Juliette, now my damn boss. I shook my head. "She kissed me the other night. I pulled away, of course, but then I noticed she got a lot more talkative after. So I've been letting her think there's a chance something could happen between us. I won't allow it to go any further."

My captain side-eyed me. "I better not find out you're full of shit and have put this entire undercover operation at risk when I went to bat for you. If you fuck this up, I'll personally make sure you can't even get a job working security at Target."

I swallowed. "Understood."

"It damn well better be," she grumbled.

"What's going on, Cap? Are you here just to check on me?"

"No. I need to give you some intel, and I need you to get some for me. There's a sit-down happening with all five families. We need to know where it's happening."

"How do you know about the sit-down but not the location?"

"Because everyone's talking in code on the fed wire taps. The meeting is going down at some place they're calling the rooster—wherever the hell that is. A big rodeo is expected—all the bosses and all the captains from each of the five families, including Salvatore Termini."

"Uncle Sal is coming back to the US?"

"That's what we're hearing. No one is allowed to miss. The chief doesn't want to disrupt our undercover operation, so we're planning to let the get-together happen. But he wants to scoop up Termini before he slips back out of the country. So we need *you* to tell us where the meeting is going to be."

I rubbed the back of my neck. "I don't know if I can get that kind of intel now. I'm not around Vince anymore. I'm limited to watching his daughter, and she's not involved in the business at all."

Captain Rourke opened the passenger door. "I don't care what you have to do to get it. Fuck it out of that girl, if you have to. But the chief wants it, and I want to be the one to give it to him." She climbed out of the car and reached into her back pocket, tossing a cell phone on the front seat. "Text me the details when you have them—and make it soon."

"I thought it was too dangerous for me to have a cell while I'm undercover? What if one of Vince's guys decides to pat me down?"

"Don't keep it on you. Stick it under the mattress while you're banging the princess." She slammed the car door without another word, not even a *goodbye* or *good luck*. And God knows, I needed all the luck I could get to save my ass now.

Six hours later, my head was still spinning when Juliette got back into the car. Not only had I allowed myself to pretend there was a shot in hell I could have a real relationship with Vince Ginocassi's daughter, I'd allowed myself to pretend she wouldn't hate me when she eventually found out I'd been working undercover for the NYPD all this time.

"Hey." Juliette smiled. "Sorry that took forever."

I turned the key in the ignition. "Not a problem."

Juliette sighed as she reached down and slipped her heels off. "That guy is such a misogynistic asshole. I don't know how he hasn't gotten canceled yet." She let her head fall back against the headrest. "Did you at least have a peaceful day in the car and continue your whistling?"

What's the opposite of peaceful? That's the day I had. "My day was fine."

I pulled away from the curb. "This morning, when you got out of the car, you kissed me."

"Did I?" Her brow furrowed as she thought back. "I didn't even realize it."

"We need to be more careful in the future."

"Okay."

Yet not two seconds later, Juliette reached over and rested her hand on my thigh.

I removed it and glanced around. "I just said we need to be more careful. Someone could see."

"My hand is below the window. Who's gonna see?"

She had a point, but it didn't ease the knot in my gut. "Let's just not touch in public at all."

"Fine."

I looked over. She was staring straight ahead, jaw tight. Clearly annoyed. But I let it be.

The drive home was quiet, and the silence continued into the house. Juliette went into her room and changed into sweats.

"Is everything okay, Wes?" she asked when she came back out.

No. Everything is fucking terrible. "I just have a headache."

"I'll get you some Advil."

"Thanks."

Dinner conversation was stilted. Every word I said felt like a lie, and I didn't have the capacity for any more today. Juliette asked me a second time if something was bothering me, and I continued with the headache story. I was relieved when she said she had some work to do and went to her room to use her desk.

She didn't emerge again until ten o'clock.

"God, I didn't realize how long I'd been working." She stretched her arms over her head and leaned to one side, yawning. "I'm tired. You ready for bed?"

I pointed toward the TV. "I think I'll watch a little more TV."

She glanced at the screen, then back to me, her brow creasing. "It's not even on."

Shit. "Right. I meant I'm *going* to watch a little TV."

She frowned, clearly unconvinced, but didn't press further. Instead, she walked over and kissed me. "Goodnight. I hope whatever is weighing on you seems lighter in the morning. If not, I'm always here to talk."

Jesus, I didn't deserve this woman. "Thanks, babe."

It was after midnight before I finally went to bed. I'd debated sleeping on the couch, but I knew that would definitely have Juliette asking questions. We'd slept together every night since we'd started having sex. So instead, I waited until I was sure she was asleep before I slipped into the room, careful not to wake her.

I stared at the ceiling, thinking back over all the decisions I'd made that had landed me here. The decision to kick the shit out of that husband when I answered a domestic-abuse call. The decision to go to the DA when Vince Ginocassi contacted me with a job offer. The decision to accept the DA's proposal to drop all the criminal charges against me, in exchange for going undercover and using Vince's offer as a way to infiltrate the Ginocassi family. At the time, it felt like the deal of a lifetime. I got to stay out of prison, keep my job, and put away a bunch of wiseguys—didn't sound like a bad idea. Until I fell for the head wiseguy's daughter.

I'm so fucked.

I hate myself.

The following afternoon, I decided the best course of action was to try to get the information my captain needed from Juliette.

It's just the location of a meeting.
It will get my boss off my back.
It's not that big of a deal.
They're not even going to raid it, just pick up a guy who's been MIA for years anyway.

But I still felt like shit, no matter how hard I tried to convince myself Juliette wasn't going to get hurt. Because deep down I knew the truth: I was betraying her. And that fucking ripped my insides apart.

Juliette was on the phone with her mom, so I figured that gave me the perfect in. I waited until she finished, then struck up a *casual* conversation.

"How's your mom doing?" I asked, strolling into the kitchen.

"She's good. My dad bought her some fifteen-thousand-dollar necklace from Van Cleef & Arpels for her birthday. That seemed to make her happy, though I'm sure it fell off the back of a truck."

I smiled. "How did your mom handle it when your dad went to prison years ago? He did like three years for assault, right?"

Juliette sighed. "Instead of making him dinner at home every night, she brought it to the prison—one set of Pyrex dishes for my dad and one set for the guard who looked the other way. I think that CO gained twenty pounds while my dad was an inmate." Juliette shook her head. "I hated going to visit him there. I was only twelve, but I remember going on family day every other week. My mom would always cry outside when we left."

I hesitated, though I was genuinely curious. "Would it make your life easier now if Vince were locked up? You wouldn't be a target anymore because he wouldn't be in power."

"I guess? But just because I hate his life doesn't mean I want him locked in a cage for the rest of it. He's still my dad."

I felt deflated. I sat at the kitchen table until a few minutes later, my phone rang. It was Vince, of all people. I swiped and lifted my cell to my ear. As usual, he started barking before I'd even said hello.

"Big meeting happening soon."

My ears perked up. "Oh yeah? What can I do to help?"

"I need Juliette in the house on Friday. All day long. You don't let her out until you hear from me."

"Tomorrow?"

"That's what I just said, didn't I?"

My eyes locked with Juliette's. She was sitting across from me, but had definitely heard what her father said. The guy spoke so damn loud, it was like he was always on speakerphone. She rolled her eyes and got up and went into the other room.

"Not a problem," I said. "Just tomorrow?"

"As of right now. Depending on how things go, the temperature could cool off or heat back up. Keep her inside until you hear from me again."

"You got it, boss."

Click.

What an asshole. The dick must've gone to the same school of manners as my captain. I tossed my phone onto the table, and Juliette came back in.

"Why do I have to be locked down again?" she asked.

"There's some sort of a big meeting happening." I paused, then added something her father and I *hadn't* discussed. "At the rooster."

Juliette sighed. "I guess it must be important. My father hates the drive to Pine Creek Gorge."

"That's Pennsylvania, right?"

She nodded. "My uncle Anthony has a country house there. They call it *the rooster* because whenever they have meetings up there, the neighbor's rooster always wakes them at the crack of dawn. My dad always complains about going. No one knows it—because God forbid the boss have any weaknesses—but my dad actually gets carsick, and it's a five-hour drive."

"Don't blame him for keeping that under wraps." I smiled. "Carsick does sound kind of wimpy."

"Would you mind taking a ride to the bookstore with me? There's a new book I might get to turn into a screenplay, and I haven't read it yet. I'd like to pick it up, especially if we're on lockdown tomorrow for Lord knows how long again."

"Sure. Just give me a minute to change my shirt."

"Okay."

Inside Juliette's room, I closed the door behind me before going to my duffel bag. I'd hidden the cell phone my captain had given me in a side compartment. Pulling it out, I turned my back to the door, in case she suddenly opened it, and turned on the phone. As soon as it illuminated, I typed in nine words.

The Rooster. Anthony Ginocassi's house. Pine Creek Gorge, Pennsylvania.

CHAPTER 19

Juliette

A day stuck in the house with Wes normally wouldn't have seemed all that bad, but he'd been a little off ever since last night. I might've thought it had something to do with the quarantine order, but we'd been through worse, and he'd never seemed this affected. Before bed last night, I'd asked him if something was wrong, and he said no, so I'd opted to go to sleep, hoping everything would be better today.

But this morning, he'd left the bed without saying anything, and when I got to the kitchen, he was uncharacteristically quiet during coffee and breakfast. Things had been going so great with us... Perhaps that was too good to be true. Maybe some of the guilt and fear that had held him back for so long had started to creep in again.

By mid-afternoon, Wes was outside installing a new mailbox for me, since my previous one had been accidentally destroyed by a delivery truck. I took the opportunity of an empty house to call my mother. I needed to vent, and she was once again the only person I could trust and who also understood everything I was going through. Mom and I had downloaded a secure app recently that allowed us to call each other and hopefully bypass any tapping. I could never be completely sure it was safe, but I told myself it was.

"Hey, honey. I wasn't expecting to hear from you today," Mom said after she picked up.

"I know." I exhaled. "I really need to talk to you, and you might not be too happy with what I have to say." I swallowed, a little nervous to admit everything.

"Now you're worrying me."

"It's nothing bad." I paced, looking out the window to make sure Wes was still a safe distance away. "Well, at least not anything you didn't already see coming."

I explained to my mother where things had gone with Wes and me recently.

"You're right that this situation is no surprise," she finally said. "I'd ask what you were thinking, but I *know* what you were thinking. That man is irresistible."

"It's not just physical, Mom. It's *so* much more than that."

"He really had me convinced he wasn't going to go there with you when I confronted him," she said. "Either he's a good actor, or you really did a number on him."

"Wes had no intention of losing control. He'd tried to stop it from happening for a long time. I've been the one who's more forward." I shrugged. "But everyone has a breaking point."

She sighed. "I just hope your father doesn't find out."

My stomach sank. "That goes without saying."

"You both need to be careful."

"We know that. Believe me."

"All right. Besides the obvious downsides to this situation... Are you happy?"

I wanted to cry. If she'd asked me that question a couple of days ago, my answer would've been much different. I'd been *deliriously* happy exploring a relationship with Wes. But today? I didn't know what to think anymore.

"It was bliss for a while. We even went away together to Palm Springs and everything. He'd been a little off here and there since then, but then last night, Wes shut down."

"What's he saying to you?"

"Nothing. That's the problem." I sighed. "He's just not his usual happy self, and it seems like he might be avoiding me. Well, as much as you can avoid someone when you're stuck in the house together. He's been busying himself away from me. He offered to put in a new mailbox, which was very random, even if it needed to be done. The change in attitude makes me wonder if he's having regrets about letting things happen between us."

"In all honesty, sweetie...he might be. And rightfully so. Whatever the cause, don't push it. No one likes being nagged. Just give Wes the space to work through it on his own, even if it's difficult for you. He's put himself in a very serious situation. And he knows it. The reality is only now setting in."

"Yeah." I gazed out the window at Wes working. "I just wish he'd talk to me about it, rather than close up."

"This is a big chance he's taking. And a big chance *you're* taking, too. We've seen this story before, Juliette, and we know how it ends."

My chest tightened. "It *can't* end that way with Wes. I won't let anything bad happen to him. I need to figure out a way to get him away from Dad. And soon."

"And how are you going to do that without your father knowing about your feelings for Wes?"

I paced. "I'm not sure yet, but there has to be a way around this."

"I think your best bet is to keep things quiet for the foreseeable future. If there were an easy way out of this, I would've taken it a long time ago, my love." She paused. "And I wish I had a solution, for your sake. I sometimes feel so guilty for bringing you into this world."

That made me sad. "Don't ever feel guilty. As hard as it is being Vince's daughter, I would never choose not to be here. We're stronger because of it in some ways. I learned from the best. Seriously, you're so cool under pressure."

"Wish I didn't need to practice that skill so much." She chuckled. "Listen, I know I warned you about getting involved with Wes when I was out in California. My concerns still stand. But I'm happy you feel like you can open up to me about anything. You know I'll always listen, even if I don't fully agree with your choices. And I love you so much."

"Thank you, Mom. I don't know what I'd do without you."

"I'll pray you never have to find out."

That sent a shiver through me. The thought of something happening to my mother freaked me out more than anything. I was an only child. In many ways, Mom was the only "normal" family I had.

After we got off the phone, I looked out at Wes putting the finishing touches on the new mailbox. He was right outside but felt a world away.

Later that evening, Wes seemed a bit more like his normal self. Earlier, when he'd come in from the mailbox project, I'd asked him again if something was wrong, and he'd denied it. But it seemed like his demeanor had changed for the better after my inquisition, as if he hadn't realized his attitude was so obvious.

Later in the evening, desperate to lighten the mood, I suggested we play a game of truth or dare as we sat together on the couch, a fun way to pass the time.

"Truth or dare?" he scoffed. "I think the last time I played that was in junior high."

"Adults can play, too." I ran a hand through his hair. "Have a drink with me."

He closed his eyes briefly as I massaged his scalp. "Now is not the time for me to be letting my guard down, Juliette."

"Just one," I prodded. "You can't get drunk from one drink. It'll take the edge off."

Wes clenched his teeth. I could tell he really wanted a drink.

"Okay." He stood and walked to the kitchen. "But if you see me going for another, you kick me in the balls."

"I like your balls," I called after him. "I'll do no such thing."

Wes grabbed a beer for him and a hard seltzer for me.

"Who's gonna start?" I asked, sinking deeper into the couch.

"You." He pointed his bottle toward me.

"Okay...truth or dare?" I asked, opening my can.

"Truth," he answered.

"What's your favorite part of my body?" I could feel my cheeks burn as I awaited his answer.

Wes took a long sip of his beer. "Your eyes."

I squinted. "Seriously?"

"Yeah."

"I thought you were gonna say something else…"

"I can't possibly choose between your tits, your beautiful pussy, and your ass. They all win in my book. But…I could look into your eyes all day."

"Well, I'll take that." I smiled. "Your turn to ask me."

"Truth or dare?" he droned.

"I'll start with truth, too."

Wes scratched his chin. "When I first moved in, did it really upset you when I took my shirt off? Or were you just putting on a tough act?"

I grinned. "It was my reaction to your shirtless chest that upset me the most. But there was nothing about looking at you I didn't like. So no, the sight of you shirtless didn't upset me. How could it? Your chest is like a work of art."

He nodded smugly. "That's what I thought."

"Cocky much?"

"You love that about me."

"I do." I winked. I took a second to think up my next question. "Truth or dare?"

"Truth," he said.

"Truth again? Are you scared of my dares or something?"

"Not really. I mean, how much trouble can we get into when we can't leave this house?"

"True." I cleared my throat. "What's one moment we've shared together that you wish you could relive?"

He stared off for a moment. "Our bike ride in Ortigia is up there. Just the two of us in the middle of nowhere riding peacefully together, getting to witness how happy you were being away from this craziness was pretty cool." He looked into my eyes. "I remember wishing I could give you that kind of life every day."

That made me a bit emotional. How I wished we could go back. "Thank you. That isn't the memory I expected you to pick, but that's beautiful."

He grinned mischievously. "You thought it was going to be the moment I said 'fuck it all', right? The first time we had sex? That was nice, too, believe me."

I smiled, crossing my legs. "Okay. Your turn."

"Truth or dare?" he asked.

"Truth."

Wes scratched his chin. "Describe me using only emojis."

I took out my phone, opened a text, then selected a heart, the eggplant, the flexing arm, a police officer, and the flame. Then I faced the phone toward him.

"Nice." He chuckled.

"Truth or dare?" I asked.

"Truth," he said.

I decided to go for the kill. "Why were you really quiet this morning? And you can't lie. You have to tell me the truth."

His face reddened.

What the fuck?

"Dare," he finally said.

My pulse raced. "Why won't you admit it?"

"Admit what?"

"That you're having regrets about what's happened between us."

He shook his head. "I promise, it's not that, Juliette, all right?" Wes let out a long breath. "We all have our moments, days even where we don't feel our best. The important thing is that the moment passed. So please, just put it out of your mind." His eyes seared into mine. "Now I'm ready for a dare."

Rather than pry, I remembered what my mother had said about not pushing things. I chose to let it go. And anyway, as the seltzer went to my head, I found myself hornier by the second. I moved over to straddle him. "I dare you to do something sexually with me that you've always wanted to but might be afraid to propose. No boundaries."

His eyes widened. "Do you understand what you're asking for when you give me that kind of liberty?"

"I do," I whispered.

He set his beer down and held his hand out, leading me to the bedroom. He kissed me hard before he pulled back just long enough to ask, "Is *anything* off-limits?"

"Absolutely nothing," I said as I reached down to rub my hand over his erection.

After taking off my clothes, I eagerly slipped my panties down my legs, ready to experience something new with Wes.

I lay back on the bed as he hovered over me and spread my legs.

He unsnapped my bra from the front and tossed it aside before lowering his head to my breasts, giving equal love to each one. Wes moved his mouth slowly down the length of my torso, kissing until he got to my swollen bud. He then circled his tongue around my clit, causing every nerve ending in my body to activate. He went lower, and I felt his tongue circling my asshole.

It tickled a little and felt foreign at first. Before I'd even adjusted to that feeling, he stuck his tongue ever so slightly inside to test the waters. I flinched a little. But as he kept moving his tongue in and out gently, I writhed in pleasure.

He stopped for a moment. "Does that feel okay?"

"Yes…" I breathed.

"Would you want to feel *all of me* in there?"

Oh. Goose bumps peppered my skin. "Yeah." I moaned. "I would *love* to feel that."

"You sure?"

"Yes." I nodded. "I want to try everything with you."

He looked up at me. "Do you have lube?"

I bit my bottom lip, embarrassed. "I only have coconut oil."

His eyes widened. "Coconut oil?"

"Yeah. It's more natural. I don't like chemicals up my hoo-ha. I use it with my vibrator."

"Okay, then." He chuckled. "I'll just imagine I'm about to fry up my cock and serve it to you." He winked.

I reached to my bedside and grabbed the jar.

Wes chuckled as he opened it and dipped a couple of fingers inside. He slathered his shaft with the creamy white oil. "Turn around," he said gruffly.

I moved to the doggy-style position, my ass in the air.

Wes teased my hole gently for several minutes, circling his cock over my opening, then inching in slowly to start.

"How does this feel?" he rasped.

"Surprisingly good."

"Have you ever done this before?"

I shook my head. "I haven't."

"Good," he murmured.

Then I felt the first real push of his cock into my ass. It burned a little.

"Fuck, you feel good," he groaned. "Tell me if you want me to stop."

My voice trembled. "Keep going."

I reached for my clit, circling my fingers around the tender flesh as Wes moved in and out of me.

He was all the way inside now, moving a bit faster, with more ease.

It was a strange sensation, but I grew more aroused by the second. I was glad my first anal-sex experience was with him, even if his girth was a bit much to take.

"I need to slow down or I'm gonna come," he said. "You're so tight, and it feels too damn good."

Rather than supporting that, I pushed my ass back against him.

"Fuck," he warned. "Don't do that."

I giggled under my breath.

When he resumed fucking me, I tightened my muscles around him.

"Shit." He gripped my side with his right hand and squeezed hard, as if that somehow might help him stave off an orgasm.

When my muscles tightened around him in climax, Wes let go, groaning as he filled me with his hot load. Though it hurt a little at first, this had turned into the most erotic experience of my life.

"Forget what I said about truth or dare." He slowly pulled out and kissed up my back. "It's my favorite game now."

The next morning, my father called and gave us the all-clear to leave the house.

I told Wes I wanted to go to this farmer's market I'd heard about. It was only open on Saturday mornings, so I wanted to take advantage. We skipped breakfast and grabbed coffee on the way, figuring we'd taste test some things at the market. Among the items I hoped to score: fresh sourdough bread, wildflower honey, and these chocolate-covered strawberries I'd heard were amazing.

Despite last night's hot sex, I found myself ruminating again about Wes's change in attitude. It seemed to be back this morning, but I also wondered if I was reading into things too much.

But as we strolled the market, I couldn't shake it. We stood at a table of farm-fresh eggs, hatched from local pasture-raised chickens, and I turned to him. "What's really going on, Wes?" I swallowed. "Are you sure you're not having doubts about us?"

He let out a long breath. "I've always been up front about the doubts I have, Juliette. Not about you, but about our ability to be together long term—for obvious reasons."

"Why were you okay with us a few days ago, but suddenly turned weird? It's like a switch flipped."

He looked down at his feet. "I might've been in a weird mood lately, but that doesn't mean you have to assign meaning to it."

I raised my voice. "But your mood changed after you spoke to my father. So that tells me it's not random. Did he say something you're not telling me?"

He shook his head. "No, Juliette."

My gut told me he was lying. I placed my hands on my hips. "You know what, if you're not going to be honest with me, I don't even want to be around you right now."

Wes crossed his arms. "Well, I'm sorry, but you don't have a choice."

"Give me some space," I huffed.

I stormed over to one of the other tables. He followed, but kept his distance.

A few minutes later, I'd just reached over to grab a bottle of honey when it felt like a truck hit me. Except it wasn't a truck—it was Wes.

CHAPTER 20

Juliette

Someone was screaming.

I blinked, dazed, before finally realizing it was *me*. Wes was on the ground, bleeding, blood pooling beneath his torso. I dropped to my knees and cradled his head in my arms. "*Wes... Wes!*"

His eyes fluttered closed as people gathered around us.

"*Someone call 9-1-1!*" I screamed. "*Call 9-1-1!*"

"I just did!" a man shouted. "They're on their way."

I slapped Wes's face gently, trying to wake him. "*Wes! Open your eyes! Open your eyes, Wes!*" Chaos swirled around me—people running, someone screaming, a dog barking nonstop—but I couldn't focus on any of it. I just kept shaking the man in my arms. "Please, Wes. *Please* wake up."

Blood spread across the ground, seeping into my clothes. But his chest was still going up and down—barely, but enough. *He's breathing. On his own.* My heart pounded as I rocked him back and forth, the world around us fading to a blur. A man knelt beside me. I think he said he was a med student. He pulled off his jacket, slipped it under Wes's body, and applied pressure to the wound, trying to slow the bleeding. Somewhere nearby, a second dog started barking. People moved around us, voices rising, footsteps pounding, but it all felt distant. Like I was underwater and everything was muffled. Sirens wailed in the distance, growing louder.

I have no idea how long it was before someone grabbed my arm. "Miss, we're the paramedics, let us take over." The guy who'd been holding pressure helped me to my feet and stood next to me, watching.

"Gunshot wound," one of the paramedics said to the other. "You turn, I'll slide. You'll hold pressure. On my count..."

One.

Two.

Three.

One paramedic rolled Wes onto his side and pressed a hand over the wound. The other slid the backboard underneath, then carefully rolled him onto it, keeping his partner's hand in place.

"The bullet definitely went through," the guy in charge muttered.

Two police officers arrived, and the paramedic spoke to them while gesturing to the gurney. "Help us carry so we can keep pressure on, all right, Mac?"

"Sure thing."

Then they were hauling ass to the ambulance. I followed as they loaded Wes into the back.

One of them looked at me. "Who are you?"

"His...girlfriend."

"Did you drive here?"

I shook my head. "Wes did."

He nodded toward the ambulance. "Get in. You can ride with us."

I climbed in, heart hammering as they slammed the doors shut behind me. We started moving before I was even settled on the bench, and the paramedic immediately began cutting Wes's shirt off and hooking him up to a bunch of wires. He slid an oxygen mask over his face and spoke to me as he worked.

"What happened? Is there any other trauma we should know about? A fight or anything before the GSW?"

I shook my head. "I don't even know who shot him or where it came from."

He nodded. "I won't shake your hand. But my name is Cal. What can you tell me about your boyfriend? Any medical issues I should know about?"

"I don't...I don't really know. He's healthy and only takes a vitamin in the morning. I know that."

"That's good." He glanced at a machine flashing numbers. "His vitals are strong. We're going to be at the hospital in less than five minutes, and then the doctors will take a look at him and probably run him right up to surgery to stop the bleeding."

"Okay."

Wes looked so pale, and it freaked me out how still he was. I sat frozen, clutching the rail like I needed it to hold me together. A few minutes into the ride, he stirred. His arms were strapped down, but he was clearly trying to move them.

"Wes." I leaned forward. "Can you hear me?"

His eyes fluttered, then opened, and he looked around, dazed and confused. He tried to lift his head and speak, but I couldn't make out what he was saying with the oxygen mask over his face.

"Easy, man. Don't try to move," the paramedic said. "You're in an ambulance, and you're okay. But we need you to stay still."

Wes's eyes met mine for a second before shutting again.

"What happened?" I asked, panicked. "He was awake."

"Totally normal. People come to and nod off again." He moved closer to Wes and spoke louder. "We're almost there. Your girl is fine, buddy."

The ambulance rocked as it sped through traffic, sirens wailing, and blue and red lights flashing on Wes's face. When we pulled up at the hospital, the back doors burst open, just like in the movies. A team of doctors and nurses swarmed, lifted Wes out, and then we were running—pushing through corridors, wheels clattering, voices calling out numbers I didn't understand. I jogged behind the gurney until a nurse held out her hand to stop me.

"You'll have to wait here."

"But..." I looked over her shoulder. Wes was already disappearing down the hallway.

"We're going to take good care of him. The best thing you can do for him now is see the clerk at the admitting desk and give her whatever medical history you know. Is this your husband?"

I shook my head. "Boyfriend."

"What's his name?"

"Wes Callahan."

She attempted to smile but didn't quite finish the job. "I'll give you an update as soon as we have one."

I nodded, feeling helpless as the gurney turned a corner and vanished from sight.

A half hour later, I was pacing in the waiting room. I'd checked in with the admitting clerk twice already, and she'd assured me someone would come speak to me when they were done examining Wes and getting him stable. But every minute that ticked by felt like an hour.

The emergency room had a set of sliding glass doors that had opened and closed a dozen times since we got here. Each time I looked up, yet I couldn't tell you what a single person who'd walked in looked like. Until now. Because this guy looked exactly like the men I grew up around—like someone from my father's crew. Or...*a rival family's*. He glanced in my direction, and my breath caught in my throat. Could he be the one who shot at me? At us? The reason Wes was lying in a hospital bed? I held my breath as he walked up to the admitting window. The clerk pointed across the room, and a moment later, he walked over and hugged a woman waiting in the chairs on the other side.

I breathed, but the knot in my chest didn't loosen.

The guy didn't seem to be a threat, but he was a much-needed reminder. *I need to call my father*.

I walked over to the woman behind the glass who had taken Wes's information. "Excuse me. Can you tell me where the chapel is?"

She pointed to a doorway. "Down the hall, take the first right, and it's the first door on your left."

"Thank you."

As I walked, I pulled my phone out and scrolled to my father's name in my contacts. Opening the door to the chapel, I was relieved to find it empty and immediately pressed the *Call* button.

He answered on the first ring.

"What's wrong?"

"Dad, Wes was shot."

"Where are you?"

"I'm at Memorial Hospital."

"Where exactly?"

"I'm in the chapel right now. I was waiting in the emergency room for them to come out and tell me how Wes is, but I realized I needed to call you. I need to get back."

"You don't leave that chapel, Juliette. Do you understand me? Is there a lock on the door?"

"I need to get back to Wes." Tears welled in my eyes. "He's all alone."

"*I don't give two shits*," Dad barked. "You stay in that damn chapel until my men get there."

"Are you even listening to me?" I shouted. "Wes was shot! He could die!" My pulse pounded in my ears. "And it's *your* fault!"

"I'll have men to you in fifteen minutes. Leave the hospital with them when they arrive."

"Go to hell!" I yelled as I ended the call.

I wiped my eyes and went back to the waiting room, regretting that I'd left.

"Hi. I'm sorry to bother you again," I said to the admitting clerk. "But I stepped out for a few minutes, so I don't know if you were looking for me about Wes Callahan. I'm still waiting to hear how he is."

She pointed with her pen to two men in suits. "No info from the doctors yet, but those two police officers asked for the woman who came in with Mr. Callahan."

Great.

They must've overheard because they walked over. "You came in with the gunshot wound?"

I nodded.

"I'm Detective Olson, and this is my partner, Detective Barkley." He flipped open a small pad. "What can you tell us about the shooting?"

I shook my head. "Nothing. One minute I was standing at a booth at the farmer's market, and the next Wes was on the ground bleeding."

"There was no argument or altercation beforehand?"

"No."

"Did you get a look at the shooter?"

I shook my head again. "I didn't see anything. Wes covered me like a human shield."

"The clerk said Mr. Callahan is your boyfriend?"

I nodded.

"And your name is?"

"Juliette."

The door that led to the back finally opened. "Person here for Callahan!" a man called.

Forgetting about the cops, I rushed to the man in scrubs. "I'm here for Wes."

"Mr. Callahan is stable, but we've taken him up to surgery. If you want to follow me, I can take you to the surgical waiting area. You can register at the nurses' station, and they'll check in with the doctors during the surgery and give you periodic updates."

"Okay." I started walking, not even noticing that the cops had joined me.

"Juliette," one said. "We're going to need to take a statement."

"I told you, I didn't see anything."

"Sometimes a witness doesn't even realize they have information that can help us find the perpetrator. Something seemingly innocuous that you saw can turn into a lead."

"I can't even think straight. I need to go to the surgical ward."

He nodded. "We'll come find you in a little while."

Three hours later, a doctor finally came out to talk to me. He lowered the mask covering his mouth and pulled off his surgical cap. "I'm Dr. Ettleman."

"Hi, Doctor. I'm Juliette Grecco."

He put his hands on his hips. "Mr. Callahan did great. The bullet nicked his liver, but I was able to repair the laceration without complication. His vitals are strong, and the minute we woke him up in recovery, he was asking for you." He smiled. "He'll be in the hospital for a few days, but I expect he'll make a full recovery."

I let out a long breath and covered my heart with my hand. "Oh, thank God. Can I see him?"

The doctor nodded. "He'll be in recovery for another thirty to sixty minutes. Then he'll go to the ICU as a precaution. He lost a significant amount of blood."

"Okay." I nodded, still trying to absorb it all. "Thank you, Doctor."

"I'll let the nurse know to come get you when he's being transferred."

He walked away, leaving me standing there, equal parts relieved and wrecked. *ICU. A significant amount of blood.* I sank into one of the waiting room chairs and stared at the floor, my mind replaying the day until a nurse finally appeared.

When I looked up, she smiled. "You can see Mr. Callahan now."

I rose so fast I nearly knocked the chair over. "Great. Thank you."

"He's still groggy," she said as we walked down a quiet hallway. "But he keeps asking for you."

I swallowed hard as we entered the ICU. The big room was bright, with a chorus of monitors beeping in the background and a faintly antiseptic smell. The nurses' station was in the middle, and the perimeter was lined with glass-walled rooms. Some had curtains drawn, others gave me a glimpse of patients connected to tubes and blinking lights.

When I saw Wes, I forgot all about the nurse and rushed into his room. His eyes were open but he looked so, so pale.

"Oh my God. How are you?"

He gave me a half smile. "Been better."

The nurse interrupted. "Don't be alarmed if he goes in and out of consciousness. The anesthesia will do that. But I'll give you two a few minutes. Then I'll need to take a full medical history." She smiled. "We still know nothing about Mr. Callahan other than he's worried more about his girlfriend than himself."

I smiled down at him. "You scared the hell out of me."

He lifted his head, but it looked like it hurt, and his voice was just above a whisper. "Is there a lock on the door?"

My face scrunched up. "The glass door?"

"Yeah. I can't protect you. I don't even know where my gun is."

I laughed and leaned down to hug him. This man was lucky to be alive after being shot, and all he cared about was protecting me. "Don't worry about anything except getting well."

"You need to call your father."

"I did."

He strained to push out words. "And listen to what he tells you to do."

I frowned.

"You have to leave and go somewhere safe."

"I'm not leaving you."

"Juliette—" his voice strained.

"I'm not leaving you. You almost died." Tears filled my eyes just from saying the words. "I don't know what I would've done if something happened. I'm in love with you, Wes."

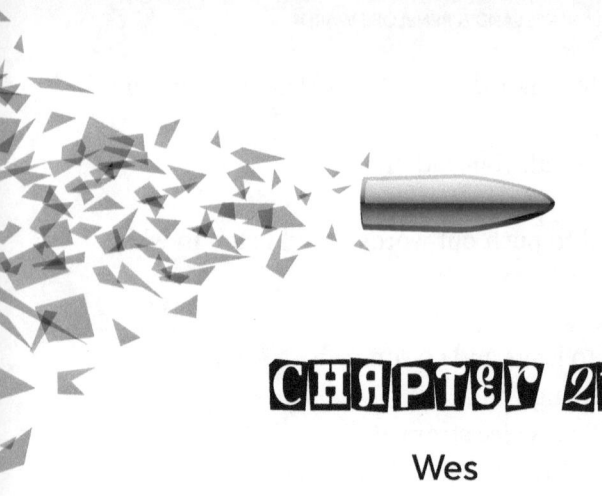

CHAPTER 21

Wes

I love you too.

That was the last thing I remembered going through my mind before I must've drifted off. I woke hours later—I could tell because outside the window was dark now, and Juliette was no longer standing next to me. Some thug was. I recognized him as one of Vince's guys—Eddie, I thought.

"Where's Juliette?" My voice sounded so damn weak.

The thug smiled. "She's fine. Tommy just walked her to the bathroom to change her bloody shirt." He chuckled. "You're hardcore, man. Took a bullet, lying in bed hooked up to all kinds of shit, and still worried about protecting her. We got her now. We'll keep her safe. You just rest."

Eddie took out his phone, pressed some buttons, and held the cell to my ear. "Someone wants to talk to you."

"Wes?"

Vince. I attempted to clear the grog in my throat so I could speak a little louder. "Hey, Boss."

"Wanted to say thank you for taking a bullet for my girl."

"Just doing my job."

"Yeah, well...it might be a job to you, but it's my only daughter. I appreciate it."

I swallowed. "You're welcome."

"I'll let you go because you sound like shit. But I also wanted to remind you to keep your fucking mouth shut to the cops."

The balls on this guy. "Of course."

"Good." *Click.*

A few minutes later, Juliette came back. She sat by my side while Eddie stood at the door.

"How are you feeling?"

"Frustrated. I keep nodding off."

She smiled. "I know. You did it before when we were talking."

"Did you at least get the honey?"

"Honey?"

"The table you were looking at in the market. You had honey in your hand. Not sure you had time to pay."

She grinned. "I actually stole it by accident. I didn't even realize I was still clutching it until I got to the emergency room."

"And here I thought you wanted to lead the straight life..."

The smile on her face made me feel better than any of the shit they were feeding me through the IVs.

"We should get going soon," Eddie said to Juliette.

She shook her head. "I'm not going anywhere."

"The boss said—"

"Save your breath, Eddie. I'm not leaving. Tell my father I'm home safe if that'll get him off your ass. But Wes nearly died for me. I'm going to sit here and make sure he is well taken care of."

It shocked the shit out of me that Eddie gave in so easily. But I guess arguing with the boss's daughter wasn't the smartest thing to do either. Since there was only one way to enter the ICU, Eddie decided to change his post from on top of me to guarding the entrance. Though a few minutes later, we got new guests. Two guys in suits that I immediately clocked as cops.

"How you doing, Mr. Callahan?" one of them asked. "I'm Detective Olson, and this is my partner, Detective Barkley. The doctor said it was okay for me to talk to you for a few minutes. We also need to take your girlfriend's statement, and we'd like to do that in the waiting room just outside the ICU."

"Now?" Juliette asked. "Can't it wait?"

"It's best to take witness statements while things are fresh in their mind."

"Can I at least stay here to give mine?"

Detective Olson shook his head. "It's standard procedure to take statements separately. Sometimes what one person says can unintentionally influence another witness's memory."

Juliette looked at me. I nodded. "I'll be fine."

She hesitated but went with Detective Barkley. Once they were out of earshot, the other detective closed the glass door.

"I'm actually the chief of Ds, Wes. I've been briefed on your situation by your captain in New York. We don't want to put you at risk unnecessarily, so no one else from my team knows you're undercover. The entire

LAPD thinks you're an ex-cop who works for the Ginocassi family."

I nodded. "Good. Thanks."

"I have a uniformed officer parked at the entrance to the ICU, right next to Eddie Guiliano. He'll make sure no one comes into the unit while I'm in here, so we should be able to talk freely."

"Do you have my gun?"

Chief Olson nodded. "The officers on scene brought it in. I'll make sure you get it back before you leave here."

"Thanks."

"Your boss wants to talk to you." He took out his cell and pressed some buttons. "Going to have her join us on a quick video call."

Captain Rourke appeared on the screen, along with New York District Attorney Ben Winston.

"This could be a good turn of events," she said. "Vince will be indebted to you for saving his daughter."

"Yeah, thanks," I scoffed. "I'm feeling fine, Captain."

"I know you, Callahan. You wouldn't admit it if you were feeling like crap, so I skipped the bullshit because we don't want Chief Olson in there with you for too long. You're supposed to be telling the cops you didn't see anything and zipping your mouth. Wouldn't want one of Vince's guys to let him know you talked to the cops for twenty minutes."

I guess she had a point, but still. "Do you know who shot me?"

"We were hoping you could tell us. LAPD interviewed a hundred potential witnesses at the farmer's market. Not a single one saw anything. Though that might also have to do with the fact that it's all over the news that the shooting was mob-related, so no one wants to get involved now."

"Was Juliette mentioned on the news, too?"

My captain nodded. "There's a video of her walking into the hospital covered in blood that's playing with the headline."

Shit. That was going to blow the cover she'd spent years building in LA. Now everyone will know who her father is.

"Did you get a look at the guy who shot you?" my captain asked.

I hesitated. "Saw a guy who looked suspicious when we first walked into the market, but I can't remember what he looks like now."

Chief Olson chimed in. "We're working the cameras in the surrounding area and going door to door. Doesn't matter if you work in New York. I consider you one of my men while you're working out here. We'll find the guy who did this to you."

"Thanks, Chief."

"Anything else you can think of before we hang up?" my captain asked.

I shook my head.

"Chief Olson, do you think you can put a few guys on the floor to keep an eye on Officer Callahan?"

"Sure thing."

I tried to lift my head but winced. "I don't need anyone watching me."

"I'm not going to leave you unprotected while you're vulnerable, lying in a bed," Captain Rourke said. "There's the off chance that the bullet struck its intended target and someone might come back to finish the job."

"You think someone was trying to take *me* out, not Juliette?"

Captain Rourke frowned. "I don't know, Wes. Did you do anything that might piss off the girl's father?"

CHAPTER 22

Juliette

Detective Barkley sat across from me in a private room at the hospital. I shivered. The room was cold and spartan, and the gray walls felt like they were caving in on me. I just wanted to be with Wes and tears threatened to fall at any moment. The reality of what had happened today came in waves. I felt like I was drowning.

"What is your full legal name?" he asked.

I clasped my hands together to stop my fingers from fidgeting. "Juliette Valentina Ginocassi."

"What is your relationship to Vincent Ginocassi?" he asked. He looked at me like he already knew the answer, and I was certain he knew a hell of a lot more than that.

I swallowed. "Vincent Ginocassi is my father."

"Do you have any reason to believe someone associated with or in opposition to your father was behind the shooting at the farmer's market today?"

I have every reason to believe that. But I needed to be careful with how I worded things. This was a nightmare. My stomach sank. "Honestly, I know as much as you do." I shook my head. "So I have no *specific* reason to believe anything. In theory, you might think it's suspicious because of who my father is. But unless you're keeping something pertinent from me, there's no evidence. I don't remember much. All I really recall is Wes covering me. He sprang into action so damn fast—like he didn't even have time to think about it. I never saw where the shot came from. And once I realized what had happened, all of my attention was focused on Wes. All that mattered was his survival." I stared across the room in a daze as my lip trembled. "I went to buy honey, and the next thing I knew, Wes had saved my life."

The detective looked into my eyes for a moment, then wrote something down. "Can you tell me where your father is currently located?"

"Vince doesn't keep me apprised of his whereabouts."

That wasn't a lie. I never knew where my father was at any given moment. *Certainly* never knew what he was up to. Didn't want to know.

"Are you aware of your father's ties to the mob?" he asked.

I laughed inwardly at that. *Am I aware*? It had only taken over my entire life and nearly killed the man I loved. It was only the bane of my existence.

I cleared my throat. "Yes, of course. That's why I have a bodyguard. There are people out there who want me dead just because I'm Vince's daughter. But that doesn't mean I'm aware of what he's up to." I exhaled. "I've spent my life trying to get away from my father's business. All I've ever wanted is to be left alone, to live independently and in peace. I've had anything but that lately, and it's making me insane."

He offered me a sad smile before jotting down a few more things. "Wes Callahan had been living with you, in addition to being your guard, correct?"

I nodded. "Yes. He's done a very good job protecting me, as he demonstrated at the farmer's market today. I owe him my life."

"You two must be close." He tilted his head. "The paramedics indicate that you were particularly distraught when Mr. Callahan was shot."

I tried not to lose my cool. "Anyone with a soul would've been distraught. He nearly died protecting me." I bounced my knees up and down. "Have you had any luck finding who's responsible?"

"I'm not able to talk about the investigation, except to say that you'll be advised if anything pertinent is discovered." He hesitated, then cocked his head again. "Any reason to believe the target was actually Mr. Callahan and not you?"

My stomach clenched. "No, I don't have any reason to believe that."

"Does that seem far-fetched to you, or might that theory hold some weight?"

I moved my eyes from side to side as I thought about that angle—it scared me more than anything. *Could Wes have been the target?* "I can't rule it out completely," I said.

Paranoia bloomed inside me. *Could my dad have found out about Wes and me and tried to have him killed?* My mind raced. *There was that photographer in Palm Springs.* Had he published photos of us that my father had seen?

My gut told me Wes couldn't have been the target, but I wasn't absolutely certain. Anything was possible when it came to my father.

"Let me word my question a bit differently," Detective Barkley said. "If there's something going on between you and Mr. Callahan, would that be motivation for someone on your father's team to have attempted to murder him?"

I shook my head as I began to sweat. "No one would know about anything going on between us."

Despite my best efforts to not address my relationship with Wes, the officer continued to dig. "*Is* there something going on between you and Mr. Callahan?"

"Wes and I are close," I answered.

"Is your father aware of that?"

I licked my lips. "I couldn't tell you what my father thinks. He hired Wes, and he knows we live together. He knows I care about Wes as more than just a bodyguard because I've expressed concern about Wes's well-being in the past. I've told my father nothing else is going on, though."

The idea of my father being behind the shooting continued to burn a hole in my brain as the officer finished grilling me. It was a terrible thing to not trust one of the people who'd brought you into this world. I knew my father would never do anything intentionally to harm *me*, but I couldn't trust him when it came to Wes. Vince Ginocassi simply didn't have respect for people who weren't related to him by blood.

After the questioning was over and I left the room, I couldn't take it anymore. I needed to call my father. I exited the hospital and walked to a corner of the parking lot, with one of my father's guys never too far behind me. I dialed and put the phone to my ear.

"Juliette," my father answered. "I didn't expect to hear from you again today. Did something happen?"

"Nothing new," I snapped, blowing a breath up into my hair. "But I need to ask you something, and I need you to be honest with me for once."

"What is it?"

"Did *you* have anything to do with the shooting at the farmer's market?" I huffed, my heart pounding faster by the second.

He raised his voice. "Are you asking me whether I ordered someone to kill my own daughter, who means more to me than anything in the world?"

"That's not what I'm getting at. I'm talking about whether you misconstrued my relationship with Wes and ordered someone to hurt *him*." I licked my parched lips.

He softened his tone. "I had nothing to do with it, Juliette. I almost wish I had because then I wouldn't be so goddamn scared that someone was still out there trying to put a hit on my daughter."

My pulse slowed a bit. I believed him for some reason, even if I could never trust him fully.

"Anyway, *why* would I be misconstruing your relationship?" he asked after a moment. "What the hell is going on between you and him?"

"Nothing," I lied. "He's just important to me. You know that."

"You're getting a little too close to the situation if you care that much about him. Your job is to live your life while my guys protect you—not the other way around. I don't want you trying to protect and cover for *them*. I don't like this one bit, Juliette."

"You actually expect me to not care about someone whose job is to guard my life? That's not natural."

"That's *exactly* what I expect," he yelled. "And I most *certainly* expect him to respect the boundaries I set when I gave him that damn job."

I rolled my eyes. As if he was doing Wes a favor by keeping him in such a shitty position. But there was no sense in arguing any further with my father. He was irrational.

"Anything else?" he asked.

"No," I muttered before hanging up.

I stood there for a while, my cheeks burning in anger. But as I walked back into the hospital, my anger turned to sadness. Tears stung my eyes again. The reality of this situation once again hit me. Wes had almost died. Taking a bodyguard position and hoping for the best was one thing. But actually proving yourself the way he had, sacrificing his life for mine, was beyond heroic. How could I ever repay him? The bullet hadn't killed him, but it very well could've killed *me* had he not been so damn selfless.

I burst into tears. An urgent need to see Wes came over me, so I rushed down to his room. But when I got there, he was sleeping. He looked so peaceful. The rise and fall of his chest comforted me. The sound of his breathing was music to my ears. That meant he was alive. But Wes needed rest after what he'd been through, so rather than risk waking him by sitting at his bedside, I wandered around a bit and ended up in the chapel again.

All the noise of the hospital disappeared the moment the chapel door closed behind me. It seemed almost completely soundproof. There was a small altar at the front of the room and some bookshelves that held bibles.

I took a seat at one of the dark wooden pews and lowered the little platform that was made for kneeling. This was the first place I'd truly felt safe in a while. Emotions flooded me as I leaned against the pew in front of me and sobbed.

After several minutes, a voice startled me. "Are you okay, young lady?"

I turned to find a priest standing there. He was tall, bald, and dressed from head to toe in black with a white Roman collar.

"Hello," I said. "Is it okay that I'm in here?"

"Of course. All are welcome here," he answered softly. "Do you have a sick loved one?"

I shook my head. "Thankfully, he's not ill. But he was injured, and he's recovering." I let out a shaky breath. "He got shot. We were very lucky."

He took a seat next to me. "Do you need someone to talk to?"

I looked into his eyes. "Can I trust you?"

He placed his hand on my arm and smiled kindly. "If you can't trust me, I'm not sure who you can trust."

He had a point.

"I'm Father Maloney."

"Hi, Father. I'm Juliette."

It might've been risky, but I unloaded the truth on this poor priest because I had to let it all out, and he was someone with no ties to the situation. While I didn't give him my dad's name, I recalled everything from the beginning with Wes up until the shooting. He listened intently and didn't interrupt.

When I finally finished, he nodded and said, "Everyone is given a cross in life, Juliette. Unfortunately, yours was handed to you directly by your father."

I nodded.

"You seem to hold a lot of resentment toward him for the position he's put you in. And I'm sure you believe it's warranted." He paused. "But resentment will sicken you like a terminal disease if you let it. It comes from within you, and you're the only one with the power to take it away. Your father knows not what he does. If he truly understood the level of sin, he'd ask the Lord for forgiveness and become a better man. You must learn to forgive your father anyway, and try your best to live a purposeful life despite him, without allowing that resentment in."

I blinked. "How do I do that when my father's actions impact literally every part of my life?"

"It's not easy. You must radically accept things as they are. As hard as that may be, everything you experience is in God's plan. Sometimes we have to go through difficult things in order to receive the gifts he has to bestow on us. It takes a bit of blind trust, and most of all... it takes time and patience to see this through."

The moment he said *gift*, my mind went to Wes. He was my one gift in all this.

"Well, this terrible situation brought me to the only man I've ever loved," I said. "So in that sense, I can understand what you mean. I would've never known Wes existed were it not for my father's terrible business. And I can't imagine never meeting him."

"That's a great example of how life works in funny ways that are perfectly orchestrated by God." He smiled. "Have faith that everything will work out in the end, and don't be afraid to seek help when you feel you can't handle things. Even if that means just coming here to pray."

I wondered if it would be too much to ask for Father Maloney's cell number. I chuckled to myself and decided against it. "Well, I appreciate you taking the time to speak with me."

"Of course." He nodded. "I'll keep you in my prayers, Juliette."

People sometimes say that, but I actually believed he would. "Thank you, Father." I shrugged. "And you never know, you might see me again."

"I would love that."

I'd never considered myself a religious person. But there was something to be said for a man who listened, who offered to pray for you. It felt like Father Maloney was as close to God as I was going to get right now, and someone up there had known I needed that talk.

I took the kind priest's words to heart. I left the chapel with a renewed sense of hope that there was still some good in the world.

When I returned to Wes's room, he was awake.

"Hey," I said as I sat by his bedside. "How are you feeling?"

"Alive but in pain." He sounded like he'd swallowed a toad.

I ran a gentle hand through his hair. "I'm so sorry."

He placed his hand over mine. "Nothing to be sorry for. You didn't do anything. This is what I signed up for."

"It doesn't matter what you say. I feel like this is my fault."

"I'd do it all over again," he said.

Wes hadn't said the words *I love you* earlier. But did he need to say them when his actions spoke so much louder?

"They're going to discharge you in a few days, right?" My voice shook. "What if after you recover fully, we run away?"

His eyes widened. "Run away to where?"

"We could go back to Ortigia or—"

"You think we can get away with that? Your father will have my head if I disappear with you."

"But wouldn't it be easier to deal with everything away from the States? Why couldn't I convince my father that we'd be safer there? He's already got his goons on my trail. Can't they guard me from anywhere? I feel like the farther from the US we go, the safer we'll be."

"You can't leave your job and everything you've worked for." He flinched in pain. "You're just scared. And it's understandable. But we have to find a better way to deal with this situation than running away. That would be like letting evil win."

My foreboding feeling about something being off with Wes continued to haunt me. Today's trouble had nearly made me forget that things weren't perfect between us at the farmer's market before everything went down.

"Can I stay with you tonight?" I asked.

"You need to get a good night's sleep. You've been through a lot, too. I think you should go home."

"I'm sort of afraid to leave the hospital, knowing that whoever did this is still out there."

He nodded and reached out his hand. "I understand, baby. If you're scared, you should stay. I was just thinking that the sooner you get back to your life, the better."

My life?

Not *our* life.

I thought for a moment and decided I couldn't let fear win. Hiding out in the hospital with no good place to sleep would've meant doing just that. I sighed. "I think I *am* gonna head home and try to rest."

"Good call."

"But I'll be back here first thing in the morning," I assured him.

"Okay." He smiled.

I bent to place a chaste kiss on his lips. "Wes…"

"Yeah?"

I hesitated. I wanted to tell him I loved him again, but I wasn't sure that's what he needed right now. "You try to get some sleep, too," I said instead. As much as I needed rest, I doubted I'd sleep much tonight.

I left for home with two of my dad's guys in tow.

The last thing I expected when I got back to my house was to see a car parked in front. I wondered why the two guards weren't freaked. But apparently, they knew what was coming. Before I could sort out anything further, the window rolled down.

I exhaled. "Dad…what the hell are you doing here?"

CHAPTER 23

Wes

Fuck my life.

A wave of pain rippled through me as I tried to adjust my position in bed. I winced, sinking back into the mattress and breathing through the ache.

"Mr. Callahan." A nurse walked into the room and took one look at my face. "Are you in pain?"

"Nah. I'm good."

She side-eyed me and grabbed the chart hanging from the foot of my bed. Flipping through a few pages, she frowned. "You haven't taken any pain medication since last night."

"I don't need any."

"When pain is uncontrolled, your body responds to the stress by releasing adrenaline and cortisol, which can slow healing and weaken the immune system."

That might be true, but the meds had also made me groggy as shit, and I needed to stay alert, especially because Juliette would probably be back soon. "If I'm in pain, I'll take the meds. Promise."

It didn't look like she believed me, yet she kicked the stopper from the door and pulled a pair of disposable gloves from the box hanging on the wall. "I need to check your wound and change your dressing, so I'm going to have you roll onto your side. I can get another nurse to help me if you don't think you're up for it."

"I got it."

It felt like all my organs were being pulled to one side as I turned, but at least I managed not to wince again while she prodded around my back for fifteen minutes. I was still facing away from the closed door when it swung open.

"Sir," the nurse said sternly. "I have the door shut for a reason."

I glanced over my shoulder to find none other than Vince Ginocassi standing there. He shielded his eyes.

"Jesus Christ. Can't you put some drawers on him? I'm looking at his bare ass."

She raised her voice. "Wait outside, sir. Please."

Vince backed out and pulled the door shut, and the nurse shook her head. "Friend of yours?"

"Something like that."

"He could use some manners, barging into a hospital room when the door's closed."

Tell me about it.

Though his manners were the least of my problems at the moment. What the hell was Vince doing here? I didn't like the idea of him nosing around, especially not when the place was crawling with cops. Yet the moment the nurse finished up and opened the door, there he was. She tried to kick the stopper back under the door to keep it open, but Vince waved her off.

"I'm his priest," he said. "Gonna keep this closed for some privacy."

The nurse's brows furrowed, and she looked to me. I shrugged. "He doesn't look the part without his collar."

Vince chuckled as she closed the door behind her. "Always had a thing for nurses in uniform. It's gonna be really screwed up when Father Vince stops on the way out and asks her if she'd like to come by my hotel so I can play doctor and examine her from the inside out."

I pressed the button to lift the head of the bed, anxious not to feel at such a big physical disadvantage in a room alone with Vince Ginocassi.

"How you feeling?" he asked.

"Like I got shot in the back," I grumbled, adjusting my posture to sit straighter. "Didn't expect to see you here. There were a lot of cops around yesterday, and they said they'd be back today since I didn't remember anything."

"Came to thank you personally for taking a bullet for my daughter. You were pretty impressive. Looked like a Secret Service man protecting our dumb-ass president."

"How do you know what I looked like?"

He pointed to the TV hanging on the wall. "It's all over the boob tube. Some kid carrying a skateboard was filming a prank they were about to pull on one of the vendors, and they accidentally caught the whole shooting on video—you covering Juliette with your body. If you hadn't done that..." He shook his head and swallowed before meeting my eyes. "I appreciate it, Wes."

"Just doing my job."

"Maybe, but there'll be a fat envelope waiting for you when you get out of here, help take care of all your pain and suffering."

"I'm not sure I'm going to be able to protect Juliette for a while."

"Already put two of my best guys on her. You take your time recovering, and then we'll talk." He gripped his hips. "What did the cops have to say?"

"The usual." I shrugged. "Asked me questions—what I saw, if I knew why someone might want to shoot at me."

"And you said..."

"Nothing. Didn't see anything. Don't know anything. They said they'd come back today to see if my memory improved."

"It better not."

It was difficult to not roll my eyes. "I know what I'm doing."

"I don't want the cops finding whoever tried to hurt my daughter before I do. Whatever punishment they'd give him won't be nearly enough. I'm going to make that fucker regret the day he was born, one chopped-off finger and toe at a time. Did you get a look at the guy?"

For a few heartbeats, I considered telling him the truth, that I might've gotten a look at the shooter a few minutes before all hell broke loose. I wanted the guy who had tried to hurt Juliette to pay, too. But something stopped me from letting Vince dole out the punishment. I shook my head. "I didn't see anyone. Wish I had."

"You think of something that could help track this dead man down, you come to me, not the cops. Understood?"

I felt like punching this asshole, yet I had to swallow every ounce of my pride. "Of course. How long you in town for?"

"At least a few days."

"What about the meeting at the rooster?"

Vince's eyes narrowed. "How do you know where the meeting was supposed to be held?"

Shit. My heart started to race, and I hoped it didn't show up on the monitors I was attached to. My captain had told me about the rooster, not Vince, and Juliette had explained where it was. I had no choice but to bluff. "You called to tell me about the meeting and said not to let Juliette out on Friday, remember? What is the rooster anyway? A bar or something?"

Vince rubbed his chin, and his eyes went out of focus. It looked like he was trying to think back to our conversation. I held my breath until he finally nodded. "Yeah, all right."

Relief flooded me. I needed to be more careful in the future. Vince and I talked for a few minutes and then the door to my room swung open again. I froze when I got a look at the man standing in the doorway. Fuck. *Chief Olson.* He stepped into the room, and his head swiveled between Vince and me. No recognition or look of surprise registered on his face. If I didn't know better, I would've sworn Olson didn't know who the guy standing at my bedside was.

"Sorry to interrupt." Chief Olson held up a hand. "I didn't realize you had a visitor." He smiled at Vince. "I'm Detective Olson from the LAPD. Just came to see if Mr. Callahan remembers anything from yesterday. Sometimes we get lucky after a victim has had a chance to settle down, and details resurface. But if now isn't a good time, I can come back later."

Vince seemed barely able to contain his amusement. "It's all right. He's all yours. I've got a nurse I need to discuss something with anyway." He winked at me, looking like the cat that swallowed a canary, and leaned down to whisper in my ear. "Dumb fucks."

Of course, the *dumb fuck* was Vince. But he left my room smiling like the devil himself. Chief Olson watched him walk down the hall before shutting the door.

"Ignorance really is bliss, huh?" He chuckled. "Unless that guy is one hell of an actor, he had no clue that I've got an eight-by-ten glossy of him hanging in my squad room, along with the rest of his buddies."

"His ego lets him believe everyone else is stupid."

Olson shook his head. "That's how most of those guys eventually fall. They get sloppy because they think they're untouchable." He lifted his chin. "How you feeling today?"

"Like the nurse came in and dug the bullet out with a spoon this morning, rather than just changing the dressing."

"They're not giving you anything for pain?"

"It's bad enough I'm sitting here with no gun, barely able to move while guys like Ginocassi are walking in and out of my room. I can't take shit that makes me groggy."

"Sucks." Chief Olson nodded. "But I guess that's a good call. What was Vince doing here anyway?"

"Came to thank me for taking a bullet for his daughter. Said he's going to be hanging around a few days."

"What about the meeting they were supposed to have? I know your captain was looking forward to picking up one of the guys in town for it."

I shrugged. "Postponed, I guess. Can't imagine they'd have it without one of the bosses."

He nodded. "Anything else? I don't want to stick around too long in case Vince and his guys are waiting until I leave. You're not supposed to have anything to tell me, so I shouldn't be here more than a few minutes."

"No." I hesitated for a few seconds before finally deciding I needed to land on the right side of this mess. "Actually...I remembered something this morning. There was a guy acting suspicious at the farmer's market, maybe five minutes before the shooting. Never saw him before. I thought he might've been tailing us. Short. Stocky. Dark hair, tan complexion with a big hook nose. Wore a leather jacket that looked like one of those old Member's Only types."

Detective Olson's eyes narrowed. "This just came back to you this morning?"

"Yeah. You know how it works—blank spots, delayed memory, things come back when the body isn't in survival mode anymore."

He crossed his arms, his expression skeptical, even though it was very common for a victim's memory to play catch up later. Eventually, he pulled out his phone and started typing. "I'll have a sketch artist come up to your room later. Might have to do it in the middle of the night, once visiting hours are over, so Vince or one of his guys doesn't pop in again."

"They could be watching the place twenty-four-seven, so maybe have him wear scrubs and hide his pad in a backpack or something."

"Good idea."

After Chief Olson left, I felt a surprising relief for the first time in twenty-four hours. Holding on to the information about the potential suspect—and not being sure who I wanted to give it to—had kept me awake last night almost as much as the pain. I sank back into the bed and let the quiet of the room finally settle around me, knowing it wouldn't last long.

Two days later, I was packing the few things I had with me into a plastic bag, getting ready to go home, when Chief Olson walked in again.

"Look at you, up and around." He smiled.

"Won't be running a marathon any time soon, but I'm glad to get the hell out of this place."

He nodded. "I'm not a fan of hospitals either. You're supposed to get rest, but all they do is wake you up to take your blood pressure and give you meds."

"What's up? Juliette is going to be here any minute."

"I have a guard at the entrance. My phone will buzz if anyone shows up. Just wanted to let you know we might have a lead. It's going to be harder to have access to you once you're discharged."

I stopped packing. "Whatta you got?"

"We canvassed the area surrounding the market and asked business owners if they had security cameras. Guy who owns a liquor store said he didn't have any. Turns out he was lying because he's going through a divorce and was afraid if anyone knew he had cameras, his wife might find out his girlfriend stops by a few times a week. But he checked the footage himself and called this morning to say he has video of a guy running from the farmer's market—short, dark hair, leather jacket, hook nose—around the same time as the shooting. I'm on my way over to take a look at the footage now. Gonna need you to check the phone your captain gave you so I can send through pics to see if you can identify the guy as the same person you saw acting suspicious."

"All right. I can do that."

"Where you heading after this?"

"Back to Juliette's."

Chief Olson's brows pulled tight. "Ginocassi put other guys on her. He's not gonna let you guard his daughter in your condition."

I shrugged. "She feels guilty for what happened and wants to take care of me. Figured it was my way to stay in the game."

His eyes searched my face. "Be careful. Getting close is good. But *too* close can be dangerous."

Tell me about it. "I know how to play it."

"I hope so, for your sake."

Two hours later, Juliette and I pulled up in front of her house. She got out of the car and ran around to offer me a hand getting out.

"Thanks. But I got it."

Up and down movements caused the worst pain, but I managed to get out on my own. Her two new guards followed as we made our way up the path to her door.

"Wes needs his rest," Juliette said. "You guys are going to have to stay out here from now on."

"Boss won't like that," Eddie warned.

"Ask me if I care." She opened the screen door and put her key in the lock. I was grateful they didn't fight her on it because all the moving around had wiped me out.

Inside, I plopped down on the couch, and Juliette brought me a blanket. "You relax while I make us some lunch."

"Thanks."

The smell of soup soon wafted through the air. I hadn't eaten much of the disgusting hospital food, so by the time she was finished, I was starving.

"Grilled cheese and tomato soup." She smiled and pulled out my chair, hovering until I sat.

"Thank you."

While I dug right in, Juliette barely touched her food. "Aren't you going to eat?"

Tears welled in her eyes. "I don't know what I would've done if anything had happened to you."

I put down the sandwich and reached across the table, taking her hand, even though stretching hurt. "I'm right here. And pretty soon I'll be as good as new."

"You almost died because of me."

I didn't know how to respond to that, so I stepped around it. "But you're fine, and I'm going to be too."

"This is why I hate my father's life so much. Innocent people get hurt."

"It's what I signed up for."

"You didn't *sign up* for it, not really anyway. You took the lesser of two evils." She shook her head. "I've been thinking about how my father deals with things. I'm sure he's grateful to you right now."

I nodded. "He actually came by the hospital to tell me he was."

"We need to capitalize on how he's feeling, use the shooting as a way to get you out, Wes. You can ask my father to be released from the deal you made, tell him you want your freedom rather than cash."

"How did you know Vince wants to give me cash?"

She rolled her eyes. "It's the way my father fixes all problems."

"I don't think your father will go for something like that."

The truth was, the same idea had crossed my mind while I was in the hospital. I could tell Vince I wasn't physically capable of protecting his daughter anymore. But even if I could get him to go for it, I still had to finish the undercover job to keep up my end of the deal I'd made with the NYPD, which meant sticking around Vince's organization long enough to take people down. Basically, I was their bitch, which meant I had to stay Vince's bitch. Any way I looked at it, I was royally fucked.

"You won't know if he'll go for it unless you try," Juliette said.

There really was no reason I couldn't attempt to break free, at least from Juliette's perspective. So I wasn't sure what to say. "Let me think about it."

"Okay." She smiled, and the glimmer of hope I saw in her eyes made me feel worse than I already did.

Hours later, Juliette asked me if I wanted to take a ride to the pharmacy to pick up the prescriptions the hospital had sent home with me. "You can just stay in the car, if you want. It's fine if you would rather stay here, but I thought you might want some fresh air."

I knew I had to check the phone my captain had given me, to see if I could identify the guy from the footage. "I'm wiped out. I think I'm going to stay."

She leaned in and pressed her lips to mine. "Okay. Is there anything else you need while I'm out?"

"No, I'm good. Thanks."

I waited until I heard the cars pull away to check the window. Both Juliette and Eddie's cars were gone. So I went to the bedroom, shut the door behind me, and dug out the phone I had hidden in my bag. Sure enough, there were texts waiting from Chief Olson. He'd sent them an hour ago.

> Unknown: Call your captain. She wants to talk to you. Let her know if this is the guy you saw and she'll relay it to us.

The photo was grainy, but I was pretty sure it was the same guy I'd seen following us earlier that day at the market. Though I couldn't be a hundred-percent positive. I stared at it for a few seconds and listened to make sure the house was still empty before dialing my captain's number.

"Hey. It's Wes."

"How you feeling?"

"Sore. But I'll live."

"Did you take a look at the photo the chief sent?"

"Yeah, it looks like him, but it's grainy."

"The video equipment the guy had was fifteen years old. But it was enough for us to run him through our facial-recognition program. We got a hit. Guy is from New York, known associate of a rival family."

I ran a hand through my hair, ignoring the pain lifting my arm caused. "Who is he?"

"I'm not going to give you his name, just in case it rings a bell and you came across him at some point when you were working with Vince in New York. I don't want to taint the ID in any way."

"How do you want to handle it?"

"I need you to meet me so we can do a proper photo array. We need to do this one by the book."

"Meet you? In New York?"

"No, I'm back out in California. I came out two days ago to lend a hand on the shooting. I didn't come by the hospital in case any of Vince's men knew my face. Didn't want them to question why a captain from the NYPD was coming to see you."

"Good idea. Okay."

"I'm staying at the Hotel Adventura. Do you know where that is?"

"Hotel Adventura? Sounds familiar. I can look it up."

"Think you can give me a time?"

"No. I need to see what Juliette is doing tomorrow. I don't want to raise any suspicions and sound like I have plans. Can we just play it by ear, and I'll text you when I'm able to get away?"

"Sure thing."

"All right, good. Anything else? Juliette only went to the pharmacy, so she'll be back soon."

"Nope. I'll wait for your text tomorrow."

After I hung up, I shoved the phone back into my bag and slid the duffel under the bed where I'd been storing it. Climbing to my feet, I listened for any sounds in the house. It would take at least fifteen minutes to get to the pharmacy and back, but I didn't want to take any chances. Hearing nothing but my own breathing, I opened the door.

And walked straight into Juliette.

"Were you just talking to someone?" she asked.

CHAPTER 24

Juliette

Wes's eyes widened. He was clearly not expecting to see me. And his surprise only worsened my growing suspicion. My stomach churned as I waited for his response.

He cleared his throat. "That was a cop investigating the shooting."

I hadn't been able to hear everything Wes was saying, but I'd heard him tell whoever it was that I'd gone to the pharmacy.

Feeling my blood pressure rise, I swallowed. "You said something about me being out of the house. Why did they need to know that?"

He looked down for a moment. "He was asking where you were. I think he wants me to keep things to myself for some reason. Maybe he thinks you talk to Vince? I think they're worried about his involvement. They want to put some distance between Vince and the investigation."

I narrowed my eyes. That seemed like a weird explanation, but I let him continue.

"We have to make sure your father doesn't interfere," he said. "Vince told me he wanted to handle it, and that's bad news. That's not the answer. He's going to botch the whole thing."

"Did my father do something since you last spoke to him?"

He shook his head. "Not yet. But Vince will inevitably fuck everything up if he thinks or even suspects he knows who did this. He could very well draw the wrong conclusion, too, since he's not working with the official investigation. Imagine if he kills the wrong person... I'm trying to cooperate with the cops so they can figure out who's responsible before Vince does anything. Your father just wants to find the person and kill them. He's trying to fight fire with fire."

While I wanted to believe Wes's explanation of the phone call, his face was red. Did that mean something, or was I reading into things? He had been through a lot recently. Maybe it was stress from all that. Despite feeling uneasy, I didn't want to say or do anything that would interfere with his recovery. I reminded myself that he'd nearly died just a few days ago. Maybe I needed to lay off.

"Okay...well..." I looked down at my shoes. "I guess I overreacted. I'm sorry." I wanted to believe my own words. But my gut wouldn't let me.

Wes moved in closer and placed his hand on my cheek. "We've both been through hell these past few days. I don't blame you for being on edge. Never hesitate to tell me what's bothering you." He lifted my chin to meet his eyes. "Okay?"

I couldn't look him in the face for long. He'd see the worry written all over mine. So I turned away.

But a moment later, I turned back. "You tell me to share what's bothering me, but then you get upset when I ask *you* to express your feelings. Don't you remember the argument we had at the farmer's market right before the shooting? We never resolved why you'd been acting differently, Wes." I shook my head, catching myself pushing when I'd said I'd back off. "You know what? Go rest. You should be taking it easy." I walked away. I needed to be alone anyway to process these feelings of doubt.

"Juliette..." he called after me.

I kept walking. "Oh, and I called the pharmacy on the way, and they said your meds weren't ready, which is why I came back. I'm gonna take a shower..." I closed the bathroom door behind me.

As the water rained down on me, more questions pummeled my brain. The longer I spent thinking about his explanation of the phone call, the more paranoid I became. Why had Wes let me leave for the pharmacy without him? It was uncharacteristic of him to not want to tag along to keep an extra set of eyes on me. What if he'd actually stayed behind so he could talk to someone on the phone without me overhearing? Worse, what if that person wasn't even a cop? A rush of panic hit. What if it was a woman? That was a stretch, given the timing. Also, I didn't take him for a cheater.

But my mind continued to race. There was that booty-call woman who'd phoned back when we were in Italy. What if she'd called him again to get together? I shook that thought from my brain. I *was* being paranoid with that one.

As I drifted off to sleep that night, I reminded myself that Wes had given me no tangible reason not to trust him. Right now, all of this was in my imagination.

Basically, I went against my gut and tried to lie to myself so I could have a chance at getting some rest.

I ended up sleeping for a few hours, at best. The foreboding feeling that Wes was hiding something won out and kept my brain busy most of the night.

And the following day, Wes brought everything to the forefront again when, in the middle of the afternoon, he announced, "I have to go meet with one of the investigators."

"Who?" I asked.

"Detective Olson."

"What does he need from you?"

"He wants me to look at some potential suspect photos."

I blinked. "They have more than one suspect?"

"Well, it's more of a lineup kind of thing, but using photos instead of real people. I think they might be close to narrowing it down to one person and need my input."

I sucked in a breath as my adrenaline surged. "That's great news."

He looked into my eyes. "I won't stop until we get to the bottom of this, Juliette."

Did he think that's why I was concerned? Maybe I *should've* been more concerned about finding the perpetrator than I was about Wes's sneaky behavior. But the latter had completely overtaken me.

"Can I go with you?" I asked.

He shook his head. "He told me I need to come alone."

"That doesn't make any sense. Why can't you bring someone? You shouldn't even be driving yet."

"I'm fine to drive." He shrugged. "I guess they don't want anyone influencing what I remember."

"I was there, too, though," I pointed out. "What if something sparks *my* memory?"

"I get why you'd think that," he said. "But you already told them you don't remember seeing anyone. I admitted that I got a glimpse of a guy right before it happened. So that's why they're focusing on what *I* remember. They likely wouldn't trust your word since you've already admitted to having no memory besides me covering you."

I swallowed the lump in my throat. *Oh my God.* His face was turning red again, same as yesterday. This confirmed that it wasn't my imagination. *He's lying.*

"Where exactly are you meeting the cop?"

He hesitated. "The police station."

I nodded, remembering the bits and pieces I could make out from his phone call. He'd mentioned the Hotel Adventura. Nothing about a police station. *Hmm...*

Wes turned away from me. "Have you seen my keys?" He scrambled to locate them, knocking into one of the end tables, seeming discombobulated.

"You have to leave right now?" I asked.

"Not yet. Like in ten minutes. But I can't go anywhere without my keys. Can't remember where I last put them. I think my brain is still fried from the meds they gave me at the hospital."

As I pretended to help him look for the keys, a crazy idea came to me. As much as I knew I shouldn't pursue it, I wasn't able to stop myself. "I, uh, have to go next door to return a book I borrowed from Pam," I said. "So I probably won't be here when you get back."

He forced a smile. "Okay. Make sure Eddie knows. I'll see you a little later then."

I nodded and walked to my room, grabbing one of Wes's black hoodies that had been hanging on a rack. When he went to use the bathroom, I snuck out the back door, somehow managing to bypass the guards' attention.

After running over to Pam's, I knocked on her door. She opened. "Hey, Juliette. I was ju—"

"I need your help." I took a deep breath.

Her expression turned serious as her dog barked, circling her legs. "What is it?"

"I have to borrow your car. Just for like an hour."

"My car?" Her forehead wrinkled. "Why?"

I decided to be somewhat honest. She either still knew nothing about my mafia ties, or had chosen not to say anything. But I could certainly play the worried-girlfriend card. *That* I knew she could relate to. Pam had a cheating husband some years ago, so I suspected she might sympathize with that angle.

"A guy I'm dating and I have been going through a little rough patch. He's supposed to be going downtown to meet a friend. But I'm not sure I trust that he's not meeting a woman." I sucked in a breath. "I want to follow him to make sure he's being honest."

Pam sighed. "Some guys are impossible to tame." She rolled her eyes. "Say no more."

"Thank you." I let out a relieved breath. "I know this seems crazy, but I appreciate you helping me out."

"You do whatever you need to, Juliette. And give him hell." She disappeared for a moment to get her keys.

"I shouldn't be too long," I told her as she handed them to me. "I just need to see where he's going. Then I'll bring the car right back."

"Be careful driving."

"Don't worry. I won't crash."

"Not concerned about the car, honey. Take care of yourself."

"Will do. Thank you, Pam." I smiled nervously. "You're a good friend."

I hid in Pam's beige Toyota Camry in her driveway until I spotted Wes leaving the house. After pulling his hood up to shield my identity, I took off and followed him.

This was probably the craziest thing I'd ever done, but I didn't see any other way to handle my growing doubts. At one point, a box truck cut in front of me, blocking my view of Wes's car.

"Damn it!" I started to sweat. If I lost him, that would be it.

When the truck turned onto a side street, I was relieved to find Wes's car still right in front of me. I exhaled.

Then it hit me that Wes wasn't going toward the police station. This was the total opposite direction. My eyes watered with disappointment and fear. He was lying to me. And this was so much bigger than a lie. Wes was the one man I'd trusted in my entire life. I'd likely never get over him breaking my trust.

When he turned off the main road, I continued to follow. A minute later, he pulled into the parking lot of the Hotel Adventura. I parked several yards behind him and watched as he went inside.

Rushing out of the car, I entered the building after him and luckily spotted him walking down a hall. Wes was moving fast, considering the injuries he'd sustained, clearly in a hurry to get to whomever he was meeting.

Slipping into a small alcove with some vending machines, I hid behind a wall and watched as Wes knocked on a door to one of the rooms.

And then I heard it: a female voice. My stomach sank. *He's seeing a woman*! This was the worst-case scenario come true. She never came out far enough to allow me a view of her face, though.

My heart pounded. After Wes slipped into the room, I wasn't sure of my next move. I took a moment to breathe as I leaned against the vending machine, which made a humming sound that vibrated against my back.

I had to hear what they were saying. Despite the risk of getting caught, I made my way over to the door and placed my ear firmly against it. But I struggled to hear because their voices were muffled.

Then a maid wheeling her cart nearly scared the crap out of me.

Damn it.

"Can I help you?" she asked. "Are you locked out of your room?"

For a moment, I considered telling her I was and having her let me in. But I wasn't ready to handle that. I needed to play my cards more carefully, and I wasn't sure I wanted Wes to know I'd outed him just yet.

I shook my head and whispered, "No."

Thankfully, she let it go and continued to push her cart down the hall.

I still couldn't hear anything. But did it matter what Wes and the woman were talking about? I'd already confirmed he was lying to me.

Devastated, I decided to head home before Wes opened the door and caught me spying. I needed time to think before facing him.

The Earth seemed to sway as I walked back to the car. I took a moment to settle my breathing before getting behind the wheel again. I had no energy to drive but couldn't risk Wes spotting me. So I forced myself to start the engine.

As I drove home, my mind raced back and forth on how to handle this. *Should I hit him with my discovery the moment he comes back? Or do I hold it in to see how much further he'll take his lie?* I started to cry, tears blurring my view of the road. This made no sense. Why would Wes save my life only to cheat on me? And maybe it wasn't exactly cheating, but what the hell was it? I might've considered that maybe it was a female cop *if* he hadn't lied about the location. Then again, there *was* a whole lot of talking going on behind that door, not sex, from what I could hear. I felt more confused than ever.

When I got back to Pam's, I parked the car out front and knocked on the door to hand her the keys.

She opened immediately. "Well?"

For some reason, I couldn't admit what I'd discovered. I felt ashamed of the whole thing and didn't want her sympathy. Plus, maybe there was something I still didn't understand.

I frowned. "I lost him. A truck cut in front of me, and that was it."

She smiled sadly. "I'm so sorry, honey. I hope you can get to the bottom of it."

"I have to go. But thank you."

"Please let me know if you need anything."

I nodded. "Will do."

When I returned to the house, both of my father's guys were out front, looking frazzled. Eddie paced with a phone to his ear, and Tommy ran over as I walked toward them. I'd been so crazed over Wes, I hadn't considered the repercussions of sneaking out unguarded. And I certainly hadn't given a thought to how they'd react.

"Where the hell did you go?" Eddie bit out.

"Sorry. I had to take care of something."

"You need to tell us if you leave," Tommy insisted.

"I'm sorry. Something personal came up, and it couldn't wait."

"If anything happens to you, it's our asses on the line." Eddie got in my face a bit and shouted, "Have the decency to at least tell us where you're going if you plan to disappear."

"Chill out…" Tommy scolded his partner. He turned to me. "Just tell us next time you want to leave, okay? If you need space, we'll follow but give you some distance."

"Okay," I muttered. "I'm sorry for the scare."

As I entered the house, Tommy followed. "Everything all right, Juliette?"

I shook my head and burst into tears.

"Hey…" He placed a hand on my arm. "Don't cry. Tell me what's going on."

"I can't," I whispered. "I just need to be alone."

"Does this have to do with Wes?"

My eyes widened in surprise. But as much as I wished I could unload everything on him, it was too dangerous to say anything. "I don't want to talk about it."

Tommy seemed nice. I certainly liked him better than the other goon, Eddie. But the last thing I needed was one of these two going back to my father about Wes and me.

"Well, just holler if I can help," Tommy said.

"Thank you." I forced a smile. "I appreciate that."

I retreated to my room and paced until I heard the front door open about twenty minutes later. Then I froze, completely unprepared for this confrontation and no closer to deciding what the hell to do.

Wes appeared in the doorway of my room.

"Hey…" He smiled, oblivious to the turmoil inside me.

The nerve of him to try to act like everything is normal.

His smile faded. He must've noticed the look on my face. "What's going on, Juliette?"

"You can't take a guess?" I spat.

He drew in his brows. "No, I can't."

"I know you've been lying to me, Wes!" I blurted. "I know *everything*." Tears stung my eyes. Apparently, there was never a decision to make because I'd had no control all along. *So much for handling this delicately.*

The color drained from his face. "What do you *think* you know?"

"I know you're having an affair." I panted. "Cheating on me."

His eyes narrowed. "Why would you say that?"

"Because I followed you and saw you with her!"

CHAPTER 25

Wes

Oh shit.

"Juliette, I swear, I'm not cheating on you." I took a step toward her, but she took one back.

"Then who was that woman? You said you were going to see Detective Olson."

I hated lying to her, hated that I'd gotten myself into this complete clusterfuck, but what else could I do? "Detective Olson was busy, so he had one of his people show me the photos."

"At a hotel?" she screamed. "What kind of a police operation meets people at a hotel, Wes?"

Fuck. Fuck. Think. Think. But it was impossible to come up with another lie while she stared at me that way. So I did the only thing I could to buy myself a few seconds. I pressed a hand to my back, covering my wound dressing, and grimaced. "I need to sit down."

Her expression cracked a little, anger softening into worry. I felt like even more of an asshole.

"Are you okay?" she asked, stepping toward me.

I nodded and sank into the nearest chair, using the time to pull my thoughts together. I needed to untangle this web of lies I'd spun before it strangled me. Once I had my shit somewhat together, I forced my voice steady. "I'm not cheating on you, Juliette, I swear."

At least *that* part was the damn truth. Saying it out loud gave me just enough footing to dump all the lies on top. "Detective Olson called when I got in the car and asked me to meet someone else from his squad. He changed the location at the last minute, so if any of your dad's guys were following me, they'd think I was meeting a woman and not working with the police." I took a deep breath. "And he was right to do that. How do you think Vince would react if he knew I was giving information to the cops and not him?"

Juliette stood there, arms crossed, her eyes scanning my face like she was searching for lies. After a long, tense moment, her shoulders dropped a little. She wanted to believe me. I could see it in her eyes, in the way her lips pressed together like she was holding back a thousand questions she might not want answers to.

"Wes..." she whispered.

It was just one word, but it gave away enough uncertainty to expose the crack I needed. I'd done it a thousand times before—talking a suspect into trusting me, convincing a perp that it was safe to believe what I'd said. But now, now I was manipulating the woman I loved.

I didn't have to fake the pain anymore as I winced. "Juliette." I stood, moving slowly. When I reached her, I touched her arm, and she didn't pull away. "I would never cheat on you. You have to know that."

Her eyes met mine, still guarded, but something flickered there. "Maybe..." she whispered. "I guess I do."

I slipped my arms around her waist and pulled her to me. Her shoulders relaxed into my hold, and I could feel the rise and fall of her breaths slow.

"I'm sorry I jumped to the wrong conclusion," she said. "I just heard you on the phone and then..."

"Shhh..." I tightened my hold. "I'm sorry I upset you. I should've told you there'd been a change in plans."

She nodded.

Hours later, things seemed ninety percent back to normal. Though, honestly, I wasn't even sure what *normal* meant anymore. Was normal sitting in Vince Ginocassi's daughter's house and holding her, feeling my chest full of love while I pretended I wasn't betraying everything I stood for? Or was normal being a cop? The lines had blurred so much, I could no longer tell where one life ended and the other began.

Juliette came into the bedroom with a basket full of supplies—gauze, peroxide, ointments, tape, pain medications that I wanted to take because I knew they would dull the stress I felt but couldn't because I needed to stay mentally sharp.

"You ready for me to change your dressing?" she asked.

I nodded and rolled to my good side, giving her access to my wound. My head continued to spin in silence as she peeled off the old gauze, cleaned around the stitches, and prepared a new bandage.

"I hate that you're doing this," I said as she finished up.

"Doing what?"

"Taking care of me."

"All done." She packed everything back into the basket. "I like taking care of you."

I rolled onto my back and reached for her. "I should be taking care of you. It's my job."

"There are two other men here to take care of me."

"I didn't mean *job* in the employment sense. It's my job as your man."

Her eyes went soft. Juliette set her basket of supplies on the floor and laid on the bed, snuggling up next to me.

"Come here," I said softly. "Put your head on my chest, like you used to."

"I don't want to put my weight on you and press your wound into the mattress more than it already is. I don't want to hurt you."

"You being close to me could only help."

She hesitated but rested her head on my chest after a moment. I stroked her hair in silence.

After maybe fifteen minutes, her breaths started to slow, and I realized she'd fallen asleep. Her breath was warm against my skin, and I should've felt comfort that my girl was back in my arms. I should've felt peace that she thought she was safe enough to drift off. But instead, my heart pounded so hard I could feel it in my throat.

Because it wasn't the truth that had calmed her; it was the lies I'd told. And I wasn't sure what was more unsettling—the ones I'd told her, or the ones I was still telling myself.

The next morning, Juliette went to a meeting with her agent to talk about damage control. Not even her agent had known who Juliette's father was until the news broke that the woman involved in the shooting was the daughter of a mob boss. Apparently, the creative community was buzzing about Juliette Grecco being Juliette Ginocassi. Her agent had already fielded two calls from clients—one who was worried about having the daughter of a mobster adapt his book, and another from someone eager to hire her to adapt his book about mob wives. They were meeting with a PR firm to figure out what kind of spin they could put on things.

I waited at the window until Juliette's car disappeared down the street, then dug out my secret phone again. Though this time, I took it with me and went back to keeping one eye on the road so I didn't get caught sneaking a call twice.

My captain had told me yesterday that she was going to send me some photos of known associates of some of the rival families, people who weren't part of an inner circle but were suspected of handling some of their dirty work from time to time. But there was no message from her yet, so I tucked the flip phone back into my bag and shoved it under the bed before grabbing the *New York Post* from the kitchen table.

Settling on the couch, I was about to flip the paper over like I always did, to read the sports section in the back. But a small photo in the front bottom corner snagged my attention. It was Vince, caught midstep, climbing into the back of a car at what looked like JFK Airport. The headline underneath it read:

Bullets and Bloodlines: Mob Boss Returns to New York after Daughter Narrowly Escapes Hit.

Acid rose in my throat. I tried to turn the page and ignore it, but my eyes kept going back to the headline and reading the same part over and over again.

Daughter narrowly escapes hit.

Daughter narrowly escapes hit.

I remembered Vince saying when he'd visited me in the hospital that he'd seen a video online of the shooting. But everything about those moments was still a blur to me. Setting the newspaper aside, I grabbed my phone and typed *Vince Ginocassi's daughter shooting* into the search bar and took a slow breath before hitting enter. A flood of results filled the screen. At the top was a YouTube link. My finger hovered for a long time before I finally got up the courage to press play.

The video opened with shaky footage of a kid carrying a skateboard. He walked to a table stacked with jars of pickles and talked to the woman behind it. When another customer came to the table and distracted her, he crouched down, pretending to tie his shoe, but instead he looped a rope around the leg of the table. A second later, there was a loud *pop pop*. Then the camera jerked, catching flashes of chaos—people panicking and ducking for cover. It steadied long enough to catch Juliette and me, just as I took her to the ground and covered her with my body.

My stomach twisted. Seeing it from the outside, how close the danger had come, was worse than remembering it. There were only inches between my back—where I took the bullet—and Juliette's head. I'd almost lost her. *Inches.* Literally inches, and that shot could've been in her skull, could've...

I swallowed, refusing to finish the thought, and hit the backspace to clear the video from my screen. But before I could close the app completely, a link to another YouTube video caught my eye. The still was of a crime scene, yellow tape sealing off the area in front of a bar, and cops standing around a body covered with a white sheet. I'd never seen the footage before, and I couldn't resist clicking. The caption below the video read:

The Don with the Short Fuse. Vince Ginocassi Allegedly Teaches His Own a Lesson for Not Following Orders.

The article went on to say that the victim had been one of Vince's runners, a kid in his twenties. His mistake? He'd fallen for a woman who was the cousin of a rival family.

I stared at the screen. Maybe that kid hadn't been the only one Vince felt the need to teach a lesson. Maybe Vince had found out that things between me and Juliette were more than just friendly. Maybe...maybe the bullet at the farmer's market hadn't been meant for Juliette after all.

Maybe it was meant for me.

CHAPTER 26

Juliette

Beep beep.

I looked around the bedroom to see where the muffled sound was coming from, but nothing obvious stood out. The shower was running in the bathroom, so I chalked it up to Wes's phone buzzing from his jeans or something. For a second, I thought about stripping out of my clothes and joining him. It felt like forever since we'd been together. But then I pictured the bandage across his back. He needed to heal, not be tempted into doing something more strenuous than he should. Instead, I took off my clothes and opened the drawer to get something more comfortable to wear. The meeting with my agent hadn't gone well, and all I wanted was a pair of comfy sweatpants and a tall glass of wine. I tossed my dirty clothes into the hamper and was about to head to the kitchen for just that until…

Beep beep.

There it was again. I turned in a slow circle. It sounded more like it was coming from the bed than the bathroom now. I lifted the pillow and checked under the blanket. *Nothing*. Bending down, I picked up the bed skirt. The only thing underneath was Wes's duffel bag, the one he'd brought when he showed up at my door that first day.

But it was empty. Wasn't it?

My heart started to race. My eyes flicked to the bathroom door, then back to under the bed. Holding my breath, I listened for proof the shower was still running. Once I confirmed that I still heard water, my pulse kicked up another notch and I reached for the bag and unzipped it. Inside, tucked into a folded sweatshirt, was a phone. Not Wes's regular iPhone, but one I'd never seen before—a flip phone. And the small LED screen glowed with *1 New Message*.

My heart thudded. *What the hell?* Why did Wes have a second phone? All the doubts I'd managed to bury about him having an affair came roaring back to life. I didn't think twice before flipping open the cell and pressing the button to play the message.

A woman's voice came through—calm, clipped, and professional.

"Hey, Wes. I forgot to mention something yesterday at the hotel. We had to pull Detective Tiramani, the other guy we had on the inside back in New York, because we heard chatter that one of Vince's guys was asking questions about him. Apparently, Tiramani ran into one of Vince's captains who was out to dinner with his nephew and his nephew's friend. The friend recognized Tiramani and asked if they'd ever met before. Tiramani lied and said no, but the truth is, he'd locked the kid up a few years ago for possession of stolen goods. We thought Tiramani pulled it off and everything was fine, but then the uncle started asking around about him a few days later. We had to be safe rather than sorry. None of this has anything to do with you, or the operation you've got going on out there with the daughter. There's no indication your cover is blown, but I wanted to let you know anyway."

Then there was a soft click, not nearly as dramatic an ending as it should've been for something that had rocked my entire world.

Holy shit.

Wes hadn't been lying about not having an affair.

This lie was worse.

So, so much worse.

He was still a cop.

And he was undercover.

Using me to get to my dad.

All this time I'd thought my father was the only crooked person in this situation. Turned out I was wrong.

Wes was the crook.

I stood frozen for a minute, the flip phone in my hand, until I suddenly realized I couldn't hear the water running in the shower anymore. Panicked, I tossed the cell back into the sweatshirt and shoved the duffel under the bed.

I barely had time to get to my feet before the bathroom door opened. Wes walked out, wrapped in a towel, hair still wet, like nothing had happened. Fury burned hot in me, yet I managed to breathe. I needed time to think. To plan. To figure out what the hell to do.

He smiled. "Hey. You're home."

"Yes, but...I forgot something at my agent's. I need to go."

"What did you—"

Wes didn't get a chance to finish his sentence as I tore ass from the bedroom, bolted through the living room, and grabbed my keys from the kitchen counter. I was at the front door before he caught up.

"Hey. Hang on. Is everything okay?"

"Fine. I just need to go."

The guards fell in step behind me as I walked out of the house and toward my car. I didn't look back as I got in, started the engine, and took off like a bat out of hell. At the corner, I nearly smashed into a stopped delivery van before slamming on the brakes. Then I drove, barely seeing the road, until I arrived at my agent's building. My bodyguards parked next to me, not looking too happy. I rolled down the window and spoke to the one in the driver's seat.

"Change of plans. My meeting is a video call. I'm doing it here from the car."

"Okay."

Rolling the window back up, I'd at least bought myself some time. Time to think, to replay every moment since the day I met Wes. What had I told him? Had I compromised my father? Given him information that he could use against him? I'd told the man about my childhood, for God's sake—confided things I'd never trusted to anyone. Because I'd thought he was one of us. On my side. I'd thought he was *mine*.

Questions spun in my head until it hurt, pounding with the worst headache.

What should I do now? If I told my father, Wes was a dead man. If I did nothing, I'd be putting my father more at risk than I already had. I hated the choices, hated how torn I felt about who to save. The man I loved had betrayed me. Everything he'd ever said or done had been an act. My tears came, sudden and heavy.

I have no idea how long I sat there, but eventually, the tears stopped. I wiped my face, cleared my head, and slammed the car into drive.

Wes was on the couch when I walked in. Dressed, hair now dry, he stood. "What's going on? Is everything okay?"

I'd rehearsed what I was going to say on the drive home, but when I opened my mouth to speak, even I was surprised at how emotionless my voice was. "Sit at the table," I said.

Wes's brows dipped. "What happened? Did—"

"Shut the fuck up and sit your ass in the chair!" My voice was loud and cold. I sounded a lot like my father.

Wes was a smart man, though. Lord knows he'd fooled me into believing I meant something to him all this time. So he walked to the table and took a seat. "What happened? Juliette, talk to—"

"Save it," I snapped. "Stop acting. I've had enough of your lies." I spelled out everything I knew—the flip phone, the message from his captain, that he'd been using me all along.

He opened his mouth to interrupt when I said that last part, but I lifted a hand and cut him off. "This is how it's going to go." I spoke with a calm I didn't feel. "You're going to get the fuck out of my house and tell Vince you're not capable of taking care of me after the shooting. Say your injury is worse than you originally thought, if you have to."

He tried to protest, to tell me things weren't what they seemed. But I was in no mood.

"Stop talking and start listening," I told him. "I'm going next door to Pam's for a much-needed drink. If you're still in this house when I get back, I will tell my father everything I know. Do you understand me? And if Vince finds out you're a cop and manipulated his only daughter, you're a dead man. Not maybe. *Dead*. He won't care if he goes to prison for the rest of his life for shooting you himself."

Wes stared at me. I could see the conflict in his eyes, the turmoil pulsing through him. For a beat, I thought I saw something that looked like love, too. But it had to be a lie like everything else.

"Don't do this," he whispered. "Juliette, I love—"

"Don't you dare finish that sentence!" If eyes could shoot daggers, he would've been on the floor. "Be gone by the time I get back."

I grabbed my coat and never looked back as I swung open the front door and walked out.

CHAPTER 27

Wes

My hands shook as I threw my belongings into a bag. Devastated as I was, I was proud of Juliette for the way she'd handled that. I deserved to be kicked out on my ass—or rather to have my ass handed to me. She'd done both and handled it like a boss.

Good for you, Juliette.

I couldn't believe I hadn't been more careful with that damn spare phone. I'd been burned out lately. And when you're burned out, you get sloppy. Anger raged inside me, even as bittersweet relief cycled through me. Lying to Juliette had been eating away at my soul, killing me inside. She didn't deserve to be deceived. When I'd agreed to go undercover, I didn't even know her. I didn't know I'd end up having to hurt the person I loved the most in this world. So good on Juliette for figuring it out and ending this fucking charade. I'd come to this operation with good intentions—to catch a criminal and earn my place back on the force. But hurting her was beyond what I'd signed up for.

I just wished I'd had the chance to tell her on my terms. I had *planned* to tell Juliette the truth, even if she might never believe that now. I wouldn't get to explain everything delicately and carefully. I'd wanted to ease her into an explanation for my actions. Instead, the news had hit her like a ton of bricks. I tried to ignore the harsh truth my gut was already warning me to prepare for. *We can't come back from this.*

She'd cut me off when I'd tried to tell her I loved her. Rightfully so. But I'd so badly wanted to say those words, to explain that I'd never meant to hurt her, and that any business arrangement I'd entered before I met her had no bearing on how much I loved her today. But I'd broken her trust for good, and the situation was most likely irreparable.

I emptied the last of my personal items from the fridge to spare her any rotten reminders of me, and then with a giant bag slung over my shoulder, I left Juliette's house, unsure whether I'd ever see the inside of these walls again.

Eddie gave me a strange look on the way out. I had no idea what those guys had been able to piece together or what they might've overheard. I had to trust that they had my back simply because they believed I was one of them. I turned and took one last look at the house before taking off.

I drove down the 405, not even knowing where the hell I was going. After a half hour, I ended up at a cheap motel. No sense investing in a room when I wasn't even sure I was going to spend the night. After checking in, I dropped my bags and sat on the hard bed, able to feel the metal springs beneath me. I stared at the wall for a few minutes before picking up the phone and doing what I knew I needed to do. Adrenaline coursed through me as the line rang.

After a few rings, he picked up. "Wes… What's going on?"

"I need to talk to you, Vince."

"We are talking," he said curtly.

I rolled my eyes and took a deep breath in. "I need to resign from my position."

Vince laughed. "That's not exactly a choice *you* get to make."

"I no longer feel capable of taking care of Juliette."

"Why? You've proven very capable. You saved her life."

"I'm grateful I was able to do that, but I'm no longer in the proper physical or mental shape to continue. I had an appointment with the specialist today who explained the long-term deficits I'll have from the injuries I sustained and my surgery. I'm going to have physical limitations that will slow me down."

"One of my other guys had the same surgery, and he's fine. It takes time. But you'll heal."

He was right. The doctors at the hospital had all said I'd eventually make a full recovery. But I needed him to believe I wasn't capable of taking care of his daughter. "Maybe. But the PTSD isn't as easy to fix. I'm already having trouble sleeping, and I startle easily. That's not safe for a bodyguard. If you choose to make me stay, you'll be making the wrong decision for Juliette's safety." I closed my eyes, knowing damn well that was a lie. I knew in my heart I was the best person to protect Juliette. Because I loved her.

"You seemed just fine when I saw you in the hospital, and that was right after you got shot."

"I think reality has had time to sink in since then. I was probably still in shock when you saw me."

"How the hell were you ever supposed to be a cop if you can't handle getting shot?"

I shook my head and muttered, "I don't know."

"PTSD." He scoffed. "I didn't take you for a weakling, Wes." He laughed angrily. "I need the strongest of my men working to protect my daughter."

"And you have that right now in Eddie and Tommy. They're perfectly capable of handling the job."

He raised his voice. "Well, if you're gonna act like a pussy, I need to let you go."

Is he serious? Now he was letting *me* go? I almost had to laugh at that. I kept waiting for the condition to come. But it never did.

"Get lost, and have a good life," he continued with a sigh. "But leave my daughter alone. Don't get any ideas now that you're no longer my employee, thinking you can go anywhere near her without conflicts of interest. *I'm* your conflict of interest and always will be. The repercussions will be just as bad as if you'd laid a hand on her while working for me."

I ran a hand through my hair. "Understood, sir."

He hung up.

I lay back on the bed and stared at the ceiling.

Holy shit.

Did he really just let me go? I'm fucking free?

It seemed too good to be true. And, in fact, it was. Because this wasn't really freedom—not when my heart was still with her. Vince "letting me" go didn't even come close to solving my problems. The biggest one currently was that the woman I loved felt betrayed by me, coupled with the fact that I was still technically part of a team intent on taking down her father.

My heart felt like it was going to explode with all the things Juliette never gave me the opportunity to say today. She'd just wanted me out as fast as possible. She might've been able to get rid of me physically, but I needed to let her know some things before I left.

I found a pad of paper in the drawer by the bed and searched for a pen. I spent the next hour pouring out my thoughts. Juliette might never read it, but it felt like I might combust if I didn't unleash them.

After I finished writing, I got back into my car and returned to Juliette's house.

I slipped the letter in her mailbox and sent her a text.

Several minutes passed, and the message remained unread.

I drove away, still having no idea where the hell I was headed.

It wasn't until I crossed into Nevada and saw a sign that I realized how damn long I'd been driving: *Leaving California.*

CHAPTER 28

Juliette

I rubbed my temples. *Jesus*. How much did I have to drink last night? My vision was foggy as I looked around my bedroom. Realizing I was still dressed in my clothes from yesterday, I blinked my eyes fully open. The clock said it was eleven in the morning, the day after I threw Wes out of my life.

When I checked my phone, he had sent me a text last night.

> I just left a letter in your mailbox. Please read it. I won't be contacting you again unless you reach out to me. I hope you do. In the meantime, I'll respect your boundaries.

I had little desire to read whatever was in that letter, yet I went to retrieve it.

I returned to my room and tucked the envelope under my pillow until I'd properly geared myself up for it.

Feeling miserable, I went to the kitchen to make coffee. When I opened the fridge, I realized Wes had even taken his food with him. He'd done exactly what

I'd asked him to do, which was to disappear. I wondered if I'd ever see him again.

After two cups of coffee and lots of staring blankly into space, I couldn't put off reading Wes's letter any longer.

I returned to my bedroom and reached under my pillow before settling in a comfortable position. As I opened the letter, I immediately noticed his meticulous handwriting, something I'd never seen before. It was just as beautiful as he was.

Dear Juliette,

I don't even know where to begin. So I'm just gonna write my heart out, since I have nothing to lose. You're everything to me, and I've already lost you, haven't I? So the worst has already happened.

Please believe me when I tell you I never intended to hurt you. When I agreed to go undercover to investigate your father, I didn't even know you. I took that position with the best of intentions. It was a way of earning respect on the force again, while also having the opportunity to take a criminal off the streets. It seemed like a no-brainer.

But then I met you. And everything I thought I knew changed. Suddenly, nothing was simple anymore. Your best interests became my interests. And, well, the meaning of "doing the right thing" wasn't so clear any longer.

From the moment we first interacted, I knew I was in trouble. I looked into your eyes and saw a beautiful, but pained, woman who didn't deserve the predicament she'd been placed in. Over time, I realized you were as kind and smart as you were beautiful. Every day we were together, I was slowly falling in love with you, even if I didn't realize it right away. In retrospect, though, I know I loved you for almost all of our time together.

I need you to understand that everything we experienced together was entirely real. It wasn't until I met you that I realized it's possible to live two parallel lives. Every moment we were together, that was the real me. If I had to slip back into Wes-the-cop for the sake of work, I did so, but never a moment went by when I didn't feel absolutely horrible about that. Deceiving someone you love, when you never set out to do that, is probably one of the worst feelings you can have.

You've wanted to know why I had a change in demeanor recently. That came to a head, as you know, the morning of our trip to the farmer's market. I wasn't able to tell you the truth then because I hadn't figured out the best way to approach it. But what you saw was me trying to work through the dilemma of how to get out of this situation without hurting you. As you and I grew closer, I no longer wanted anything to do with taking down your father. All I wanted was to love you freely, to protect you. And that included protecting you from the harm I knew telling you the truth would cause. I was struggling, trying to figure a way out, and apparently, I did a terrible job of hiding my torment in the process. I'm sorry I didn't have the courage to tell you the truth when you all but begged me to. But please know my intention, even in hiding the truth, was always to protect you.

Possibly having saved your life will always be the greatest thing I've ever accomplished. I would do it all over again. I don't regret a single moment with you, good or bad. I only hope that someday you can find it in your heart to forgive me for the misjudgments I made along the way.

I love you so much, Juliette. If you take nothing else from this letter, please believe that.

I don't know what's next for me. I just hope that by some miracle all roads lead back to you. That may be a pipe dream, but it's one I'll never give up on, even if it takes a while.

I love you, Juliette. Never forget that.

Yours,

Wes

Tommy must've heard me sobbing because he knocked on my bedroom door. "Juliette? Are you okay? I was just out here eating a sandwich and heard you crying."

Sniffling, I wiped my eyes. "I'm fine."

"I saw Wes drop something off last night," he called from behind the door. "Does this have anything to do with him?"

I hesitated. "Wes quit. And I'm just...upset...because we were close."

"I can be your friend, too, you know."

I scowled. As nice as Tommy was, I had no interest in a personal relationship of any kind with him. From the very beginning, I'd had such natural chemistry with Wes. Nothing had ever felt forced.

"I appreciate that, Tommy. But what I really need right now is some space."

"Okay. Gotcha. Well, holler if that changes, okay?"

"Thanks. I appreciate you checking in."

Getting under the covers, I wallowed in my bed for a while until my phone rang.

My heart skipped a beat as I considered whether it might be Wes. But when I looked at the caller ID, it was my father.

I inhaled and picked up. "Hi."

"I let Wes go."

I narrowed my eyes. "What?"

"I wasn't sure if you knew. But I'm letting you know I fired him. He's not competent enough for the job anymore."

"He told me he was quitting."

"He can't quit," my father snapped. "I fired him."

Right. In some ways, my father was like a toddler you had to coddle. I played along with his delusion.

"Well, I agree that was the best decision...to let him go. He wasn't able to work after the shooting."

"I didn't like how tight you seemed to be with him, either. So this is for the best."

"Is that the only reason you called...to tell me you fired Wes?"

"Yes."

"All right, then. Have a good night."

After I got off the phone, I stared into space. I knew for certain that Wes was better off not working for my father anymore—or rather, better off not *pretending* to work for my father while he really worked for the cops. Despite how this had ended, I was happy that he'd gotten away. In fact, I was envious that Wes had the option to detach himself from Vince, something I'd do if I could. *An eye for an eye*, I supposed. Wes had saved my life, and I'd saved him.

Only now I had to live with the guilt of not stopping my father's inevitable capture.

After moping around my room most of the day, I eventually made my way out to the living room. I looked down and found that in his haste to leave, Wes had actually left something behind: one of his signature black hooded sweatshirts. Picking it up off the floor, I held it in my hands.

Don't do it.

But it was too tempting. I lifted it to my face and took in a long whiff of his delicious, masculine scent. It was fascinating how one smell could bring on a deluge of memories and feelings.

Deep down, I did believe he'd never meant to hurt me. Tears once again rolled down my cheeks. Always the glutton for punishment, I slipped the sweatshirt over my head and wrapped my arms around myself. As I closed my eyes, for a moment I imagined it was his arms around me. I doubted anyone would ever make me feel so safe and protected again.

Speaking of self-punishment, I opened my laptop and decided to read some of the news articles I'd been avoiding. Articles with titles like:

Bodyguard Nearly Dies Saving Mafia Princess
Ginocassi's Guard May Have Been Target
Hollywood Hit: When the Mafia and Tinseltown Collide

After scouring every word, I realized just how close both Wes and I had come to dying. I'd been so incredibly mean when I kicked him out yesterday. And he deserved better for the sheer fact that he'd saved my life.

I returned to my room and read his letter a few more times. I accepted the truth of his words about how he felt about me. I wondered where he'd been when he'd written the letter, whether he'd eaten anything, whether he'd cried. I wondered a lot of things I might never know now.

Tempted to call him, I must've picked up the phone a dozen times only to put it down again. What good would calling him do? Wes needed a clean break. And despite understanding how he'd gotten himself into the undercover predicament, I probably wouldn't ever fully trust him again.

I needed to leave well enough alone.

I needed to let him go.

CHAPTER 29

Wes

Three months later

I looked around at my empty apartment one more time. I'd lived in this little place in Brooklyn since I first joined the force. It wasn't much, but it had always felt like home. I suppose it was fitting that I was moving now because nothing had felt right since I'd walked out of Juliette's house three months ago. Coffee tasted bitter. The City sounded different at night. And the badge I'd been so proud to wear had grown too heavy.

I picked up the final box, took one last glance around, and pulled the door shut behind me. Forty minutes later, I pulled up at my next-to-last stop. Mom opened the door, and the smell of meatballs wafted out onto the porch.

"Perfect timing," she said. "I just put the pasta into the water."

"You didn't have to cook."

"Nonsense. I love cooking for you."

"Thanks, Ma." I followed her into the kitchen and found a cooler on the table. Inside was a bunch of Tupperware.

"I made you six different meals," she said. "I guessed that was about how long it would take you to drive from New York to California."

Shit. "Sorry, Ma. I should've told you there was a change in my plans. I'm not driving anymore. I'm flying because I need to be out there sooner than I thought to start my new job the day after tomorrow."

"Oh my gosh. You got a job! I've been so worried about what you were going to do for money out there in California, now that you quit the force." She pointed to the packed Yeti. "I even hid some of the money I'd been saving to blow with my girlfriends next month in Atlantic City at the bottom of the cooler. It's in a zippy bag. I knew you wouldn't take it if I tried to hand it to you."

I smiled and pulled my mom in for a hug. "You're the best, Ma. But you don't have to worry about me. I've got a nice little nest egg, and this new job pays better than the NYPD."

She leaned back. "You're not working for one of those crooked guys again, are you?"

The week after I returned to New York, I'd unloaded the truth about what I'd been doing with Vince and the NYPD on my poor, unsuspecting mom. Even though I no longer worked for the Ginocassi family, I still couldn't trust just anyone with the truth, and I'd really needed to talk to someone about my messed-up life. Mom had been the one to inspire me to not give up on Juliette so easily.

"No, Ma. I'll never get involved with people like that again. Promise. You don't have to worry."

Her shoulders relaxed. "Thank goodness."

"I'm actually going to be working for Tom Chalder, my old sergeant from the police academy. Do you remember him?"

"I do. I met him at your graduation ceremony. Red hair, right?"

I smiled. "It's almost all white now, but yeah. He and I stayed in touch, and he's been sort of like a mentor to me. Last year he retired from the force and moved out to the West Coast to be near his daughter who lives in LA. She and her husband just had a baby. Tom's got rheumatoid arthritis, and the winters here were tough on his joints. Anyway, he was never one to sit still, so after a few months in LA, he decided to open a private-security business, and it took off pretty fast. I'm going to be guarding celebrities, actors, and musicians, probably some rich tech people, too. My first assignment starts Monday, so I'm taking a late flight tonight."

"Oh, that's wonderful, Wes." She dug into the cooler and came up with a zippy bag full of hundreds. "Now I can go to battle with the one-armed bandit."

I chuckled. "I appreciate that you were going to give up your slot-machine money for me, though."

Mom and I had an early dinner together, and I managed to pack two of the meals she'd made into my backpack.

"I'm gonna head out," I eventually told her. "I want to stop by the cemetery to say goodbye to Luke before I make my way to the airport."

Her face softened. "Tell him I'll be there to do some weeding next weekend."

"Will do."

"Before you go, I just want to say that I think what you're doing—giving up everything for the woman you love—is very romantic, Wes. Hang in there. The best things in life don't always come easy."

"Thanks, Mom."

She opened the front door. "Good luck, Romeo. Go get your Juliette!"

I kissed my mother's cheek. "Let's hope this Romeo and Juliette story has a better ending."

"Thanks again for doing this." I stood and extended my hand to my mentor. We shook.

"Are you kidding? You're helping me." He came around the desk and put a hand on my shoulder as we walked toward the door. "I didn't expect my business to take off so fast. I'm not complaining. I like the action and all, but I don't want it to take over my life the way the NYPD did. I got a grandkid that I babysit two days a week now. So believe me, I'm glad to have someone here I can rely on."

I smiled. "That's awesome. And I'm happy to take on whatever you need, especially since, unlike you, I have *no* life out here in California...yet."

"Everything you need is on the assignment sheet I gave you. Job starts at noon today, and the pick-up is at the client's house in the Pacific Palisades. Good luck with your first gig. The guy you're protecting is sort of a dick. So you're gonna need it."

Back in my car, I put the key in the ignition and checked the time on my watch. It was still only nine o'clock, so I had a couple of hours to kill. Putting my hand on the gear shifter, I realized I had no place to go except my mostly empty apartment. I'd shipped my boxes and car, and they weren't scheduled to arrive for another ten days, so I didn't even have unpacking to keep me busy. The envelope Tom had given me sat on the passenger seat. Since I was in no rush, I decided to learn about the celebrity I was going to be protecting.

The top left-hand corner listed the date and time of the job's start, along with the address, but when I moved on to the client's name, I froze.

Bradley Wilson.

No way. The douchebag actor that had given Juliette a hard time. The guy had kept making her do rewrites just to feed his ego. What were the odds? There had to be tens of thousands of actors out here in LA, and I just *happened* to get assigned to *him*? I scanned the assignment sheet again. I'd be picking Bradley up at his house, then accompanying him on a three-day local press junket—media interviews, photo ops, late-night talk shows, the works. The paperwork didn't mention the title of the movie, but just being assigned to him felt...oddly significant. Or maybe a little like fate. So I decided to lean in, take a detour before heading over to Bradley's. It had been three months since I'd last seen Juliette—unless you counted all the times I'd stalked her social media—and even just catching a glimpse of her house in person would be great.

When I pulled up outside her place, though, I almost didn't recognize it. The tan house had been painted bright blue, and the front yard, which used to be patchy dry grass, was now alive. There were even a few flowers planted. The garage door was open, and while I sat idling, Juliette walked out carrying a pot of flowers in one hand and a small trowel in the other. I should've slipped down in the driver's seat or hit the gas and moved on so she didn't spot me, but I couldn't bring myself to take my eyes off her.

Juliette walked over to a flowerbed, seemingly oblivious that a man was watching her not thirty feet away. Sadly, so was her trusted bodyguard, Eddie, who sat in his car, busy stuffing his face, and didn't even clock me idling. Juliette dropped to her knees and started digging, and I thought I was going to get away with stealing a glance at her, but then she suddenly sat up and turned her head. And her eyes landed right on me. For a second, her face lit up, and my heart started to race. Then, just as quickly, everything changed. Her eyes narrowed, her lips pursed, and her posture said *don't you dare*.

The smart thing to do would've been to wave and drive away. But *smart* wasn't the way I'd ever handled things with Juliette Ginocassi. So instead, I pulled closer to the curb and killed the engine. The look on her face told me I should stay in the car. So what did I do? Of course, I got out and ambled over.

"Hey," I said softly. "How are you?"

She stabbed the trowel into the dirt. "What do you want?" *Icy.*

"Do you think we could talk for a few minutes?"

"No."

I swallowed. "Could you listen then? I won't take up more than a minute of your time."

"Get off my property."

"Juliette, I—"

She pointed toward the street and raised her voice. "Off. My. Property."

I lifted my hands and showed her my palms. "Okay, okay."

She didn't wait for me to retreat before turning back to her planting. Deflated, I started the walk of shame toward my car, but it hit me that if I was ever going to have any chance with her again, I needed to say my piece. I hadn't planned on coming here today, hadn't planned on laying my heart on the line this morning, yet now I felt desperate to do it. So I stepped off the curb, cupped my hands around my mouth, and yelled to her.

"I'm off your property now. I just need to say a few things, and then I'll leave."

Juliette's head whipped around, and she scowled. "Keep it down. My neighbors are going to hear you..."

I shrugged. "What choice do I have when you won't let me come closer so we can talk quietly?"

Her eyes narrowed to near slits.

I took that as an invitation to continue, this time even louder. "Three months ago, when I left California—"

She abruptly stood and pulled off her gardening gloves. "Five minutes, Wes. I'm not kidding."

I smiled, which only made her scowl deepen, and walked back onto her property.

Juliette gestured to the garage. "In there, so nosy ears don't hear you."

That was better than yelling from the curb, and I'd take what I could get. Inside the garage, she folded her arms across her chest.

"How are you?" I asked.

She rolled her eyes. "No small talk. Say whatever it is you came to say."

I opened my mouth, but she held up a hand, stopping me. "Wait. I'm going to set a timer."

"A timer?"

"I'm giving you five minutes. That's it." She pulled out her cell phone, swiped a few times, and brought up the big digital clock. After she pushed a red button, the seconds started to tick down. "Well, go ahead," she said. "Time is ticking."

I dragged a hand through my hair. "I'm not even sure where to start."

"You better figure it out, because..." She lifted the phone and showed me the screen. "*Tick, tick, tick.*"

That stupid clock made me more nervous than I'd ever been as a cop. I tamped down what I felt, took a deep breath, and dove in. "I quit my job with the NYPD."

Her face cracked, just the slightest bit. "Why?"

"Because you'd never trust a man who works for the police department, not with your father's line of business."

"Not that it matters, but how do I know you're telling the truth? This could be you undercover again."

I nodded. I didn't blame her for being suspicious. Hell, if I were her, I wouldn't believe me either. I took out my phone, scrolled to *Mom*, and hit speaker, holding the phone between us.

It rang twice before my mother answered. "Sweetheart? I didn't expect to hear from you this soon."

"Hi, Ma. Quick question—why did I quit the NYPD?"

"I don't understand."

"I'll explain later. Can you just tell me why I quit?"

"You moved out to California to be near Juliette."

Juliette's eyes flicked between me and the phone.

"And why do I want to be near Juliette?"

"Because you're crazy about her, and you picked a chance at true love over your career. I hate that you gave up a good job, but I'm proud of you for following your heart. It's so romantic."

I kept my eyes locked with Juliette's. "Thanks, Mom. I'll call you tomorrow." I ended the call and spoke in a low voice. "I've spent every single day missing you since I left California, Juliette."

Her face softened. Then she seemed to catch herself, and the angry mask she'd been wearing slid back into place as she cleared her throat. "Three minutes and counting."

"I never got to apologize to you in person. I am so sorry for hurting you, Juliette. I never wanted that—not for a second. The truth is, you caught me completely off guard. Every day I fell for you a little more, and then suddenly it hit me all at once, and I didn't know what to do about it. You might've come into my life as part of my job, but somewhere along the way, it stopped being about work. It stopped being about anything but you. You made everything else fade into the background and become unimportant. I wish I could take back the hurt. Every single word, every lie by omission. But all I can do now is tell you the truth. Every part of me longs for you, in a way I never knew was possible because I didn't understand what love was before you walked into my life…"

I felt myself getting emotional, and my gut reaction was to try to push it down. But I couldn't. It was too powerful. Tears spilled down my face and my voice broke. "I am so damn sorry, Juliette. And I will do anything and everything in my power to prove that you can trust me again. I'm here, and I'm staying."

Juliette looked down. I saw glimpses of emotion in her face, but the walls she had up weren't going to come down that easily—if ever. "Anything else?"

I shook my head.

"Okay, then." Her voice was low. "You should go."

I waited until she looked up and our eyes met. "Can I come back again? Maybe just for another five minutes? You can set another timer."

"That's not a good idea."

I nodded. "I'm leaving because I want to respect your wishes, and you gave me five minutes I didn't deserve. But I'm not giving up that easily, Juliette."

She didn't say a word. Just turned and walked out of the garage, going back to planting her flowers. I'd already gotten more than I should've, and I knew it wasn't the time to push any more than I had, so I went back to my car. When I pulled out onto the street, though, I slowed in front of her house and watched her as I passed. Juliette didn't look my way. I caught one last glimpse of her in the rearview mirror, and only then did she turn and watch until the car disappeared from view.

A few miles down the road, I saw a little nursery tucked off the side of the road. Before I even thought about it, I turned in. Flats of flowers were stacked all over—red, yellows, blues, and bright purple. An older man looked up from behind the counter.

"Can I help you?"

"Yeah," I said, glancing around at all the color once again. "I'll take a hundred flats."

He raised a brow. "A hundred *flats* of flowers? You know, a flat is the full plastic tray. There're eighteen individual cells in one flat."

I smiled. "I know."

"Alrighty, then. Any particular kind?"

"Doesn't matter." I shrugged. "Just something that lasts."

"You want them delivered to a jobsite? We can deliver them the day after tomorrow, on Wednesday."

"No, thanks. I'm going to be planting them tonight."

The next morning, I was running on fumes. I'd worked security from twelve to twelve and then spent the rest of the night planting until the first light of dawn. When I was done, I parked two houses down from Juliette's place so she wouldn't spot me right away. I just wanted to see her face when she came out and saw what I'd done while she was sleeping.

A few hours went by, and I nearly drifted off more than once. But then the front door opened. Juliette stepped outside, walked down the stairs, and froze. Her brows furrowed as she took it all in: beds packed with rows of fresh flowers, a rainbow of color where there had only been three plantings the day before. She stood for a moment, staring. Then she turned and scanned the street, and her eyes landed on my car.

I couldn't help but smile. I lifted a hand in a small wave, then turned the ignition and shifted into gear, driving off before she could decide whether to smile back.

CHAPTER 30

Juliette

"Shit..." I was running late for book club.

I wasn't really in the mood for it tonight, but I'd fallen into a funk over the last week since I'd seen Wes, so I was forcing myself to go.

I grabbed a bottle of wine, walked over to Pam's, knocked on the door, and waited.

When she opened, she had a funny expression on her face. And when I looked over her shoulder into the living room, I knew exactly the reason why.

I put the bottle of wine on an end table as I stormed inside. "What the hell are you doing here?"

Wes sat in the circle with a shit-eating grin on his face.

"Wes joined the book club," Pam explained.

I looked back at her before returning to glare at him. "Why?"

"I had fun the last time I was here." He popped a cheese curl into his mouth.

"We don't have any rule that men can't join," someone said.

"I thought he was a friend of yours," another woman chimed in.

Clearly, Pam hadn't made the connection that the guy I'd needed to follow in her car that one night was Wes. And I was a little relieved. Either Pam hadn't seen the news about us, or if she had, she was good at playing dumb. But the fact that she'd invited him tonight made me pretty certain she was clueless about my identity.

Wes smiled over at me as I took a seat in the circle of chairs. Since I was late, the book discussion was already underway.

One of the members tilted her head. "Wes, as you were saying...before Juliette arrived..."

"Yeah." He cleared his throat. "I think the concept of a why-choose romance makes a lot of sense. I mean why choose one when you can have both hot guys?"

I rolled my eyes.

He reached for the book he'd placed under his seat. "I actually annotated my favorite parts."

To my shock, there were, in fact, colored tabs throughout the paperback.

He flipped through the pages. "Pink for sex scenes, blue for parts that made me swoon, and green for things I was curious to get your thoughts on."

I sniffed the air, noticing a familiar smell. "You brought smoked sausage, didn't you?"

Wes grinned. "How did you know?"

"I can smell it."

He nodded. "Stopped in West Hollywood to get it."

"Better here than in my fridge."

He smirked, and I rolled my eyes before someone interrupted our moment.

"What was your favorite part of the book, Wes?"

Without skipping a beat, he shifted gears. "I loved how Aiden actually helped Marina see Adam's perspective when Adam fucked up. Aiden convinced her that sometimes lies of omission aren't personal. Sometimes they're meant to protect. Adam was doing what he had to, but Marina took it personally, when she shouldn't have." He looked over at me. "That said, she was totally right to be angry with him. But Aiden helped her see that Adam really loves her and never meant to hurt her. It surprised me, though, that it was Aiden who stepped up to help Adam when they'd originally been competing for her love."

He grinned and bit into a piece of chocolate. "I thought maybe the two guys were going to start fucking after that, but realized this wasn't that type of book. It's MFMM—not MMMF."

I turned to him. "Impressed that you know the lingo..." I wanted to be angry, but there was something truly adorable about the fact that Wes had read this book cover to cover and done his research. I also couldn't help but notice how damn hot he looked tonight. He seemed more tan and less stressed than he had when he was working for my father.

But that reminded me of *why* he'd been so damn stressed while working for Vince; Wes had been lying to me the entire time. I sighed.

After the book discussion, I went over to the appetizer table and begrudgingly took a piece of the smoked chorizo Wes had brought. As strong as it smelled, it did taste damn good.

He came up behind me. "Happy you're still willing to eat my sausage, despite everything we've been through."

I glared at him.

He raised a brow. "Too soon?"

"Much too soon." I lowered my voice. "Seriously, what do you think you're doing infiltrating my book club?"

"How else am I gonna get to see you? And there are no five-minute timers here." He winked. "Is that a hint of a smile?"

I pursed my lips, staving off any shred of amusement that tried to peek through. "No."

Wes raised his chin. "If you hate me so much, why are you wearing my cock and balls around your neck?"

"What?" I blinked.

"The cactus necklace I bought in Venice."

Crap. I clutched the charm. I'd forgotten I'd been wearing it a lot lately.

"I'm taking it as a sign of hope," he added, then looked around. "I'm a little disappointed that they didn't read another bodyguard romance." He winked. "I kind of like those."

"Even when the hero turns against the heroine?" I bit into the chorizo angrily.

"Yes. Especially when she gives him a second chance," he whispered into my ear, sending a chill down my spine. "And then they live happily ever after."

I pulled away. "Too bad that doesn't happen in real life."

I walked back to the other room, but after several minutes of trying to immerse myself in conversations that didn't include Wes, I could no longer avoid him. It was time to go.

"Can I walk you home?" he asked.

Not wanting to make a scene, I nodded.

"Where are you living now?" I asked as we strolled back to my house.

"At the Magnolia Apartments off of Sunset."

As we passed all the flowers he'd put in, I stopped. "Thank you for these, by the way. But it wasn't necessary."

"Again, just a way I could still be connected to you, when you're otherwise making it tough."

We resumed walking. "What other creative ways are you going to come up with to invade my life?"

He looked down at his feet a moment. "Actually, speaking of that..."

I stopped again. "What, Wes?"

"I'll be at the early screening of your movie next week. And before you think it's a stalking situation...I have no choice. I've started working for a private security firm, and they assigned me to none other than Bradley Wilson."

My eyes went wide. "You're kidding..."

"No. Believe me, I have no desire to work for that douche. But here we are." He sighed. "So, yeah. That's why I'll be at the early screening—not to stalk you." He paused. "Congratulations, by the way. You're obviously going, right?"

I nodded. "Yes, of course."

"Tommy going with you?"

"He's following me."

"Since we're both going to the same event, would it be possible for me to pick you up and take you?"

"I'm actually going with someone else."

His expression fell, and I didn't elaborate.

When we got to my door, Wes didn't say much else before he walked away, looking defeated.

The following week, I was a barrel of nerves as I got ready for the early screening of *Autumn's Husband*, which was the first feature film made from one of my screenplays. It had been tweaked quite a bit by other writers, yet I'd adapted the majority of it from the novel and was extremely proud. But my nerves tonight had nothing to do with the film.

Not only would I have to see Wes, I would be bringing a date—a film agent a friend had connected me with. Allan Kraft and I had started talking casually over the phone a few weeks ago. When we realized we were going to the same event, he asked if we could go together. I'd agreed to the date before I knew Wes was working for that private security firm, though now he'd think I'd brought a date just to stick it to him.

I shouldn't have been thinking about how Wes was going to react, but I couldn't help myself.

That evening, when Allan picked me up, he had no idea that Tommy would be shadowing us.

"You look amazing, Juliette," he said as we got into his car. "I'm so glad this worked out."

"Me too." I smiled nervously, still preoccupied with Wes.

"You said this is your first feature film?"

I shrugged. "Yes. Not my first adapted screenplay, but the first full-length project that's been produced."

"Amazing. Do you have family attending?"

My family attending. Yeah, right. "No…" I shook my head. "They're all on the East Coast."

By some miracle, it also seemed Allan hadn't been privy to the news coverage about me. I kept feeling him out to see if he was playing dumb, but he seemed genuinely unaware. And I certainly wasn't going to volunteer that information.

"How long have you been an agent?" I asked.

"About ten years. I love it, but it's cutthroat. Generally, once a client hits it big, other agents try to swoop in with incentives to jump ship. I've had very few loyal, big-name clients over the years."

"That stinks."

He glanced over at me. "Well, that's show business, as they say, right?"

Within minutes of arriving at the auditorium, I spotted Wes standing near the door. I could hardly breathe with how damn amazing he looked in a dark suit.

His eyes met mine, and his mouth curved into a smile—which faded the moment he noticed Allan next to me. Allan placed his hand at the small of my back, and Wes almost immediately turned away. I couldn't blame him.

During the screening, I was barely able to think of anything besides Wes. When the show ended, Allan spoke into my ear. "That was fantastic. You must be very proud."

"I am. Thank you."

"How about we hit the after party?"

I opened my mouth, prepared to forge ahead, but then I shook my head and made an executive decision for my mental health. "I'm not feeling so great, actually. So if you don't mind, I'd like to head home."

"That's too bad." He frowned. "But of course."

Allan drove me home, and when we got to my door, he leaned in to kiss me.

I moved back.

"I'm sorry," he said. "I—"

"No. I'm the one who's sorry." I shook my head and inwardly cringed. "It's not you. I'm just not ready for this. I apologize if I've led you on. I'm just getting out of a relationship. I thought dating would be good for me, but I misjudged, and I'm so very sorry you got dragged into it."

"I totally understand." He smiled sadly. "And I think you're fantastic, so if at any given point you find yourself ready to date again, you know where to find me."

"Thank you, Allan." I nodded. "That's very sweet of you." I waved as I closed the door behind me.

But alone in my house, I wondered if I'd ever be ready for another man as long as Wes was alive.

CHAPTER 31

Juliette

A few days after the screening, I was flopped on my couch, still unable to stop thinking about Wes. He hadn't come by again. Not that I could blame him after I'd shown up with a date the other night...

As I flipped through the channels, trying to put my mind on something else, I felt like I was going crazy. Nothing worked to distract me, so on impulse, I decided to go see Wes at his new place, though I had no clue what I was going to say or do when I got there.

I noticed Tommy getting into his car to follow me as I'd once again given him no information when I left the house. Eddie and Tommy had gotten used to having to scramble when it came to me.

I parked just down the street from Magnolia Apartments, where Wes had told me he was living now. My plan was to walk into his building and attempt to figure out which apartment was his. Unfortunately, I didn't make it to the building. Before I got there, I spotted him at the café on the corner. My heart nearly stopped at the sight of Wes sitting across from an attractive blonde.

The Earth seemed to sway. *He's on a date?* This was my fault. I'd led him to believe I was moving on with Allan, when that couldn't have been further from the truth. But right now I needed to move before he saw me staring through the window like a creeper. So I forced one foot in front of the other, and rather than going to his building to wait for him, I hung my head and went back down the street to where my car was parked. I couldn't bear to risk witnessing him taking that beautiful woman back to his apartment.

Oh God. I felt sick.

As I drove home, my mind churned. *What the hell did you expect?* I asked myself. *That a gorgeous, virile man like Wes was going to just stay celibate, pining for you in perpetuity?* I'd given him the green light to move on by showing up with Allan at the screening. Wes didn't know I was still hung up on him.

When I got home, Tommy pulled in behind me a minute later. He'd obviously been on my tail and had seen my bizarre behavior. I just didn't know if he'd figured out what I'd been up to.

"Everything okay?" he called from behind me as I was about to enter my house.

I stopped short of my front door and stared down at the ground. "Yeah. Everything is fine."

"I saw you looking in the window of that café." He paused. "I also saw Wes there with someone."

Damn. I turned to face him. "I don't know what to say, except that I don't want to talk about it."

"There's no way he moved on that fast, Juliette. There's got to be another explanation. I mean, all the flowers he planted outside this house? The man is crazy about you."

"Yeah, well, there's a lot you don't know. This situation is more complicated than you could imagine, Tommy."

"Complicated? When it comes to *your* situation?" He arched a brow. "You don't say..."

I sighed. "I'm pretty sure Wes just realized he's better off without me."

"Well, like I've told you before, if you need someone to talk to, I'm here."

"Thank you."

I was about to open the door when he called out again. "Juliette?"

"Yeah?"

"No man is better off without the woman he loves."

A week later was the official premiere for *Autumn's Husband*. This was an even bigger event than the early screening, and much more formal. Since I'd totally blown off Allan last time, when he asked me to accompany him again tonight—just as friends—I decided to give it a go. I figured it was one way to try to forget about Wes moving on. *Try* being the operative word. Plus, showing up alone seemed miserable.

Unfortunately, though, once we arrived, I realized quickly that there would be no forgetting about Wes tonight. I spotted him across the red carpet, this time looking even more gorgeous in a tux. *I should've known he'd be here.* He was working for Bradley, after all, who was expected tonight. And not only was Wes in attendance, but he was on the arm of the same beautiful blonde I'd seen him with at the café. I didn't realize security guards could bring dates when they were on the clock.

Was it rude to leave the premiere of a movie you'd adapted? Because I was this close to getting the hell out of here. My head spun with jealousy. But I reminded myself that this was the bed I'd made when I'd refused to give Wes a chance after he returned to LA. And anyway, Wes was probably better off with someone else, since my father would make it impossible for us to live in peace. That thought hurt my chest.

When he and the blonde moved to a central spot on the red carpet for photos, a flurry of flashes surrounded them. It occurred to me for the first time that she must've been a celebrity.

I leaned over to Allan. "Who is that blonde over there in the pink gown?"

"That's Shelby Warner," he replied. "She's on that new show that's doing really well, the one about the wives who cheat on their husbands with each other. The name escapes me..."

Wes is dating an actress? I supposed I shouldn't have been surprised in this town.

I let out a long exhale as I waited for my turn to be photographed. My red evening gown complemented my dark hair, but I felt like I was suffocating in it. Poor Allan once again unknowingly found himself the victim of my preoccupation with Wes.

As we entered the theater, I remained in a daze over Wes's red-carpet debut. After the introductory speeches, the lights dimmed in the theater, and the opening credits began to roll.

About fifteen minutes into the movie, I nearly flew out of my seat at what sounded like a gunshot behind me. My adrenaline spiked, and the lights in the theater flashed on. The movie stopped and chaos erupted.

Next thing I knew, Wes came rushing through the crowd toward me. He reached out and wrapped his arms around me. "Are you okay?"

"Yes." I spoke into his chest, feeling my nervous system calm from just being in his arms.

He looked around. "What the hell was that noise?"

"Speaker malfunction," someone shouted.

He panted as he looked down at me. "I thought..."

"I know what you thought." I cradled his face. "Thankfully, this time it wasn't that."

"I was so fucking scared," he admitted.

"How the hell did you get to me so fast?" I asked.

"I'd been watching you the entire time."

Our eyes locked. I was hopelessly in love with him.

Clearing my throat, I asked, "Are you dating that actress?"

He chuckled. "No, Juliette. I couldn't stand working for that asshole Bradley any longer. One more day and I was going to end up injuring him myself. So I requested a reassignment. They put me with Shelby. I just met her the other day, and this is my first assignment with her."

"She's pretty."

"Pretty sure she'll fire my ass after I ditched her just now."

The lights in the theater began to darken again.

"I'd better go," he whispered as he placed his hand under my chin.

I closed my eyes, cherishing his touch. When I opened them, Wes was already gone—and so was Allan.

CHAPTER 32

Wes

"What the fuck happened last night?"

My boss did *not* sound happy. Though the call didn't come as a total surprise, not after the earful I'd gotten from Shelby yesterday evening when I returned to my seat. What could I expect after running to protect someone other than the person I'd been hired to protect?

But I'd heard what I thought was a gunshot and reacted on instinct.

I sighed. "I fucked up, Tom."

"Obviously, since I just got my ass chewed by Shelby Warner, who says she never wants you working for her again. What happened?"

"A speaker blew. It made a loud pop sound. I thought it was gunfire and ran to cover...the wrong woman."

"Who the hell did you run to?"

"My...ex. She wrote the screenplay for the movie. I didn't even think about it. That's just where I went."

"Did you know she was going to be there?"

I swallowed. "Yeah, I did."

He heaved a sigh. "Then you should've told me you couldn't work the job when I assigned it. You know better than that. You can't commit to provide protection for someone when you've got a conflict of interest. Your instincts are compromised."

"I know. I'm sorry. I guess I was thinking about this job as more protecting actors from the paparazzi, not gunshots. But the job is protection. Period. I fucked up. I understand if you need to fire me."

"I *should* fire your ass. But I'm not gonna. Because if I were in your shoes, I'd have probably done the same thing. Though I *wouldn't* be in your shoes since I would've seen the conflict and avoided it. Let this be a lesson learned, though."

"Thanks, Tom. I appreciate it."

We finished our call, and a few minutes later I went on the grocery run I'd been putting off since I arrived in LA. I stepped outside, and my phone buzzed as I climbed into the car. I ignored it at first, but when it buzzed a second time before I could get the key in the ignition, I frowned. *Who the hell is texting me multiple times in thirty seconds?*

I pulled out my phone and saw that two different people had texted me, and a third message came through as I looked down—this one from my mom.

Mom: Is Juliette okay?

My pulse kicked up. *What the hell is she talking about?* I clicked open the text and saw my mother had posted a link. In preview, I could read the headline.

Mob Boss Arrested.

What the...

I tapped the link, and a photo of Vince Ginocassi filled the top half of the screen—brown bathrobe hanging open with his hands cuffed behind his back as two agents wearing FBI jackets walked him to an unmarked car. The caption below read: *Mob underboss turns against his family. Alleged crime boss Vince Ginocassi is taken into federal custody after feds flip long-time lieutenant Anthony "Tony Tall Tales" Mariano.*

My heart thumped as I scanned the rest of the article. The murder charges stemmed from an unsolved case that dated back almost a decade ago. At the bottom were links to related articles. Clicking on a video, I watched Vince being led out of his house while Juliette's mother stood in the doorway crying.

Fuck. Juliette. What if she thought I had something to do with this? I swiped to the phone screen and scrolled down until I reached her name. Hitting call, I waited impatiently while the phone rang. *Once. Twice.* After the third time, it went to voicemail. So I switched over to text and thumbed off a message to her.

> **Wes: I just saw the news. I'm sorry. I hope you know I had nothing to do with your dad's arrest.**

The text went from *Sent* to *Delivered*, then a few seconds later turned to *Read*. I waited and waited, staring at the screen, willing the phone to ring. But it never did. My chest ached as I thought about what she must be feeling right now. After ten minutes of sitting in the car, the suffocation I felt wasn't just in my head anymore. The air was thick, the walls closing in around me. I needed to start the engine or roll down the window, do *something*. But what the hell could I do? I wasn't a cop anymore. I couldn't just call a buddy at the precinct for the inside scoop. And Juliette... Well, she clearly didn't want to talk to me.

So I continued with the only thing I *could* do—go to the market, like I'd planned. I started the car, shifted into reverse, and eased out of the parking spot. Rolling down the window as I switched into drive, I let in some desperately needed fresh air. It helped, just not with the knot in my gut.

A block from the market, my phone buzzed, and my heart jumped. For a split second, I was sure it was her. But the screen lit up with *Mom*. I exhaled, disappointment settling in before I finally swiped to answer. "Hey, Ma."

"Hi, sweetheart. Are you okay? I saw the news and got worried."

"Yeah, I'm good. Sorry. I should've texted you back."

"How's Juliette?"

I frowned. "I don't know. She didn't answer when I called."

"Have you spoken to her since you got back to California?"

"I have. She wasn't thrilled about it, but she did give me a few minutes to apologize, at least." I pulled into the grocery store lot and parked. "She's seeing someone."

"Oh, Wes. I'm so sorry."

I rubbed the back of my neck. "It's my own fault."

"What are you going to do about it?"

"You mean about the guy she's seeing or the article?"

"Well...both."

"I'm not sure there's much I can do about either."

My mom let out a quiet sigh. "That doesn't sound like the Wes I know. The one I raised never stood by while people he cared about fell apart."

"What am I supposed to do?"

"If you love her, don't let her go through this alone. You might not be able to fix what happened, but you can *show up*. Even if she pushes you away, at least you'll know you tried."

I stared out the windshield, watching people walk by but not really seeing them.

"You always wanted to protect people," she continued. "Sometimes protecting someone doesn't mean throwing yourself in front of a bullet. Sometimes it means being there when they need a shoulder to cry on."

I swallowed hard. "Yeah. You're right."

"Of course, I am. Mothers always are."

I chuckled. "Thanks, Ma. I gotta go."

Forgetting all about the market, I started the car again. My pulse climbed as I shifted into reverse and backed out of the spot. I wasn't sure what I was going to say when I got there—*if* she even let me in—but I suddenly couldn't get to Juliette fast enough. I hit the gas as I turned onto the main road, driving way too fast for a civilian. My thoughts were a mess as I merged onto the highway—Juliette in her kitchen, face streaked with tears, her mom crying alone back in New York, the smug look I imagined on the FBI agent's face as he'd led Vince Ginocassi from his mansion wearing nothing but a bathrobe. He could've let the guy throw on a shirt, maybe a jacket, but no—the agent probably enjoyed stripping the dignity from his collar.

When I finally turned onto Juliette's street, my stomach dropped. Two news vans were parked along the curb, satellite dishes on top. *Shit*. I hadn't even thought about that. Of course they'd be here. Now that

Juliette's identity was public, it made sense they'd want a shot of *the mob boss's daughter* looking broken.

I parked a half block away and stepped out, keeping my head down as I walked. Tommy stood at the front door, arms folded across his chest. As I passed the first news van, the passenger door swung open, and a woman jumped out carrying a microphone. "Sir! Are you connected to the Ginocassi family?"

I ignored her and kept moving to the house.

Tommy lifted his chin. "How you doing, Wes?"

"I've been better," I said. "Is she home?"

He nodded once. "She know you're coming?"

I thought about lying but decided against it. "No. And she might not be happy about it. But I want to be here for her."

A grin tugged at the corner of his mouth. "I was busy fending off the photographers, and you helped yourself inside the house. That's the story if she gets pissed."

"You got it."

Tommy stepped aside, and I pushed open the door. Inside the house was quiet, with the faint smell of freshly brewed coffee. I found Juliette sitting at the kitchen table, hands cupped around a mug. She looked up, saw me, and her bottom lip began to tremble. I wanted more than anything to wrap her in my arms, but I also didn't want to get my ass kicked to the curb the second I walked in.

"Hey," I said softly. "I didn't want you to be alone right now."

Her face was blotchy, eyes puffy from crying. "You shouldn't be here."

"Maybe not," I said, meeting her gaze. "But I am. I'll leave whenever you tell me to, but I know there aren't a lot of people you can confide in."

She swallowed, and tears welled in her eyes. "I feel so conflicted. If he did what they say he did, he should be in prison forever. But he's my father, and I don't want him to spend the rest of his life behind bars."

"Of course you don't. There's no right answer when it comes to family."

A tear slid down her cheek. "I keep thinking of when I was seven and he coached my soccer team. The regular coach had broken his ankle and had to have surgery, so my dad stepped in and took over the job. He had no idea what he was doing, but he hired the kid down the street who played on his college soccer team to come teach him the rules. He was out in the backyard every night for hours, even after it got dark, trying to learn the sport." She smiled and wiped her cheek. "We were a terrible team, didn't win a single game, but he kept trying."

I smiled and took the seat across from her.

Juliette stared off at nothing. "He had the ice cream man come after each game, and he even gave us all a pep talk, telling us how good we'd played and how we'd almost won." She shook her head. "I keep asking myself if any of it was real."

"It was real, Juliette. No matter what else he did, those moments were real. You don't have to erase the good times just because there were bad ones, too."

She met my eyes. "But how do I live with a man who can do both?"

"You don't need to figure that out today," I said. "One thing at a time."

She laughed, and it somehow turned into a sob. Before I could second-guess it, I was out of my chair and pulling her into my arms. Juliette collapsed against me, her forehead pressing into my chest as she bawled her eyes out. I held her tight, feeling her whole body shake.

"It's okay," I murmured, stroking her back. "It might not feel like it, but everything is going to be okay one day." I held her for the longest time. When she finally pulled back, she let me wipe tears from her cheeks. "Did you eat today?" I asked.

She shook her head.

"How about I make you some bacon and eggs? There's nothing better than breakfast for dinner."

She sniffled and nodded her head. "Would you mind if I took a shower while you do that?"

I smiled. "Not at all."

Juliette disappeared down the hall, and I pulled out everything I'd need to cook. I cracked eggs, fried bacon, and took comfort in the little I could do to help her feel better.

Everything was done by the time she came back out, her hair wrapped in a towel. She offered a small, tired smile. "It smells good."

I winked. "Me or the bacon?"

Plating the food, I poured juice into glasses and took the seat across from her. "I hope you don't mind. I wasn't planning on eating, but the smell of bacon got me."

She smiled. "Sure, you weren't. Coming over to check on me at dinnertime was probably just a ruse because your refrigerator is empty."

The teasing felt nice, normal, even. Juliette dug in quietly while I sat across from her, enjoying whatever I could get. After a few bites, she looked up at me, her eyes still shiny but the tears less threatening. "Thank you for coming."

"Of course. I'll always be here when you need me."

After we finished, I wasn't sure what to do. I didn't want to overstay my welcome, but I also hated to leave when she was in such a fragile state. Her phone buzzed on the table, and both our eyes went to the flashing name. *Mom.* She looked up, seeming uncertain whether she should answer.

"Take it," I said. "I'll clean up."

"Thank you." Juliette went into the other room and talked for a while. I couldn't help but overhear some of the conversation since the kitchen and living room were open to each other, though I drowned out most of it running water to do the dishes.

When there was nothing left to clean, I found Juliette on the couch, no longer on the phone. "How's your mom?"

"She's okay. Sadly, I think she's used to him getting arrested. She told me he'd probably get bail and be home in a day or two. Though, I think she might be delusional this time, don't you?"

I hated to be the bearer of more bad news, but I also couldn't lie to her. "Capital murder and a history of arrests, I would think it would be tough."

She sighed. "That's what I figured. She's going to call me after she meets with his lawyers in the morning."

I nodded, looking at her a moment before I finally spoke. "Juliette, I want you to know I had nothing to do with your dad being arrested. None of this stemmed from anything I learned while I was working for him."

She gave a small, sad smile. "I know."

"Thank you." Physical relief washed over me. Tension drained from my shoulders, and the giant knot in my neck loosened. "Is it…okay if I stay for a little while?"

"Only if I set the timer on my phone."

I looked up at her, and she grinned. "Kidding. Sit down, Wes. It's weird when you tiptoe rather than bulldoze."

I took the chair across from her, and for a long time, we were both quiet. Then she began to speak, telling me about the first time her father was arrested in front of her—in the middle of her tenth birthday party, with a dozen of her friends sitting around a pink-frosted cake about to sing happy birthday. I listened, letting her continue without interruption, offering reassurance only when I thought she needed it. Minutes blurred into hours as we talked about her childhood, her complicated relationship with her dad, and all the chaos of growing up the way she had. At some point, she yawned—a big, long yawn with a stretch, and I realized it was almost midnight.

"Why don't you get some sleep? If it's okay with you, I'll stay out here for a while, just to make sure you don't need me." She looked hesitant, so I added, "I promise, no funny business. I know you're seeing someone. And I'll be gone before you wake up. I promise."

She nodded and stood. "Thank you for being here, Wes."

"Anytime, sweetheart."

It looked like she was debating how to say goodbye, but eventually she waved. "Goodnight."

"Goodnight."

She walked to her bedroom door and looked back over her shoulder. "Wes?"

"Yeah?"

"I'm not dating anyone. The guy you saw me with didn't even make it to first base when he drove me home the night of the early screening."

I couldn't help it—I smiled.

Juliette rolled her eyes, but there was a hint of a grin at the corners of her mouth. "You were doing so well. Don't ruin the evening by gloating."

I smiled again. "Get some sleep."

CHAPTER 33

Juliette

The next morning, disappointment settled in my chest when I walked into the living room and found no sign of Wes. It was probably for the best, but it didn't make things any easier. The house felt empty without him.

I started the coffeemaker and leaned against the counter, waiting for the pot to finish brewing. I pulled out my phone to check for flights to New York, and just as the airline schedule loaded, it buzzed in my hand. *Mom.*

I steadied myself before answering. "Hi, Mom."

"Your father's lawyer thinks the judge is probably going to deny him bail."

I sighed. "I'm not that surprised. He's accused of a very serious crime. This isn't breaking Vito Antonelli's nose."

"The hearing isn't going to be until tomorrow. Dad's attorneys want some time to talk to the prosecutor before they all go before the judge."

"Okay. Have you talked to Dad yet?"

"I will this morning. His attorney is going to see him now, and he said he'll call me after."

"I'm going to fly home to New York tonight."

"You don't have to do that, sweetheart."

"I want to. I looked up flights, and there's one at three. It won't get me into JFK until midnight with the time change, but I prefer that to the redeye."

"Your father ordered more security for us. He's concerned that one of his enemies might try to take advantage of the current situation."

"That's not necessary, Mom."

"You know how your father is."

I sighed. It didn't really matter since I'd be in New York by the end of the day.

"How are you holding up?" Mom asked.

"Okay. At least as okay as I can feel with everything going on."

"When we spoke yesterday, you mentioned Wes was there. I didn't think you were seeing each other anymore?"

"We aren't. But he was here for me."

"You never did tell me what happened between the two of you."

I hated to lie to my mom, but it was too risky to tell her Wes had been a cop. "We just... We had very different lives, and I didn't think it was a good idea to get serious."

"Your dad and I had very different lives, and look at us. We've been married for thirty years."

"Umm, Mom... You're in love with someone else, don't even live in the house with Dad, and now he might go to prison for the rest of his life."

"Don't say that."

"Which part?"

"Your father is not going to prison. He didn't do the things the government is accusing him of."

I honestly wasn't sure if my mother was that naïve, or if she needed to believe that to get through this. Either way, we were on a line that could easily be tapped, so it wasn't a conversation we should be having.

"I need to pack and book my flight," I told her. "I'll text you the info when I have it."

"Okay, sweetheart. I'll see you soon."

A little while later, I had my flight booked and took out my suitcase. Before I started packing, I texted my travel information to my mom. She responded almost immediately.

> Mom: I'll pass it along to your extra security so they can travel with you.

I closed my eyes. *Whatever*. Some extra goon could sit a row or two away from me, and I'd just ignore him like always.

After a whirlwind of preparation, I was on my way to the airport with Tommy. He looked in the rearview mirror, catching my eye. "Your new security detail is meeting you at the terminal. Boss wants Eddie to stay out here and take care of a few things. I'll park the car and meet you at the gate."

I sighed. "Great."

He smiled, and that was the last we spoke until we pulled up at the airport. Tommy turned back toward me as I got out. "I'll see you in a bit, Ms. G. Hope you like your new security detail."

"Trust me," I mumbled as I gathered my things, sliding across the backseat to exit on the curb side. "I won't."

"We'll see about that."

The rear passenger door opened, and a man held his hand out to me. Instead of taking it, I climbed out on my own—only to be met by a familiar smirk.

"I was only offering my hand, sweetheart. Not my dick."

My mouth dropped open. "Wes? What are you doing here?"

"Your mother hired me as your security."

CHAPTER 34

Wes

"I don't have to take the gig if you don't want me to," I assured her. "Just say the word, and I'll leave." My heart pounded as I waited for her response.

Please don't tell me to leave.
Please don't tell me to leave.

It felt like years that I stood there anticipating her answer while people rolled their luggage by us.

"Okay. Yeah." Her expression softened. "Better than a stranger."

Juliette's smile seemed genuine. It included her eyes, which was always my gauge. *God, I love her.*

As we checked in and went through security, Juliette and I stole glances at each other. When she smiled at me again, relief settled in my gut. The smile thing was becoming a trend. For the first time in a long time, I felt hope that this situation was turning around. Maybe she could forgive me.

On the flight to New York, I looked out at the clouds from my window seat, which was fitting, since at the moment I felt on top of the world. Juliette said she preferred the aisle, which I didn't really understand. Tommy sat behind us, so I got the seat next to Juliette. Pretty sure by now Tommy knew what was up between her and me. I kept noticing the way he watched us, and I wondered if Juliette had spoken to him. At the very least, he'd watched me plant that freaking garden exhibition outside her house in LA. That had to have given my feelings away.

It was later in the day, yet I'd opted for a coffee when the beverage cart came around, and the caffeine had made me totally buzzed. Juliette had opted for a glass of wine, and I wondered about its effect on her.

At one point, she and I placed our hands on the armrest at the same moment, brushing against one another. To my shock, she took my hand and intertwined our fingers. I turned to her, and her expression held a calm I hadn't witnessed before. Was it that little bit of wine, or had she finally come to terms with her doubts about me? My gut was even more certain that everything was going to be okay.

I felt more peace now than I had in all the time we'd known each other. I hated to say it, but this had to be at least partly because Vince was locked away. Maybe that was the entirety of the reason. All I knew was it felt like a brand-new day, and I was here for it.

"I never acknowledged the letter you sent me right after I kicked you out," Juliette finally said.

I nodded. "It wasn't meant to garner a response. I just needed to make sure you knew where I stood. I was feeling really hopeless when I wrote it, even if I was still determined not to lose you forever. Driving out of California after dropping it off was one of the hardest things

I've ever done." I smiled. "Even if I didn't end up being gone for very long."

"I'm glad you came back, Wes."

"I had to tell my mother everything. She helped convince me I needed to lay it all on the line with you."

"I'm so happy she didn't hold the fact that we lied to her about our relationship against me."

I shook my head. "She loves you." I smiled. "She's not the only one."

"You promised to never give up on me." Her eyes glistened. "You've really proven that."

"I'll never give up on you, Juliette."

She squeezed my hand. "What now?"

I thought about how I wanted to answer that. "Back when I was hiding my real job from you, I used to discourage your suggestion that we could run away together. I couldn't make promises when I didn't know how you were going to react to finding out the truth." I sighed. "But nothing is off the table now. I'll do whatever it takes to make you happy and safe. I'll follow you to the ends of the Earth."

Juliette stared at me for several seconds. I'd expected her to say something in return, but not, "I'll be right back." Yet that's what she told me before she got up and went down the aisle to the bathroom.

Had I upset her? I practically counted the seconds until she'd return. Then a text came in.

Juliette: My zipper is stuck. Can you come help me?

I stood from my seat and rushed down the aisle.

The moment I slipped inside the lavatory, Juliette wrapped her arms around me and pulled me close. I realized quickly that this had nothing to do with a zipper. My dick hardened, a reminder of just how long it had been since I'd buried myself inside her.

"I never *properly* thanked you for saving my life," she muttered over my lips. "This seems like a fun way to do it."

"Well, if this is the way you thank me, I have to warn you that one time isn't going to be nearly enough to pay off the debt."

I backed Juliette against the sink. With barely any room to move, I kissed her like my life depended on it. Every ounce of me surrendered to the immense pleasure of being back in my happy place. Her smell. Her taste. I was drowning in endorphins and loving every bit of it.

She fumbled with my belt, and within seconds, I was inside of her. I paused for a moment to relish the warmth of her pussy before thrusting in and out with so much force that when the plane hit turbulence, it felt like it could've been caused by *us*. I'd normally be a little freaked out when a plane shook like this. But at the moment? I didn't have a care in the world, other than escaping inside this woman. With each movement, I let out more and more of the frustration I'd harbored during the time we'd been apart.

"I've missed fucking you so much," I murmured.

Juliette responded by moving her hips faster.

When I came, it was sudden and hard. My body shook, and I felt her hands tighten around me just before the muscles between her legs pulsed around my shaft. I pumped in and out slowly until I had nothing left to give.

As we recovered from our mile-high-club debut, I set her down and softly kissed her neck.

"I'm never letting you go again," I whispered.

I opted to leave first and return to my seat, and I tried to pretend I didn't notice Tommy smirking at me. I couldn't have cared less what he thought at the moment.

About five minutes later, Juliette emerged from the bathroom. Her hair was mussed, and I knew mine must have been tousled, too. She looked like she'd been properly fucked, and I was proud to say, she had.

For the rest of the flight, Juliette leaned her head on my shoulder. We were sated and at peace. It was bliss.

We decided to turn on a movie for the last couple of hours, and the universe must have been playing with us, because the first one that popped up on the screen? *Goodfellas*.

The three-story house in Mill Basin, Brooklyn, had a stucco façade and was surrounded by a large, black, wrought-iron fence. It looked like something out of Beverly Hills stuck in the middle of New York. According to Juliette, her neighborhood was known for its Christmas-light displays during the winter months. Even though I'd lived in Brooklyn, I'd never spent too much time in this neck of the woods. To the average person, this would've seemed like a nice, wholesome home, but of course, I knew better.

Two luxury SUVs sat parked in the driveway out front. I assumed one of them was Vince's, and it occurred to me that he might not be driving it again for a very long time. That thought was bittersweet. As relieved as I was to have him safely locked away, I'd always feel bad for Juliette. He was still her dad.

It was late, past midnight, but Frannie was bright-eyed and bushy-tailed when she opened the solid mahogany door to greet us.

"There's my baby!" she cried as she wrapped her arms around her daughter. Her nails were perfectly manicured and painted red. She winked at me as we entered. "Welcome, Wes. Hey, Tommy."

I looked up at the winding staircase and crystal chandeliers as Frannie ushered us inside.

"It's so good to see you, Mom," Juliette said.

I took in a waft of Frannie's strong perfume.

"How was the flight?" Frannie asked.

"Really rocky, but *so* worth it." Juliette grinned over at me.

So freaking worth it, indeed.

"It's always worth it to see family, isn't it?" Frannie sighed. "I don't love to fly, but I don't have to think twice about getting on that plane to see my beautiful girl across the country."

I took in a whiff of something else in the air. Tomato sauce and a hint of coffee, maybe.

"Hope you're hungry," Frannie said as she led us through the house.

"It's past midnight!" Juliette laughed.

"I know. But I figured you'd be hungry after that flight. And I drank a ton of coffee waiting up for you guys. Anyway, it's never too late to eat. You can sleep in as long as you need to in the morning. You have nothing planned for tomorrow, right?"

Juliette shook her head, and Tommy rubbed his stomach. "I could eat."

The only thing I craved tonight was a hot shower, followed by another round of amazing sex with Frannie's daughter.

As Tommy retreated to the kitchen with Frannie, Juliette tugged my arm and showed me around. The more I saw of it, the more I realized this house looked exactly like I'd imagined, with leather furniture and shiny gold accents. The outside featured an in-ground pool and a large patio, and farther back on the property was a small pool house, where Juliette said her mother lived. The walls were lined with photos of Juliette at every stage of her life, and my heart nearly burst at the sight of mini-Juliette. It made me want a little girl with her someday.

We ended up in Juliette's old bedroom. As we'd passed through the kitchen on our tour, Frannie had made it clear that she'd set up Juliette's room for us—meaning Juliette and me. That proved her hiring me was a sham if she knew I'd most likely end up sleeping in the same bed as her daughter. But I was relieved to know I wouldn't have to sleep apart from her tonight, especially after the taste of her I'd gotten in that airplane bathroom.

Juliette's room was exactly as I might have imagined it: pink and frilly and fit for a mafia princess. It didn't match her style now, of course, but it screamed teenage queen. And everything remained untouched from a decade ago.

"Welcome to my time capsule," she said.

I lay back on her bed and looked up at the ceiling. "Glow-in-the-dark stars...nice."

"I used to love to look up at those before going to sleep, mostly while wishing for a different life. I know that sounds terrible because I was so privileged, but..."

"You have every right to have wanted something different," I told her. "We can't help what we wish for at night when no one else is around."

She reached into the drawer next to the bed and took out several small journals.

"What's all that?" I asked.

"This drawer is filled with my diaries. They're from different stages of my life."

Juliette opened a random one and read me some of the passages, many of which lamented the fact that her life had to revolve around Vince. Not much had changed in that respect. The one she'd chosen was one of the oldest, and she came upon a section where she'd written about the type of guy she hoped to meet someday.

"Don't laugh, but listen to this," she said. "*I've started to figure out the kind of guy I want to end up with. He has to think I'm funny. He has to look at me like I'm the most delicious cannoli he's ever seen. He has to text me all day. He has to stand up to my bully father. He has to like dogs. He has to have hair like a Disney prince. He has to be smart. I don't care if he has money, because money only causes problems. So, to summarize, I want a poor Disney prince who looks at me like I am a cannoli. Thank you.*"

I shook my head. "God, you were cute...and a little weird."

"Cute? That is the most pathetic thing I've ever read. In my defense, I probably wasn't even twelve when I wrote that."

I reached for a pen and found a blank spot on the page next to that passage. "Let me," I said before writing a response into the journal.

After, I read it aloud to her.

"*Dear Twelve-Year-Old Juliette, This is your boyfriend writing from the future. I'm happy to report that you turned out a lot smarter than one might've guessed based on this entry. That said, I can attest to the fact that while I do think you're funny, I much prefer being the one to make YOU laugh. Also, you look far more delicious than a cannoli (you're at least the level of the finest tiramisu). You taste better than that, too. Trust me, you don't want me to be texting you all day—that would be annoying—but I will always be here for you, if you need me. I love dogs and hope to get one when we get our first house together. I don't have hair exactly like a Disney prince, but I'm built better and could take down any one of them in a fight. As luck would have it, I am not rich, so no worries about money ruining us. But you asked for a smart guy. If you're talking about street smart, I'm your man. I'm not the most book-smart guy you've ever met, but I hope I make up for that in the way I protect you, in the way I love you. So, to summarize, I'm hotter than a Disney prince, and holy cannoli, I love you."*

xo,
Wes

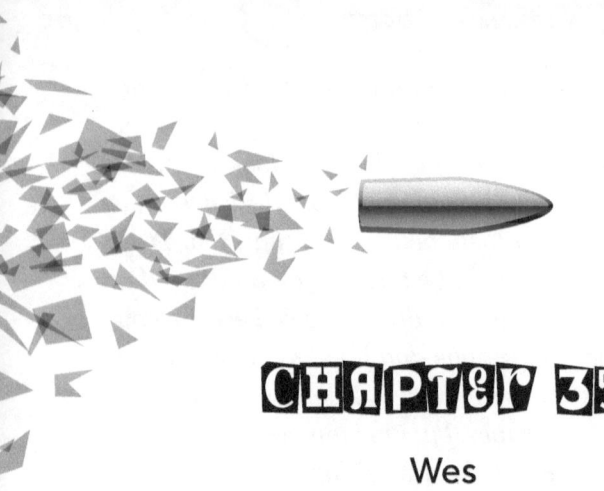

CHAPTER 35

Wes
Three months later

"Why can't they just do the training over Zoom?" Juliette sat down on the edge of the bed next to my half-packed suitcase.

I folded a pair of jeans and a Henley, set them inside, then tossed in socks and underwear before flipping the top shut. "They want me to demonstrate some things in person," I explained, zipping the bag. "Most of the actors they hire have never held a gun or crashed through a door."

A lot had changed over the last three months. I was no longer doing private security. Instead, I was teaching actors how to *look* like real cops on TV and in movies. The week after we'd gotten back from New York, I'd worked a security gig for a big-shot producer. We started talking, and when I'd mentioned I was a former NYPD detective, he'd asked if I'd check out some footage for a new *Law & Order*-type series he was producing. One of the actors was supposed to be in a high-speed vehicle pursuit, but he came off more like he was playing a video game. I gave the guy a few pointers, and the next thing I knew, other producers and directors were calling me to consult on their shows. That single afternoon had snowballed into a lucrative business pretty fast, and as of next week, I was already bringing on another former cop to help me keep up with the workload.

Juliette let out a sigh. "I just... I like when you're here at night."

There was nowhere I liked being more than next to her. And that's exactly where I'd been for the last three months. We hadn't spent a single night apart since I'd flown to New York with her to see her mom after her dad got arrested. I didn't want to leave her now. And lying about why I was going back to the East Coast made me feel a hell of a lot worse.

I swallowed. "It's only one night. I'll be back late tomorrow before you go to bed."

"Where did you say you were doing the training?"

I hadn't. "It's an on-location shoot, somewhere downtown."

"Oh."

I avoided her eyes, focusing on getting the rest of my crap together. I just couldn't look her in the face and lie—not again. Been there, done that, and I'd sworn I'd never go down that road with her again. But this particular white lie felt like a necessity.

I looked at my watch. I was going to get to the airport way earlier than necessary, but that was better than digging myself any deeper with Juliette. Leaning down, I brushed my lips over hers.

"Traffic is going to be a bitch, so I'm gonna get on the road."

"All right. Call me later."

"Love you."

She smiled. "Love you too."

Her words warmed my chest. I didn't think I'd ever get tired of hearing them.

Outside, Tommy was sitting in the car. When he saw me coming with my suitcase, he got out and started up the walkway. We met halfway, and he set a hand on my shoulder.

"Take good care of my girl while I'm gone," I said.

"Will do. And good luck, man." He lowered his voice. "With the boss."

The metal detector beeped and lit up bright red.

The corrections officer sighed and pointed to my feet. "Probably the boots. Steel toe aren't allowed."

Shit. They are steel toe. I bent to untie them, figuring they'd just run them through the conveyor belt like they did my wallet and jacket, but the officer shook his head again. "Step off the line. You're going to have to find other shoes."

"I can't just take them off and run them through the machine?"

"This facility doesn't allow steel toes."

"Rikers allows 'em."

His eyebrows lifted. "This ain't Rikers now, is it?"

"So, what? I'm supposed to go in barefoot?"

"Nope. Shoes required."

"What if I don't have another pair?"

"Sounds like a *you* problem." He jerked his chin to the person behind me. "Next!"

What a dick. This might've been the first time I'd wished I still had a badge to flash since leaving the force.

Though something told me not even that would've softened this guy. Luckily, I'd packed a pair of sneakers in my bag, in case I wanted to go for a run. My suitcase was in the rental car, though, a solid hike across the parking lot. By the time I made it back and got through the metal detector, it was more than thirty minutes later, and the officer acted like he'd never seen me before. *Fine.* Whatever. I was just glad to get in. I'd been a nervous wreck all day waiting for this.

After clearing security, I joined yet another line to get into the actual visiting room. When it was my turn, I gave the name of the prisoner I was here to see. The officer scanned his clipboard and pointed to a wooden table backed by a thick glass panel. A phone dangled from a hook on the wall beside it. "Seat thirteen. The inmate will be brought out."

The room smelled like industrial cleaner, and the plastic chair creaked every time I shifted—which was often since I was nervous as shit. Ten minutes went by, and a few men wearing khaki-colored prison uniforms came and went on the other side of the glass. Then eventually, the door buzzed at the far end and Vince Ginocassi stepped in. The CO escorted him to the seat across from me and uncuffed his wrists. He didn't look too surprised to see me, probably because he wasn't— I'd had to request to have him put me on his visitors list. Though he didn't look happy about it, either.

His eyes locked on mine through the glass. No nod. No smile. Just the same cold stare he'd perfected long before landing in here. I picked up the phone and brought it to my ear. After a long beat, Vince did the same. His jaw was tight, and he didn't say anything.

"Hey." I smiled nervously. "How you doing?"

"What do you want?"

Okay, then. Straight to the point. I shifted in my seat and cleared my throat.

"I, uh, called in a favor with a guard who's an ex-cop. Met him before his shift started this morning. You'll have some fresh food waiting in your cell when you get back. I went to Defonte's and got you the Nicky Special—Italian bread with capocollo, salami, ham, fried eggplant, provolone, and marinated mushrooms."

He licked his lips. "Sounds like you're trying to butter me up."

"I just figured it was a good peace offering."

His eyes shifted back and forth between mine. "What are you really here for? I know you didn't come all the way to make sure I had a good meal and shoot the shit."

I shook my head. "No, you're right. I didn't." I took a deep breath. "I came to tell you...I've been seeing Juliette."

"If that's all you've got to say, you wasted a trip. I already know that."

My eyes widened. "You do?"

He rolled his eyes. "I know everything that goes on with my family, blood and otherwise, even while I'm on the inside."

I wanted to ask *how* he knew. Was Tommy the leak? Did Frannie tell him? But none of that mattered right now. What mattered was that Vince knew...and I was still breathing.

Vince leaned back in his plastic chair, studying me. Eventually he shrugged. "So?"

I wasn't sure what he was waiting for—more details, an apology... I hesitated before answering. "So...I'm in love with her."

"And you want *what* from me?" He leaned in, his voice low. "Say what you came to say. You might not ever get an opportunity like this again. There's nothing I can do about whatever it is you feel the need to discuss."

My knee bounced under the table, and I forced it still. "I'd like to get rid of her security detail. I can handle protecting her."

He arched a brow. "Oh, you can, huh? I thought you weren't capable of that anymore. PTSD and shit. Isn't that what you told me?"

"It is. But I'm a hundred percent now, and I won't let anything happen to her." I met his eyes. "I would lay down my life for her."

Vince held my gaze for a long, silent moment. Then he nodded, almost imperceptibly. "I'll make a call."

Relief washed over me. "Thank you."

"That it?"

That wasn't it—not even close. Asking for a security change was only the tip of the iceberg. But things had gone better than I'd expected...so far. I swallowed again. "Someday, I'm going to ask her to marry me."

He didn't respond. Instead, he looked up at the clock on the wall. "Looks like your time's almost up."

I glanced at my watch. "There's still twenty—"

"It is for this conversation." He pulled the phone from his ear, stood, and lifted his wrists for the guard—never breaking eye contact with me as the cuffs clicked closed.

I still had the receiver pressed to my ear as he took a step, then paused. He gestured to the guard for a second, lifted both bound hands to the phone and brought it back to his ear. "Next time, bring the Joey Bishop hero. The Nicky Special gives me heartburn."

And just like that, he was gone.

I sat there a moment longer, his words rattling around in my head. After replaying our conversation a few times, a slow smile crept over my face.

At least there would be a next time. *Baby steps.*

EPILOGUE

Juliette
Two years later

I opened the door to find our new neighbor, Patrice, standing there with a scowl on her face.

"What the hell is burning?" she asked. "I almost called the fire department until I saw your husband out back, apparently up to no good."

"It's not a fire. My *boyfriend* is smoking sausage in the backyard."

"Well, tell him he needs to do that somewhere else. I can't stand the smell of smoke."

"I'm sorry. I'll let him know you stopped by." I closed the door.

I walked out back to meet Wes by the smoker he'd set up. "The neighbor came by to complain about the smoke."

"I'll drop some off for her when I'm done. Once she tastes it, she'll never bitch about it again."

"We should've moved to the middle of nowhere like I wanted," I said. "Then you wouldn't have to worry about anyone complaining."

Wes and I had just bought a house in Irvine, about an hour away from LA. I'd wanted no neighbors at all. But we didn't have the luxury of moving too far from Los Angeles. We needed to be close enough that Wes could still commute to his movie-consulting gigs. This was at least away from the hustle and bustle. I also needed to be relatively close to the city for the occasional meeting; although, I pretty much wrote from home full time now.

We'd had two requirements for a house: more than one bedroom and space for a basketball court. We'd managed to get both.

Today would be the first time we'd had guests since moving to the new place. I was hosting book club for my old LA crew. We normally got together in the evenings, but we'd planned a Saturday noontime gathering today since traffic during the week to get to where we lived was a bitch.

And as we were no longer close to Wes's infamous sausage guy in West Hollywood, he'd recently learned how to smoke his own and was smoking some today for the ladies. Up until now, though, the only sausage they'd ever really been interested in was the one in his pants. Pam did know that Wes was my boyfriend now, so at least we didn't have to pretend he was just a friend anymore.

When the four ladies arrived, both Wes and I went to the door to greet them.

"Wes, it's so good to see you again!" Pam said as she hugged him, the other three ladies following her in.

"You, as well." He smiled. "Make yourself at home."

My nerves were really on fire today, and it had nothing to do with hosting my first gathering. The ladies didn't realize the book I'd suggested for this month's meeting was *mine*. *Guarded* was a romantic thriller I'd written under a secret name, a pen I'd carefully selected since it had a ring similar to Ginocassi: Gina Wesley. I thought it would be fun to incorporate Wes into my pen name, too, since he'd been my biggest inspiration to start writing books after my transition from screenplays. But more than that, this book was about seventy-five percent *our* story with some fiction mixed in. For instance, in my book, they'd caught the person who'd shot at the heroine, whereas in reality, there'd never been an arrest for the shooting at the farmer's market. I'd changed all the names and altered enough of the circumstances that no one could figure out that it had anything to do with Vince Ginocassi.

I'd come to trust this group's judgment about books after years of reading together, so they were the perfect test subjects for my novel-writing debut. I was both bracing myself and eager for their feedback.

Once we got underway, Sandy read one of her favorite passages. "This novel was a little different than the bodyguard stories we've read in the past," she said. "It was *so* much more than a romance. It had everything. Mystery, intrigue..." She sighed. "When you find out that he was actually still a cop? I mean, I didn't see that coming. Did you?"

Pam shook her head. "Not at all. I loved every second of this one."

I filled with pride as the discussion continued.

"The part when he wrote her that letter?" Karly placed her hand on her chest. "My heart broke for him."

"I know," Maria agreed. "He really never meant to hurt her. His hands were tied."

Pam turned to Wes. "What did you think about it? What was your favorite part?"

He put down his plate. "You know... It's hard to pick a favorite part of this one. What I'll say is that even the hard things they went through sort of seemed necessary to get to where they end up, you know? I'm just glad it had a happy ending." He exhaled. "Had me sweating there for a while. You know those books where you have no idea how the hell the author is gonna get her characters out of a sticky situation? Kudos to the writer for working it all out so well." He looked over at me and winked.

I clasped my hands together and looked around the room. "Well, I'm relieved you all loved my choice." I wished I could've said, *be sure to leave a five-star review*, but that would've been weird.

By three PM, everyone had gone. After Wes and I cleaned up, we still had much of the afternoon left to chill. I'd planned a surprise for him later, but it was contingent upon a UPS delivery. Our neighborhood was usually one of the last ones the delivery truck reached, so it could be as late as nine PM, or maybe seven at the earliest. I had some time to kill.

Wes threw a dish towel over his shoulder. "Want to shoot some hoops?"

"Sure." I grinned.

I still remembered that the first time we'd visited Jersey, Wes's mom had told me that if he and I ever lived together, we would need a basketball hoop out front. She'd said he threw himself into shooting hoops when he needed to blow off steam or work something out. Come to think of it, he'd seemed a bit anxious this afternoon. And now his suggestion that we go out and play basketball made me wonder if he was stressed about something.

"I just got a new ball," he announced. "So it should feel nice and tight, freshly filled with air."

"Cool."

We took the new ball outside and threw it around for a while. Could have been my imagination, but it seemed like he was trying to let me win today. He kept missing shots and passing me the ball when it should have been his turn.

Then, at one point after he passed it to me, I froze. I couldn't tell you why we'd been out here for ten minutes, and I was only *now* just noticing it. But in black ink on the ball where the logo would normally be, it said: *Will you marry me?*

My hands shook, and the ball bounced as it slipped from my grip. By the time I looked over at Wes again, he was a foot away from me, down on one knee.

He looked up, his eyes sparkling in the sun. "Baby, I don't even know how to put into words how much you mean to me. I hope I've proven to you by now that I will always love, honor, and protect you. Please say you'll be my wife, so I can continue doing that for as long as we live." His chest rose and fell as he awaited my answer.

"Oh my God. Yes!" As he stood, I wrapped my arms around him. "You really surprised me. I knew this was coming…but not today!"

Wes held me tight in the middle of the driveway, the ball having rolled into the grass. I looked down at the gorgeous, pear-shaped diamond on a gold band. At the end of my book, where the couple got engaged, I might've snuck in details about my favorite diamond shape. Good to know he'd been paying attention. Although, of course, when it came to love, the ring didn't matter. Wes could've given me one that came out of a bubblegum machine, and I would've been just as happy.

I pulled back for a moment. "It's beautiful."

"I'm happy you like it."

"Like it? I love it."

He kissed my forehead. "You've been long overdue for a beautiful piece of jewelry. The only other piece I've ever gifted you was that cheap cock and balls from Venice."

"I thought it was a cactus."

Wes smirked. "It was *always* a cock and balls. It was *my* cock and balls you've been wearing around your neck all this time."

"I knew I should've gone with my first instinct. How was I so gullible? I've worn that thing to church!"

He cackled. "I think you should wear it when we get hitched."

"I might." I laughed.

My attention then turned to an ice cream truck approaching in the distance. I'd never seen one in this area before. When I looked over at Wes, the smile on his face told me this was planned.

It parked right in front of the house, music blaring. I was certain our neighbor was going to be pissed at us yet again today.

I turned to him. "What's going on?"

"The final surprise." Wes beamed as he took my hand. "You once told me your dad used to have the ice cream man come after all of your soccer games when you were younger. That was one of your good memories about him." Wes grinned. "He sent this for you today."

I covered my mouth. "He did?"

He shrugged. "With a little help from me, yeah. Since...you know...he can only do so much from where he is. But it was his idea."

Wow. That warmed my heart.

Wes took my hand as we walked toward the truck. "He gave his blessing, by the way."

Warmth flooded me. "Oh, I hadn't even thought about whether you'd asked him..."

"Well, he gave me his permission—right after he told me he'd have me killed if I ever hurt you."

I shook my head. "That sounds like my father."

Wes let go of my hand. "Let's order a celebratory ice cream."

As I perused the menu on the side of the truck, the window where you order slid open.

"Surprise!" someone yelled.

My jaw dropped. "Mom!"

My mother ran out of the truck to wrap her arms around me. "Hope this is a good surprise. Wes wanted me to help you celebrate the engagement."

"I can't believe this." I squeezed her. "This is the best day of my life."

"Do we have room for one more person?" my mom asked.

"I thought you were no longer using Paulie..."

She shook her head. "Not Paulie."

"Surprise!" Wes's mom shouted as she came out of the truck as well.

"Oh my God!" I ran to her. "Joanna!"

She hugged me tightly. "I think you can call me Ma now."

"I'm so lucky to have two beautiful moms." I looked at each of them before smiling over at Wes.

After Wes embraced them both, I turned to him. "How the hell did you pull this off?"

"I've been orchestrating it for weeks."

Wes explained that he'd hired a friend to pick up both our mothers at the airport and drive them here in the ice cream truck.

As the four of us entered the house together, all I could think about was the surprise I'd planned for *him* tonight. I hadn't expected there to be an audience, but perhaps the more the merrier.

Later that evening, Wes had cooked a delicious Italian dinner with a side of smoked sausage for the moms. We'd finished eating, and I was chomping at the bit, looking out the window for the delivery man.

When I finally saw the lights of the truck pulling up outside, I rushed out to fetch the box, my heart pounding.

Our mothers and Wes were sitting at the dining room table, still lingering over dessert when I entered the room carrying the box.

Here goes.

"Look what just came!" I opened it in front of them and took out the single copy of my novel.

"It's your book," Wes said, confusion on his face. "But we already have a zillion copies in the garage. I don't get it."

"This isn't just *any* copy, though. It's a new, one-of-a-kind special edition."

"Ah." He nodded. "Cool."

I offered it to him, and he flipped through the pages as our mothers looked on. "It looks the same, though." His eyes narrowed. "What's different about it?"

I swallowed. "The dedication."

"Oh..." he said as he flipped back to the beginning.

My mother leaned in. "What is it?"

I braced myself as he read it out loud.

"To Wes, this is our story, but the best part—created by both of us—didn't make it to print." His lip trembled as he looked up at me and whispered the last line. "The next chapter will be coming in nine months."

ACKNOWLEDGEMENTS

Thank you to all of the amazing bloggers, bookstagrammers and BookTokers who helped spread the news about *Crooked*. We are so grateful for the book community and all you do to support authors!

To our rocks: Julie, Luna, and Cheri – Thank you for always being there and for more than a decade of friendship.

To our agent, Kimberly Brower – Thank you for helping to get our books into the hands of readers internationally.

To Jessica – Thank you for always perfecting our words with your editing skills.

To Elaine – An amazing editor, proofer, formatter, and friend. We so appreciate you!

To Julia – Thank you for polishing our stories and making them shine.

To Kylie and Jo at Give Me Books Promotions – Thank you for making sure our books find their way into readers' hands!

To Sommer – Thank you for giving Wes and Juliette's story a cover that does the gorgeous photo justice and for the beautiful illustrated version.

To Brooke – Thank you for organizing this release and for taking some of the load off of our endless to-do lists each day.

Last but not least, to our readers – You could've spent your time anywhere, but you chose to spend it here—with these characters, this story, and us. That's pure magic, and we are endlessly grateful for your trust.

Much love,
Vi and Penelope

OTHER BOOKS
by Vi Keeland and Penelope Ward

Denim & Diamonds
The Rules of Dating
The Rules of Dating My Best Friend's Sister
The Rules of Dating My One Night Stand
The Rules of Dating a Younger Man
Well Played
Not Pretending Anymore
Happily Letter After
My Favorite Souvenir
Dirty Letters
Hate Notes
Rebel Heir
Rebel Heart
Cocky Bastard
Stuck-Up Suit
Playboy Pilot
Mister Moneybags
British Bedmate
Park Avenue Player

Other Books
from Vi Keeland

The Exception
Indiscretion
Someone Knows
The Unraveling
Jilted
What Happens at the Lake
Something Unexpected
The Game
The Boss Project
The Summer Proposal
The Spark
The Invitation
The Rivals
Inappropriate
All Grown Up
We Shouldn't
The Naked Truth
Something Borrowed, Something You
Beautiful Mistake
Egomaniac
Bossman
The Baller
Left Behind
Beat
Throb
Worth the Fight
Worth the Chance
Worth Forgiving
Belong to You
Made for You

OTHER BOOKS
by Vi Keeland and Penelope Ward

Denim & Diamonds
The Rules of Dating
The Rules of Dating My Best Friend's Sister
The Rules of Dating My One Night Stand
The Rules of Dating a Younger Man
Well Played
Not Pretending Anymore
Happily Letter After
My Favorite Souvenir
Dirty Letters
Hate Notes
Rebel Heir
Rebel Heart
Cocky Bastard
Stuck-Up Suit
Playboy Pilot
Mister Moneybags
British Bedmate
Park Avenue Player

OTHER BOOKS
from Vi Keeland

The Exception
Indiscretion
Someone Knows
The Unraveling
Jilted
What Happens at the Lake
Something Unexpected
The Game
The Boss Project
The Summer Proposal
The Spark
The Invitation
The Rivals
Inappropriate
All Grown Up
We Shouldn't
The Naked Truth
Something Borrowed, Something You
Beautiful Mistake
Egomaniac
Bossman
The Baller
Left Behind
Beat
Throb
Worth the Fight
Worth the Chance
Worth Forgiving
Belong to You
Made for You

OTHER BOOKS
from Penelope Ward

Taylor's Father
The House Guest
The Rocker's Muse
The Drummer's Heart
The Surrogate
I Could Never
Toe the Line
Moody
The Assignment
The Aristocrat
The Crush
The Anti-Boyfriend
Just One Year
The Day He Came Back
When August Ends
Love Online
Gentleman Nine
Drunk Dial
Mack Daddy
Stepbrother Dearest
Neighbor Dearest
RoomHate
Sins of Sevin
Jake Undone (Jake #1)
My Skylar (Jake #2)
Jake Understood (Jake #3)
Gemini

Vi Keeland is a #1 *New York Times*, #1 *Wall Street Journal*, and *USA Today* Bestselling author. With millions of books sold, her titles are currently translated in twenty-seven languages and have appeared on bestseller lists in the US, Germany, Brazil, Bulgaria, and Hungary. Three of her short stories have been turned into films, and two of her books are currently optioned for movies. She resides in New York with her husband and their three children where she is living out her own happily ever after with the boy she met at age six.

Connect with Vi Keeland
Facebook Private Fan Group:
https://www.facebook.com/groups/ViKeelandFanGroup/)
Facebook: https://www.facebook.com/pages/Author-Vi-Keeland/435952616513958
TikTok: https://www.tiktok.com/@vikeeland
Website: http://www.vikeeland.com
Twitter: https://twitter.com/ViKeeland
Instagram: http://instagram.com/Vi_Keeland/

Penelope Ward is a *New York Times*, *USA Today*, and #1 *Wall Street Journal* Bestselling author. With millions of books sold, she's a 21-time New York Times bestseller. Her novels are published in over a dozen languages and can be found in bookstores around the world. Having grown up in Boston with five older brothers, she spent most of her twenties as a television news anchor, before switching to a more family-friendly career. She is the proud mother of a beautiful girl with autism and her amazing brother. Penelope and her family reside in Rhode Island.

Connect with Penelope Ward

Facebook Private Fan Group:
https://www.facebook.com/groups/PenelopesPeeps/
Facebook: https://www.facebook.com/penelopewardauthor
TikTok: https://www.tiktok.com/@penelopewardofficial
Website: http://www.penelopewardauthor.com
Twitter: https://twitter.com/PenelopeAuthor
Instagram: http://instagram.com/PenelopeWardAuthor/

www.ingramcontent.com/pod-product-compliance
Lightning Source LLC
LaVergne TN
LVHW040132080526
838202LV00042B/2887